P

'Yet again Tessa Harri[...]
known corner of WW[...]
Sarah Steele

'Gripping, compelling and beautiful'
Emma Cowell

'I was completely immersed in this book from start to finish'
Kathleen McGurl

'Beautifully written and immaculately researched,
with characters that jump off the page.
I couldn't put it down!'
Lana Kortchik

'A fascinating read'
Glynis Peters

TESSA HARRIS read History at Oxford University and has been a journalist, writing for several national newspapers and magazines, for more than thirty years. She is the author of 12 published historical novels. Her debut, *The Anatomist's Apprentice*, won the Romantic Times First Best Mystery Award 2012 in the USA. She lectures in creative writing and is married with two children. She lives in the Cotswolds.

Facebook: Tessa Harris Author

X: @harris_tessa

Also by Tessa Harris

Beneath a Starless Sky

The Light We Left Behind

The Paris Notebook

The Tuscan Daughter

TESSA HARRIS

ONE PLACE. MANY STORIES

HQ
An imprint of HarperCollins*Publishers* Ltd
1 London Bridge Street
London SE1 9GF

www.harpercollins.co.uk

HarperCollins*Publishers*
Macken House, 39/40 Mayor Street Upper,
Dublin 1 D01 C9W8

This paperback edition 2024

2
First published in Great Britain by
HQ, an imprint of HarperCollins*Publishers* Ltd 2024

ISBN: 9780008640491

Printed and bound in the United States

For Franca

and for the women in Italy
who fought for freedom, 1940–45

A woman with a voice is by definition a strong woman. But the search to find that voice can be remarkably difficult.
Melinda Gates

Prologue

Emilia-Romagna, Italy

April 1944

'They're watching us.'

The warning rasped from the corner of her mouth, dry with fear. The skin beneath her mink coat prickled with sweat. Despite the snow lingering on the Apennine peaks, the air was warm, but it didn't stop her shivering. Fighting the urge to run to the drumbeat of her heart, she clutched Cristo's small hand tightly.

The limousine lay ahead of them, its engine throbbing. The driver, in a chauffeur's peaked cap, at the wheel. This had to be the longest walk of Lizzie Thornton's life. Just how she, a governess from England, became embroiled in such an outlandish plot to rescue a child from Mussolini's fascists, she wasn't quite sure. But now the plan had succeeded – almost. They were nearly there. Just a few more paces across cobbles worn smooth by five hundred years of footsteps and she'd feel safe. Safer.

The great medieval tower of the Rocca at Castell'Arquato cast a long shadow over their path. The prison stood brooding above the surrounding landscape, a symbol of unfettered power and brutal authority. For the past two days and nights it was where the fascists had been holding Cristo in shackles. They'd locked him in a cell for carrying messages for the partisans. They'd threatened to shoot him. He wouldn't have been the first boy to die by firing squad. Now he was free. But for how much longer?

Behind her, above the pounding of blood in her ears, Lizzie heard Vincenzo's footsteps. They were measured, authoritative, arrogant; just how a fascist general's should sound. He'd played the part magnificently. In his dark *gerarca* uniform, a chest full of medals and black hair slicked back under a gold braided cap, Vincenzo Baldini looked very convincing.

How dare they hold his son – a boy Il Duce treats as his own? There'd been a terrible mistake. The governor would pay. Release the boy at once.

But then . . .

'Excellency!' A call from behind.

Lizzie froze with Cristo, while Vincenzo turned to see one of the guards approaching in a hurry. Her nerves were dancing on a knife edge. Somehow, she held it together.

'Allow me, sir,' said the soldier, his hand now resting on the handle of the back passenger door of the Lancia.

Vincenzo gave him a nod and the car door was opened. He ushered Lizzie and the child inside first, then settled beside them. The door clicked shut and the soldier's arm flew out in a salute.

Lizzie wound down the passenger window to her right. She thought she might pass out with relief as Cristo piled in next to her. She needed air, but first she held him tight. 'You're safe now, my darling,' she whispered in his ear. She saw tears in Vincenzo's eyes, too, as Cristo nestled his curly head against her like a frightened puppy. She wasn't the only one who loved the boy like a son.

'Slowly does it,' Vincenzo told the driver as the clutch was engaged smoothly and the Lancia purred into life. They mustn't seem in too much of a hurry to get away. That would arouse suspicion.

They were off. *Thank God.* Or so Lizzie thought, until . . .

The shrill ringing of a telephone in the guardhouse just as they began to move away sliced through her aching brain and alerted her to more danger. A soldier answered the call and, with the receiver to his ear, his look switched instantly towards the car. As soon as she saw his startled glare target the Lancia, Lizzie realised. The game was up.

'They know!' she cried.

'Let's get out of here,' yelled Vincenzo.

The driver slammed his foot on the throttle and the limousine shot off, gathering speed in a billow of choking black fumes.

A sharp left swerve took them down a narrow backstreet where a flower seller set her stall. Instinctively the driver yanked the wheel to avoid her. She jumped for her life, but he clipped the stall, toppling buckets and sending flowers flying through the air. As the car bounced over the cobbles, Lizzie feared it might take off any second and veer out of control. Her stomach lurched, jumping into her chest. When it landed, the vehicle shaved the kerb and began fishtailing as the driver wrestled with the steering wheel to right it.

Vincenzo twisted round, eyes to the rear window, picturing guards rushing to their trucks by the prison. Orders would be bellowed, weapons loaded, but right now it was looking as though they might just . . .

'Bloody hell!' yelled the driver.

The first shot whistled past the Lancia, smashing a shop window, shards of glass shattering across the street. Then a second and a third.

'Get down,' screamed Vincenzo, throwing himself sideways on top of Lizzie, forcing her and Cristo to lower their heads and cower below window height.

Up ahead the portcullis came into view, but on the other side of it two Germans leapt out onto the road. The driver's pilot training kicked in. Instinctively he drove full pelt right at them.

Before they had time to aim, he'd forced them to dive out of the way. But it didn't stop Nazi semiautomatics screaming their fury at the limousine as it tore passed. Bullets were falling like rain. Harsh cracks sounded as a two or three ricocheted off the bonnet. Revving hard, the driver powered through until another bombardment. This time the boot was clipped.

On the backseat Lizzie clung to Cristo. With each wrench of the wheel, they were tossed left and right. Throttle. Brake. Throttle. Brake. With every swerve the boy screamed, like a passenger on a fairground swing boat.

Vincenzo, daring to raise his gaze and glimpse behind, spotted more guards. They huddled together then dispersed, their rifles primed. 'Faster,' he yelled. 'Faster.'

Lurching and pitching through the back streets the car sped, swerving to avoid a bent old woman crossing the road. Up ahead lay the archway that marked the border between the old and new towns; between the impossibly narrow lanes and tightly packed houses and the wider, smoother roads. The driver's foot thrust the throttle hard to the floor, but just as he did, upstairs shutters were flung open. Another hail of bullets rained down from above. A shot shattered the rear window. Vincenzo flinched and clutched the side of his head. Lizzie screamed as a thousand spears of glass lanced through the air and a heavy weight fell against her. But it was only when she saw the spatters of blood on her fur coat that reality dawned. Vincenzo was hit. Cristo screamed at the sight and struggled to sit up, but Lizzie gripped his shoulders like a vice.

'Get down,' she snapped, snatching at the scarf around her neck and holding it to Vincenzo's head to stem the blood. Then to the driver, 'Vincenzo's hit. Hurry, please. For God's sake, keep going.'

Chapter 1

Lucca, Tuscany

September 1942

Sitting in the gloom of her bedroom in the Villa Martini, the cicadas drumming outside the shutters and the smell of late roses heavy on the air, Lizzie re-read the message for the tenth time. She still couldn't believe what it said. *Hugh was dead.* The stark news, typed in black ink on a thin strip of paper, was delivered via the Swiss consulate. It shot through her like a bullet to the chest. The man she once planned to spend the rest of her life with was dead; his plane downed over Tobruk four months before. He'd been dead all that time and she hadn't known. Hadn't sensed something was wrong. It made her feel even more guilty. Her gaze dropped to the emerald engagement ring on her left hand.

'To match your eyes, darling Elizabeth,' Hugh had said when he'd proposed one magical night at the Café de Paris in London. He'd always called her Elizabeth, even though everyone else called her Lizzie.

More than at any time over the past two years, since war was declared, she felt trapped. When she'd first taken up the post of tutor, Italy had been the sun-kissed land of Dante and Michelangelo. Now it was her prison.

She would never forget standing in the Piazza dell'Anfiteatro as Mussolini's words boomed out over the loudspeaker that scorching June day in 1940. *'An hour marked by destiny is striking in the sky of our country.'* She'd been on a simple errand but had accidentally found herself caught up in a crowd. Carried along on a tide of excitable people, she'd barely been able to breathe. Milling among them were the Blackshirt bullies, coshes in hand, ready to strike anyone who stepped out of the fascist party line. At the time her stomach had clenched with fear. She'd been right to be afraid. As an Englishwoman, overnight she became an enemy of the Italian state. But there was no way back. Hitler's invading armies had already blocked her path home and continued to do so.

The paper felt slightly soggy between her fingers as Lizzie, wiping away her tears, returned it to the bundle containing all Hugh's previous letters. They were tied together with red ribbon. She'd loved him once. She really had, and at first, she'd thought the distance would only make her love him more. But it hadn't. In his last letter, sent just before he joined the Royal Air Force, he'd seemed as ardent as ever. He'd written about their future, imaging their life together, with children of course. For most women the picture he painted seemed idyllic, and, for a short while, it had for her. After her father walked out on her mother when Lizzie was just six, she craved stability. She'd accepted that marriage, for a woman, was in most cases as predictable as London fog, and had been happy to play by the rules, until, that is, she'd been tempted away by something far more exciting.

Italy, with its art and culture, had made her realise there was more to life than an Edwardian villa in suburbia and changing nappies. Da Vinci crooked his enticing finger at her and beckoned her to Tuscany. And it had turned out every bit as alluring and mesmerising as she'd imagined, until of course war had shown its ugly face. She'd known for a long time she wasn't ready for marriage. Perhaps she never would be. That meant, even though she remained terribly fond of him, she'd have to break off her engagement to Hugh. The thought of hurting his feelings meant she kept putting off writing the dreaded letter, even though ending it all would have been the kindest course in the long run. She just hadn't known how or when.

Returning the letters to her drawer, Lizzie switched off her bedside lamp to settle down, even though she doubted she'd sleep. It was then she noticed her door was slightly ajar – a chink of moonlight wedging itself onto the tiles. And just beyond the reach of the beams stood a silent figure in white. It jumped back as she bolted upright. It was the figure of a child.

'Cristo?' she gasped, scrambling up from the bed. 'Cristo, is that you?'

Moving blindly through the immediate darkness, her arms outstretched, she headed for the door.

'Yes, Miss Lizzie,' came Cristo's trembling voice as he rushed forward. Flinging his arms around her, he buried his face in her nightgown. The child was her pupil. He was only nine years old and had lost his mother at the age of just seven. His father, Count Antonio de Falco, had engaged her to be his governess at the Villa Martini, but she'd soon become so much more. She knew it wasn't her place to fill the late contessa's shoes as his mother, but she found they fitted so easily it was hard not to at times.

Hot tears seeped through Lizzie's nightgown as she folded the child into her arms. 'What is it? Did you have a bad dream?' she asked, stroking his tousled curls. 'Come and sit down.' She guided him over to the bed and he clambered up onto the mattress, his feet dangling over the edge.

'What is it?' she asked again in a low voice, anxious not to wake the household.

The little boy lifted his face to hers. 'They say we will have to fight to protect our mothers, and sisters. They say the English will kill all the women and then the Jews will come and make suits and dresses from their skin.'

The vile words gushed from Cristo's mouth in a torrent until his anguished outburst broke into sobs.

'Wait! Wait, Cristo!' cried Lizzie, her voice louder than she'd wished. 'No. No. Who told you that? The sergeant?' She pictured the leering roughneck in charge of the Lucca GIL, the fascist youth group compulsory for all youngsters.

Cristo nodded and flung his arms around her again, hugging her tight. 'They won't kill you, will they? I won't let them kill you. I'll protect you.'

'Oh, my dear Cristo,' she soothed, stroking his head again. 'No one's going to kill me. I'm safe here and so are you. The war is a long way away. You mustn't worry yourself with it.'

'But they say the British and Americans are going to invade.'

Lizzie knew that was true. The Allies had bombed Naples and Milan especially, and thousands of civilians had been killed. What if the Allies now had Lucca in their sights, too?

'The bombs are aimed at factories and railways, Cristo, not homes. They won't touch us here,' she told him. 'The Englishmen who fly the planes aren't interested in us.' She hoped he hadn't picked up on the quaver in her voice as she thought of Hugh.

Looking down at Cristo, his black head nuzzled on her shoulder, she wanted to rail against his arrogant father and all Mussolini's cronies who'd taken Italy into this war. Children like Cristo were being brainwashed by murderous monsters. The fascists were telling them contemptible lies about other countries and other people – Jews in particular.

She hugged the child. 'It's going to be all right, dear Cristo. No one will harm us.' She kissed the top of his head. 'Now, back to bed with you.'

Taking him by the hand, she led him to his room, three doors along the corridor, and without switching on the light, tucked him in.

'Sleep well and don't worry,' she told him stroking his head.

Cristo nodded but said nothing before she saw him close his eyes. As she walked along the corridor and back to her own room, Lizzie looked down and noticed a fat black scorpion scuttle along the skirting. When she'd first arrived in Italy, she would have screamed and recoiled at the sight. Not now. She didn't even flinch. Nowadays she knew there were other monsters in Italy which were far more terrifying. Despite what the GIL taught him, despite his father's politics, Cristo was as much a victim in this madness as anyone else. He and poor Hugh.

Chapter 2

Two weeks later, Lizzie woke to the smell of freshly baked brioches and followed her nose to the kitchen where Maria, her silver hair drawn back from her plump face, was bringing out a batch from the oven.

'You come just in time, Signorina Lizzie,' the cook chortled as she set the tray on a marble slab by the sink.

Lizzie spotted Cristo on a nearby stool eagerly tucking into an earlier batch of brioches. 'I'm not the only one,' she replied.

Maria laughed, a deep, throaty chuckle, and flapped a tea towel in the air before it flopped over her shoulder. 'He's a growing boy!'

It was true. In the past year Lizzie's pupil had grown to reach her elbow. She poured herself a coffee from the espresso kettle on the stove – nowadays she so much preferred it to tea – and walked over to him.

'Good morning, Master Cristoforo,' she greeted playfully. 'Maria is right. You need fuel for your brain.' She pointed to his temple, hidden under a fringe of dark curls.

Cristo smiled at her broadly. 'Hello, Miss Lizzie,' he said. When she'd first arrived at the villa, the child couldn't pronounce the *th* in Thornton, so she'd told him to call her Miss Lizzie instead.

A splodge of jam had settled on his cheek and, taking a napkin from the table, Lizzie wiped it away.

He leaned sideways and, still seated, threw his arms around her waist, hugging her tight. Lizzie darted an embarrassed look at Maria before gently pushing him back. The count didn't encourage public displays of affection.

'I've told you, Cristo, your papa says you are too old for this,' she said lightly.

The boy retreated, shaking his black curls. 'Forgive me,' he said in such a way that, yet again, he made her feel like a heartless monster. Lizzie exchanged looks with Maria once more, as if to confirm that Cristoforo de Falco had both of them firmly under his thumb.

'Now go with Violetta and I'll see you at eight o'clock for your lessons,' she told him sternly, trying to hide a smile.

Cristo had barely left the room with the young maid when Signora Cortina, the housekeeper, glided into the kitchen like a ghost, dragging her keys behind her. The woman's customary black clothes always seemed to match her mood. Lizzie had rarely seen her smile.

'Miss Thornton,' she greeted Lizzie. 'The count wishes to see you in his study.'

Her heart missed a beat. No one ever said no to Count de Falco. Not even women. *Especially not women*, thought Lizzie, judging by the stream of attractive female visitors to the villa. He was very rich and very powerful and as well as being on the Grand Council of Fascism, or perhaps because of it, he was a personal friend of Mussolini. He was everything she loathed in a man, yet she was bound to do his bidding.

The count held the door of his study open for her. He was wearing the uniform of a *gerarca*, one of the highest offices in the National Fascist Party. The well-cut jacket with a sash, wide grey breeches, long leather boots and fez suited him, accentuating his aristocratic features. It also made him look every bit as arrogant

11

as he actually was, Lizzie thought. But she relied on his discretion to keep her employed. She knew of so many other English citizens who'd been banished to internment camps in remote areas of Italy. She was one of the lucky ones, even though her fate depended solely on the count's whim. Since the outbreak of war, he'd barely been at the villa, regularly being called to Rome by Il Duce. She liked to think he was far too busy to bother about her.

In the study, another man with dark hair and wearing a pale blue linen jacket sat with his back to her. He rose as soon as she walked in the room and turned to face her. His lips twitched in a smile.

'Miss Thornton. I'd like you to meet Cristoforo's new tutor,' said de Falco. 'Signor Vincenzo Baldini.'

Lizzie's stomach flipped and her face betrayed her confusion as she stared at the bespectacled man. The sunlight glinted on the gold round rims of his glasses, so she couldn't see his eyes properly. She turned to the count and said, 'New tutor, sir? But I don't . . .' Was she being sacked? Or, worse still, might she be sent to an internment camp like some fellow Britons? As the war progressed, had de Falco had second thoughts and decided it was time to ban his English governess? But no.

Instead, he announced, 'I've decided my son needs a male tutor as well, someone who can teach him manly pursuits.'

The news came from out of nowhere. 'A male tutor?' she repeated. Since Mussolini's rule, it seemed women in Italy had become invisible.

The count nodded. 'He's coming up to eleven now and—'

'Ten, sir.' Lizzie interrupted.

'What?'

'Your son is nine years old. He will be ten in November.'

De Falco arched a brow. 'No matter. It is high time he grew up. I trust that you will show Signor Baldini the classroom and Cristoforo's routine, Miss Thornton.'

Lizzie did her best to conceal her anger at not being consulted

prior to any decision on Cristo's education. The count had dimin-
ished her in front of a stranger. 'Of course, sir,' she replied. She
threw a grudging smile in the new tutor's direction and self-
consciously tucked a wayward strand of hair behind her ear. 'I'd
be glad to. This way, Signor Baldini.'

She led the way through the hall to floor-to-ceiling French
windows at the back of the villa that opened out onto the terrace.
The new tutor paused to admire the view of the city that lay
before them.

'What a sight,' he said. He unhooked his glasses, wiped them
with a handkerchief, then replaced them again as if he wanted
to take in every detail of the vista.

'I never tire of it,' replied Lizzie, appreciating the green spires
of cypress trees and the city's solid Roman walls and medieval
towers more than usual. But she knew no amount of small talk
could address what she needed to say. She was annoyed at this
man's appointment, and she wanted him to know it.

They walked briskly to a separate stone building in the grounds
of the villa. It was modelled on a classical temple and lay at the
bottom of a gently sloping lawn at the edge of a reed-fringed lake.

'This is where we have our lessons in summer,' she told him,
once inside. 'It's cool and quite practical. As you see, the count
has installed fitted cupboards and bookshelves.'

Baldini's eyes swept the room, taking in the work bench, the
poster of the periodic table and the map of the world on the
wall. He nodded and seemed happy enough, silently inspecting
the facilities.

'And Cristoforo,' he said, picking up an ammonite on a nearby
shelf. 'What is he like?'

Lizzie was taken aback. 'You haven't met him.'

'Not yet. I was only officially offered the job this morning.'

'I see,' she replied. The situation was even more unsatisfactory
than she'd first supposed. 'Cristoforo is . . .' She paused. 'I call him
Cristo. He's a lively boy, but sensitive. I expect the count told you

his mother died about two years ago. Naturally, he's always had a particularly strong attachment to female staff members here.'

'To be expected,' said Baldini, replacing the ammonite on the shelf and turning to look at her with a smile. 'You spoil him, yes?'

Lizzie wasn't sure if that comment was meant as a criticism, but privately she had to admit it was an accurate assumption. Her relationship with Cristo was a constant balancing act between maintaining discipline and providing the love and emotional support he so needed after the contessa's death.

'I have established boundaries, Signor Baldini,' she countered, sounding almost indignant. Was he putting her professionalism on trial? The way she should be addressed, the way the boy should behave towards her and how much was expected of him; they were all rules the count had laid down. While she herself kept to a tight routine and upheld good discipline, she would never raise her voice or use threatening behaviour towards Cristo. Nor would she ever admit to loving the child as if he were her own.

'Of course,' the new tutor replied. 'I'm sure you are an excellent teacher of the Arts, Miss Thornton. It will be my task to concentrate on the sciences,' he told her. 'And on sport.'

'Sport?' repeated Lizzie, as if sport had never really occurred to her as something Cristo should be taught.

'*Mens sana in corpore sano*,' quoted Baldini.

Lizzie didn't need to be reminded 'a sound mind in a sound body' was beneficial, but the only proper physical activity she'd ever seen Cristo do was rowing her across the lake in the little boat.

'I shall teach him to swim and run,' he told her.

Both her brows raised in surprise. 'He'll like that,' she replied, realising adjustments to the timetable would be needed to accommodate these new activities.

'And backgammon and chess. Very good for strategy and problem solving,' he told her earnestly. 'The count is keen his son learns to think like a solider.' The words sent a chill through her. The thought of Cristo going to war filled her with dread.

'I'm sure,' she replied, troubled by this new approach, although she tried to mask her disquiet. 'It sounds as though you intend to keep Cristo very busy.'

Baldini answered her with another saying. 'Idle hands are the devil's tools.'

She agreed with him, of course, but she didn't say so. She still wasn't at all sure how she felt about Signor Baldini.

They returned to the villa in slightly awkward silence. 'Did the count say when you might start?' Lizzie asked as they reached the French doors.

'On Monday,' Baldini replied. 'I have some affairs to settle beforehand.'

'Of course,' she replied, entering the hall. *Affairs to settle. What could that mean?* 'And will you be seeing Cristo before then?'

In the next breath her question was answered.

'There you are!' The count's deep voice carried loudly across the hall's marble tiles. 'Signor Baldini. I have someone here to meet you.'

Cristo stood in the doorway of his father's study. Lizzie could see the child was looking slightly nervous, fidgeting as he stood unsmiling on the threshold.

'That will be all, Miss Thornton,' the count told her.

Baldini turned to her and bowed once more. 'I look forward to working with you,' he told her.

With that he strode towards the count's study to meet his new pupil. The door was shut firmly in her face. Lizzie stood for a moment, still nonplussed by her encounter with the new tutor. He seemed very professional and, she had to admit, rather charming. But she still couldn't quite get over the fact that she wasn't consulted about his appointment. It was a reminder of how vulnerable she was as an Englishwoman in Italy at a time of war. The count had put her well and truly in her place with the appointment of a male tutor. But call it female intuition, a sixth sense, or whatever, she also found something puzzling about Vincenzo Baldini; something that didn't ring true. He was a contradiction. On the one hand this new tutor had treated her with courtesy and respect. He also seemed to have Cristo's best interests at heart, wishing to broaden the curriculum. On the other, he appeared eager to do the count's fascist bidding, and might well see his role as steering his pupil away from childhood to turn him into an arrogant bully. He might pose a threat, not only to her position, but to Cristo as well.

Chapter 3

Lizzie had promised Cristo a gelato for trying so hard with his English comprehension. Despite the war, they found the city centre busy with tourists. As well as queueing to go up the city's famous Guinigi Tower, small crowds were gathered around newsstands and noticeboards anxious for updates. All men under the age of thirty had been called to arms. At the Villa Martini, Marco, the son of Giuseppe the gardener, who helped the old man in the garden, had been one of them. Lizzie supposed Signor Baldini was slightly older and therefore exempt from conscription. However, even though she believed him a supporter of Il Duce – the count wouldn't have employed him otherwise – she also knew most ordinary Italians didn't back Mussolini. Despite the fascists' best efforts to tear them down, posters and handbills declaring *MORTE DEL FASCISMO! Death to Fascism!* kept appearing relentlessly all over Lucca.

Strolling along the city wall Lizzie and Cristo came to the botanical gardens and found a gelato seller on a bicycle by the main gates. Cristo chose a large cone filled with chocolate ice cream, topped with strawberry sauce and a sprinkle of chopped nuts. But as soon as he walked into the sun, the gelato began to melt, running in rivulets through his fingers.

'Let's go and find somewhere cooler,' Lizzie suggested, mopping Cristo's hand with her handkerchief as she spoke. She'd once heard someone say *Life is like an ice cream. Enjoy it before it melts.* Her life with Hugh had melted before it had even begun. He was a whirlwind who'd gusted in and blown her away with his charm and his humour. On reflection it was all too quick, all too dizzying. By nature, she had always been a cautious person, willing to toe the line, and Hugh seemed the opposite. At least that's how she'd started to feel when she'd arrived in Lucca, shortly before Britain went to war. In those heady few months before Italy, too, joined the conflict, the country had got under her skin. She'd relished everything about it; its food, its culture, its climate. The thought of being a housewife in a dull English suburb quickly lost its appeal.

Entering the formal gardens, they soon settled in the shade of a magnificent Lebanese cedar tree so Cristo could lick the ice cream at his leisure.

'Let's take a look down there, shall we?' Lizzie suggested as soon as the gelato was eaten.

While Cristo raced ahead towards the pond, Lizzie followed at a more sedate pace through the various species of trees in the arboretum, still trying to come to terms with losing Hugh. She'd met him at a polo match through a mutual friend in the spring of 1939. When he'd asked to see her again, she'd told him she'd just signed a contract to teach for a year in Italy. She was to leave for Lucca that August, she'd explained. But it hadn't put him off. If anything, it had made him even more eager to take her to dinners and dances. She considered him witty and good-looking. He could make her laugh when she was down, often buying her chocolates and flowers. He was from a well-respected family and had a good job in the City too. There'd been talk of war with Germany, but few took it seriously and when his proposal came, she'd thought long and hard about staying in England and not going to Italy at all. But her mother had died suddenly the year

18

before, leaving her a small legacy, and she'd needed a change; *wanted* a change before she settled down to the inevitability of marriage. She spoke near-fluent Italian and longed to explore the country that so excited her. It was to be her last hurrah.

She tried to assure Hugh time would fly. 'It's only for twelve months,' she'd insisted. 'And you can visit me. It'll be wonderful.' How wrong she had been. War had come between them. And now Hugh was dead. It wasn't her fault. If she'd stayed in England, it wouldn't have changed anything, but even so, a sense of guilt wormed its way into her brain when she recalled how she'd intended to break off their engagement months ago. She just couldn't bring herself to do it by letter.

'Come on,' called Cristo, with a wide sweep of his arm. Once again, she wouldn't be left alone to grieve.

Lizzie sighed deeply, but just as she upped her pace, she spotted movement from the corner of her eye. Turning, she spied two men in the shadows. They were deep in conversation behind a tree. An older man in a Panama hat was leaning on a cane, while the younger one seemed familiar.

Cristo remained impatient. 'What is it?' he asked, running back to her.

'Nothing,' she replied quickly, switching to face him, and taking his outstretched hand.

The trouble was she sensed it was *something*. As she tried to hurry the child along, the younger man stepped out of the shade and the sun coloured his jacket. It was pale blue, and Lizzie's suspicions were confirmed. It was Vincenzo Baldini.

Cristo saw the men, too, just before Lizzie grasped him by the hand and pulled him along. 'Isn't that Signor Baldini?' he asked, pivoting round for a better look.

Lizzie hurried to the next turning through the trees and, wide-eyed, stopped to clamp her forefinger to her lips. She couldn't be certain what she'd just witnessed, but whatever was going on, she had the distinct impression she shouldn't have seen it.

'No, Cristo,' she whispered, taking the boy by the shoulders, and wheeling him in front of her. 'You're mistaken.'

'But . . .' protested the child, trying to wriggle out of her grasp.

'He only looked like Signor Baldini,' she insisted. They headed back towards the gates. 'Let's hurry now, or we'll be late back for Maria.'

They walked on in the direction of the Porta Sant'Anna, Cristo's hand in hers. But Lizzie was so lost in her own thoughts that the first she knew of a large vehicle coming up behind them was the roar of an engine on the left. She glanced over her shoulder to see a truck less than a metre away as it pulled over to the kerb. She recognised it instantly. It was one of those unmarked vehicles that cruised around the streets of the city, picking up people who'd fallen foul of the *fascisti*. Her heart thudded as she watched four men in black uniforms scramble out and rush into a nearby apartment block.

'Come on, Cristo,' she insisted, tugging at the child's hand, but he remained rooted.

A moment later there was a hammering on a door swiftly followed by shouts and screams from a woman. The few passers-by paid no attention. Or, if they did, they weren't going to let on.

'What's happening?' asked Cristo.

Lizzie tried steering him away. 'Take no notice,' she said. But it was too late. They both saw a handcuffed man dragged out of the building. When he protested, he was silenced by a blow from a baton.

'*Basta!*' cried one of the brutes before shoving his helpless victim into the waiting truck, blood gushing from a head wound. Lizzie had just witnessed the OVRA in action. Mussolini's secret police had never been busier.

'What are they doing?' asked Cristo, jerking his hand out of hers.

Lizzie span round. 'The poor man had a nasty accident,' she lied. 'They're taking him to hospital, and we must go home.'

She clenched Cristo's hand once more and together they walked back to the sanctuary of the villa. Fascist Italy had become a frightening place for her, let alone a nine-year-old boy.

Chapter 4

Vincenzo Baldini started teaching Cristo the following week as planned. Lizzie still taught the child in the mornings; Baldini in the afternoons. At the end of lessons on the first day, Lizzie walked down the lawn to look out over the lake. Cristo had gone inside the villa with Violetta to ready himself for his GIL meeting. Lizzie hated seeing him trussed up to fight, but she had to force herself to hide her revulsion. She took the opportunity for a moment's quiet reflection to think about Hugh and how her life would be so different if she'd stayed with him in England.

The staff had been kind to her when they'd learned of her loss, even though Hugh had died fighting against Italy. Signor Sacco, the count's rather effete valet, who looked down his long nose at everyone, had offered condolences. The two kitchen maids – Nina, with dark eyes and olive skin, and Bianca, younger and much taller – had shown great sympathy, as had old Giuseppe, the gardener. Even Jacopo, Marco's temporary replacement who did odd jobs around the villa and kept to himself, also expressed his sympathies. Luigi, the count's self-opinionated driver with his lantern jaw and rather hostile manner, had been kind, too, and their kindness was much appreciated, but it didn't take away the isolation Lizzie felt.

As she stared at the dark water, she realised it mirrored her future right now. She'd no idea what it held, and the thought terrified her. Mussolini's Italy was no longer a place for a woman, let alone a single English one. Just as she felt she might cry, she heard footsteps approaching.

'Miss Thornton.' It was Signor Baldini. He was standing close to her right shoulder.

Lizzie brushed away a stray tear that had inconveniently broken loose and managed a tight smile as he drew alongside her.

'I just heard about your loss. Please accept my deepest sympathies.' He bowed his head, and she could see, behind his large lenses, the sincerity in his eyes. 'I understand you were engaged to be married.'

Maria must have told him, she guessed.

'Yes. Yes, I was.' She dared not turn and look at him in case she broke down all together.

They stood in silence for a moment and Lizzie appreciated it was an awkward situation for them both, but just then a family of ducks, a mother and father and a brood of six ducklings, paddled into the shallows and the tension seemed to break.

'I am sure Cristo will be of comfort to you at this difficult time,' he said.

The comment surprised her, but of course Baldini was right. In the circumstances, dear Cristo was her rock, even though he was too young to realise it. 'Yes. Yes, I'm sure he will,' she replied, still watching the ducks. Then she surprised herself by asking, 'Do you have children of your own, Signor Baldini?'

There was a slight pause and Lizzie turned to detect a shadow flit across the tutor's face. She realised she may have overstepped the mark.

'Why do you ask?' He held his hat in his hands and began to finger the rim, awkwardly.

'Because you are so good with Cristo. There seems to be this bond betw—'

He looked up and cut her short. 'Do you not also have a bond?'

She shrugged, instantly regretting their conversation had become so intimate. 'Yes, but as a woman it's more natural for me. Besides, I've known him a lot longer.'

He nodded and for a moment, Lizzie thought he might open up a little. The way he fixed his eyes on her made her think he might trust her with something as yet unspoken. Vincenzo Baldini was an enigma. He may talk like a fascist, but he had secrets. Yet she doubted he was ready to share them with her.

'Miss Lizzie, I can't find my cap.' Cristo, now dressed in the uniform of the fascist youth movement, cut through the tension.

Saved by his pupil's arrival, Baldini stepped away from her. 'Hello, young man,' he greeted.

'Sir,' said Cristo, before turning to Lizzie once more. 'Violetta said it wasn't with the rest of my uniform last week.'

'Then let's look together,' Lizzie suggested, holding out her hand to him. She glanced over her shoulder at Baldini, who remained by the lake.

As they walked briskly back up to the villa, Cristo asked, 'Miss Lizzie, you like Signor Baldini, don't you?'

The question was so unexpected, so out of the blue, that Lizzie didn't know quite how to deal with it. She paused her step. Of course, she'd been angry at first about not being consulted over his appointment, but the professional arrangement seemed to be working well.

'Of course, I like Signor Baldini,' she replied.

The boy looked thoughtful and nodded. 'I think he likes you, too.'

Over the next few days, life for Lizzie – at least her professional life – settled down into a routine. In the mornings she and Cristo would study English vocabulary, followed by English poetry, then composition. They'd also just begun to read *The Wind in the Willows*, which he seemed to enjoy. 'Mr Toad is funny,' he said, after Lizzie had just read the part where Toad proudly shows off his new motor car, living the life of a rich playboy. *Just like your father*, she thought.

Lizzie only usually saw Signor Baldini at a distance, striding up the hill from the classroom at the end of the school day, his satchel slung over his shoulder. If he happened to see her, he would raise his hat, but rarely stopped to talk. Once she saw him swimming in the lake with Cristo. She'd waved at them from the shore and Baldini waved back, but no more. Lizzie knew Cristo liked him, too, because it was obvious from what the little boy told her. *'Signor Baldini timed me when I ran today. Signor Baldini said my geometry is improving. Signor Baldini says he will start to teach me chess next week.'*

Admittedly Lizzie found it slightly odd that she felt she was only getting to know the new tutor through Cristo. The little boy was becoming a link in the chain. With all the upheaval of war and the daily diet of death and destruction in the newspapers and on the wireless in the kitchen, it seemed to her Cristo was forging something solid between all three of them that was holding their lives steady. And yet, despite this new tutor having been in post for almost a month, he remained a ghost; a shadow that flickered past from time to time, never leaving any trace. It was time to take the initiative, she decided. It was time to get to know Signor Vincenzo Baldini better.

At the end of another school day, Lizzie positioned herself on the terrace so Baldini couldn't avoid her as he walked back from the classroom towards the villa after lessons. The air was breathless, and the heat still searing. Her hands were planted on the hot stone of the balustrade as she pretended to scan the shimmering Tuscan skyline. The broad-brimmed hat she was wearing shaded her eyes, so Baldini couldn't know she was tracking him as he approached. With his dark hair, bronzed skin and jacket that was a little on the large side for him, he looked *different*. Unlike any other teacher she'd ever encountered when she taught at an

English prep school. There was no sign of a slight stoop, nor leather patches at the elbows of a tweed jacket. He wasn't socially awkward, nor did he seem self-opinionated and patronising, like so many males in her profession. She found him intriguing – that was the word – and that afternoon she decided to try to break down some of the barriers surrounding him.

'You seem to be settling in well, signor,' she remarked lightly as he approached.

Baldini paused just in front of her and smiled easily. Under his arm, he carried some textbooks. He took off his hat to address her and squinted against the sun. Sweat plastered his dark hair to his forehead.

'Cristoforo is an eager student,' he said. 'Too easily distracted, but I'm sure he will settle down.'

'Where is he now?' asked Lizzie, glancing at the summerhouse.

'On his way,' Baldini replied, looking over his shoulder just as the boy appeared running up the hill towards them.

'Good,' replied Lizzie. 'He has a GIL meeting in an hour.'

'Ah yes. The Italian Youth of the Lictor.' Lizzie noticed the corner of Baldini's mouth lifted in a crooked smile as he spelled out the acronym. There was something in his manner that made her think he didn't approve of the fascist youth movement either, although she didn't want to press him further. Instead, she explained: 'Maria needs to give him his supper before he goes.'

'Of course,' said Baldini, just as Cristo reached them both.

Lizzie noticed the pockets of the child's short trousers were bulging. 'What have you been up to, Cristo?' she quizzed.

The boy smiled, first at her, then at his new tutor. 'Signor Baldini told me to count the spirals in pinecones,' he replied.

'The Fibonacci sequence,' Baldini explained.

Lizzie laughed. 'An innovative maths lessons. Very good,' she said as Cristo whisked past her towards the back door. 'But I'm not sure Maria will want them in her kitchen,' she called after him. She couldn't be certain he'd heard her. Shaking her head, she turned back to Baldini. 'You seem to have captured his interest, signor.'

Lizzie saw his eyes light up behind his spectacles, appreciating the compliment. He nodded. 'I do my best,' he replied. 'Now if you'll excuse me, Miss Thornton.' Returning his hat to his head, he started off towards the path that led round to the front of the villa. Lizzie gathered he lived somewhere in the city, but suddenly found herself wondering if he was going home to a wife. He'd dodged her earlier question about having children of his own. Perhaps he was a bachelor. She shook such silly speculation from her head and went inside, realising she had failed again to find out anything at all about the mysterious new tutor. Besides, she had more pressing concerns, like making sure Cristo put those pinecones out of Maria's way and washed his hands before sitting down to eat. For the time being at least, Signor Vincenzo Baldini would have to remain an enigma.

Chapter 5

Wearing his grand uniform, Count de Falco pulled on his leather gloves on the steps of the Villa Martini. He'd told Signora Cortina he didn't know when he would return. America had joined the war the previous December and now threatened to drop its bombs on mainland Italy. Once again, he'd been called to Rome.

Cristo was also dressed in his uniform – in the dark shirt and shorts of the GIL. The outfit was topped off with a fez, just like the count's, and the child waited patiently on the front doorsteps to bid his father farewell. But when Luigi pulled up in the Lancia, the count barely bothered with his son. Instead, he just called out, 'Make me proud of you,' as he climbed into his waiting limousine. Moments later he disappeared out of the gates in a cloud of dust.

Lizzie liked it when the count was away. His presence in the villa seemed to cast a shadow over everything. His strict rules and regulations kept the staff in check. Over the next two weeks, her teaching became much more relaxed and informal. One day she even suggested a trip to the greenhouse to see Giuseppe's fruits and vegetables, thinking he might show Cristo how to plant and tend seeds.

In the slow warmth of a late autumn afternoon, Lizzie took Cristo to the kitchen garden at the back of the villa. The perfumed air was alive with the sound of buzzing bees, but the dazzling palette of colours was fading. Orange pumpkins and swollen green and yellow squashes still splashed the well-tended beds. There were red pomegranates on the trees, too, but many leaves were wilting and turning brown. They reminded Lizzie that winter was coming.

The garden was criss-crossed by narrow paths, bordered in places by neat, low hedges, but Giuseppe was nowhere to be found, so Lizzie followed a tapping sound at the far end of the garden.

'Come on,' she told Cristo, who'd been distracted by a dead lizard on the path.

Hand in hand, they went to a low stone building screened by a high hedge in the corner. There they found Jacopo, the handyman, hammering nails into a door frame.

'Hello,' greeted Lizzie.

The man, his eyes bulging out of a gaunt face, looked surprised to see visitors and laid down his hammer. Lizzie also thought she glimpsed fear scud across his pale face, although she'd no idea why.

'We're looking for Giuseppe,' she explained. 'We hoped he could show us how he grows his vegetables.'

Jacopo shook his head. 'He's taking his nap,' he told them sharply.

Lizzie, surprised by the unfriendly tone, nodded and bent down to Cristo. 'We'll come back another day,' she told him as they began to turn.

'No. Wait,' Jacopo called after a moment, his tone softening.

Lizzie looked back to see him beckoning.

'Please. I can show the young master something he might like.'

Cristo's eyes lit up and he looked at Lizzie. 'Yes? Can I?!' he exclaimed, rushing forward.

Lizzie followed as Jacopo opened wide the door frame he'd been repairing. The space seemed pitch-black at first, but when their eyes adjusted to the light, she could see dozens of tools, in all shapes and sizes, hanging on hooks from the walls. Shelves held pots of paint and oil. Planks of wood leaned in one corner, while in another Lizzie noted an iron-framed bed with a coverlet and bolster. She supposed it was where Jacopo slept. But it was what lay on the work bench that made Cristo suddenly gasp. A large wooden model of an aeroplane occupied almost the entire area.

'It's magnificent,' said Lizzie, bending down to examine it. 'You made it?'

'I did.' Jacopo nodded proudly.

'You are very clever,' remarked Cristo, spellbound by the craft as he walked around the workbench.

'If you are trained, it's not so hard,' came the reply.

Lizzie looked at the man questioningly. An air of intangible sadness seemed to float around him, like the imminent feeling of decay around the autumn garden.

'I was once an engineer,' he explained.

'Once?' repeated Lizzie, wondering why someone so highly skilled would be working as a handyman, especially when Italy was at war.

Making sure Cristo wasn't listening, Jacopo shrugged and shook his head. 'I am no longer welcome in my own country,' he told her softly.

It was then Lizzie realised what he was trying to tell her. 'I see,' she whispered. Jacopo was a Jew and, for the past few years, Jews had been banned from many professions in Italy.

'What model is it?' Cristo chirped up, still enthralled by the aircraft.

'A Macchi Thunderbolt,' explained Jacopo. 'One of our finest fighter planes.'

'I want to be a pilot one day,' piped up Cristo. Lizzie smiled but was reminded of Hugh and secretly hoped the boy would never have to go to war.

'Then you must study hard,' replied Jacopo. 'Look. I've almost finished the bodywork, then I must paint it,' he told him, adding; 'You can help me, if you like.'

Cristo gasped again and looked at his governess. 'Can I, Miss Lizzie? Please?'

Lizzie smiled. 'I'm sure you can, after lessons of course.'

'Come one day next week. Thursday, let's say,' said Jacopo, stroking his chin.

'It should be ready for the first coat then.'

'Thank you very much, Signor . . .'

'Levi,' said Jacopo, his dark eyes turning to crescents as he smiled.

Lizzie took her charge by the hand. 'What do you say to Signor Levi, Cristo?'

The child turned. 'Thank you, sir, for showing me your model,' he recited, adding excitedly, 'I can't wait to paint it.'

While Lizzie felt she could relax in Count de Falco's absence, clearly Signor Baldini did not. He seemed to retreat into his own shell. Whenever she saw him, he was preoccupied, always writing and barely having any time for her. She began to think that maybe, with news of Allied victories against Italy, he too, was coming to regard her as an enemy. It made her feel very uncomfortable, although she had to admit, even more intriguing to her. And the intrigue only grew when one afternoon she came downstairs to see the count's study door slightly ajar. She thought it very odd. Treading as softly as she could on the marble tiles, she stopped outside and put her ear to the crack. Drawers were being opened and shut. Someone was inside.

Taking a deep breath, she flung the door wide, hoping to catch an intruder off guard. Without his glasses he looked very different but there was no mistaking him.

'Signor Baldini!' she blurted, unable to hide her surprise.

Baldini stepped back from the desk, like a child caught with his hand in a biscuit jar. 'Miss Thornton,' he said with a stiff bow.

Lizzie waited a moment to allow the tutor time to offer an explanation. When it came – eventually, after a very awkward moment – she found it highly implausible.

'The count invited me to help myself to any books to prepare

Cristo's lessons,' Baldini explained. He gestured towards the wall of leather-bound volumes on his right.

Lizzie's eyes followed his hand to the bulging bookshelves. She nodded. 'How generous,' she replied, the sarcasm in her voice letting it be known she didn't believe him.

He shrugged slightly, then reached out towards the shelves and plucked out a hefty tome. Lifting it up triumphantly, he said: 'Here. This is what I was looking for.'

Lizzie tilted her head so she could read the spine. 'Really?' she said, suppressing her surprise. 'I don't think even the count would approve of you showing Cristo his copy of *One Hundred Erotic Illustrations* by the Marquis de Sade,' she added, trying to keep a straight face.

Baldini's eyes widened at the same time as he realised what the book contained. 'Oh, my mistake,' he said clumsily, patting his jacket pockets. 'I didn't have my spectacles on me.' He returned the volume to the shelf.

Even though Lizzie wasn't taken in by his unlikely excuse, she decided to let the matter drop. She looked at him squarely. He looked directly back. For the first time she could see his eyes properly. They were large and brown and fringed with long lashes, and they were pleading with her.

'Please. You won't . . .' he said.

She narrowed her gaze on his. She'd caught him red-handed in his employer's study, going through desk drawers, obviously searching for something.

'I'm not sure what you're up to, Signor Baldini,' she told him with a shake of her head, 'nor will I ask you, but what I do need to know is that you'll always do what's right for Cristo.'

At the mention of his pupil Baldini's brows shot up and his fearful expression dissolved into offended disbelief. 'Have I done anything to make you think otherwise, Miss Thornton?'

Lizzie was relieved to hear the hurt in his voice. She believed it to be genuine. 'No. No, you have not,' she conceded.

'And I can assure you I will never do anything to jeopardise Cristoforo's well-being,' he shot back.

'Very well, Signor Baldini,' Lizzie agreed. 'We'll say no more about this.'

In reply Baldini looked at her intently. 'Thank you,' he said, before taking a step towards the door. But something made Lizzie stand in his way.

'Just one more thing, Signor Baldini,' she said. Now she was sure he wasn't hired as the count's yes man to sing from the fascist song sheet, she had to let him know. She had to warn him, and she palmed her hand to stop him in his tracks.

As he pulled up, Lizzie's fingers brushed lightly against his jacket. He looked down at his sleeve, showing her he was aware of what had just happened, then lifted his gaze to meet hers.

'Yes, Miss Thornton?'

She took a deep breath. 'Please be careful, Signor Baldini,' she said. 'The secret police are everywhere.'

Every day for the past week, Cristo had kept reminding Lizzie about Thursday. 'Don't forget, miss,' he'd say. 'I need to help paint the model.'

'I won't forget,' Lizzie had always replied. It was good to see Cristo so excited. Signor Baldini was doing a good job of engaging his new student, but the prospect of painting the wooden aeroplane seemed to trump everything else, for the time being at least.

When lessons ended on Thursday, Lizzie needed no reminding it was finally time to pay a return visit to Jacopo's workshop. Smoke hung in the autumn air and Lizzie presumed Giuseppe had lit a bonfire. A plume of black smoke rose above the trees and the sound of flames crackled like snapping sticks as they approached.

Cristo bounded ahead of her on the path through the vegetable garden, but Lizzie saw something suddenly made him stop dead. As soon as she caught up, she could see why. Luigi, the driver, was throwing what looked like rags onto the fire, then poking the blaze with a pitchfork. She stopped in her tracks, too, the acrid smoke making her eyes sting. What had caught Cristo's attention wasn't the bedding that was being burned, nor the few books that fuelled the fire. What had turned the child's excitement to horror was the sight of a large wooden model of a single-seater Macchi Thunderbolt being hurled onto the blazing pyre and consumed by flames.

Chapter 6

The count's Lancia limousine had broken down. Luigi was trying to fix the gearbox, but with Jacopo's engineering skills no longer available because he'd been forced to leave, it was taking longer than expected.

'So how will Cristo get to his GIL meeting this evening?' asked Maria. She was sitting in her rocking chair in the kitchen, stroking Milo the cat on her knee.

Violetta, washing dishes at the sink, shrugged. 'He will have to miss it,' she said, with a toss of her long, dark hair.

'What?' barked Luigi, striding in with an oily cloth in his hand. Everyone knew the count was particularly keen his son attended the GIL meetings without fail.

'I'll take him,' volunteered Lizzie. She hated what was taught at the meetings but knew if de Falco discovered Cristo had missed one, he would blame her. 'I could do with the exercise. Besides, it's less than half an hour's walk away.'

Cristo remained quiet as they strode along the cobbled streets to the drill hall where the youth of Lucca congregated twice a week. Lizzie understood he was confused and upset about the burning of the wooden model and Jacopo's expulsion from the villa. An earlier thunderstorm had brought heavy rain and

35

without warning he stamped in a puddle, splashing his uniform socks and shorts.

'Cristo!' Lizzie scolded. 'Look at you. Why did you do that?'

'Why did they burn Jacopo's plane?' he countered. Lizzie bit her lip. How could she defend the indefensible? 'Why did they send him away?'

'He probably got a better job,' she lied. She hated herself for not explaining the reality of being a Jew in Italy, but she didn't think Cristo would understand the fascist racial laws, which his father now insisted were followed to the letter. It also made her worry about her own position. How long would it be before there was a knock on her own door and she was carried away as an 'enemy alien'?

The child brought his gaze up to hers, as if he knew she was hiding some terrible truth.

'It was because he was Jewish, wasn't it?'

They were standing outside the drill hall. Keen to avoid any more awkward questions, Lizzie tried to hurry her pupil inside. But Cristo persisted.

'It was, wasn't it? I heard Signora Cortina say so.' The boy's voice was climbing higher with exasperation. 'I heard her say he wasn't to be trusted, but Jesus was Jewish, and he was God's son, so I don't understand.'

The truth was nor did Lizzie, but before she was forced to reply, a GIL thug appeared on the hall steps. He ushered Cristo in, berating the youngster for his mud-spattered uniform as he went. For once she was grateful to one of Il Duce's henchmen. Thoughts of Jacopo and his model were hastily swept away from Cristo's head. *But for how long?* she wondered.

Lizzie decided to fill the next two hours with a stroll around the city. The mid-October air after the downpour was being warmed by a weaker sun, and the pavement *caffès* were beginning to fill up again. If the official Italian newspapers could be believed, although most of the time they couldn't, back in England

36

Hitler had just begun dropping tons of bombs on London. Yet here, in this beautiful ancient Roman city of golden stone, life went on as normal. Hugh was dead, but people still drank their espressos, smoked their Muratti cigarettes and strolled along Lucca's sun-kissed walls.

As she rounded the corner into a central piazza, Lizzie caught sight of a familiar figure. Signor Baldini, a satchel over his shoulder, was also emerging into the piazza from a side street. She waved, but he didn't notice her. Opening her mouth, she was just about to call out to him, when something stopped her.

He dropped by one of the *caffè* tables to talk to a heavily built man already seated. When he looked up, she could see that under his hat he had a beaked nose and high cheekbones. It was the sudden idea that she could learn more about Signor Baldini by saying nothing, that seized her then. During his time at the villa, he hadn't mentioned his home or his family once. Spying him with the elderly man in the botanical gardens and catching him in the count's study had made her curious, and that curiosity once again got the better of her.

He didn't join the man at the table, but after sweeping the piazza with a glare, simply handed over a brown paper bag, nodded and, without seemingly saying a word, made off through a nearby archway. Lizzie realised this was her chance to find out more. She would follow the new tutor.

Baldini kept to the back streets, powering along the narrow lanes and occasionally stopping to look over his shoulder. Lizzie managed to keep up, diving into doorways now and again, or flattening herself against yet another wall plastered with anti-government posters. It was quite early in the evening. Children played on the cobbles and the kitchen smells of ragout fought with the stink of drains in the warm air.

The tutor marched determinedly through the maze of lanes, ducking down under low arches and snaking through dark alleyways until at last a small square opened up before him. He headed for a large, solid building in the diagonally opposite corner. It looked like a factory to Lizzie, and she watched him disappear down some steps into, she presumed, a basement. She followed, keeping to the long shadows. Moving closer she bent down to peer through a low window. Once her eyes had adjusted to the light, she could make out some sort of machine. It was making a rhythmic, clattering sound. As she squinted through the glass, she realised what she was looking at.

A printing press. Her mind flashed to the antifascist bills on the walls that often appeared across the city overnight. They called for people to resist the government and take up arms against it. Luigi always said the communists were responsible for them. *Could Signor Baldini be a communist?* She was just pondering the thought when, from somewhere behind her, a rough hand clamped over her mouth, robbing her of breath. She struggled to get free, but the arm round her neck kept pulling towards the door. Lizzie's body was rigid with fear. She was no match for the man who now dragged her down the rest of the steps. Inside, the sound of the machinery was so deafening no one would hear her scream. But then as soon as the darkness lifted, she realised there would be no point struggling because Vincenzo Baldini was rushing towards her, a horrified look on his face.

'*Basta!*' he shouted over the noise of the press. 'Leave her!' he yelled. The man's grip loosened, and he backed off. 'Miss Thornton,' Baldini cried with a frown. 'Please, forgive him. Enzo can be a little too zealous at times.'

Despite realising there'd been a misunderstanding, the incident still unsettled her. 'Zealous?' she repeated. 'Is that what you call it?'

Baldini nodded his understanding. 'If the fascists find out what we're doing here . . .' He lifted his shoulders in a shrug and left the consequences to her imagination. 'Let us talk somewhere quieter.' As dozens of handbills continued to spew off the press to be bundled by another man, he led her away.

Lizzie followed him.

'Please.' He gestured her into a chair in a small office, while he took a seat behind the desk. In his hand he held one of the flyers that had just come hot off the press. He placed it in front of her. Immediately she realised what it was – a call to resistance. Antifascist propaganda. *MORTE DEL FASCISMO!* Looking up she saw Baldini leaning forward, an apology on his face. He blinked and raked his fingers through his dark hair. 'I can explain.'

Lizzie took a deep, steadying breath. 'Please do,' she agreed, giving way to curiosity. Perhaps Baldini would finally answer the questions that had been swirling around in her head ever since she'd caught him in the count's study. 'I'd like to know who you really are, Signor Baldini.'

He nodded, pushed his glasses up the bridge of his nose and cleared his throat. 'That is the easy part,' he told her. 'I am a democrat and I'm not alone. We call ourselves the Action Party. We are many in our group. Lawyers, doctors, students. We loathe Mussolini and his fascists, and we intend to fight to the death to restore our country to its people.'

Lizzie remained silent for a moment, digesting what she had just been told, then said, 'I saw you in the botanical gardens, before you started work at the villa. You were talking with an older man. It all seemed very hush-hush. Where does he fit in?'

'You saw me?' Baldini was shocked.

'The OVRA is not the only one who sees things done in secret, Signor Baldini,' she replied, feeling she had the upper hand.

He nodded and reached for a newspaper lying on the desk and turned it so she could read the front page. It was a publication she hadn't seen before. He read the title out loud. '*Freedom and Justice,*' he said. 'You could be jailed for reading it.'

She looked up at him, then down again to see a large photograph of an elderly man on the front page, under the headline '*The Professor arrested*'.

'But he's the man you . . .' Her voice trailed off in shock.

'Yes,' replied Baldini, sliding back the newspaper and jabbing the image with his finger. 'Professor Lodato, the joint head of the Action Party in Lucca. We are against the fascists and for freedom and democracy.'

'And now this Professor Lodato is in jail.'

'Yes, and while there are those working for his release, I must carry on publishing the newspaper.'

Planting his elbows on the desk, he pushed his spectacles back up his nose once more and leaned forward again. 'It seems you and I are on the same side, Miss Thornton.'

'If you mean I oppose the fascists and all they stand for, then yes, I do,' agreed Lizzie. She needed to put his mind at rest. 'I will not betray you, Signor Baldini, if that is what worries you.'

He smiled then – a wide, generous smile. 'I never doubted you would do that, Miss Thornton. I know you are a woman who believes in democracy, too, yes? You agree with Mr Churchill? Hitler and Mussolini must be stopped.'

'Yes, of course, but . . .' Poor Jacopo's gaunt face appeared in her mind's eye. Not only must the fascists be stopped. They had to be defeated, but other than by bombs and guns – neither of which she had – how? Was he setting a trap for her? 'What are you saying, Signor Baldini?' she asked, her heart starting to race again.

Baldini tilted his head and removed his glasses to fix her with his dark eyes. She felt a pulse thumping in her temple as she anticipated his question but instead of swerving away from him, something deep inside compelled her to hold his gaze. Even so, when the words came, they were even more terrifying than she'd imagined.

In a low, steady voice, he said: 'We need strong women like you to help our cause, Miss Thornton. Will you stand with us?'

Chapter 7

Count de Falco's anticipated return from Rome a few days later set the household abuzz. Maria ordered Giuseppe to harvest tomatoes, lemons and zucchini from the greenhouse and Signora Cortina worked Violetta and the other housemaids all hours, polishing the silver and scrubbing the floors. Cristo had been so excited when he'd learned of his father's return after so many weeks away, he found it hard to concentrate on his schoolwork. Lizzie caught him daydreaming more than usual, so she suggested he write an account of everything that had happened in the count's absence. Cristo's letters may have been unruly, but his sentiment touched her deeply. *'Miss Lizzie looked after me when I was sad and missed Mama.'*

With the colder weather approaching, it had also been decided to hold classes indoors. Lizzie and Signor Baldini were packing books in the pavilion in anticipation of the move when news came that de Falco was due to arrive that afternoon. Cristo was already inside the villa, so Lizzie took advantage of one of the rare moments alone with the tutor.

Signor Baldini's secret was, of course, safe with her. She admired his courage and commitment and would never alert the fascists to the printing press. She loathed them just as much as he did. Nevertheless, her first duty remained to Cristo.

'I respect you, Signor Baldini, and I have given careful thought to joining . . .' She hesitated to say 'the resistance' in case someone was listening. 'But I need to know more,' she told him, arranging textbooks in a box ready for the to move to the villa.

He smiled then; one of his deeply disarming smiles and nodded. 'I apologise, Miss Thornton,' he replied, hefting another large box, as if he had anticipated her response and was happy to accept it. 'I should not have asked you. Please, forget I ever did.'

He was about to turn away, heading for the door, when Lizzie felt herself suddenly reaching out to him. Taken aback, he looked down to see her hand resting on his sleeve. She seemed as shocked as he was and quickly withdrew as the colour rose in her cheeks. 'I cannot forget, Signor Baldini. That is the trouble.' She had witnessed fascist brutality close up, first with the OVRA agents and then with Jacopo's treatment. She shook her head. 'The more I see around me, the hatred and the cruelty, the more I want to protect Cristo.'

Baldini's smile was gentle. Understanding. 'The decision is yours, Miss Thornton,' he told her. 'You must do what your conscience dictates.'

'Signor Baldini.' A croaky voice sounded from outside. It was Signora Cortina. She was beckoning in an agitated way, summoning them up to the villa. Their conversation would have to be resumed another time.

For the duration of the winter, the music room was to be the classroom. Up until now, the count had decreed the room strictly out of bounds. It was once the late contessa's favourite space, where she would spend hours playing her beloved Puccini pieces at the piano. De Falco had not wished it to be disturbed.

Once inside the villa, Lizzie and Cristo joined Signora Cortina by the locked door as she examined the keys on her belt in silence. Finally settling on one, she inserted it in the keyhole. The door swung open on creaky hinges to reveal a room clothed in darkness and trapped in time.

'Please.' The housekeeper's bony hand gestured Lizzie and Cristo inside.

The shutters were closed and the internal blinds on the long casement windows were down. Lizzie sniffed. The air was musty and slightly damp, but dried lavender had been placed along the sills to ward off any scorpions. Yet she detected another perfume lingering on the air. Something more sophisticated, more smouldering. Patchouli, perhaps with a hint of vanilla. The late Contessa de Falco's Paris perfume, she assumed. Then she spotted her portrait hanging over the fireplace. Lizzie walked over to study it. The woman was in her early thirties, she guessed, and strikingly beautiful with dark lustrous curls, just like Cristo's. She'd been painted looking away into the distance. There was a wistful, melancholy expression on her face. It made Lizzie wonder if she'd been happily married to the count, although judging by what she'd witnessed, she suspected de Falco's fondness for female company had started prior to his wife's death.

Signora Cortina crossed the marble floor to lift the blinds and open the shutters. The low sunlight of an autumn afternoon bathed the room in a golden glow. There were a few other paintings of bucolic scenes on the walls and a marble bust on a plinth but at the centre, covered by a white sheet, stood a grand piano. The housekeeper removed the sheet with a slow reverence, gathering its folds into her arms, to expose a magnificent Steinway.

'The contessa would play it for hours,' she mused, standing back to admire the instrument. Turning then to Cristo, she said: 'You remember, don't you?'

'Yes. Yes, I do,' replied the child. 'Mama played like an angel.'

Signor Cortina regarded Cristo with something like fondness. There was a warmth in her look that Lizzie had never seen on the housekeeper's face before. 'And now she is one herself,' she said softly.

Lizzie paused for a moment, feeling like an unwelcome intruder, encroaching on memories of a woman she had never known. 'We will treat everything with great respect,' she assured the housekeeper, touching the piano lid lightly.

Signora Cortina shut her eyes for a moment, as if conjuring an image of the contessa in her mind. 'Yes,' she said softly. 'I trust you will.'

Lizzie watched the housekeeper leave before setting down her books on the large desk by the French doors.

'Where should I sit?' asked Cristo.

Lizzie looked around her at the sparsely furnished room.

'We'll find you a desk and chair,' she told him just as the door was flung wide open. Baldini stood in the doorway, a huge box in his arms. He entered and set it down on the tiled floor, then straightened himself to take stock of the room. It seemed to Lizzie that he was reacquainting himself with it, even though she knew he couldn't have possibly been inside it before. She especially noticed his gaze snag on the contessa's portrait before sniffing the air. For a fraction of a second his eyes closed, too, as if the lingering scent Lizzie noticed earlier had triggered a memory.

'The contessa was very beautiful, wasn't she?' she said.

'Yes. Yes, she was,' the tutor replied, allowing his gaze to remain a little longer on the painting.

'Is everything all right, Signor Baldini?'

His head turned quickly, and, on his face, Lizzie noticed the same look he'd given her when she'd caught him in the count's study. But before he could reply, Signor Sacco called through. The count's car was coming up the drive.

Within seconds the staff had hastily lined up on the villa steps to greet de Falco's limousine. Flanked by two motorcycle outriders, it roared to a halt outside. Cristo insisted on wearing his GIL uniform to welcome his father. He stood ramrod straight with his small hand raised in a salute. But when de Falco stepped out of the motor car, he didn't even look at his son standing proudly

44

on the steps. Instead, he swept into the villa and through the hall. Cristo's hand dropped wanly by his side, but, still desperate to see his papa after so many weeks, he began tugging at Lizzie's arm like a puppy on a leash.

'Not now, Cristo,' she told him, watching the count storm into his study. 'Your father has important affairs to attend to.' Taking the child's hand in hers she started to lead him gently away to the music room. But just before she did, she saw through the half-open study door that de Falco was on the telephone. In his left hand he held a ragged poster, torn at its top edge. A shiver coursed through her as she recognised it was one of the antifascist posters – one of Baldini's.

'Go and get your exercise book out,' she instructed.

'But . . .' Cristo tugged at her again.

'No buts. I'll be along in a moment.'

As soon as the child huffed off leaving her in the hallway, Lizzie was able to hear what was said in the study. As the staff filed back to their duties, she loitered outside the study a moment longer to catch de Falco bark down the line, 'Get me the mayor, now!'

A short pause followed but then, 'I don't care if there are dozens of them. Hundreds. I want every single one of these filthy posters destroyed and whoever put them up arrested. You hear me? Or it'll be *you* in front of a firing squad.'

Back in the classroom, Lizzie found it hard to concentrate on Cristo's lesson as de Falco's words replayed in her mind. Signor Baldini was in the count's sights. So, too, was the printer as well as all the brave men and women who ventured out under cover of darkness to tell the citizens of Lucca their leaders were tyrants. As for Cristo, he'd completely withdrawn, upset that his father had ignored him. It seemed that no amount of coaxing would bring him out of his shell.

It was a huge relief when, a few minutes later, Baldini finally returned from the outbuildings, where he and old Giuseppe were looking for a suitable desk. They'd found one.

'Well, what have we here?' he asked, seeing the child in his GIL uniform.

Cristo leapt up from the piano stool and stood to attention, his arm extended in a salute.

'What a fine young man you are,' he remarked with a nod, even though Lizzie knew he was putting on a show.

The child beamed at this response and, although she hated to see Cristo wearing his uniform, Lizzie smiled, too. He could not be blamed for conforming. The sins of his father were not his.

'Now, soldier,' said Baldini, 'why don't you change out of your uniform, so we can go rowing?'

Cristo's face lit up with excitement. Gone was the despondent expression, and in its place an eagerness to please.

'Rowing? Yes, sir,' he cried, saluting once more.

Baldini took out a fob watch from his pocket. 'You have ten minutes to complete your task,' he said, raising his hand, then chopping the air. 'Go!'

As soon as Cristo was out of the room, he edged towards Lizzie and removed his spectacles. 'You were saying you wanted to protect Cristo, Miss Thornton.'

Lizzie frowned, remembering what she'd told him earlier. *Was she really so transparent?* 'Yes. Yes, I do. Very much,' she came back quickly.

He smiled. 'We have worked together for a little while now. I think we understand each other.'

'I believe we do,' she replied. 'And that is why I must tell you.'

He lowered his voice even more. 'Tell me what?'

She took a deep breath. 'I overheard the count on the telephone earlier.'

'Yes?' Baldini seemed interested. He tilted his head but still didn't look at her directly.

'He was speaking with the mayor. He's seen your posters around the city, and he's angry.'

'Good,' he replied with a nod.

'But then he said . . .' She paused, worried how to frame her news. 'He said he wanted whoever was responsible for them arrested.'

Baldini coughed out a laugh. 'I'm sure he does,' he replied lightly.

He doesn't understand the danger, thought Lizzie. She tried again. 'He said if the mayor didn't see all the posters were destroyed, he would *also* be shot.'

A shake of the head then, but still the smile lingered. 'De Falco doesn't frighten me. Yes, he can shoot me, but there are many others to take my place. There are hundreds in this city who will risk their lives to overthrow Mussolini.'

'You are very brave, Signor Baldini,' she told him. Hugh had been brave, too, she thought. He'd died a hero, but this was a different kind of heroism.

'Courage comes easily to those who have no choice,' Baldini replied. His eyes, so often hidden behind the shield of his glasses, suddenly reddened and, for a second, Lizzie thought he might even give in to tears. 'It is for Cristo I do this, Miss Thornton,' he said finally. 'This war has been foisted on Italians by one man's ego. Fighting doesn't come naturally to me, either, but fight I will and to the death, if I have to, because I want children, like Cristo, to grow up free.'

His voice carried such conviction that she found herself moved by it. Determination was written on his face. He meant every word and what he said made her feel small and inadequate. She, too, wanted the very best for Cristo.

'Signor Baldini,' she said a moment later.

'Vincenzo, please.'

'Vincenzo.' His name sounded soft on her tongue. 'Please call me . . .' She hesitated. 'Please call me Lizzie,' she said, 'like Cristo does.'

His gaze was intense. 'Yes, Lizzie.'

'I wanted to say . . .' She drew a deep breath. 'I wanted to say I wish to join you.'

Baldini's brows suddenly knitted together, and he held her gaze. 'You wish to join the resistance?'

'More than anything,' she replied, looking deep into his brown eyes.

But he began shaking his head, as if he suspected her motives. 'Please, you don't have to do this. I asked too much of you. Italy is not even your country.'

She also shook her head. 'That's where you're wrong, Vincenzo. I have come to feel more Italian than English. That is why I have decided to help you, if you'll let me.' She'd been afraid she might falter, but the words tumbled quickly from her mouth and the tutor's stern look dissolved into a smile.

'You are sure? You know the consequences if—'

'I've never been more certain of anything.'

'Then I am indebted to you, Miss Thornton. Lizzie. I'm so grateful to you for—' He broke off. 'I respect you, you see.'

Respect. No man, Italian or English, or indeed of any nationality, had ever told Lizzie they *respected* her before. Male colleagues had complimented her, but come to think of it, usually on her appearance. *What a pretty blouse you're wearing today, Miss Thornton.* Or *Have you done something different to your hair?* Now here was a man – a brave, good man – telling her he respected her. His words made her feel taller; made her believe anything was possible.

Drawing herself up to her full height she told him, 'Thank you, Vincenzo. I appreciate that.' He would never know how much it meant to her.

From that day on, it was as if Lizzie had shed a heavy old coat and slipped on a summer dress. Despite the cooler weather, she felt a sense of freedom she'd never had before. But with that freedom came another sensation – fear. Vincenzo had asked her if she could contribute to the newspaper and she'd willingly agreed, although she'd no idea what it might involve; only that the role came with risks. Great risks. Yet, despite the dangers, with Vincenzo at her side, she also felt invincible.

A few days later, Lizzie went to read Cristo a bedtime story in his room, but before she knocked, she paused when she heard a sound. Pressing her ear against the door, she listened. Was Cristo singing? She smiled. She'd never heard him sing to himself before. She listened again. Could it be Puccini? Without waiting for a reply, she walked in. But the sight that greeted her came as quite a surprise.

'Cristo? Cristo, what are you doing?' she asked, finding the boy in his pyjamas, lying on his stomach. He didn't respond to her immediately and it was only when she drew nearer, she discovered why. Haloing his head was a thin metal ring and discs covered his ears. He was huddled over something on his counterpane.

Edging over to the bed Lizzie touched him on the shoulder. He jumped and let out a little squeal, then scrambled upright, immediately jettisoning the earphones.

'What have you got there?' she asked, looking at the strange contraption on the bed. It consisted of a coil, a tube and some wire.

Cristo grinned. It wasn't his normal reaction when he'd been caught doing something he shouldn't. In fact, on this occasion, he seemed eager to share his excitement.

'It's a crystal set,' he replied, proudly holding it up.

Lizzie joined him on the bed to inspect the odd device and took it from his hands. On a small wooden board, a pencil lead was attached to a safety pin pressing against a razor blade.

Of course, she'd heard of crystal sets. They were rudimentary radio receivers that didn't need any external power. But how on earth had Cristo got hold of one? And, just as importantly, what was he listening to? Both questions were answered swiftly.

'We made it in my physics lesson,' the child informed her. 'I can listen to Radio EIAR now.'

Lizzie's brows lifted simultaneously. The state radio station broadcast music and entertainment as well as Il Duce's speeches.

'So Signor Baldini taught you how to make this?'

'Yes.' The boy held out his earphones. 'Would you like to listen?'

She nodded and took them from him, clamping them onto her ears. The sound was not very loud and slightly scratchy, but it was audible. A Puccini aria was playing.

'Isn't it *sublime*?' said Cristo, mimicking one of Signor Sacco's favourite words.

Lizzie had to agree. 'Yes. It certainly is,' she replied, unhooking the earphones and smoothing down her hair. Secretly, however, she was still processing the surprise. This, she guessed, was how Vincenzo obtained most of the latest news to fill *Freedom & Justice*. He would have his very own crystal set and it would be tuned into an Allied radio station. Instead of the usual fascist propaganda broadcast by Mussolini and his lackeys, he would be able to hear the true version of events; the Italian defeats and casualties never aired and the Allied victories taking so long to materialise. Suddenly everything was falling into place. Thanks to Vincenzo Baldini, she had hope once more.

Chapter 8

At the start of November, the autumn sun disappeared behind grey clouds, and cold rain fell incessantly. The River Serchio hurtled down from the mountains and became a raging torrent and all over Europe the war raged too, pouring into northern Africa, and reaching deep into the desert. Cristo's tenth birthday – ignored by the count – was marked by a small party in the kitchen. Shortly afterwards, de Falco left for Rome once more. It made it easier for Lizzie to speak more freely with Vincenzo and to learn more about her new role in the resistance.

She had been right about the radio. It turned out Vincenzo kept one hidden in the attic of his home. It was tuned to Radio Londra, the British Broadcasting Corporation channel started shortly before the outbreak of war. For obvious reasons, the wireless in the kitchen at the Villa Martini was tuned to the official government station which spewed out constant lies. Now, thanks to Vincenzo, Lizzie had her very own crystal set and could listen to British radio in her room at night. It was good to hear the truth from a trusted source and she would willingly spread the word through her pen as soon as Vincenzo showed her how.

A week had passed when they met one evening in the music room to discuss Lizzie's role on the newspaper. Vincenzo suggested she sit at the piano. He would stand by her side. That way if anyone entered, they could say they were arranging a piece of music to teach to Cristo.

She had already written two articles from material she'd gathered from the Radio Londra broadcast and now awaited Vincenzo's verdict. It felt odd being the pupil, watching his owlish eyes scan her handwritten prose in silence as she held her breath. But when he looked up, took off his spectacles and smiled broadly, she felt calmer.

'These are excellent,' he told her, slapping the paper enthusiastically. 'But then I knew they would be.'

'They are not too . . .' She searched for a word. 'Academic?'

Vincenzo shook his head. 'The tone is *perfetto*,' he told her.

'And it's not too long?'

He raised a hand. 'We shall see. This is where I need to teach you about headlines, fonts, point sizes and printers' marks, so that you can prepare copy for the press.' He counted on his fingers as he thought of what she needed to know.

'Copy?' she repeated with a frown. He was talking in a foreign language.

'Another word for an article,' he replied. But when he saw she was anxious, he paused and looked into her eyes to reassure her. 'It's not hard. Really it isn't, and if anyone can learn quickly, it's you, Lizzie.'

He had a wonderful gift of making her feel she could do anything she set her mind to.

'Cristo tells me you are a very good teacher,' she teased. 'I can see he is right.'

Vincenzo rolled his eyes and laughed a little. 'True, but my pupil has to be eager to learn,' he told her, smiling as her nerves seemed to miraculously disappear.

Working secretly in the evenings, Lizzie would make notes on the Allied news bulletins, and, where necessary, translate them into Italian. Her articles were then printed in the antifascist newsletter

52

read in hundreds of homes around the city. At first, she was careful to work only in her room, and to hide any manuscripts in a shoebox in her wardrobe. There were those on the villa staff who certainly couldn't be trusted. But when the count was away, as he so often was these days, and wasn't expected back until January, she allowed herself to relax a little.

It was the end of another school day, shortly before Christmas, and, by the light of an oil lamp, Lizzie hunched over her desk in the music room, shivering as she tried to control the pen clutched between icy fingers. Vincenzo sat opposite. In the Tuscan mountains to the north the snow lay thick, according to reports, but in Lucca the few flakes that fell turned to water when they hit the wet ground. Nevertheless, the cold crept into everyone's bones and as the war dragged on, into everyone's soul. News had also come of Marco's death. Giuseppe's son had died of exposure in the Albanian mountains. Nina and Bianca had cried on and off for days and poor Giuseppe, who had lost his only son, retreated into his own silent world to mourn.

That evening Cristo had been driven to another drill meeting and she, a thick shawl round her shoulders, had set to work. It had been dark for a while and the only sound she heard was the rain beating against the shuttered windows. But she was not alone. Glancing up she saw Vincenzo at work on the opposite side of the table. If anyone walked in it would look as though they were both marking Cristo's textbooks. The reality was very different. He was editing the latest edition of *Freedom & Justice* and Lizzie was helping him. As well as writing pieces, she'd been proofreading articles by other activists for the newspaper. Some of them were typed, some were not, but they all needed to be marked up and corrected before they were printed.

On the newsstands in the street, the fascist newspapers kept hailing victories and lauding Il Duce. In reality, that winter, Mussolini's dreams of restoring the Roman empire in the Mediterranean seemed to be fading. The articles Lizzie wrote told the other side of the story; of the suffering of the conscripted soldiers and the hungry, homeless civilians, as well as any progress the Allies made.

Vincenzo told her he admired her work, while she admired his bravery and his tenacity, but there was something more that had been growing between them; a mutual understanding, an ease in each other's company. It was a strange feeling and one she'd never experienced before. With Hugh everything had been so rushed, so dramatic. When she'd first realised she was attracted to Vincenzo, it was an unhurried response, like being carried gently along on a broad river, but their time together was snatched and occupied by work on the newspaper. Yet that evening, as they sat opposite each other, working by candlelight, an overwhelming need to touch him had gathered inside her. She could bear it no longer. Even though she knew she was playing a dangerous game, she set down her pen and reached out to him, laying her cold hand on his.

Taken by surprise, Vincenzo looked down before his gaze travelled up her arm to her face. He smiled, then, and took off his spectacles before clasping her other hand in his. The lamplight's glow made his large eyes glisten. But just as he opened his mouth to speak, the door swung wide without warning and Violetta appeared. Lizzie snatched back her hand.

'Signora Cortina sent me to close up. I didn't realise . . .' Her voice faltered awkwardly. It was clear to Lizzie the maid had caught them together.

'We'll see everything is in order,' Vincenzo replied with a reassuring nod, adding, 'Thank you, Violetta,' in such a way as if silently begging her to say nothing about what she'd just witnessed.

The trouble was neither of them could be sure of her loyalty. From now on they both knew they would need to be extra careful in each other's company.

*   *   *

The encounter with Violetta was a wake-up call. Vincenzo suggested their contact should be confined to between lessons or occasionally in the evenings when Cristo was at his GIL meetings. Lizzie knew it was the sensible reaction, but it only made her long for him more. Every time he walked into the room, she caught her breath. Every hour spent without him was longer. In his presence it was as if Hugh's sensible, solid, wifely Elizabeth had never existed. She'd been replaced by a bolder, more independent Lizzie who drew her courage from the light Vincenzo Baldini had kindled inside her. He was putting his trust in her. She doubted if Hugh ever had. It made her stronger.

As Christmas approached, Lizzie sat at the kitchen table, helping Cristo string coloured pasta through thin red ribbon as decorations. In recent days Cristo had stopped asking if there was any news of his father, knowing that he would not be returning for the festivities. Lizzie was determined that he should enjoy the forthcoming celebrations no matter what and suggested Giuseppe cut a small cypress from the garden to set in the hall. Together she and Cristo were making ornaments to hang on it, just as she had as a child, and painting pinecones silver for a table display.

On Christmas Eve, all the staff who were not away fighting sat down on the long table in the kitchen to enjoy a traditional meal together. Maria cooked a fish supper and supplemented it with roast potatoes, pumpkin with herbs and fried mushrooms. No one seemed keen to talk about the war although Signor Sacco proposed a toast to those who were fighting for their country, and they all thought of Marco. Lizzie thought of Jacopo, too, turned out of his home for being a Jew, but no one ever mentioned his name.

She sat opposite Vincenzo. They kept their conversation formal in front of everyone else. 'So, your fourth Italian Christmas, Miss Thornton,' he remarked, taking a sip of red wine.

'Yes,' replied Lizzie. 'Quite different from an English one.'

'But most of your customs are German, surely, from Queen Victoria's husband, Albert?'

Lizzie played with the stem of her glass and smiled a little awkwardly, aware Signor Sacco was taking an interest in their conversation and would willingly hijack it with his fascist propaganda.

'That is true. The tree, the stocking and many of our carols are borrowed from Germany.'

'Then let us drink a toast to our German allies,' suggested Sacco. No one dared contradict him, so everyone stood and raised their glasses to the Nazis. 'To Herr Hitler,' he cried.

'And to Marco – and all our brave brothers who've lost their lives,' Luigi added.

When it was time to eat, Cristo joined in enthusiastically and helped Maria and Violetta put dishes on the table before sitting down himself.

'This one is specially for you,' Violetta told Vincenzo with a coquettish smile. She set down a plate of baked aubergine in front of him. It seemed to have more mozzarella than the others.

'Eh. No favourites!' Maria called over, shaking her plump finger.

There was a gale of laughter from the other housemaids and Giuseppe. Vincenzo just smiled, taking it all in good spirit.

Talk turned to past Christmases and what people did when they were children. Maria remembered when her father gave her an orange and Signor Sacco recalled seeing his mother dress for Midnight Mass and looking 'sublime'.

'What about you, Signor Baldini?' asked Cristo. 'What about your mama and papa?'

Vincenzo shrugged and seemed a little embarrassed. He looked deep into his glass, as if seeking an answer. 'I lost them long ago,' was all he said. Vincenzo's background remained a closed book to everyone, including Lizzie. Even though they'd grown closer over the past few weeks, she was none the wiser about his family; aunts and uncles and cousins, if not a wife and children. She understood. The less he said about his personal life, the better. The OVRA would not hesitate to arrest any of his loved ones and make them suffer, too.

Cristo's eyes lit up. 'Why don't you stay with us, and we could sing songs and play games?'

Another smile from Vincenzo. 'Thank you, Cristo. We shall see.'

After the meal Giuseppe sat in his usual chair by the stove, smoking a pipe. Maria flopped down in another chair beside him, her legs splayed under her voluminous black skirt. The housemaids chattered as they tidied away the plates. Seeing the fire was dying, Vincenzo poked more life into the embers and added more logs from the nearby basket.

'Can I, miss?' asked Cristo, cryptically. He was bursting with excitement, hopping from one foot to the other. Only Lizzie understood why.

Vincenzo shot her a questioning look and she replied with a smile. 'Yes, you can.'

Scampering over to a cupboard, the boy flung open a door and pulled out a large red stocking. It had been patched with felt holly leaves and berries. Lizzie had spent a rainy afternoon decorating it with her pupil.

'It is something children do in England,' Cristo explained as he hung the stocking on a hook on the mantel shelf. 'And if they are good, they are visited by Father Christmas who leaves a present as a reward.'

'Well, well,' said Vincenzo, returning the poker to its stand. He smiled at Lizzie standing behind the boy, her hands on his shoulders, as she watched Cristo adjust the brightly coloured stocking. The wine had left her face flushed, and from the corner of her eye she sensed he was looking at her.

'What a beautiful custom. Goodness rewarded,' he said.

Perhaps it was the glow of the firelight or possibly the wine, but rekindling the warmth that memories of past Christmases brought her made her dare to think of the future. She could suddenly see what it might be like with Vincenzo, and she turned to meet his gaze. There'd been a tenderness in his eyes as he watched Cristo and now, she realised what she thought was a glint in his eye was a tear. It spilled out and he quickly wiped it away with the flick of a finger. She guessed he felt the same as her. He was worrying for Cristo, too. She longed to hold this kind, good man, who seemed to care for the child as much as she did. But in that moment, all she could do was comfort him with the warmth of her look.

When he moved a little closer her heart fluttered.

'Merry Christmas, Miss Thornton,' he said softly.

'Merry Christmas, Signor Baldini,' she replied.

There were just two people in the room. All the others seemed to melt away. It was only Violetta, pouring milk into a jug by the sink, who noticed what passed between them.

Chapter 9

When Lizzie walked into the kitchen at the Villa Martini one bitterly cold morning, all hell seemed to have broken loose. Count de Falco had finally returned home the previous week and ensconced himself in his study for hours on end. The household had been wearing its straitjacket of rules and regulations once again but suddenly Signora Cortina was presiding over organised chaos, pointing and shouting like a traffic policeman in central Rome. Maria appeared more stressed than usual, arguing with herself over which dishes should be fetched. Giuseppe had just arrived with a basketful of dried herbs and was toing and froing from the pantry, while Nina and Bianca had been put to work cleaning the silver on the table. Violetta was ironing napkins.

'What's happened? *Che e successo?*' Lizzie asked anyone who might answer. Pino, the pigeon-toed assistant gardener back on leave from the army, had just barged past carrying a leg of lamb over his shoulder.

'We have guests tomorrow,' Violetta explained, the words escaping from the corner of her full lips to avoid Signora Cortina's detection.

Guests, repeated Lizzie in her head. The only guests the count had ever entertained were the female variety. They normally spent time on the chaise longue in his study to emerge two hours later with their hair freshly brushed and their lipstick newly applied. These guests must be much more important, she told herself.

She was just digesting this information when the housekeeper caught her eye, but instead of shooing her away to allow the kitchen staff to get on with their tasks, she beckoned to her.

'Yes, signora?' asked Lizzie, puzzled.

'The count wishes to see you, Miss Thornton.' Her head was tilted at an imperious angle like an undertaker trying to soften the blow of a death. 'He is in his study.'

Lizzie swallowed hard. The count rarely asked to see her, and she immediately assumed she was in trouble. Her thoughts turned to Vincenzo. Did de Falco suspect him? Had Vincenzo been revealed as the man behind the posters and newspapers in the city? Even though it was a cold day, sweat prickled her neck.

A timid knock on the study door was answered by a measured '*Avanti*,' and Lizzie entered to find, much to her surprise, Cristo standing by his father's desk. The room was wreathed in smoke from the count's cigar. It masked the usual lingering smell of expensive French perfume.

'Good morning, Miss Thornton.' De Falco greeted her in English as he rose and invited her to sit in the chair in front of him.

'Sir,' she replied with a nod, her eyes scooting to Cristo. She was relieved to see he was standing with a smile on his face.

'I shall be brief,' said the count, returning to his seat. 'I have invited some very special guests to dine here tomorrow evening and I would like to provide some entertainment.' His head inclined towards his son and Lizzie raised a brow. Surely, he wasn't going to ask Cristo to perform like some dancing bear?

'You look bemused, Miss Thornton, but what I propose is quite straightforward. Cristoforo will sing "Giovinezza", accompanied by your good self on the pianoforte.'

This time Lizzie raised both brows. '"Giovinezza"?' she repeated.

'Yes,' replied the count with a nod, adding, 'wearing his GIL uniform of course.'

Lizzie said nothing at first. 'Giovinezza' had become the Italian Fascist anthem, a poem set to music that lauded Mussolini and the Fatherland. Her gaze rested on Cristo, his round face split by a broad grin. He looked so happy it broke her heart to see him being exploited by his father. But there was nothing she could do. After a moment's hesitation she replied: 'Of course, sir. We do not have much time, but . . .'

The count clapped his hands and rubbed them together. 'Exactly. You need to start practising,' he told her, passing over a printed copy of the words and music. 'The performance must be perfect,' he said, his expression stern. 'You understand, Miss Thornton?'

His look sent a cold shiver coursing down Lizzie's spine. From the sound of it, these guests were high-ranking fascist officials. Their presence would be of interest to Vincenzo.

'Of course, sir,' she replied. 'We will do our very best,' she added, throwing a nod at Cristo.

'Good,' he said, switching on a smile and ruffling his son's hair. 'Because only your best is good enough. Now, off you go,' he told him. He reached into the ashtray for his half-smoked cigar and gave it a triumphant puff.

Lizzie also rose, slipped Count de Falco a tight smile then followed her pupil out of the study in silence. Had the count's words carried a threat? Or was she just imagining it? Either way, a sense of dread powered her every step out of the study.

When Lizzie told Vincenzo about the guests, he whipped off his spectacles. 'He didn't say who?'

She'd caught him alone in the music room. Cristo was with Violetta. They wouldn't be interrupted. 'No, but he said they were very important. He's asked Cristo and me to perform "Giovinezza" for them.'

'What?' Baldini frowned. 'So, you, an Englishwoman, will get to meet them?'

Lizzie stood quite still. 'Yes. Yes, I will.'

The prospect clearly troubled Vincenzo. 'But your position. You are . . .' His voice trailed off in concern.

Lizzie understood what he was driving at. 'I know I'm here at the count's discretion, Vincenzo, but don't you see? I can listen to what they say. It's rumoured on the radio German reinforcements are on their way to Mussolini's units in North Africa. They might discuss matters that could be useful to us.'

Still, the tutor seemed unhappy. 'It could be a trap. I don't want . . .'

Suddenly she felt his hands clasping her arms. A tingling sensation shot through her as she glanced down at them, then looked up again. She shook her head. 'You said yourself, we are not alone, Vincenzo. You told me the Action Party is in touch with a British agent. I must find out what I can, so you can pass on any intelligence.'

She found his touch calming and reassuring, yet thrilling at the same time, so that as she held his gaze, she felt her chin tilt towards his face. The next moment his hot mouth pressed hard on her open lips and his body was firm against hers. For several heavenly seconds her whole being took flight. Any fears seemed to drift away, and an energy, absent for such a very long time, flooded her body, lifting it up, as if it was liberating her, bringing her out of the shadows. In Vincenzo Baldini's embrace she had surfaced to the light: she was finally made to feel equal.

Lizzie seated herself at the stool in the music room early the following morning. Taking a deep breath, she reverently opened the piano's lid. Cristo stood at her side as she propped up the sheet music on the holder and read the lyrics. No matter how much she reviled the sentiments in the song, she appreciated that Cristo saw this as a chance to prove himself to his father.

'Well,' she told him. 'What an honour your papa has given you.'

Cristo stuck out his chest like a pouter pigeon. It was clear he wanted to make de Falco proud in front of his important guests and Lizzie would do everything in her power to help him achieve that goal.

'I know the words already,' he told her eagerly. 'We learned them at GIL.'

'That is good news,' she replied. She only wished she could be as confident of her own musical abilities. Never having played the anthem before presented her with a challenge. 'But I'm afraid I don't know the music, so you'll have to bear with me for a few moments.' She took out her reading spectacles and hooked them over her nose. 'Why don't you just look over the lyrics quietly while I familiarise myself with the piece?' she suggested. She pointed to an upholstered chair in the corner.

Lizzie began fingering the keys. It was a few years since she'd last played the piano and the ivories felt cool and smooth to touch. The Steinway seemed perfectly in tune, too, despite the fact that the Contessa de Falco died almost four years ago. She began to play – hesitantly at first, but by the time she reached the end of the first chorus she was feeling much more confident when, without warning, the door was flung wide open. Vincenzo stood in the doorway and the room fell silent, but not before Lizzie caught his expression. He seemed slightly bewildered, as if the sound of the piano had triggered a memory. He approached and smiled at her before turning his attention to Cristo seated in the corner.

'Well, young man, I understand you are greatly honoured. Singing "Giovinezza" in front of distinguished guests.' Vincenzo extended his hand and the boy hurried forward to shake it. 'Congratulations,' he said, bending low so that his face was level with Cristo's. 'And do you know who these special guests might be?'

The child gave his head a quick shake. 'Papa said I was to tell no one before I've sung.'

Vincenzo raised a brow to look impressed, before straightening himself once more. 'Then they must indeed be very important, and I must not keep you and Miss Thornton from your rehearsals.'

Cristo nodded and Vincenzo turned towards Lizzie. 'I look forward to hearing all about the performance,' he told her pointedly.

'And I look forward to telling you,' she replied. True, she had agreed to work with Vincenzo for Cristo's sake and to defeat fascism and all it stood for, but it was also something she wanted to do for herself; to prove that she could take control of her own destiny in a way that she chose. Rising from the stool she accompanied him to the door.

Vincenzo's large eyes blinked at her and made her want to kiss him again so badly. But by now they had reached the door. 'Take great care, *mia cara*,' he whispered, before breaking away from her gaze to wave at Cristo. 'Good luck, young man,' he called, then, again to Lizzie, 'Please be careful.'

Chapter 10

The convoy thundered through the gates of the Villa Martini at precisely seven o'clock the next evening. Two motorcycle outriders escorted a Fiat Torpedo, while an armoured truck followed behind. The vehicles pulled up on the circular drive below Lizzie's bedroom window. Their very important passenger was in the back seat.

Four guards poured out of the truck's tailgate to assume positions by the gate and on the front steps. When the back door of the car was opened, arms were flung out in the now familiar fascist salute. The count's guests were indeed special. First to leave the limousine were two high-ranking generals. Lizzie could tell from their epaulettes, but then they were followed by someone else. There was no mistaking the broad hulk of Benito Mussolini himself, sporting a fez and weighed down by his many medals.

Hardly able to believe her eyes, Lizzie watched with morbid fascination as Il Duce and the other officers were greeted by de Falco. Her nerves were already frayed and now, setting eyes on Mussolini in person – with his bullish neck and lantern jaw – they were almost shredded.

The count had insisted Cristo spend all day rehearsing with her. Normal lessons, including those with Signor Baldini, were suspended in order to practise. Cristo had faltered at first. He kept tripping over words and hit the wrong notes several times, but by the afternoon Lizzie had seen a huge improvement. Even so, the boy was every bit as nervous as she was. One slip on the keys, one wrong note, one missed word and she knew the evening could turn very sour.

She'd chosen a plain dark blue gown and wore her fair hair up in a no-nonsense style so as not to distract from Cristo. After all, the count was not the only important fascist with a reputation for being a predator.

As loud voices and laughter boomed down below, Lizzie decided to check on Cristo in his room. Violetta was helping him into his freshly pressed black shirt. He was already in his grey-green trousers.

'How are you feeling?' Lizzie asked.

'There are butterflies in here,' the boy complained, patting his stomach.

'Of course. It's only natural,' said Lizzie, sympathetically. Her own stomach was a raging cauldron that was churning unrelentingly. She noticed her hands were shaking as she passed Violetta an azure handkerchief to tuck into Cristo's shirt pocket. Finally came his fez – a miniature version of the one worn by Mussolini himself. The child's curls, usually covering his ears, were shorn on his father's orders. With his short hair he looked older than his ten years.

'What a brave soldier,' remarked Violetta, as Cristo stared at himself in a full-length mirror.

Lizzie, however, felt her heart might break at the sight. She couldn't help but think Cristo, her dear, sweet Cristo, dressed in this ridiculous uniform, was like a lamb being prepared for slaughter.

A knock at the door from Signor Cortina told them the time had come, so Lizzie and Cristo went down to the music room to ready themselves. Four chairs had been arranged in a semi-circle around the piano. Lizzie put on her spectacles to cast her eyes over the music then ghosted her fingers over the keys, while Cristo performed the vocal warm-up exercises she'd taught him. A few minutes later, boots were heard outside on the marble floor and the door opened to reveal the count with Mussolini at his side. They entered the room in a cloud of tobacco and leather and Signora Cortina showed the two other officers their seats.

Lizzie rose from the piano stool and Cristo stood to attention, his little arm outstretched in a salute.

'Il Duce, may I present to you my son Cristoforo?' said the count proudly.

Mussolini looked at the boy, his arm still outstretched, then returned the salute. 'He is a fine young man,' he remarked.

Lizzie's stomach tightened as the count nodded at her. She kept her spectacles on as if they offered her some protection against Il Duce's glare. She felt his eyes upon her as de Falco said, 'And this is his teacher, Miss Thornton.'

A pause, then, and Lizzie dared not look up.

'English?' Mussolini queried with a frown. 'Hmmm. Technically an enemy.'

Lizzie froze as a fat hand under her chin forced up her head and she found herself caught in Mussolini's penetrating stare. He was studying her like an insect, and she wanted to squirm. This was what Vincenzo had warned her about – the sense of ownership he had over any woman who came into his sphere.

The count looked uncomfortable, too. 'Miss Thornton came to us before war was declared, Duce,' he replied. He was eager to make it known she'd been given the job before she was technically an enemy alien.

Mussolini narrowed his eyes and Lizzie held her breath. But then just as suddenly as he had swooped, he seemed to dismiss the subject with a wave of the hand and took a seat to watch the performance. De Falco sat at his side. Nothing mattered more in that moment to Lizzie than giving a perfect performance for

Cristo's sake. Flexing her hands over the keys, she took a deep breath and played the first few notes.

Cristo's eyes slid towards hers and she gave the signal. He came in strongly at exactly the right beat and sang with confidence.

> *Hail, people of heroes,*
> *hail, immortal Fatherland,*
> *your sons were born again*
> *with faith and the ideal.*

Soon they were at the chorus and the boy was really in his stride, even making gestures with his hands as he sang. To Lizzie's great surprise Mussolini joined in and began to clap in time. The count sang, too, and the men built up to a crescendo at the end. As soon as the last note finished, the Duce applauded. 'Bravo,' he called. 'Bravo!'

Cristo's nerves completely disappeared. Now Lizzie thought he might explode with happiness. He looked over to his father, who was clapping in a more measured way, then at Lizzie. She smiled at him with relief more than anything else.

Mussolini stood to shake Cristo's hand. 'The future of the Fatherland lies with young men like you,' he told him. The child looked at his father for permission to touch the hand of the leader he regarded as Italy's saviour. As soon as de Falco nodded, Cristo pulled back his chest, lifted his chin and took the tyrant's hand.

Lizzie flinched at the thought of Mussolini's touch, but mercifully it did not come. Instead of thanking her for her playing, he ignored her altogether and a wave of relief swept over her as she watched him leave the room. A second later, a sudden tap on her arm made her turn quickly to see a beaming Cristo. She bent down and hugged him tight. This time she didn't care who saw.

'You sang beautifully,' she told him, straightening the fez that her enthusiastic embrace had sent askew. 'I'm so proud of you and so was your papa.'

'Thank you, miss,' replied Cristo, before he began rubbing his eyes. She could tell he was tired and seeing Violetta hovering on the threshold, Lizzie told him, 'It's late, so off to bed with you. Great singers need their sleep.' It was time she left, too.

While the count took Mussolini into his study – Lizzie presumed to discuss campaign strategy – she retreated to her room, her nerves still tight as violin strings. In the semi-darkness she waited, listening to every door slam, every footstep. The performance had gone well. As well as she could have hoped, but still, she couldn't sleep. She mustn't. She had work to do.

It was a cold night and the icy air made her skin tingle. Slipping out of her bedroom in dark clothes, an hour or so later, Lizzie made it unseen down the main stairs. Male voices could be heard in the study, punctuated by the occasional loud laugh – Il Duce's she presumed. Then light footsteps. Violetta was carrying a tray of coffee for the guests. As soon as she opened the study door, Lizzie scurried through the hallway to the servants' stairs. Dashing past the kitchen, where Nina and Bianca were washing up the dinner dishes, she made it unseen out through the back door.

Now in the grounds, her plan was to skirt round the front of the house to the study where she would watch the men through the window. The shutters were closed, but she managed to squint through a crack to see into the room. The count stood by the very blackboard on which she regularly wrote his son's spellings. But tonight, de Falco had fixed a map on it and was using her pointer to show Mussolini and his generals various locations. While she couldn't hear what he was saying, Lizzie could see the map was unmistakably of northern Africa. But most chillingly of all, several swastikas had appeared pinned along the coast.

From listening to Radio Londra, Lizzie knew Tobruk and Benghasi had been retaken by the British, so could the Germans really be persuaded to send reinforcements to help Italian troops in their North African campaign? Troubled by what she'd learned, she was just about to retreat into the villa when a dog's ferocious

69

bark shattered the calm. Whipping round, she saw a guard struggling to control a frothing hound straining on its leash. Scrambling into the shadows of a nearby doorway, she leaned backwards, her heart barrelling in her ribcage. The dog kept tugging at its lead and the guard kept yelling as it came nearer. It had her scent. As soon as it cornered her it would attack. But no. She gulped down a lungful of breath and stood statue-still as hound and handler darted passed. Only then did she realise, to her great relief, she wasn't what the beast was snarling at. Milo the cat had just scampered along the wall, setting the dog into attack mode. Taking advantage of the distraction, Lizzie escaped back to her room undetected, her heart still racing in her chest.

It was two o'clock in the morning before she heard a door open, and voices fill the hallway. Il Duce was leaving. Padding over to the window she crouched below the sill to listen to his parting words. Gravel crunched beneath boots. An engine started. But under it all Lizzie picked up Mussolini's final comment to the count.

'So, the Americans will be on the receiving end of Rommel's army. That'll show them up for the cowards they are.'

'Yes, Duce.'

'North Africa is as good as ours again.'

The limousine's engine revved then, and de Falco's reply was lost. Nevertheless, piecing together the scant information she had gleaned from the evening, Lizzie knew what she had seen and heard could prove vital to British intelligence. She was sure Vincenzo would know what to do with it.

Chapter 11

At breakfast the next morning, the mood seemed to be one of relief. Mussolini's visit had seemingly passed off without incident. Nina and Bianca were giggling and chatting as they filled buckets of water to start cleaning. Luigi went out singing a Verdi aria and Signor Sacca, normally so stony-faced, could be heard muttering, '*Sublime. Quite sublime.*' Meanwhile, at the stove Maria was humming as she made brioche. It was only Violetta, starching collars in the corner, who seemed quieter than usual.

'Il Duce said her tiramisu was as good as his own mother's,' Giuseppe told Lizzie, glancing at the singing cook as he set down a basket of apples.

'Praise indeed,' she replied, even though she'd no idea about Mussolini's mother's culinary skills. She smiled at her pupil. 'And of course he was very impressed by Cristo's performance.'

Maria laughed. 'Why do you think the young master gets two brioches this morning?'

'Yes. We are all very proud of him,' said Lizzie. She looked towards the corner. 'Aren't we, Violetta?' she made a point of asking.

The maid lifted her gaze to see Lizzie waiting for a reply. Her eyes were red rimmed but instead of agreeing, she flung down the shirt in her hand and ran out of the room in tears.

Puzzled, Lizzie looked first at Maria, then at the other maids. 'What's wrong? Is she unwell?' she asked.

Nina and Bianca pretended not to hear, while Maria shook her head. 'Man trouble, I expect,' she suggested, adding, 'It usually is with Violetta.'

A week later, after breakfast, Signora Cortina appeared at the kitchen doorway to say the master wanted to see everyone in the hall. Once more, Lizzie's stomach flipped. Ever since Mussolini's visit, she'd been on edge. She'd handwritten her account of all she'd seen and heard discussed that night, drawing particular attention to the map of northern Africa and Il Duce's parting words. But deception didn't sit easily on her shoulders. Being an informant called for cunning and guile – traits that she didn't naturally possess. And now she found new meanings in every look and gesture addressed to her and was terrified her words or actions might betray vital resistance secrets.

Everyone gathered in the large hallway and Vincenzo, coming from the city centre, was last to arrive. He and Lizzie swapped wary looks as the count stood on the stairs, glowering down on his staff. In his hand he held a newspaper. When he lifted it up and she saw the title, Lizzie thought she might faint. It was a copy of *Freedom & Justice*.

'Some of you may be familiar with this despicable publication,' began the count, his face like thunder. 'If you are, you know it is full of Communist lies. A filthy rag, good for the gutter.' His glare travelled steadily over everyone present. Lizzie tensed. De Falco mustn't see her shaking. 'You will also know that this villa was honoured by a very special guest the other night. You were all sworn to secrecy about Il Duce's visit and yet . . .' He held up the broadsheet again and slapped it making the paper rustle. '*German reinforcements for North Africa?*'

The hall was so silent that a moth trapped in the window frame could be heard fluttering its terrified wings. The count's gaze continued to bore into everyone, looking for signs of guilt, or weakness. Lizzie, instead of dipping her head to avoid de Falco's searching eyes, looked straight ahead. But there was no escaping his words, delivered with vitriol and hatred, as they boomed out across the hall.

'If someone here is responsible for this; if someone here is a spy, they will pay for their treachery.'

A shiver ran down Lizzie's spine. Vincenzo's days could be numbered. And so could hers.

After the count's speech, the cool atmosphere at Villa Martina, which had temporarily thawed, turned icy. Lizzie was grateful Vincenzo managed to snatch a few stolen words with her in the music room between lessons later in the day.

'Keep calm. Say nothing. Deny everything.'

Lizzie looked at him. 'It's so easy for you. You're used to this, but I'm not, Vincenzo, and I'm petrified.'

He removed his glasses to look at her straight and took her hands in his. Instantly, she felt calmer. 'If anything happens. If anything is said, I will take the blame. I will keep you safe.' He lifted her hand to his lips and kissed it. 'Trust me, Lizzie. I won't let anyone harm you.'

Despite knowing deep down that he couldn't possibly protect her if the count ever found out she was the source of the newspaper article, at that moment Lizzie found herself believing Vincenzo implicitly. She knew love did that to people; made them blind. It was the first time she'd admitted to herself just how deeply she cared for him.

'I do trust you,' she whispered. She was going to add that it didn't stop her worrying. But before she could, he pressed his lips on hers in a tender kiss and suddenly all her fears dissolved.

Lizzie was just beginning to think the storm may have passed at the Villa Martini when, a few days later, Vincenzo failed to turn up to teach Cristo. Worry started to take hold again. She prayed he was sick, but she didn't know how to reach him. He'd never told her where he lived. He'd said it was safer that way, but surely, he would have been able to get a message to her somehow? Then, when one day's absence turned into four, then six, the gnawing fear set in and with each passing day it grew. When she'd asked Maria if she knew where he lived so she might check on him, her enquiry drew a blank. Old Giuseppe simply shrugged, and it was left to Nina to give her the only sensible piece of advice. 'Why don't you ask the count? Signora Cortina says he returns from Rome the day after tomorrow.'

De Falco had left the villa shortly after his terrifying speech but as much as she hated the idea, asking him about Vincenzo's whereabouts on his return seemed her only option. So, when the count did arrive back at the Villa Martini with all the fanfare befitting a high-ranking fascist, Lizzie decided to act.

Pennants flew and arms were flung out in salute, as guards stood to attention. But the count had already given orders that no one was allowed near him, apart from his adjutant and secretary. There were many telephone calls. After those came the meetings. Officers and dignitaries visited in a constant stream and Lizzie was beginning to doubt whether de Falco would even ask to see his only child, let alone answer her questions about Vincenzo's whereabouts.

'Where is Signor Baldini?' Cristo kept asking when Vincenzo had failed to turn up for a tenth day.

'I've told you, he's sick, Cristo, but he will be back with us just as soon as he feels better,' she would reply, even though the excuse was wearing thin. She didn't know how much longer she could offer it.

When on the fourth day of his return de Falco summoned her to his study, Lizzie didn't know whether she should be hopeful or nervous. She assumed the meeting was to discuss Cristo's academic progress. It would also be an opportunity for her to ask him if he knew what had happened to Vincenzo. But when Signora Cortina knocked and held open the study door, Lizzie was surprised to see Violetta walking towards her. She caught her eye as they passed on the threshold, but the girl was red-faced, and she dipped her gaze. Had she been crying again? Lizzie could not be sure, but her behaviour made the knot in her chest tighten.

'Sit, if you please, Miss Thornton,' directed the count, standing by the window. As soon as she did, he turned abruptly and stalked towards her.

Lizzie swallowed hard and did as she was told as de Falco perched on the corner of his desk.

'I understand, Miss Thornton, you have been making enquiries as to the whereabouts of Signor Baldini.' The count leered over her as she sat cowering below. He sounded angry with her for caring about a fellow tutor.

'Yes, sir,' she replied, keeping her eyes to the floor and clasping her hands together to stop them shaking. 'He hasn't been at work for over a week now and I—'

The count broke in with a flap of his hand and stuck out his chin. 'He hasn't been at work because he is behind bars,' he told her flatly.

'What? I . . .' The bluntness of the statement momentarily stunned Lizzie.

'You heard, Miss Thornton. Signor Baldini is in prison, arrested by the OVRA for his traitorous activities.'

'But I . . . but he . . .' Lizzie's mind was in turmoil. Her worst fears were founded.

'If I were you,' de Falco intervened, leaning in and hooking his forefinger under her chin to jerk up her head, 'I would keep that pretty mouth of yours shut. I would also remind you consorting with traitors is a crime punishable by firing squad.'

Alarm bells rang in Lizzie's brain. Everything was unravelling. The count took a step back to lance her with a sharp glare. 'Violetta has told me about you and Baldini.'

Oh God! The room span. She wanted the ground to open up and swallow her, but the count continued. 'You came with the highest recommendation from England, Miss Thornton. To say I am disappointed in you is an understatement.' A half-smoked cigar lay in an ashtray on the desk. 'What do you have to say for yourself?' He struck a match and lit the stub, then returned to his chair to listen to Lizzie's response.

Feeling more like a schoolgirl than a teacher, Lizzie shook her head. Violetta was jealous. Lizzie had seen the way the maid looked at Vincenzo. They'd been betrayed by her, yet there was nothing else for it than to deny their affair. They would not be the only ones to suffer if they were ordered behind bars. The newspaper and all its contributors would be in danger, too.

'I don't know what Violetta is talking about. The relationship Signor Baldini and I have is purely professional.'

When the count next opened his mouth to answer her, his words came out in a billow of smoke, so that Lizzie couldn't see his eyes clearly at first.

'That is good to hear, Miss Thornton,' he told her. 'If I thought you had anything to do with the printing press that was raided, it would be a different matter. Please be aware you remain in your post purely at my discretion. Technically you are an enemy of the Italian state. Many other British citizens are languishing in camps as we speak. I have decided you may remain as Cristoforo's tutor for the time being because the child is so fond of you. But be warned.' He sat upright and leaned forward. 'Make no mistake. One false move and you will join Signor Baldini in jail.'

The colour leached from Lizzie's face as the reality hit her like a blow to the stomach. De Falco must've ordered a raid on the printing press and found evidence to connect it and the newspaper to Vincenzo. She gripped the arms of her chair. Not only was the man she loved being held in jail, she could also soon follow him.

Chapter 12

In the classroom the following morning, Lizzie noticed Cristo was pale and subdued and when she asked him to read to her, he burst out crying.

'Whatever is wrong, Cristo?' she said, fearing his tears probably had something to do with Vincenzo. She'd hoped the count might concoct a reason for the tutor's absence, but then when Cristo had asked his father outright, the answer he got was brutal.

'Papa says Signor Baldini is a bad man. He said he was trying to hurt Il Duce,' he sobbed.

Lizzie put her arm around the boy. How could she contradict his father? If word got back to him, she would probably be carted off to a labour camp.

'He says he's never coming back.' Cristo's bottom lip jutted out as he spoke and seeing him so terribly distraught took Lizzie close to crying as well.

'Oh, my dearest Cristo,' she told him, dabbing away his tears with her handkerchief. She couldn't let the child believe that the one man in his life who'd taken any genuine interest in his well-being, was a traitor. 'Signor Baldini cares for you very much and is so sorry he is not here with you. He will be back with us again just as soon as this war is over.'

'You promise?' The child cheered up a little.

Lizzie faltered and searched Cristo's large brown eyes. How could she swear Vincenzo would come back when for all she knew he could, God forbid, already be dead? She bit her lip. 'I give you my word,' she said, even though she wasn't sure she could keep it.

For the next few days Violetta shunned Lizzie as if she had the plague. The maid ate her meals at different times in the kitchen and avoided eye contact. The situation couldn't go on if the two women were to continue living under the same roof. One evening they confronted each other unexpectedly in the narrow staff corridor near the kitchen. Someone had to give way. Lizzie was determined it wouldn't be her. She blocked Violetta's path.

'Why did you do it?' she asked bluntly.

The maid's eyes jumped to the floor. 'Let me pass, please miss.'

'No. I will not. Not until you tell me why you betrayed me and Signor Baldini.' Lizzie grabbed the girl's wrist in desperation.

Violetta's eyes widened as she looked down at her arm and realised Lizzie wasn't going to let her go until she'd spoken.

'It was the count. He made me. He told me I'd lose my job if I didn't speak the truth.'

'The truth,' repeated Lizzie, finding a hidden strength and tightening her grip. 'And what was the truth?'

'I'd seen the way Signor Baldini looked at you. I knew there was something.'

Lizzie narrowed her eyes. 'You were jealous. That was it, wasn't it? You wanted him for yourself, didn't you? And if you couldn't have him, then no one could.'

Tears sprang from the girl's eyes. 'I didn't mean . . . I didn't think . . .'

Lizzie let go of Violetta's wrist in disgust. 'May God forgive you,' she hissed. But the damage was done, and, in truth, her anger and bitterness were wasted on the girl. Fighting the urge to cry herself, she stood aside, and the maid ran off sobbing.

Lizzie was treading on eggshells. If Violetta had betrayed her, then what about the others? Luigi's steel-grey eyes must be watching her every move. Signor Sacca's, too. Not to mention corpse-like Signora Cortina. She was careful not to say anything that could be misconstrued to Cristo, as well. The child might inadvertently repeat something she'd said in class, and it could be taken the wrong way. *'One false move and you will join Signor Baldini in jail.'* The count's warning hammered at her brain.

Behind her anxiety there was always the thought of what Vincenzo was going through. Where was he? What had become of him? She recalled the man she'd seen arrested the day war was declared; how he was beaten with a baton, how his face turned to a bloody pulp. No doubt they would torture Vincenzo. She'd heard stories, terrible stories that chilled the blood in her veins. But he wouldn't give in. She knew that. He would never betray his friends in the resistance network.

With Vincenzo gone, it only made Lizzie even more determined to continue his work. Editing the newspaper on her own would be difficult, but possible. The problem was, she just didn't know how to contact anyone else from Vincenzo's resistance group. There was only one thing for it. She would have to trace them herself. But how?

Chapter 13

Seated at a table in the busy piazza where she'd caught Vincenzo liaising with the man with the beaked nose, Lizzie ordered a *caffè d'orzo*. She was growing used to the earthy taste of ground barley, even though it bore little resemblance to real coffee, as sought after these days as da Vinci paintings. What she really wanted was a brandy to steady her nerves, but that would give the wrong impression. She needed to be alert, too.

The bell in the nearby clock tower tolled seven. The waiter brought her the coffee. She looked up at him, then around her at the tightly packed tables. Four suited businessmen shared a bottle of wine to her left, while two well-dressed women drank limoncello at the next table. By them an elderly man in dark glasses supped a beer. There was no one who looked remotely like the man she had seen before with Vincenzo. But maybe he was there – somewhere in the crowd by the gelato vendor, or on the steps of the church. Or perhaps he was lurking on a street corner in the long shadows, just waiting to make his move. Her breath juddered as she sighed heavily and self-consciously lifted her cup to sip her coffee. Her red lipstick left a crimson crescent on the porcelain. It reminded her of the blood she'd seen spilled when the OVRA dragged a man from his home. She thought of Vincenzo.

Ten sips and ten minutes later no one had showed up. She would try again tomorrow – maybe slightly later. It had been a long shot, she knew that, but she had to keep on trying. The newspaper was too important to fail. She owed it to Vincenzo to continue its publication and she very much hoped whoever met him at this *caffè* before would help her.

Taking out her purse, she secured a fifty-lire note under the ashtray and was about to leave when, out of the corner of her eye, she noticed a man moving towards her. It only took one glance, and she stayed put as he squeezed into a seat at the next table. But as he did so, he caught Lizzie's handbag and it fell to the ground.

For a split second she feared she was being robbed, but no. He handed back the bag to her with a smile.

'Forgive me,' he said. It was the heavily built man with the beaked nose and high cheekbones.

This time when Lizzie rose, it was in the knowledge that this seemingly clumsy man had slyly slipped a piece of paper into her bag that could contain everything she needed to know. Possession of it could also probably get her killed. She hurried back to the Villa Martini without daring to look at it. But at least now she might find out what she had to do next.

Since the raid on the printing press, she'd learned Vincenzo's colleagues had managed to lay their hands on a mimeograph, a small portable printing machine. Once in her own room she read the brief note. On it was the name of a church, a date and time. She assumed someone would be there to take delivery of her articles for the publication. Clenching the details in her hand Lizzie felt a new sense of purpose. Vincenzo may be in jail, but the *Freedom & Justice* would continue telling the people of Lucca and beyond the truth about the fascists. The newspaper was back in business.

* * *

81

Lizzie sat on a bench in the botanical gardens. Still no word of Vincenzo. It was early spring, and buds were bursting into life. Everything was green and vibrant, but she wasn't there to admire the trees and plants. She was making a drop of the latest edition of *Freedom & Justice*. This week's edition – her first in sole charge – featured Mussolini's meeting with Hitler in Salzburg. Rumour had it Il Duce's morale was fading. She hoped it was true. Editing the newspaper was her way of justifying the trust Vincenzo had placed in her and a continuation of what she had started with him. For the first time ever, he had shown her what it was really like to have a cause and to fight for it. Throughout the long, lonely days since his arrest, he'd inspired her to continue to play her part in the fight to defeat Mussolini.

The OVRA were keeping themselves busy. Whenever she set foot within the city walls, she'd witnessed at least one of their dreaded trucks. Each time one slowed down there'd be people nearby who'd look about them, wondering if they'd be dragged away next. The fear on the streets was as real as the market stalls. But there was no word of Vincenzo. Nor of Professor Lodato, the joint head of the Action Party in Lucca, who'd been arrested before Christmas.

The first drop went without a hitch. The second took place the following week in a park. The nearby clock struck four as she waited. She wondered how long she should stay after the appointed time. Someone would surely be watching her. As her eagle eyes darted from one bush to another, she felt exposed and vulnerable. And when, after another ten minutes, no one had approached, she decided it was too dangerous to remain. She was about to leave when a shabbily dressed man in a beret limped up to her and sat down at the other end of the bench. He was clutching a copy of *Il Popolo d'Italia*, the fascist daily, under his arm. But instead of reading it, he laid it down on the bench beside her.

Lizzie instinctively locked on to the courier. Up until then she hadn't really bothered to look at his face, but now she saw clearly. The man who was risking his life to print the resistance newspaper was Jacopo, the handyman who'd been turned out of the Villa Martini because he was Jewish. As he pretended to rest, Lizzie slid an envelope containing the sub-edited copy into the folds of *Il Popolo*. She walked away as calmly as she could, hoping Jacopo wouldn't be stopped by the OVRA before he made it to the mimeograph.

Over the next few weeks, Lizzie continued to work on more articles based on the Radio Londra broadcasts she listened to late into the night. Sometimes Jacopo would take them as he passed a *caffè* table where she sat. Sometimes the big man with the beaked nose would bump into her by the cathedral, or in a park. But then, one day, Jacopo didn't show when he was supposed to. Lizzie waited on a bench in the gardens at the Palazzo Pfanner but moved on after half an hour when there was no sign of him. Something was wrong. A terrible feeling of dread swelled inside her, but there was nothing she could do without putting others in danger if she tried to find out. As it happened, she didn't need to look far. In the next edition of *Il Popolo d'Italia*, a three-lined report, tucked deep inside, told her the body of an unidentified Jew had been fished from the Serchio three days before. He had been bludgeoned to death.

Jacopo's murder only reminded Lizzie, as if she needed reminding, the work she was undertaking was dangerous. But she still found herself running needless risks. The following week, in the early hour of the morning, she sat up at her dressing table. With her back to the door, she was wearing headphones and taking notes as she listened to the crystal set in the soft glow of a lamp. She was just writing down a particular phrase when a shadow crossed her notepad, suddenly blocking the light.

Instinctively she jettisoned the earphones and her head jerked up straight away to see a figure standing beside her. It took her a moment to realise who.

'Cristo!' she cried, her breath sucked from her lungs. 'You startled me!'

'I had a nightmare,' he shot back, his cheeks glistening with tears in the lamplight.

'Oh, you dear boy,' she whispered, drawing him to her. She remained seated as his head rested on top of her shoulder until his body suddenly stiffened.

'You've got a crystal set,' he said excitedly, pushing away from her. 'It's like the one I made with Signor Baldini.'

Horrified, her gaze switched back to the device. There was no hiding the truth. 'That's right. I like to listen to music at night. It helps me sleep.'

He frowned in reply. 'Then why weren't you in bed?'

She smiled and shrugged her shoulders. 'I was just going,' she told him, covering up her notepad with a romantic novel she was supposedly reading.

Cristo looked at her oddly then. She couldn't be sure that he believed her, so she tried a different approach. 'What would your papa say if he could see us now? It's gone two in the morning and we're both out of bed.'

Cristo stuck out his bottom lip. 'He would be angry.'

'He certainly would,' agreed Lizzie. 'I'll tell you what. I won't say anything about you, if you don't . . .'

Cristo's head suddenly shook. 'No. I won't tell,' he said.

'Good. That's settled,' replied Lizzie, although from then on, she didn't take any chances. She listened to the crystal set and made notes under the covers. Editing and proofreading the articles were done between lessons. But no matter where she worked, gathering the information and writing the reports brought her closer to Vincenzo, wherever he was.

One evening in early May, when Luigi had driven Cristo to another drill meeting, Lizzie, a shawl round her shoulders, had started editing an article in the music room. She was confident she wouldn't

84

be interrupted. The next edition of *Freedom & Justice* was due to go to press shortly, but she still had to proofread a piece. A pile of Cristo's exercise books sat on the table, just in case she was disturbed and needed to look occupied with marking his homework. It was just as well because no sooner had she finished with her red pen than she heard the familiar sound of keys clanking outside in the hall. There was just enough time to conceal the typed article inside one of Cristo's textbooks before Signora Cortina entered the room.

'*Buonasera*, Signorina Thornton,' greeted the housekeeper unsmilingly.

'Signora.' Lizzie nodded courteously as she approached, but not before she had cast a swift eye over the table to ensure nothing incriminating was in sight.

'I am come to tell you that the count plans to return on Tuesday for a few days. He would like you to report on Cristoforo's academic progress.'

'Of course,' replied Lizzie, suddenly distracted by a wayward typed sheet. 'I shall compile one for him,' she said, surreptitiously sliding the paper into an exercise book she'd previously marked. 'I'll get to work on it straight away.'

Tuesday arrived and the count returned to the villa in the afternoon, as Signora Cortina said. It was the evening when Lizzie received a summons to his study. When she saw de Falco standing by the window, looking out, his hands laced behind his back, and he didn't even greet her when she entered, something told Lizzie he didn't want to discuss Cristo's report.

'Sit,' he snapped, still looking out of the window.

Lizzie obeyed, perching herself on the edge of the chair as the adrenaline pumped round her body. Her mouth was dry, and her palms wet as she sat prone. On the desk in front of her was the report she'd submitted on Cristo's schoolwork, together with a pile of his exercise books.

After a moment, de Falco returned to his desk and sat down opposite her. He glanced at her handwritten report, then reached for one of Cristo's exercise books next to it. *English composition*. The count slid it across to her.

'Do you recognise this, Miss Thornton?' he asked.

Lizzie stared at the familiar book. 'Yes, sir. It's Cristo's composition book. He's very good at—'

A palm was lifted in front of her. 'And do you recognise what was found in this book, Miss Thornton?' The book lay open and from it he removed a folded sheet of paper. Lizzie thought she might be sick.

'Is this what you have been teaching my son, Miss Thornton?' de Falco asked, unfolding the sheet to reveal the article she'd been about to proofread for the newspaper. He read the headline out loud. '*German and Italian forces in Tunisia surrender to British.*' His eyes burned into her. 'What have you to say?'

Lizzie couldn't think straight. She was speechless. The evening in question spooled quickly through her mind. She'd been distracted by Signora Cortina's arrival in the music room and hidden the article between the pages of the exercise book. She thought she'd retrieved it all when the housekeeper left the room but must've missed the first page. It remained inside. Not only did the report detail Italian losses, it was marked up in her own hand, in red ink, ready for the printer. It was surely enough to condemn her.

'I . . . I cannot say,' she replied. He'd caught her on the back foot. There was no time to concoct a story. But even if she had, the count would never have believed her.

He shook his head. 'No matter. There is no need,' he told her, dragging once more on his cigar. He pulled the cord by his desk that usually summoned Violetta. Only on this occasion in staggered Vincenzo Baldini, flanked by two guards.

'Oh God, no!' Lizzie cried, her eyes wide with horror. Almost two months had passed. Each day had been full of fear and anxiety. Not knowing if Vincenzo was alive or dead had taken its toll on her, and now he stood before her, a mockery of the man she loved.

His beautiful aquiline nose had been broken, a jagged scar ran down his left cheek and one of his front teeth was missing. It was as if someone had smashed a puppet against a stone wall, breaking it in pieces then tried to put it together again.

One of the lenses of his glasses was broken. His hair was ruffled, and his hands were shackled behind his back. The look he gave her was so full of despair she felt her heart cracking.

I'm so sorry, he mouthed.

Jumping up from her seat, she bolted over. But before Lizzie could reach him the count raised a palm to signify he had seen and heard enough. 'Take him away,' he ordered, and Vincenzo was hauled from the room.

'No!' she cried. But her cries fell on deaf ears and as she watched Vincenzo disappear, it felt as if he were taking a piece of her heart with him. 'Please, no,' she whispered. Turning quickly to the count, she cried, 'What will happen to him now?' She laid her palms flat on the desk and pleaded. 'Don't let them hurt him anymore.'

The count's lips lifted in a smirk as he lit a cigar. 'How touching, Miss Thornton. But if I were you, I'd be worried about yourself. You have been implicated in a serious crime. Treachery against the state. What have you to say for yourself?' He picked up the typed page again then dropped it in disdain. 'And, perhaps more importantly, who gave you this?'

She stepped away from the desk to stand up straight and stuck out her chin. 'I don't know,' she hissed.

De Falco puffed on his cigar. 'Really? How odd,' he said. 'Because I do.'

Lizzie's forehead furrowed. 'How . . .?'

'And so do the secret police. They arrested one of your newspaper contacts shortly after he left the botanical gardens.'

The count kept his eyes trained on her, watching for a reaction. Lizzie's mind flew straight to the man with the beaked nose.

'No matter. He will reveal his name and contacts under torture.' De Falco smiled as he spoke, and it took all of Lizzie's willpower not to wipe it off with a slap. 'But it's you I must consider, right now.'

Lizzie squared her shoulders. She had to be strong. Whatever terrible fate the count had in mind for her, she wouldn't crumble. *I won't tell, Vincenzo. I won't tell*, she repeated over in her head, before she spat out her feelings. 'You can do what you want with me, but you'll never win.'

He laughed at her then. 'How very noble, you are. Spoken like a true British citizen,' he mocked. Pausing for a moment, he pointed his cigar at her.

'Please. Sit, Miss Thornton,' said the count, his mood inexplicably swinging.

Lizzie frowned and allowed herself to breathe again, even though she wasn't sure what would come next. Slowly easing into the chair, she tried to compose herself. She had to tell him what really mattered to her before it was too late. 'You see, sir, I don't care about myself, but I do care about Cristo,' she began. Vincenzo's absence had affected the boy badly, but her heart ached at the thought of how he would react if she were to be taken from him, too. His whole life would be turned upside down. Clasping her hands together she pleaded, 'Please let me continue to teach him. I beg you.' She held her breath, waiting for a reply.

To her surprise de Falco nodded. 'I have decided it would be best if you both went away until the war is won.' He clenched the cigar between his teeth.

'Away?' she repeated, puzzled but relieved. At least she and Cristo would remain together. But where?

'Lucca is no longer safe. Cristoforo would be much better off on my country estate in Emilia-Romagna. The boy can continue his education there, away from the threat of enemy bombs. You must go with him.'

Lizzie was confused. Was the count really going to let her leave Lucca with Cristo? Vincenzo was facing torture and possible death and yet she was being allowed to depart for the relative safety of a country estate.

'I don't understand,' she blurted. 'I . . .'

The count pressed a finger to his lips. 'If I were you, I would stay silent, Miss Thornton. You have already said enough. As I told you before, it is only because my son cares so much for you that you are not behind bars, too.' Setting down his cigar once more he began to rearrange the papers on his desk. He made it clear he had dealt with her and wished to move on.

Stunned, Lizzie hesitated for a moment and de Falco, noticing, looked up once more. 'Now you better pack your things,' he said with a flap of his hand. 'You leave for Emilia-Romagna tomorrow.'

Chapter 14

May 1943

The imposing gates of Count de Falco's country estate, Castello di Castiglione, towered in front of them. A high brick wall surrounded a huge campanile and the bulk of the massive mansion. On her first visit to the medieval estate, nearly four years ago, Lizzie had thought of it as somewhere exciting; an adventure playground to be explored with Cristo. They'd stayed there for six weeks, walking, riding and paddling in the river. Now, however, she realised it was to be her prison.

Despite knowing she would accompany him, Cristo had been reluctant to leave Lucca and the familiar comforts of his home. He'd clung to Violetta, telling her he didn't want to go. But the girl had promised to visit him as soon as she could. Bianca painted him a picture of the villa and Nina knitted him a pair of socks with his initials on them. Lizzie had managed to coax him into the back of the limousine. Maria's hamper of little cakes and fruit was very welcome, but it was well into the long journey before he finally rested his head in the crook of her arm and gave in to sleep.

Only then did Lizzie allow herself the luxury of quiet tears. As the driver powered along – *not Luigi, why not Luigi?* – she'd realised the other silent, suited man who sat next to him in the front passenger seat may well be an OVRA agent. His eyes were trained on the rear-view mirror. On her. She turned away from his gaze to think of Vincenzo.

An hour after leaving Lucca, the car turned off the main road north, by the great white marble mountain at Carrera. They headed east into the mountains. The way became flanked by forest, and it wasn't until they'd reached the gentler plains that the landscape turned into rolling plains, then flatter fields of green corn. On her last visit, the golden wheat was waist-high and the grapes were turning deep crimson on the vines. Cristo had been happy in those few weeks. So had she. Happier at least. The small estate farm had provided the child with endless hours of entertainment. Cristo had fed the chickens and pigs and had even been presented with his own pony to ride. They'd both needed to learn to be alive again; Cristo after the loss of his mother and she after the death of hers. That autumn of 1940, Castello di Castiglione had given them both the space they needed. How different things were now.

The gates opened wide, as if some unseen hand had pulled them back and the limousine clattered over the cobbles in the courtyard. The juddering woke Cristo. Now roused, he strained to look out of the window.

'Where are we?' he asked, rubbing his eyes.

'At Castello di Castiglione, Cristo,' Lizzie replied, trying to inject some enthusiasm in her voice. 'We had fun here. Remember?'

Cristo did not reply at first, as if processing his own memories. 'Is Isabella, here?'

Isabella was the pony he'd learned to ride, and a sudden rush of relief overcame Lizzie. She'd telephoned ahead to find out. 'Yes, she is, and you can ride her again. She's waiting for you.'

The child's eyes lit up. 'Then I must see her,' he said, grabbing the handle and opening the car door to scramble out.

The driver was already standing by to help Cristo alight, even though he'd kept the engine grumbling. Lizzie slid along the seat to follow, but when she tried to put a foot down on the cobbles, a palm was flattened in front of her.

'*Non!*' snapped the driver.

Shocked, Lizzie craned her head out of the car window. 'What do you mean? Let me pass, if you please.'

Behind her she heard the passenger door open and glanced over her shoulder to see the OVRA agent sidling into the back seat beside her.

'What's going on?' she asked, panic in her voice. The reply was delivered by a hypodermic needle. A sharp pain stabbed her thigh and as she yelped, she caught sight of the syringe. Her eyes followed it back to the hand of the agent.

'What?!' she cried, horrified.

'Miss Lizzie, come on!' she heard Cristo call. She lunged towards the open car door, but the driver slammed it shut.

'No!' she screamed over the noise of the car engine. 'Cristo!' She balled her fists and hammered on the side window as the vehicle accelerated. 'No! Cristo!' she screamed.

Cristo, confused by what was happening, rushed towards the car, but Signora Cortina appeared from inside the castle, and snatched him back roughly.

'Miss Lizzie!' he yelled. 'Come back! Miss Lizzie!' But inside the limousine Lizzie was powerless to act. Her head was pounding, her body was heavy, and she was seeing double. Cristo was screaming, waving frantically, as his body remained clinched in the arms of the housekeeper. If Lizzie had the strength she would have cried out. She did not. It was the last she saw of the child before everything went black.

Even before she opened her eyes Lizzie shivered. She was somewhere cold, lying on a hard surface. Her head throbbed mercilessly, and her mouth was full of sawdust. Then she remembered what happened. She'd been drugged. The recollection made her eyes pop open to face bare stone. Lying on her side, she was up against a wall. Slowly she turned, feeling like a piece of porcelain. One wrong move could break her. As soon as her eyes managed to focus, she saw light pouring in from a single window high up in the wall. Opposite was a wooden door with a small grille in it. And something else. A wooden crucifix with a bronze Christ nailed to it just to one side.

When she heard a bolt slide and the door creak open, she realised someone must have been watching her. Light footsteps came towards her. Drawing herself up on her elbows, she saw a young woman carrying a tray. But not just any young woman. This one was dressed from top to toe in a long white robe, while her hair was hidden under a sort of headscarf.

Lizzie cleared her throat. 'What . . . What is this place?' she asked in Italian as the tray was set down on a nearby table.

The girl in white didn't look at her. 'A convent,' she replied, with downcast eyes.

A convent? So, the girl must be a nun.

'But why am I here?'

The nun finally raised her gaze and let her large brown eyes slide towards her. *She can't be more than eighteen*, Lizzie thought.

'The Lord sent you to us,' came the unconvincing reply.

'The Lord?' repeated Lizzie. If she wasn't feeling so weak, she would have laughed at the remark. She slung her feet over the side of the bed and tried to push herself up but had to sit down again immediately when the room span. Her head dropped into her hands. 'I was brought here against my will.' she groaned.

The nun's timid expression gave way to a frown. 'I'm sorry,' she said. 'All I know is Mother Superior will visit you shortly when you've had something to eat.' On the tray she'd just delivered were bread and cheese, along with a small bunch of grapes and a pitcher of something to drink. 'You'll feel better then, God willing.'

'Wait,' called Lizzie as the cell door opened once more. 'I'm being held against my will,' she repeated. 'I was kidnapped.'

The young nun hesitated on the threshold, then shook her head. The latch clicked behind her.

Lizzie managed to heave herself up to stagger after her. She made it to the door and put her mouth to the grille.

'Please. Come back,' she called, but it was no use. Her legs buckled under her, and she collapsed in a heap on the stone floor.

As she lay dazed, a bell rang out five o'clock. She must've been unconscious for at least six hours. Moments later, the sound of footsteps echoed along the corridor outside. Suddenly Lizzie was aware of the door opening again. It pushed against her, forcing her to shuffle backwards. The young nun had returned, only this time she was accompanied by a much older, portly woman in a black habit, who carried herself very upright with an air of authority. A large silver crucifix hung on a chain around her neck. Her arms were crossed, with both her hands tucked into the voluminous sleeves of her habit.

Lizzie assumed this was Mother Superior. She dragged herself back towards the narrow bed.

'Welcome to the Convent of the Madonna del Rosario, Miss Thornton,' said the woman with a muted smile. A plump hand emerged from its sleeve to signal the young nun to help Lizzie up from the floor. She struggled to her feet once more, not wanting to appear even more vulnerable than she already was.

'You need to know I was brought here against my will,' Lizzie croaked. 'I was kidnapped.'

Mother Superior laughed lightly at the suggestion. 'Kidnapped, Miss Thornton? You are not being held prisoner here.' She gestured towards the door. 'It is not locked.'

Lizzie frowned and felt a little foolish, imagining the door was kept bolted. 'Then I choose to go,' she said, a tremble in her voice. 'Please arrange to take me back to . . .' She was going to say Castello di Castiglione, but she'd be rearrested. Nor could she return to Lucca.

Mother Superior tilted her head. 'I'm afraid it is not that easy, is it? The war,' she said. 'You must stay here, but you are free to come and go within our convent walls.'

Within our convent walls. At this Lizzie felt her limp body stiffen. 'So, I *am* a prisoner.'

The nun's features tightened. 'You are English and there are many who regard you as an enemy,' she replied firmly. 'It is not safe for you here in Italy and we are under instructions to offer you refuge within our walls until the war is over.'

'Whose instructions?' snapped Lizzie. 'Count de Falco's by any chance?'

Mother Superior's lips flattened for a moment until she angled her head and replied, 'The count is one of our most generous benefactors.'

'Of course he is,' Lizzie muttered cynically.

The nun returned both her hands into the folds of her habit and regarded Lizzie haughtily. 'I am sorry you do not appreciate the count's protection,' she replied. 'May I suggest you pray to the Almighty for the gift of fortitude to help you endure your stay with us, Miss Thornton, however long it may be.'

With those words, she turned and walked serenely out of the cell. The young nun, who was holding open the door, shot Lizzie an apologetic look. It was as if the sister was trying to offer her a ray of hope, but it still didn't ease her anger. This was all the count's doing. It was her punishment for collaborating with Vincenzo. How naive had she been to think banishment to Castello di Castiglione was enough? To be walled up in a convent for the duration of the war – away from Cristo and Vincenzo wasn't merely punishment. It was torture. A wave of anger surged through her and somehow, through the haze of pain, she managed to pick up the enamelled pitcher from the tray and hurl it against the cell door. It clattered on the cold stone floor below. She had to face it. She was trapped.

*   *   *

Later that same evening there was a timid knock at Lizzie's cell door.

She sat up. 'Come in,' she called weakly.

After her angry outburst had come thoughts about what to do next. She'd quickly realised that, for the moment at least, the convent offered a refuge until she'd worked out a plan.

The young nun stood by the door again. 'I am to see if I can get you anything,' she said nervously. She wrung her hands as she spoke.

Lizzie was sorry for her. She was barely an adult, but she presumed she'd already signed away her life to the Holy Order. 'No. Thank you,' she replied, her eyes on the suitcase. Whoever carried her unconscious into the cell had also delivered her belongings. At least her clothes and personal effects were inside.

The nun nodded and made to leave but paused with her hand on the door latch. She turned abruptly. 'I can show you round if you like,' she said. 'Round the convent, I mean.'

Surprised by the offer, Lizzie let out a little laugh, but the irony was wasted on the young woman.

'I'm sorry, Sister . . .'

'Sister Cecilia. I am a novice,' she replied softly.

The girl had not yet taken her vows. That explained why she was wearing white robes and why her elfin face wasn't trussed inside a wimple. A wave of sympathy washed over Lizzie. Leaving her family and her home, never knowing when or if she might see them again, must, in its own way, have been almost as terrifying as her own experience. She felt herself softening towards her. This novice wasn't a jailer, but in a way, a prisoner, just like her.

'Yes, I would like you to show me around. Thank you,' she replied.

'Tomorrow morning then.'

For the first time Lizzie thought she detected a smile hovering on the novice's lips. 'Yes,' she replied. She was warming to Sister Cecilia.

That night, loneliness wrapped itself around Lizzie like the coarse wool blanket she'd been given. It scratched at her skin and stopped her from sleeping as she lay on the plank of wood that was her bed. That's when, as the church bell rang one, she finally gave in to tears. She cried for Cristo, deprived of love, and for Vincenzo, facing the daily terror of detention and torture. She even cried for Hugh, killed for doing his duty for his country. But most of all she cried for herself and the prospect of being shut within these cold stone walls, helpless and alone, for as long as war raged. She cried so hard that by the time the bell marked two o'clock she was fast asleep.

Chapter 15

The tour of the convent took place, as Cecilia promised, before the Angelus was sung at noon. The building was large and very old, but with modern additions and extensions. The forty nuns took their meals at a long table in the refectory and prayers were said four times a day in the chapel.

'On Sundays we're allowed to celebrate Mass from here,' said Cecilia, gesturing to a galleried area on the first floor. The space overlooked a bigger church but was separated from it.

'Why can't you join in with the others?' asked Lizzie. She was still exhausted from lack of sleep and her eyes were red and swollen from last night's tears.

Cecilia looked surprised. 'Because we are a closed Order, Miss Thornton. We never leave here except if we are gravely ill or are being transferred to another convent. And we are only allowed to communicate with the outside world in certain circumstances.'

Lizzie's eyes widened. The thought of being completely isolated for life sent a shudder through her entire body. 'And that doesn't bother you?' she asked.

The novice shrugged. Of course it bothered her, Lizzie could tell as her face darkened, but all she said was, 'It is the will of God.'

They walked out into the grounds where the scent of roses

filled the air. As they strolled through the cloisters Lizzie asked the novice, 'Do you miss your family?'

Cecilia shot her a sideways look. 'Jesus is always with me,' she replied quickly. 'God has called me, and I must obey.'

Lizzie sensed something forced in her eager reply. 'Do your parents want you to take your final vows?'

Cecilia hesitated. 'My family is very poor. There were too many mouths to feed.'

'So they sent you away?' Lizzie knew poverty rarely gave its victims any choice. If the whole family was starving, it made sense to send at least one member somewhere they would be fed.

'I was *called*,' Cecilia countered, a little tetchily.

There was an awkward pause, but Lizzie was glad to have caught a spark underneath the novice's meek exterior. A sudden breeze sent apple blossom cascading through the air like confetti. Cecilia raised her hands to catch the petals like a child and smiled. Some landed on her sleeves, making Lizzie smile, too.

'And what about your family?' Cecilia asked after a moment.

Lizzie paused by a fountain and thought of Vincenzo, but she didn't mention him. She thought of her beloved Cristo, too, and how he was like a son to her, but she didn't mention him either because if she had, she might have cried. When she'd asked Mother Superior if she could write to her pupil, her request had been turned down flat. No communication with the outside world was permitted. Instead, she said, 'My mother died almost five years ago and my fiancé was a pilot, but his plane was shot down at the beginning of the war.'

'I'm sorry,' said Cecilia. 'That must've been very hard for you.'

'The war is hard for everyone,' replied Lizzie.

The novice led her through a door off the cloisters. Down steep steps they went to a basement where they were hit by a wall of hot air and the tang of carbolic soap. The laundry. A large copper cauldron filled with boiling water was steaming away in the far corner. Two nuns with baskets of washing on their hips walked past towards a sorting area, while more nuns gathered sheets ready for ironing. As she watched some sisters heat irons by a blazing fire, Lizzie noticed that on a nearby line hung several men's shirts. Alongside them on a separate drying rack were dozens of men's socks.

'Those shirts . . .' Lizzie began.

Cecilia nodded. 'They belong to the prisoners of war,' she said matter-of-factly.

Lizzie switched to face her. 'Prisoners of war?'

'Yes. The orphanage next door has been turned into a camp. There are many captured men there,' she said, as if they were very unremarkable neighbours.

'Where are they from?' asked Lizzie, holding up a khaki-coloured shirt.

'From America and Australia, I believe. And from Britain.'

'Britain,' echoed Lizzie.

'Yes. They have very smart uniforms.' Cecilia smiled as she threw a shirt into a basket marked *British Army*.

'And you do their laundry?'

'Yes. We do.' Cecilia's slight shoulders twitched in a shrug. 'We send them notes sometimes, too.'

'Notes?'

'Yes. In their socks or shirts. We tell them we are praying they will see the error of their ways and ask the Madonna del Rosario to bless them. Mother Superior says it helps them.'

Lizzie couldn't hide her astonishment. 'I'm sure it does,' she replied, her tongue firmly in her cheek. 'If I were a prisoner, I'd be very grateful.' She found herself smiling at the thought of Hugh discovering such a note in his socks and how he'd react. She imagined he'd hit the roof at the sheer nerve of it. Instead of trying to mend his ways, he'd be looking for ones to escape. But then she remembered he was gone, and the smile disappeared. Nevertheless, what the novice had just said lingered. They were

Allied troops being held next door. Some from Britain. It set her wondering. Perhaps, just perhaps, someone may have known her fiancé.

Chapter 16

The smell of incense hung heavy in the chapel air. On the altar stood a large statue of the Virgin Mary. She was holding the Infant Jesus. With his dark curls and large eyes, he reminded Lizzie of Cristo. The only lights came from the tabernacle on the altar and from the many votive candles burning on a wrought-iron stand nearby.

Lizzie had gone to the chapel not so much to pray, but for a change from her cell. The space gave her a chance to gather her thoughts. Her troubled mind took her back to memories of Hugh, shortly after their engagement. They'd been lunching in a little restaurant in Kensington, when, without warning, his knife and fork clattered on his plate and he grasped her hand to say, 'Don't go to Italy, Elizabeth. Stay here with me, in England.'

His forcefulness surprised her, yet she managed to smile politely as she delivered her reply. 'You know I have a contract, Hugh,' she'd reminded him.

He kept his eyes trained on her as he dabbed his moustache with a linen napkin, then blurted, 'Blow the contract. I'll pay to get you out of it. You don't belong there. Your place is here, with me, as my wife.'

Realising he was on the verge of anger, she was startled.

'But I can't stay here, Hugh,' she'd come back. His tone grated on her. 'As I said, I have signed a contract of employment and I intend to stick to it.' She supposed she could have wriggled out of it, somehow, but, in truth, she didn't want to. The thought of spending the next twelve months in Italy excited her.

He narrowed his eyes. 'Wilful, eh?' But then his frown turned to a smile, and he seemed to relax a little. 'I like that in a woman.' He winked at her then, but she found his reaction irritating. Was he patronising her?

Despite the distance, their courtship continued by letter. Hugh wrote to her every week for the first month, until, that September, Britain declared war on Germany. Sending letters to civilians abroad became nigh on impossible. She'd heard from a friend of his mother he'd joined the RAF.

'Would you like me to hear your confession?' came a man's voice from out of the darkness. Lizzie turned to recognise the priest who'd said Mass the other Sunday.

The question took her by surprise. 'My confession?' she repeated.

The priest gestured to her. 'You are kneeling in the House of God by the confessional box. I thought . . .'

She nodded. 'Of course, Father, I . . .' She was about to explain she had just been seeking a quiet place for reflection when she stopped herself. She needed to talk to someone without fear of being reported to the authorities. To unburden herself of all her troubles. 'Yes. Yes, Father. I would like to make a confession.'

Taking a deep breath, she opened the door of the large rosewood confessional. Inside the box it was dark and cramped. Much to her own surprise, Lizzie found herself unthinkingly making the sign of the cross as soon as she knelt. The nuns crossed themselves so often, the habit seemed to have rubbed off on her.

'Bless me, Father, for I have sinned,' she recited in Italian. The screen in front of her was made of mesh and she could see the silhouette of the priest on the other side – Father Salvatore was

103

his name. Lizzie knew she didn't have to be a Roman Catholic to make a confession. She also knew the priest was bound by the Seal of Confession. That meant anything she said to him could never be revealed to another living soul. Father Salvatore had to keep secret whatever she told him, no matter what. What he couldn't give her was absolution, but of course she wasn't seeking forgiveness. What she wanted was a sense of closure.

Lizzie clasped her hands, not because she was praying, but to stop them trembling. A memory of her confirmation into the Church of England hovered in her brain. She'd been fourteen and in preparation had made her first – and to date, last – confession. Just then, however, her sins were a million miles from her mind. Anything she divulged inside that small, stuffy box would go no further. Suddenly she felt safe.

'You wish to speak in English?' the priest enquired. Lizzie was surprised at his near-perfect accent. 'I studied at a seminary in Cornwall,' he explained.

His words went some way to calming her remaining fears. 'Thank you, Father. Yes.' He might be more sympathetic if he was familiar with the English way of doing things.

'What is it you wish to tell the Lord?' He was skipping the formalities and cutting to the chase. Was he inviting her to talk about herself? He was reaching out to her. Perhaps she should take his hand.

Picturing his features on the other side of the mesh helped her focus on what she had to say. Swallowing down her hesitation, she launched in. 'I know I'm a sinner, Father, but I really shouldn't be here, at this convent, I mean. I've been taken away from my job and my home and the people I care about and brought here simply because I am English.'

She held her breath until finally the priest said, 'Go on.' His silhouette nodded.

'I am a prisoner in this convent because my government is at war with yours. Next door are many of my fellow countrymen

104

who are deprived of their liberty for the same reason.' It felt so good to speak her mind freely.

There was a short silence, as if the priest was processing his reply to her unexpected statement. She heard him sigh before he leaned closer to the mesh. 'I am a prison chaplain. I hear the confessions of tortured men and I know they are not the evil ones,' he told her. 'I like this war no more than you. Mussolini is an evil tyrant and the Devil incarnate. I will do anything I can to help you. What is it that you want of me?' Any previous doubts disappeared. He was on her side. 'If you need my help, my child, then you have it.'

Lizzie paused for a moment before she continued. 'Can you tell me if there are any British prisoners next door, Father?'

His reply was measured but encouraging. 'There are many hundreds of men from several Allied countries, and yes, they are mainly British, I understand.'

Lizzie's heart skipped a beat. 'Are there any Royal Air Force crews among them?'

A nod through the mesh. 'At least two dozen air crew, I think.'

'Air crew,' repeated Lizzie.

'Yes. Seven or eight navigators and the rest pilots, I believe.'

'Pilots?'

'Yes?' There was a question in the priest's voice.

She was surprised to hear the tremble in her reply. 'I was engaged to be married to an RAF pilot once, Father,' she explained. 'But he was shot down several months ago.'

'He will be with the Lord now,' he told her, thinking he was offering comfort.

'Thank you, Father,' she replied. 'Perhaps . . .' She faltered a little. 'Perhaps some of them, the air crew I mean, might have served with my fiancé. It would be of great comfort to me if I could speak with someone who knew him.'

'I can make enquiries,' replied Father Salvatore. 'What was his name?'

A strange sense of relief rippled through Lizzie's body at his words. What the priest revealed was far more valuable than giving her absolution. Father Salvatore had just become her powerful ally.

'Flight Lieutenant Hugh Codrington, No. 83 Squadron,' she said.

Chapter 17

Two weeks later, Father Salvatore returned with news. He insisted on delivering it face to face. Lizzie walked nervously into the convent visitors' parlour to see the priest standing in the middle of it. His expression was hard to read. Ever since she'd asked him to make enquiries about Hugh, Lizzie had been churning the past over in her head. Being parted from her fiancé for so long had helped deaden the pain of his loss, but it hadn't lessened the guilt she'd felt. He'd died never knowing her intention to break off their engagement and while Lizzie was glad of that, it still made her feel awkward. By speaking to someone who knew Hugh well, she hoped it would bring her peace.

'What have you to tell me, Father?' She couldn't wait to find out. If she could only learn just how Hugh had died from someone who'd been there, it might bring her proper closure. 'Have you found anyone?'

Ignoring her question, Father Salvatore's features remained neutral as he bade her sit. The room was hot, and he shoved two fingers down his tight priest's collar as if trying to circulate some air. Lizzie declined his invitation. She was too on edge.

'As you wish,' he said, drawing a steadying breath. 'Flight Lieutenant Codrington,' he began.

'Yes.' Lizzie's heart started to race.

'His plane was shot down in May last year. He was piloting a Blenheim bomber over Bardia in northeastern Libya when it was hit by anti-aircraft guns . . .'

So, it was true. Her eyes dipped for a moment's reflection. She hoped it had all been over quickly; that he hadn't suffered. Another 'yes'. Then raising her head, she noticed the priest was looking at her rather oddly, almost as if he were playing a game with her.

'But there's more,' he teased.

'More?' snapped Lizzie. She found her patience was being tried. 'I don't under—'

'He survived the crash.'

Lizzie gasped and her hands flew to her mouth, and she felt her legs crumple beneath her. 'You mean he's alive?'

'Please. You must keep calm,' pleaded the priest, helping her to a nearby chair.

'I'm sorry. It's just such a . . . such a shock,' she replied.

The priest paused to allow Lizzie to compose herself before he started to speak again. 'Of course,' he said with a nod, pouring her water from a nearby jug.

She took a sip then frowned when a new thought crowded in. 'If Hugh's alive, does anyone know where he is?' she murmured to herself as much as to the priest.

Father Salvatore took a deep breath and looked at her straight. 'Not only did the Lord choose to spare your pilot's life, he brought him to the camp next door.'

Lizzie, her head bowed till then, jerked up. 'What? You mean . . .?'

'I mean Flight Lieutenant Codrington is being held prisoner not five hundred metres away from here.'

She stifled another cry of shock. Hugh was alive. What's more he was just the other side of the convent wall. A thousand thoughts swam round her head. This was not the outcome she'd expected from her enquiry, and she wasn't sure how to react. Guilt melded with surprise. She was delighted, of course. It was wonderful news that Hugh was alive, but she needed time to address her own thoughts.

'Can I speak with him?' she asked after a moment. Her conscience wouldn't allow her to be so close to him without letting him know. After all, she was next door, and, for all Hugh knew, as soon as this ghastly war was over, they would still be married. He'd no idea she'd given her heart to another man. She knew she was plunging herself into an awkward position, but she considered it only fair on her fiancé.

'You could write,' Father Salvatore suggested. 'I can get a note to him.'

'Oh, could you? Yes. Yes, please,' said Lizzie, still shaking her head in disbelief.

Hugh was alive. But was Vincenzo?

Lizzie's pen had remained poised over a small scrap of paper for the past ten minutes. Her single candle cast a weak puddle of light on the page, but still it was blank. Hugh was alive and she had the chance to write to him, but what should she say? Four years ago, just after she'd agreed to marry him, it would have been easy. She would have told him she loved him – because she thought she did – that their years apart had been miserable and that she couldn't wait to return to England to spend the rest of her days with him. Now everything had changed.

Falling in love with Vincenzo Baldini had been the best thing that had ever happened to her. Hugh had been so persuasive, so charismatic that she'd allowed herself to be caught up in his net. He'd hauled her in. Hook, line and sinker. She hadn't put up a fight, believing him when he'd said her future was in England, with him. She'd thought it was, too; never questioning the solid prospects of a home and children that lay ahead of her. But then Lizzie had fallen in love with Italy and out of love with Hugh and the lifestyle he'd promised her. Then, quite out of the blue,

109

along came Vincenzo. He'd shown her a different side of life. What's more, he had treated her as his equal. They were partners in their work to nurture Cristo and in their work for the resistance. And as for his touch and his kiss, they had electrified her in a way Hugh's never did. He excited her in a way Hugh never had. But he'd been cruelly snatched from her. The irony of it was now she knew Hugh had survived his plane crash, Vincenzo might have died in jail.

In her head she wrestled with the dilemma. It would have been easier if she'd never thought of asking about Hugh, but his survival changed everything. Now it was only right to reach out to him. She presumed he would still love her, after all, even though she no longer loved him. Not in the way she did. She cared for him, of course, but her love had died long before she thought he'd died, too. She just hadn't had the courage to tell him. Vincenzo's arrival in her life meant love had put on fresh clothes, spoken a different language and taken on a whole new dimension. Time alone would tell if he had survived torture and imprisonment. Meanwhile, she clutched her pen tighter and with a strong hand began unequivocally:

Dear Hugh
  This is a letter I never dared to dream of writing . . .

The reply came a week later, on Father Salvatore's return from his regular visit to the men's camp. Lizzie read the familiar writing with trembling hands.

Dearest Elizabeth
  I can't tell you how overjoyed I was to hear you are alive and living in the convent next door. The angels truly brought me to you, my love. If I told you everything, I would quickly run out of paper. (It's in short supply, as I'm sure you know!) Suffice to say, as soon as war broke out, I joined the RAF.

110

Following pilot training I was sent on a mission over North Africa but was shot down and captured by the Italians last year. I spent a long time in hospital, then several months in a hellish camp before they transferred me here a few weeks ago. But now I know you are only a few yards away, my life will be so much more bearable.

Father Salvatore is a good man. We can trust him to be our courier. I can't wait to hear from you again, dearest Elizabeth. Suddenly I can just about stand these four walls but live for the day I can hold you in my arms once more.

Your ever-loving
Hugh

Lizzie gripped the single sheet of tightly written script to her breast. What had she done? It was as if by contacting Hugh and discovering he still loved her, she'd opened her very own Pandora's box. It was full of emotions and impossible dilemmas. *He loves me. He still loves me*, she repeated over and over in a panic. But she thought he'd died almost a year ago. Her life had moved on. The embers of her love for him had long grown cold but now here he was trying to rekindle them.

Her thoughts switched to Vincenzo and tipped the day into sadness. She pictured him every night before she went to bed. Whenever he was beside her, she'd felt herself light up, like an electric bulb. No one had made her feel that way before, and now she'd experienced real love, she yearned for him more and more. Lizzie knew her heart no longer belonged to Hugh – just how on earth was she meant to tell him?

Chapter 18

Hugh's letters came every other week via Father Salvatore. They were often funny. His friend Tuffers, or to give him his full title, Flight Lieutenant Giles Tufnell, provided much of the merriment, the way he would dupe guards into handing out more rations and mimic them behind their backs. There was news of an amateur dramatic club and the supervised walks the prisoners were allowed to take. But as well as light-hearted chat, there was romance, too. There were lines of poetry and reminiscences about their engagement. And there was talk of the future. That was the hardest thing of all. Lizzie didn't know how to respond to Hugh's hope to *'pick up where we left off'* because she simply couldn't. She had cared deeply for Hugh, and in some ways, she still did. She'd be completely callous if, in some corner of her heart, there wasn't something that lingered, even if it was only a fond memory. When she thought he was dead, her mourning had been real, too. Even so, it was a different kind of feeling she harboured for him nowadays; a completely platonic one. But how could she tell him in a letter she had no wish to wear his ring again? She simply couldn't bring herself to act so harshly. Not while they were both held captive. But then, in his next letter, he came up with an idea.

My Darling,

The thought of you next door but out of reach is driving me simply crazy. I must see you again and so I've formulated a plan.

That was so like Hugh, she thought. His devil-may-care approach to life was admired in an RAF pilot, but in everyday life he could easily hurt people. He had to get his way at all costs.

On feast days and certain saint's days, we chaps gather at our windows to watch the young gals in the congregation walk from the church to visit the nearby cemetery. The oldies think they go to pay their respects to the dead, but they're dressed in bright colours and carry posies of flowers, supposedly to decorate the graves, and the little minxes don't look in the least bit sad. Everyone knows they're only parading in front of us POWs to tease us.

Of course, we're not allowed to watch them and if the guards see us, they shoot over our heads, but it's tremendous fun. If you can pull it off by joining the procession next week, my darling, it would be the most wonderful thing. I'll be looking out for you.

Lizzie read the letter again. Part of her was slightly indignant that Hugh was asking her to take part in some sort of beauty pageant for the gratification of his fellow prisoners, but part of her understood what it would mean to him – and, if she were honest – to her, to see him again, even if it was only a glimpse. She found his presence nearby reassuring; like an anchor in stormy seas. In all truthfulness, she probably needed him as much as he needed her right now. More so, even. At least Hugh was surrounded by his comrades who could bolster each other's morale. The only person she was drawn to was Cecilia, but she still hadn't confided in her. Perhaps it was time she did.

On Thursday, a church feast day, Hugh would be standing at the fifth window from the right on the second floor. It didn't matter that they'd both need a pair of binoculars to see each other's faces, he'd told her. The mere thought of being able to set eyes on her, if only in outline, was exciting enough.

Lizzie had sought permission to take flowers to the mausoleum. By a quirk of fate, an old teacher who'd once taught her Italian was laid to rest there – or so she told Mother Superior. Her story had, much to her amazement, been believed and she would shortly be able to see Hugh for the first time in almost four years.

Wearing a green dress and a bright blue headscarf, she'd written telling him to look out for her. She would be at the end of the line of women making the pilgrimage to the cemetery where the graves were stacked one of top of each other into the walls. That way he would know to look out for her. The feeling of freedom once she was out of the convent gates was almost overwhelming. In a few short steps she walked along the path at the back of the convent and managed to draw level with the camp. Looking to her right, she saw the windows where the prisoners clustered. With her heart racing she counted them. Three, four, five. And just as she set eyes on a single man standing at the frame, a sheet was unfurled with her name on it, written in red. She couldn't make out his face, but just knowing Hugh was there, only a few yards away, was somehow reassuring, until . . .

A burst of gunfire echoed inside the prison and Hugh disappeared along with the banner. Lizzie held her breath. Some of the girls in the procession screamed, although she knew it was a routine show of force by the fascist guards. A moment later Hugh was back again at the window; his arm raised in a wave, then in the next he was gone. But it was enough. She felt happy to see him. She really did, especially after thinking he was dead. Yet it was also strangely unsettling and confusing. When she asked herself the question that had been hovering over her like a great bird ever since she'd been told her fiancé was alive: would she rather have seen Vincenzo standing at that window? the answer that came back, without a shadow of a doubt, was yes.

Lizzie decided to confide in Cecilia about seeing Hugh. At first, she'd been afraid the news that she was in touch with a prisoner next door might somehow get back to Mother Superior. But now she believed she could trust her young friend, so after dinner in the refectory, she sought her out. She found the novice sitting quietly alone on a cloister seat. Lizzie could tell immediately something was wrong. Her eyes were red and swollen.

Lizzie sat beside her and touched her arm lightly. 'What is it?'

The girl turned to her tearfully and shook her head.

'You can tell me,' said Lizzie gently.

'I heard today . . .' Cecilia sniffed back more tears. 'I heard that two of my brothers are dead.'

A pain jabbed at Lizzie's heart. 'I'm so sorry,' she said, instinctively putting an arm around her. But Cecilia flinched and pulled away.

'It is not allowed,' she muttered through her grief.

'Forgive me,' said Lizzie, feeling utterly helpless. She understood the hard edges of sorrow could sometimes be softened by the touch of another human, but these nuns were denied that, even in their greatest hour of need.

'They died two days apart, fighting in Tunisia,' Cecilia explained. She brought out a handkerchief from her habit to dab her cheeks.

'Can you at least go home to comfort your parents?' asked Lizzie.

The same words were repeated once more. 'It is not allowed.'

For a second time, Lizzie's heart ached for the young novice. Her face was a study in suffering and yet she was forbidden from being with her family at such a terrible time because of the strict rules of her Order. At least Lizzie had the comfort of knowing that

Hugh was next door. Despite her change in feelings towards him, his letters had kept her going over the past few weeks of captivity. She decided now was the right time to open up to the novice.

'Don't give up hope,' Lizzie said.

Cecilia frowned. 'What do you mean?'

It was then Lizzie told her about Hugh and how, for almost a year, she'd believed him dead, only to discover he was very much alive and living next door.

'But that's ... that's a miracle,' Cecilia cried, her red eyes widening in surprise.

'Yes. Yes, I suppose it is,' Lizzie replied. The coincidence was so huge that even she had entertained the idea some divine intervention was at work.

'I will pray that you can both be together again soon,' said Cecilia.

Lizzie sighed. 'I wish it were that simple,' she muttered. Cecilia wasn't supposed to hear, but she picked up on her negativity.

'What's wrong?' asked the novice. 'You're not happy?'

Lizzie looked ahead of her at the high wall that stood between her and Hugh. A white rose with vicious thorns was climbing up it, so no one else could. 'I've been a coward,' she confessed.

'A coward? What do you mean?'

'I should have broken off our engagement a long time ago, but I just didn't have the courage.'

Cecilia nodded. 'I see. You no longer love this man?'

Lizzie shook her head. 'But he loves me and when we are free, he still wants me to be his wife.'

The novice was quiet for a moment before she said, 'You must listen to your heart.'

Lizzie switched back to her. She thought it ironic advice coming from a young girl who clearly wasn't listening to hers. If she had, she would be with her parents right now, offering them comfort instead of being walled up in a convent, where even the caring touch of another was forbidden.

'Yes, you're right,' Lizzie agreed. 'I ought to listen to my heart.' She reached out and took Cecilia's hand and squeezed it. It was small and cool in hers, reminding her that this young woman was little more than a child. 'And maybe so should you, too,' she added.

Chapter 19

The increasing numbers of aircraft flying overhead in the brilliant blue July sky were a sure sign to Lizzie and the prisoners of Camp 49 that the war had taken a new turn. One day, as she was walking in the orchard, about to pick cherries, she heard loud cheers coming from next door. Making sure there were no nuns around, she scrambled up into the nearest tree and could barely believe what she saw over the wall, behind the barbed wire. The mayhem was being caused not by the prisoners but by their Italian guards. She caught the sound of a chant. *Arrivederci, Benito! Arrivederci, Benito!* It couldn't be true, could it?

Confirmation came the following day from Father Salvatore in a letter from Hugh. After supper in the refectory that evening, when the air was thick with heat and dust and the incense in the chapel overpowering, Lizzie walked with Cecilia and shared the momentous news.

'Mussolini has been arrested.'

'Oh,' was all the nun managed at first.

'It's a good thing,' said Lizzie, encouragingly. 'It means that the beginning of the end could be in sight.'

Cecilia nodded. 'We must pray that is the case,' she said, but Lizzie noticed her voice was tinged with sadness.

'What is it, Cecilia? What's wrong?' she asked.

The novice shrugged. 'When the war ends you will be free,' she replied weakly. 'I will be happy for you, but I will remain here.'

The prospect brought Lizzie up sharply. Freedom meant different things to different people. She knew Cecilia was due to take her final sacred vows by the end of the year, after which she may never leave the four walls of the Madonna del Rosario again.

'God has chosen you,' Lizzie told her, thinking it was what her young friend wanted to hear.

Cecilia nodded. 'Of course,' she replied, but her gaze fell to the ground. For the first time Lizzie thought she detected a slight waver in the novice's conviction.

For the next few weeks, as summer rolled into autumn, hope that the war might come to an end returned to Lizzie. Her morale was boosted when another mighty armada of planes flew over the convent. She was working in the vegetable garden at the time and knew from their enormous size the aircraft had to be American. Hugh's letters became more encouraging, too. The Allies, he wrote, were ashore near Reggio di Calabria in the south. At last she dared to dream, then finally on a sweltering afternoon on 8 September, as Lizzie was washing her face in her room in a vain effort to keep cool, she heard shouts, followed by gunfire. Rushing outside, she climbed up the tree once more to look out across to the camp, even though she couldn't see much. But the noises which seemed to be coming from there sounded joyful rather than aggressive, although they didn't last more than ten minutes. Then there was silence once more.

The following day in the small walled garden under the shade of the olive trees, Father Salvatore approached her. 'There is news,' he told her breathlessly, looking around to make sure no one was watching. '*Un armistizio*,' he muttered. The word needed no translation. Lizzie's eyes widened. The priest continued, 'General Badoglio has asked General Eisenhower for an armistice, and it's been granted. All hostilities between Italian and Anglo-American forces have ceased.'

Lizzie suddenly felt joyfully alert. It was as if for the past four months she'd been asleep and now news of the Armistice had woken her. Just like the story of the Sleeping Beauty, she'd been left alone in the convent, imprisoned by a wall of thick, twisted briars and any moment now someone would come riding along on a charger and hack away at the thorns to free her.

'Here,' said Father Salvatore, handing her another note from Hugh. 'I believe it contains instructions.' He smiled nervously. No one knew what might happen over the next few hours. 'May God go with you.'

It was hard for her not to run back to her cell. Forcing herself to walk slowly, so as not to attract attention, she returned directly to her room. Once inside, she read Hugh's note.

It seems our chaps are expected to make airborne landings at Rome and Milan. Sea landings could be made at Genoa and Rimini, too. The Italian colonel in charge is a good sort and reckons we'll be able to walk out of here very shortly, although it seems the Germans might not play fair. They're not at all happy about the Armistice and are threatening to invade. We all need to be on our mettle.

Lizzie didn't like the sound of that. If the Nazis descended on the region, at best she'd be taken prisoner and sent to a labour camp and at worse she'd be killed on the spot. In between, as a woman, there was always the threat so horrifying she couldn't even think about it. And as for prisoners like Hugh next door – it would take more than a handful of half-hearted Italian guards to fend off the brutish Germans. There'd be a blood bath.

She returned to Hugh's note.

In the meantime, the bar is open and doing a roaring trade.

He always made light of tricky situations. *Nothing*, he would say, *is ever as bad as it seems.* On this occasion, she really hoped he was right.

I'll be waiting by the plane tree in the avenue outside at three o'clock this afternoon.

Just a few more hours and we'll be together.

Just a few more hours. The words swam on the page before her as her whole body was rigid with anticipation. The waiting would soon be over. But what would freedom look like? She couldn't even think about it right now. All she had to do was pack and ask to leave. *Easier said than done?* She would find out soon enough. In the meantime, she also did something she'd barely done since her confinement in the convent – silently she began to pray.

Heaving her suitcase from under her bed she threw in the few possessions she had with her when there was a knock on the door. It was Cecilia. Lizzie guessed she must have seen her meet with Father Salvatore in the garden.

'Come in.' She took a deep breath. Her friend would find out what had happened soon enough, she guessed. She may as well tell her now.

'Is everything all right?' asked the young nun, looking anxious.

Lizzie smiled and hurried forward, with her arms open wide. At that moment, she really didn't care for the Order's strict rules.

'It's over,' she said, trying to keep her voice low while hugging Cecilia tightly. 'They've declared an armistice.'

'An armistice?' repeated the novice, her body rigid to Lizzie's touch. She pulled back, looking uncomfortable and bewildered. 'Does that mean you are free to go?'

'I hope it does,' Lizzie said, but she knew her reply was a double-edged sword because it meant she would have to leave Cecilia. She would soon be moving on, but for the novice little would

121

change. In fact, after she'd taken her vows, her routine would only be stricter and her life harsher. For her the end of the war did not mean the end of drudgery and isolation. It meant more of the same, only worse.

Lizzie touched her friend lightly on the arm and Cecilia returned her gaze.

'I will never forget you,' she whispered.

This time when Lizzie hugged her, Cecilia did not flinch, but allowed herself to be comforted. Lizzie only wished she could take her with her when she left, but she knew it was not to be. They had both made their choices in life. Hers was to escape alongside Hugh. Cecilia's was to stay with her Order. Whether either of those turned out to be the right decisions, only time would tell.

Chapter 20

Two hours had passed since Father Salvatore delivered the news and when the summons she'd been expecting from Mother Superior didn't come, Lizzie grew edgy. Around noon a bugle sounded three notes next door. A signal? Or maybe an alarm. Climbing into the fruit tree once more, she pulled herself up onto the highest branch to look into the camp. What she saw unsettled her. The only people she could see were Italian soldiers setting up machine guns and scuttling into slit trenches around the perimeter. It appeared they were preparing to defend themselves, just as Hugh said. It could only be against the Germans. The Nazis must be on their way.

Time was slipping away from her. She needed to leave immediately. She was just about to clamber back down the tree to tell Mother Superior of her intention when a movement in the far corner of the camp caught her eye. One of the prisoners was hobbling along. He seemed injured and she tracked his progress to a small huddle of men. At first, she couldn't be sure, but the harder she looked, the more certain she became. They'd cut their way through the barbed wire perimeter fence and were exiting the camp one by one.

Lizzie's heart beat faster as she scrambled down from the tree.

There was no time to lose. Hurrying back to her room to collect her suitcase, she dashed to Mother Superior's office. One of the sisters tried to bar her way, but she ignored her and barged in.

'Mother Superior, forgive the intrusion,' she began breathlessly, dropping her suitcase to the floor. 'But I've learned German troops are expected any moment now. I must leave.'

The nun, seated at her desk, looked up slowly from her papers. She resented the interruption and frowned. Her chair creaked beneath her weight as she shifted in it. Then, very deliberately, she laced her fingers in front of her to show she was in no hurry to grant Lizzie's request.

'You seem very sure, Miss Thornton,' she remarked coldly.

'I am,' Lizzie replied, trying to hide the fear growing inside her.

'Come back tomorrow and we can discuss your release then, but at the moment as you can see . . .' She pointed to a stack of papers on her desk. 'I am rather busy. In the meantime, I suggest you go to the chapel to pray for your safe delivery.'

Lizzie stood her ground. She stuck out her chin defiantly. 'God helps those who help themselves,' she responded. 'You no longer have any right to hold me here against my will.'

Below her wimple, Mother Superior arched a brow. 'I haven't received any authorisation to release you,' she countered.

Lizzie took a juddering breath. 'If that is a refusal, then I shall take matters into my own hands.'

The nun leaned forward. 'You would disobey me?' she hissed.

Lizzie was shaking inside. 'I must remind you I am not one of your Order. An armistice has been declared, so you no longer have authority over me.'

Mother Superior leaned back then, just as Father Salvatore appeared at her study door, looking anxious.

'Miss Thornton wishes to leave us,' the nun announced. 'What do you say, Father?'

The priest darted a troubled look at Lizzie then replied with a warning. 'I say she must go at once, Mother Superior. The

124

Germans are furious about the Armistice. They feel betrayed and there are reports of them approaching along the Via Emilia. They're about ten kilometres away from the town.'

There was no time for goodbyes. Lizzie grabbed her suitcase and rushed to the entrance hall of the convent to be let out through a back door. Briefly she turned to see if Cecilia was around, but she was nowhere to be seen.

'May God go with you,' said Father Salvatore, extending his hand to make the sign of the cross. 'I will pray for you.'

'Thank you, Father. For everything,' said Lizzie, watching one of the sisters unlock a side gate and open it wide. She took her first steps into the outside world knowing she was going to need not just prayers but luck, guile and guts if she hoped to survive any forthcoming Nazi onslaught.

There was the plane tree on the avenue. But no Hugh. Lizzie waited under its shade. The convent's bell struck three o'clock, reminding her that each minute under the tree meant the German tanks were drawing closer. As she waited, all sorts of terrible scenarios ran through her head. What if Hugh didn't turn up? What if he'd been prevented from leaving the camp? What if for one out of a million different reasons he couldn't make the rendezvous? She would have to go alone. But where would she go? Count de Falco's estate was fifteen kilometres east of the town. Cristo was there, she hoped. But it was a risk because, despite Mussolini's arrest, the count could still be free. On the other hand, if he wasn't and she reached Castello di Castiglione that evening, perhaps she could stay there for a while. Her head felt it was about to burst when suddenly . . .

'Elizabeth.'

She heard her name – her old name – called in a loud whisper, then turned sharply to see Hugh standing in the shadows, a few metres away. Picking up her case she ran to him and felt his arms around her.

125

'Oh Hugh.' Tears of relief sprang up to fill her eyes. 'It's so good to see you again.' She drew back to look at him. His moustache was bushier, and his brows were thicker. His body was thinner and the lines around his eyes were deeper, but it was still the same Hugh Codrington who had proposed to her four years before.

'It's all right now, my darling,' he said, cupping her face in his hands. 'My God, I've missed you,' he told her, planting his lips on hers so suddenly she'd had no time to protest. His moustache still tickled her the way it had before, but, thankfully for Lizzie, the kiss was cut short.

'Codrington!' A voice from a little farther down the road called and Hugh broke away.

'We've got to go,' he told her, grabbing her suitcase and taking her hand in his. 'This way.'

In the scorching heat, she had trouble keeping up with the pace he set down the street, the dust flying up behind him. Soon he was turning left onto a footpath that skirted the camp. The man who'd called out was waiting for them at the corner.

'This is Tuffers,' said Hugh. 'We're in the same squadron.' Tuffers was a redhead and a little taller than his fellow pilot. He nodded to Lizzie, but there was no smile. He gave the distinct impression he wasn't thrilled by the prospect of having her as a travel companion.

'We need to hurry,' he snapped.

'Where are we going?' asked Lizzie as they set off.

'Anywhere. Just away from here,' Hugh replied, still hefting her suitcase.

They'd taken a few more paces forward before Lizzie said, 'I know somewhere.'

The two men stopped dead.

'What?' said Hugh. 'Where?'

'Castello di Castiglione. West of here. It belongs to the count whose son I tutored.'

'Balderdash,' barked Tuffers. 'We need to go north. That's where everyone else is headed.'

Hugh set down the suitcase and turned to Lizzie. 'You're sure we can get food and supplies there?'

Lizzie hesitated for a moment. The situation was so fluid, but as long as de Falco wasn't there, she hoped the staff would give them refuge. 'Yes,' she said, looking at Tuffers. 'If we hurry, we can make it in less than four hours.'

The other pilot remained unconvinced and pointed to the fields ahead of them. 'The chaps are going that way.'

'But what if the Germans are coming from that way, too?' asked Lizzie.

The question unsettled Tuffers. 'We'll take our chances.'

'Hugh?' she said, looking at him. He seemed to have the casting vote.

He glanced back at his friend, then at Lizzie once more. 'I say we go to this estate first off. We can regroup there.'

Tuffers sucked breath through his teeth and shook his head. 'Then, I'm off, old boy.' He held out a hand. 'Good luck and see you on the other side.'

Even though he was clearly shocked by his friend's abruptness, Hugh took the offered hand. 'You can't be persuaded?' he asked forlornly.

'You know what they say. Two's company and all that,' Tuffers replied, tossing a disdainful look at Lizzie. 'Best get cracking,' and with those words he set off once more, breaking into a run to catch up with a group of escapees who were a few hundred metres ahead.

'Well,' said Hugh with an awkward smile. 'The count's estate it is.' Digging into his pocket, he produced a folded piece of cloth.

As she peered at it, Lizzie could see there was writing on it. 'A map of the area?' she asked.

Hugh chuckled then turned away slightly so she couldn't look at it. 'Women and maps don't mix, darling,' he joked. 'I told you we were allowed on walks, and I managed to cobble this together from memory. If we are going west, we head that way out of town.' He pointed behind her. 'Let's get going, shall we?'

Chapter 21

The town was eerily quiet, as if it had paused to hold its breath, expecting the roar of Panzer tanks to roll down its wide main street at any moment. A stray cat crossing the road and an unseen hand closing shutters were the only signs of life. They had to be as inconspicuous as possible, so they kept to the shade of trees as they made their way out of Fontanellato and onto the flat plains surrounding it.

The vast fields were criss-crossed by irrigation channels. They proved hard for Lizzie to negotiate in her skirt that stopped just above her ankles. Hugh was finding her suitcase a hindrance, too. She knew what she had to do. Crouching down into one of the dry ditches, she opened the case and took out the only pair of trousers she possessed and quickly slipped them on. Rescuing two warm jumpers and a scarf, she abandoned the case.

Hugh had already clambered up a nearby bank and turned to offer her his hand. Lizzie took it and together they set off once more, keeping to the margins lined by tall poplars. Some of the fields had already been ploughed, but in others the corn was high and ripe and ready to be gathered. They passed a party of *contadini* harvesting it with sickles. One by one the peasants stopped as they noticed this strange couple marching across the field, following the line of a ditch. But then one of the men waved an arm.

'*Buongiorno!*' he called.

'*Buongiorno,*' replied Lizzie, equally enthusiastically.

It seemed to satisfy the working party. A few of the workers waved at them, too, but there was no attempt to engage them in conversation and for that Lizzie was grateful. She was not yet used to the idea of freedom and nor was Hugh. They both knew they were vulnerable and could be detained at any moment by random fascist sympathisers they encountered, despite the Armistice. They hurried on but had only progressed about a mile out of town when the silence was broken by machine-gun fire. Their heads spun round simultaneously to see smoke rising from the town.

'Christ!' muttered Hugh. 'Jerry must've reached the camp.'

The Germans had made more progress than they could have imagined. They were right behind them. The crack of gunfire and the rumble of tanks grew louder. They hurried on.

By four o'clock the heat was almost unbearable. Dehydration had given Lizzie a terrible headache, and, exhausted, the pair stopped under the shade of a line of vines. Hugh stared at a stagnant puddle at the bottom of one of the ditches.

'What I wouldn't give for a pint of cool bitter, right now,' he said wistfully.

'You'll have to make do with chilled white wine,' replied Lizzie, thinking of the cellars at Castello di Castiglione as she licked her parched lips.

'I'll settle for that,' he said with a smile, quickly drawing her close to him. 'God, it's good to see you again.' He moved to kiss her on the mouth, but she ducked, and he brushed her forehead with his lips.

'And you,' she replied. Even with his hair plastered with sweat and his forearms covered in mosquito bites, she still found Hugh handsome. She could see why she'd been so attracted to him, but although they'd only been reunited for a few hours, it was almost a relief to know the spark she'd once felt was no longer there. Managing to duck out of his grasp, she put him off with, 'We've got four years of catching up to do, but right now, we must keep going.'

They walked on, even though their pace had slowed. The stutter of machine-gun fire seemed to be fading, but they weren't willing to take any chances. Keeping to hedgerows and poplar groves where they could, they trudged on, not even daring to ask for water from a farmhouse they passed. The risk of being handed over to the Germans wasn't worth it.

The bell at the campanile of Castello di Castiglione was marking seven o'clock as they staggered into the surrounding village. Ahead of them stood the count's forbidding castle. They plodded up the cobbled driveway to the great gates and Lizzie tried the latch before she saw a huge padlock that kept them firmly shut. The place looked deserted. Even the lazy cats were nowhere to be seen. With a sense of trepidation, Lizzie tugged at the bell rope.

Seconds turned into minutes as they scanned the castle windows, then walked around the corner to try a side gate. It was then Lizzie saw a flash. Someone was at the window. Someone she knew. 'Maria,' she gasped, then remembering she couldn't be assured of a welcome from everyone, she simply waved.

A moment later there was the clatter of boots on the cobbles and another familiar face from the Villa Martini emerged into the courtyard.

'Giuseppe! Giuseppe, is that really you?' cried Lizzie in Italian, unable to suppress her relief. She was grasping the iron bars of the side gate with excitement.

'Miss Lizzie.' The old gardener greeted her with a smile, but underneath lay a puzzled look. 'What . . .? What are you doing here?' he asked, eyeing Hugh suspiciously.

'It's a long story, Giuseppe,' she replied through the bars. 'This man is a friend. But is Count de Falco here?'

His grizzled head shook. 'We haven't seen him for weeks. He was arrested alongside that tyrant,' he said, narrowing his eyes.

It was clear he meant Mussolini. So, de Falco had finally got his comeuppance, too, thought Lizzie. She only hoped he wouldn't be released any time soon. 'And Signora Cortina?' recalling the housekeeper's part in her kidnapping.

'Back in Lucca. You are safe here,' Giuseppe assured her.

Lizzie believed him. But for how much longer?

The old man grappled with the stiff gate, but after a moment the padlock finally yielded, allowing Lizzie and Hugh to enter.

'It's so good to see you,' she said, clutching at the gardener's shirtsleeves. 'And Cristo? Is he here?'

Before Giuseppe could answer there were more footsteps – lighter and faster. They echoed around the courtyard and a boy appeared framed by a nearby arch. His dark curls had been tamed and his expression seemed troubled, but Lizzie knew he was unmistakably her beloved Cristo.

Without a word she ran and flung her arms around him. To her surprise she found he'd grown up to her shoulder. After a moment she pulled back to look at him, her hands bracketing his face.

'Cristo! Oh, my dearest Cristo!' she gasped, tears filling her eyes.

Cristo smiled and allowed Lizzie to fuss him. Normally he would have returned her embrace, but he didn't seem at ease being watched by Hugh. He slid him a sideways glance and replied, 'What happened, Miss Lizzie? Those men. Where did they take you?'

Lizzie shook her head and thought back to the last time she had seen Cristo. She wondered what he had been told about her disappearance. 'Those men who brought us here, they took me to a convent not far away. I didn't want to go, believe me. And then I wasn't allowed to write to you. Oh, dear Cristo!' She reached forward again for another hug.

Maria now joined them, waddling across the courtyard, frantically waving a tea towel.

'Miss Lizzie. Miss Lizzie,' she cried, embracing her with open arms. 'Miss Lizzie. You are free!' She wiped away sudden tears with her apron.

'Yes. The Armistice. They let us go. It's so good to see you all.' Lizzie leaned forward to kiss the cook on the cheek. 'And this is' – she looked at Hugh – 'this is Flight Lieutenant Codrington. He's my—' She broke off. Aware her relationship with Hugh was now hard to describe, she settled on, 'He's a good friend.'

She caught Hugh's puzzled look as he nodded to acknowledge the welcoming smiles, but clearly couldn't follow most of what was being said. 'I'm afraid his Italian is not good,' explained Lizzie. Then, turning to Maria she asked, 'But why are you here and not in Lucca?'

The cook leaned in and lowered her voice so that Cristo couldn't hear. 'The count said it was safer for us,' she said before adding, 'But not for him. They took him away six weeks back.' She winked and a smile planted itself on her wrinkled face once more. 'First we eat, then we talk. Yes?'

They all crossed the cobbles, gabbling excitedly as they walked towards the kitchen. Much to Lizzie's delight Cristo looped his arm in hers. 'Have you heard anything about Signor Baldini?' he asked.

'Signor Baldini,' she repeated. It was a name that hadn't passed her lips for a while and her heart stuttered at the mention of it. For some reason it felt odd even thinking about the man she loved in Hugh's presence, as if he could read her mind.

'Baldini?' Hugh arched a brow – the name seeming to trigger an interest.

'A tutor, too, but he was arrested a few months ago,' she explained before turning back to Cristo. 'No. No, I haven't heard anything about him.'

Giuseppe and Maria looked at each other. 'Poor man,' said Maria reflectively, raising her eyes heavenwards. His likely fate seemed to be something unspoken in the household. 'We haven't either,' she mumbled, then began again, lightly this time, 'So, I have pasta with my special sauce. Let's get you some.'

Seeing Hugh tense at the mention of pasta, Lizzie said, 'We cannot stay long. We're afraid the Germans are close by. But food would be most welcome.' She glanced down at her mud-caked slacks as she spoke. 'And maybe some clean cl—' But Lizzie didn't finish what she was saying. A sudden warning was shouted from the high tower above them.

'*Il Tedesco! Il Tedesco!*'

All eyes looked up to see a young man waving binoculars and leaning over the parapet of the campanile. 'Tanks on the Via Emilia!' he cried.

The Germans were swarming south faster than a horde of ravenous locusts. Fear dropped like a blanket over the castle.

'You have to leave,' said Giuseppe.

Hugh certainly got the gist of what the old gardener said. 'We certainly must,' he shot back, knowing that as an escaped prisoner the Germans might execute him without a second thought.

'But where do we go?' asked Lizzie.

Maria took her by the hand. 'My brother, Franco, has a farm, not far from here, near Vigoleno.' Lizzie remembered Maria mentioning him before. The poor man lost his wife a while back and his four sons had all been conscripted. Two had recently died in action. 'You need to head twelve kilometres north. Tell him I sent you,' she said. 'Everyone knows Franco Moreno round there. Just ask anyone for directions. He will take good care of you and your friend.'

'Thank you,' said Lizzie just as Nina, who'd disappeared a moment before, returned with food and a flask of water in a canvas bag.

'May Santo Cristoforo bless you both,' said Maria, making the sign of the cross.

'And you, too,' replied Lizzie. She stopped to look at Cristo one last time. 'Stay safe, my dearest,' she told him, taking his head in her hands. She kissed the top of his crown and felt his arms encircle her waist.

'Don't go,' he whispered. 'Please don't leave me again.'

His words jabbed at her heart, and she drew back, telling herself to be strong. 'Oh Cristo,' she told him, peeling away his arms. 'You can't come with us. You'll be much safer here.' She reached for Maria. 'And I know you'll take good care of him.'

The cook squeezed Lizzie's hand before patting Cristo's shoulder. 'Of course I will,' she replied. 'Now you must go.' She touched Lizzie lightly on the arm once more. 'Give my love to Franco,' she called after her. 'Tell him I will cook his favourite stewed wild boar as soon as this war is over.'

The sound of a truck horn broke through their goodbyes. It was followed by a rumble that grew louder by the second.

'They're near the church,' the young lookout yelled down again.

There was no time to lose.

'This way,' said Giuseppe. He was shooing them down a path that led towards the back gates.

Lizzie turned one last time. 'I'll be back!' she called out to Cristo, even though, after everything that had happened, she wasn't sure he would believe her.

Chapter 22

Giuseppe directed them through an archway at the corner of the courtyard then down some steps that Lizzie never knew existed. There was a torch at the foot of the stairs and the old man lit it with a match. Now Lizzie could see they were at the mouth of a low tunnel with a vaulted ceiling.

'It's been used to escape from the castle for hundreds of years,' explained Giuseppe with a wicked smile. 'It runs for two kilometres, and it'll bring you out near the Stirone, then follow the river north for another five kilometres to a track through the woods. That'll take you to Franco's farm.' He grasped Lizzie by the arm. 'God's speed, signorina,' he told her, before quickly clenching his jaw to stop it quivering.

Lizzie nodded as Hugh took the flaming torch from the old man's hand.

Crouching low in the darkness they made their way over pools of water. Rats squeaked in the gloom. One scuttled across their path, but Lizzie wasn't afraid. She had no choice but to carry on until eventually a pinprick of daylight appeared up ahead.

'There's our light at the end of the tunnel,' remarked Hugh with a laugh in his voice.

Lizzie had always found his optimism so comforting. It was one of the things that attracted her to him. But that was then.

Extinguishing the torch in a puddle, Hugh clambered out first, then, grasping her hand heaved her up, too. They emerged amid a clump of trees in an otherwise treeless landscape. The copse was surrounded by arable land that offered little or no cover, but thankfully the fading light played to their advantage.

Hugh took a swig of water from the flask and swatted away the flies that buzzed around them. 'Now, where's that farm?' he said.

Lizzie, also keeping by a tree, scanned the horizon to settle on a ridge of hills ahead of them on the other side of the river. 'Up there! That must be Vigoleno,' she replied. She shaded her eyes against the red glow of the setting sun that turned distant medieval walls into burnished gold. 'If we hurry, we can make it before dark.'

Once again, they were forced to navigate through the network of irrigation ditches until the farmland gave way to unmanaged ground, covered in gorse bushes and bracken. They trudged on until finally the track began to rise, taking them away from the wide, reed-fringed riverbed of the Stirone. In winter it raged with ice-melt, but now, at the end of a long hot summer, it was almost completely dry.

As the sun dropped below the horizon, they tramped up a steep path that led into dense beech woods. The trees had already begun to turn. The fallen leaves formed a soft carpet of brown and yellow underfoot. They were on an ancient shepherd's track and if it hadn't been for the knowledge that the Germans were just a few kilometres away, the evening would have been idyllic.

'You all right, darling?' asked Hugh as they stopped to rest on the brow of a hill. He wiped the sweat from the back of his neck with a handkerchief then offered her the flask of water.

'I'm fine,' she told him, slumping on a tree trunk. 'I just can't quite believe we're free.'

137

Hugh raised a sceptical eyebrow and she saw his moustache twitch. 'Let's see if we can keep it that way, shall we?' he said. 'We need to get to this bally farmhouse first.'

They'd both just clambered to their feet when they heard the rustle of leaves not far away. 'What was that?' snapped Lizzie.

'A squirrel maybe?' suggested Hugh, looking around him. 'Or a boar. They have them round here, don't they?'

'Yes. Yes, they do,' she said uneasily, starting off once more, her head moving from left to right. But she soon stopped again. 'Did you hear that?' Twigs cracked to her left.

Hugh peered through the growing gloom and shook his head. 'Not far now, anyway,' he told her cheerfully. 'I reckon we're only half a mile from Vigoleno. Maybe we should make camp for the night, then find the farmhouse tomorrow.'

Lizzie looked surprised. 'You mean sleep out here.'

Hugh smiled. 'It'll be fun. Girl guides and all that,' he told her, putting an arm around her and drawing her close. 'Nothing bad will happen as long as I'm here to protect you.' She looked up at him and suddenly his lips were on hers. But the kiss was dry and although Hugh was urgent, she was not. Inside she felt quite cold and as soon as she sensed his body relax, she took a step back. He frowned.

'What is it, my darling?' he asked, reaching out to her again. 'I love you so very much, you know.'

She let him pull her into his arms again. 'I know, Hugh,' she replied. It was hard to pretend that nothing had changed between them. But every time she looked at him, and saw how he looked at her, how his eyes still burned with love, she couldn't bring herself to tell him how she really felt.

'Let's take the weight off our feet, shall we?' he suggested, turning towards a fallen tree trunk. They walked over to it together and sat down, side by side.

'It must've been hard for you in that camp,' said Lizzie, picking up a stick and prodding the dead leaves at her feet.

Hugh took her free hand in his. 'It wasn't a bed of roses, but the worst thing was being cooped up all the time.' He chuckled to himself. 'I used to daydream a lot; picture myself sipping a pint of bitter in The Coach and Horses, after a long day in the office, then hopping on the train and home to you and the children.' He winked at her then. 'You'd be waiting for me in that cocktail dress, you know, the black lacey one that shows off your figure.' His hand moved up to the back of her neck and traced its curve, before leaning in for another kiss. Lizzie turned awkwardly and Hugh's lips brushed hers. He hugged her for a moment, hoping she would relax, but she didn't. When he finally loosened his arms, it was because he noticed she wasn't wearing her engagement ring.

'Where is it?' He sounded wounded. 'Where's the emerald?'

Lizzie swallowed and thought quickly. 'They said you were dead, Hugh,' she replied defensively. 'I put it away safely. It's still at the villa in Lucca.'

'Hmmm,' he growled. 'In that case, I'll have to improvise.'

Lizzie smiled. 'Improvise? What on earth are you doing?' she asked as she watched him pluck a stalk of grass, form it into a circle and secure it with a knot.

'Elizabeth. Darling Elizabeth.' Without warning, he was dropping on one knee. 'After all that we've both been through, this time let's make sure we're never parted. Please, my love, say you still want us to marry.'

The gesture took her completely by surprise. She stared at the makeshift ring, then recalled the original emerald at the Café de Paris. *To match your eyes.* One night in her cell at the convent, after she'd made contact with him, she'd fleetingly wondered how she would react if he asked her to marry him again. But she'd brushed the thought aside. She'd certainly never imagined it would be so soon after their reunion. It would have been a lot easier if she'd told him her true feelings in a letter from the convent. Heartless, perhaps, but at least she wouldn't have to look him in the eye and tell him she no longer loved him.

'Oh Hugh. I . . . I . . .'

He'd taken her left hand in his but seeing her reaction, was hesitating to slip the ring on her finger.

'What is it? What's wrong, Elizabeth?'

Elizabeth. She didn't like being called that name anymore. Sensible Elizabeth. Dependable Elizabeth. Lizzie made her sound more independent, more willing to take risks. No longer was she needy and compliant to the will of everyone else. She should tell him now. Get it over and done with. But no. Once again, her courage ebbed away.

'Oh Hugh,' she began again. 'We've been apart so long and I thought you were . . .' She couldn't bring herself to say the word 'dead'. 'Perhaps it would be better if we got to know each other again. Took it slowly. Didn't rush into anything.'

Hugh jerked back and rose to his feet. 'But I still love you, Elizabeth. Nothing's changed.' He paused, frowning. 'Or has it?'

Lizzie nodded and took a deep breath. 'Well, it's . . .'

Another rustle in the trees. Much closer. The chance was lost. 'What was that? Did you hear it?'

The sound of a twig snapping under foot made Hugh take notice, too. 'Quick,' he said, taking Lizzie by the hand and pulling her with him. 'Over there.' They backed up against a tree trunk as a strange whirring sound grew nearer. Lizzie nodded towards a nearby stone wall that had partly collapsed. They were about to dive for cover when Hugh exclaimed, 'Good God!'

Lizzie followed his gaze to see the whites of two eyes staring out at them from the gloom. The creature to which they belonged seemed too large for an animal but too small for a man.

'Miss Lizzie.' The voice came in a whisper at first.

Lizzie craned her neck. 'Cristo? Cristo, is that you?'

'Yes. Yes, it's me,' replied the disembodied voice, before, a second later, the boy emerged from the trees onto the track in front of them.

'Oh Cristo!' cried Lizzie, rushing towards him. 'You shouldn't be here. It's dangerous,' she scolded in Italian.

'I know, but I couldn't lose you again.' She felt his lean body heave in a sigh as she put her arms around him. 'Please don't make me go back,' he pleaded in English.

'I'm afraid you're going to have to, old chap.' Hugh stood at the boy's back and slapped him on the shoulder.

Cristo's head whirled round. 'No. Please. I can be useful to you,' he told Hugh. 'I can be your scout. I have that, see.' He pointed to a bicycle propped up against a tree.

'Is that how you got here?' asked Lizzie.

'Yes,' he replied with a nod. 'I can go places and not be stopped. I slipped out of the castle just as the Germans came up the hill. They didn't give me a second look.'

Lizzie glanced at Hugh to gauge his reaction, but before she could say any more, Cristo butted in again. 'And I know where Maria's brother lives.'

'You do?' said Lizzie.

Cristo nodded. 'Yes, we went to visit him a few weeks back.'

Lizzie was impressed and a little relieved. She turned to Hugh. 'What do you say?'

Hugh scratched the back of his head. 'Well . . .' He sucked air through his teeth. 'All right, but just until the farmhouse.'

Lizzie beamed and hugged the boy once more. 'You must do what Flight Lieutenant Codrington tells you. Is that clear? He is your commanding officer from now on.'

Cristo glibly stood to attention and saluted. 'Yes, sir.'

Hugh wasn't amused. It was clear he wasn't entirely satisfied that being joined by Cristo was such a good idea. 'One wrong move and it's back to the castle with you. Understand?' he said sternly.

'Yes, sir,' replied the boy, this time in all seriousness.

They sat on the trunk of a fallen tree to eat Maria's focaccia. Cristo added some plums and a salami he'd smuggled out of the kitchen. They spoke in English, but in whispers.

'Have you been at the castle since I left you?' Lizzie asked Cristo.

'Not all of the time. Papa's been away a lot, too.'

Lizzie understood the boy had not been told about his father's imprisonment. 'What about your lessons? Have you had any schooling?' She recalled Signora Cortina, holding Cristo back as he screamed.

The child's expression changed. 'I was sent to a seminary in Milan, but I ran away. Twice. And by the time I came back here Papa had gone.'

Lizzie shook her head. 'Oh, you poor thing. Was it so terrible?'

Cristo glanced at Hugh. 'It was worse zan terrible,' he replied in broken English. 'After that I stayed in ze castle. I cycle and read books. Lots of books.' He smiled at her then. 'I do that for you, Miss Lizzie.'

She reached for his hand, and the boy took it, shooting another look at Hugh, as if he regarded him as a rival. Lizzie sensed he did not like him. She saw mistrust written on his face. When Cristo spoke again it was in Italian.

'I tried to find out about Signor Baldini, too,' he told her.

Hugh's head jerked up, unhappy that he was being excluded from the conversation. He narrowed his eyes at the mention of the name Baldini again.

Lizzie frowned and touched Hugh lightly on the arm. 'It's all right. Let him tell me in Italian. He's been through so much.'

'Very well. But in future . . .' He huffed.

Ignoring Hugh, she turned back to Cristo. 'You said you tried to find out about the signor.' She deliberately didn't say Baldini again because just the mention of his name made her want to scream it out loud. She longed to know where he was. Hugh was with her now, of course – the man who still wanted to spend the rest of his life with her. But the mere thought of what had become of Vincenzo Baldini sent her world into freefall. Where was he?

'Maria said he might be in Le Nuove,' Cristo told her.

'Le Nuove,' she repeated.

The name sent a shiver down Lizzie's back. The jail, in Turin, was notorious for its brutal torture of anyone opposed to Mussolini. Vincenzo, she knew, would be lucky to get out alive.

Chapter 23

Now and again great flashes lit up the sky as far as the eye could see. There were explosions, too, that echoed in the valley and bounced off the hillsides. The Nazis were on the move, and it was hard to sleep. Lizzie, Hugh and Cristo were hunkered in a hollow on the leeward side of the stone wall; Lizzie and Hugh lying side by side and Cristo a little way off. But Lizzie could only snatch a couple of hours rest and it wasn't just the distant gunfire that kept her from slumber. Propping herself up on her elbow, she studied Hugh as his chest rose and fell in a gentle sleep, while her own mind was a tangled mess of thoughts and emotions. How could she tell him she no longer wanted to be his wife, knowing that he still loved her? Surely that made her not only a coward but heartless, too. Reaching over, she brushed a leaf from his hair and the movement made him open his eyes.

'Tell me I'm not dreaming,' he said, looking up at her and taking her hand. He sat up and kissed her on the lips. 'Tell me you're not an angel.' As he spoke, he stroked her cheek and looked deep into her eyes. But Lizzie was afraid he might see something she didn't want him to and turned away quickly.

'Cristo's awake,' she replied and to her relief, Hugh's hand dropped as the boy stirred and sat up. They all rose quickly to eat what scraps were left over from the previous evening then moved back onto the trail where Cristo had left his bicycle.

'Lead on,' Hugh instructed the boy, coolly. Lizzie could tell he still resented his presence.

Cristo insisted on riding his cycle, keeping a little way ahead of them on the track. They'd only been moving for ten minutes when a deafening screech blasted out of the woods. Up ahead Lizzie saw the child swerve as a wild boar careened in front of him. It disappeared as quickly as it had come, to the other side of the track, back into the woods. But Cristo had been catapulted off his bike and was lying on his side.

'Cristo!' shouted Lizzie, hurrying to him. He remained on the ground and when she drew closer, she realised he was hugging his arm.

'Are you all right?' she asked, helping him up.

'It hurts,' he moaned.

'You'll be fine. Stiff upper lip and all that,' said Hugh, rather unhelpfully.

'Perhaps you should wheel your cycle from now on,' Lizzie suggested.

Cristo nodded, then grimaced as he reached for the handlebars to right his bike.

'Are you sure . . .?' Lizzie began.

'Stop fussing, Elizabeth,' snapped Hugh. 'He'll tell you if he isn't all right.'

She bit her tongue. Hugh was back to his old tricks; taking command and ignoring her own contributions. But she didn't want to row with him. Not so soon after their escape. She needed to bide her time. They set off again, but shortly afterwards, Cristo took a turn where the path opened out. On a cleared patch of ground ahead of them lay three small houses. One to the right and two to the left. All the shutters were closed. They appeared to be uninhabited, but a few chickens remained pecking at the baked dirt and a basket of apples lay under one of the orchard trees.

'Not far now,' Cristo reassured Lizzie as she and Hugh walked tentatively through the hamlet. They both peered in through arches and gates as they passed and looked up at windows, expecting to see a shutter open, but none did. The silence was uneasy, and Lizzie sensed curious eyes upon her. Just like them, the unseen inhabitants were watching and waiting for the Germans to come.

A few minutes later, after ascending a steep track, Cristo nodded to a ramshackle collection of stone buildings clustered around a farmhouse nestling in a dark hollow. Unless the boy had been with them, Lizzie was sure they would never have found it.

'Signor Moreno's house,' he said. The roof in one corner of the three-storey house had fallen in and been strangled by ivy. It was surrounded by lop-sided barns and the skeletons of outbuildings, their roof rafters exposed to the sky. Next to one of them stood a great woodpile, half-covered under tarpaulin. Nearby a tall, brawny man wielding an axe cleaved fat logs in two. When he stopped for a moment to catch his breath, he noticed he had visitors.

'Cristo? Cristoforo is that you?' he called, dabbing the sweat from his brow with a filthy kerchief.

'Yes, signor.'

'What are you doing here, boy?' Letting the axe fall to the ground, he drew himself up to his full height and puffed out his enormous chest. He looked beyond Cristo to Hugh and Lizzie and frowned.

'Signor Moreno, we are friends of Maria,' Lizzie explained. 'We are English. Your sister said you would help.'

Leaving the axe on the ground, Franco wiped his big hands on his thighs and strode forward. 'English, eh? You are the tutor, yes?' His voice was deep, and he reminded Lizzie of a character from a Caravaggio painting – all muscle and shadow.

She nodded, knowing Cristo must have mentioned her to him. 'That's right. I'm Miss Thornton and . . .' Once again, she hesitated, not knowing how to introduce Hugh. He was no longer her fiancé, but she wasn't sure what he was to her anymore. She settled on the bare facts. 'This is Flight Lieutenant Hugh Codrington. He has just escaped from the prison camp at Fontanellato.'

Franco's eyes turned to slits against the sun's glare. 'You know the Germans are coming?'

Lizzie nodded. 'Yes. Yes, we do and that's why we're here. We hoped we'd be safer in the mountains until we worked out what to do.'

A grunt escaped from the back of the Italian's throat. He rubbed his unshaven chin in thought. 'You better come in,' he said, a smile emerging from between the stubble. He led the way towards a side door of the farmhouse without hesitation.

It took a moment for Lizzie's eyes to adjust to the dark, but when they did, she saw a large room with a long wooden table at its centre. At one end there was a cast iron cooking stove. Dirty pots and pans were piled up in a sink. Cobwebs festooned the corners, and the floor was covered in straw and chicken droppings. It was then she remembered Maria had told her Franco was widowed and now lived on his own.

'Sit,' he said in English. He gestured to the chairs around the table and from a nearby dresser pulled out four pottery mugs to fill with red wine from a bottle as if it were water.

'You heard the news?' he asked in Italian, sitting astride a stool.

'About the Armistice?' said Lizzie, looking at Hugh as she spoke. By now he was very familiar with the word *armistizio*. 'Yes. That's how we escaped. A lot of prisoners took their chances, but now the Germans have arrived and . . .'

Franco lifted his hand to silence her. As he rose his stool scraped along the stone floor and he lumbered over to a curtain near the range. Lizzie assumed it was some sort of larder, but when he drew back the curtain and opened a cupboard door, she gasped.

'A wireless set!'

'Good show!' exclaimed Hugh.

'This is how I get my news,' Franco explained to Lizzie. 'There is a new station for people like me who hate the fascists. Last night I listened to our king, Victor Emmanuel.' He bowed his large, matted head. 'He has left Rome for Brindisi in the west. But that doesn't help us here. The Germans are now in Castell'Arquato. They've set up their headquarters in the elementary school.'

Lizzie knew the town was only a few kilometres farther up the valley. She turned to Hugh to translate and when she did his face dropped.

'All the villages and farms within fifty kilometres of here are now under their control,' Franco told her.

'So we're trapped.' The blood rushed from Lizzie's head.

'Si,' replied Franco as she opened her mouth to translate. She didn't have to. Hugh had understood perfectly well.

'Basically, we're in a spot of bother,' he said, always a master of understatement.

'You could say that,' she replied.

Franco returned to his stool at the table and downed his wine in one. Slapping his palms on his knees he turned to Lizzie. 'So, signorina, what is your plan?'

'Our plan?' she repeated. She looked down at the mess on the floor; the straw and the droppings and a broken egg shell. It occurred to her that for the past twenty-four hours simply being free – and of course with Cristo – had been enough. But beyond that . . . She looked at Hugh. 'Do we have a plan?' she asked in English.

Hugh seemed uncomfortable and stroked his moustache, something he often did when he needed to think. 'There was talk of our chaps landing at La Spezia. Perhaps if we headed there . . .' He broke off when he saw Franco had begun to shake his head at the mention of the westerly port city.

'Non. La Spezia, non. Instead, they land in Sicily, many kilometres to south,' he replied in broken English.

148

The news took the wind out of Hugh's sails and his shoulders slumped.

Lizzie turned to him. 'Surely that's where we need to head. South.'

Hugh scowled. 'But that'll take weeks, months.'

She shook her head and looked at him with desperate eyes. 'What other way is there? We can't stay here forever. The Nazis are bound to find us.'

Cristo, following the conversation in English, flinched at the thought and hurried over to Lizzie to put a protective arm around her shoulder.

As the argument went backwards and forwards between Lizzie and Hugh, Franco's umber eyes darted between them. Finally, he lifted his large hand and slapped it on the table again. The thud got everyone's attention.

'There are men,' he said.

'Men?' repeated Lizzie. 'I don't understand.'

'Italians. Like you, they have escaped from prison, or they are soldiers who have deserted. I hear them,' he said, cupping his ear and pointing to the wireless, once more concealed by the curtain. 'They hate the fascists and the Germans.' He raised a clenched fist. 'They want . . .' When he couldn't think of the right English word, he punched the air.

'To fight them?' volunteered Hugh, arching a brow.

'Yes. Fight them,' agreed Franco with a nod.

'A bunch of Italians against the Third Reich's Panzers?' Hugh smirked. 'I don't think so.'

Franco, understanding just enough of what the Englishman had said to toss him a disdainful look, addressed his next remark to Lizzie in Italian. 'They plan to sabotage the German operations.'

'*Sabotare*?' repeated Hugh. It was one of the few Italian words he understood. 'Good luck with that,' he mumbled grudgingly, crossing his arms.

Lizzie frowned at him. 'These men, are they organised? Do they have any weapons?'

'There are not many,' replied Franco. 'But they are being joined all the time as Italian troops are sent back from the front to their homes. They plan to wage a guerrilla war on the Nazis and of course the fascist pigs who keep on fighting.' He turned his head to spit on the floor.

Lizzie bit her lip. 'Do you think they would help us escape?'

Franco's mouth turned down and his palms lifted in a shrug. 'Perhaps, but what would be in it for them?'

It was a question Lizzie hadn't expected. She hesitated for a moment. 'Maybe we could communicate with the British military and get supplies,' she suggested, before adding weakly, 'somehow.'

The burly Italian nodded and poured himself more wine. 'I'll drink to that,' he said, lifting his mug. '*Salute.*'

'What did he say?' asked Hugh, clearly frustrated by his lack of involvement in the conversation.

Lizzie could see he resented having to rely on a woman to translate for him. It only made matters worse.

'He was talking about men who might be able to help us get away.' She narrowed her eyes at him then. 'The resistance fighters you don't seem to have any time for,' she pointed out.

Franco heaved himself away from the table. 'You hungry, yes?' he asked.

'*Si. Si, signor,*' Cristo replied eagerly, nodding.

Franco laughed and ruffled the boy's hair. 'Come, help me cook. You can show me how my sister makes such good polenta.'

Left alone at the table, Lizzie could see Hugh was worried. 'Before we left Fontanellato our commanding officer told us we could either head north to the Swiss border or join our chaps as soon as they've landed here.'

Over wooden platters of polenta and tomato sauce, plans were discussed. Both of Hugh's options would involve hundreds of miles of trekking through unsafe terrain. Lizzie had another suggestion. 'Perhaps we should stay put until we can make contact with these friendly Italians of Franco's. They will know the landscape round here. There'll be trails we can take.'

Hugh took another slug of wine. 'Perhaps you're right. I don't see we've got much choice.'

Lizzie was glad they were agreed to remain at the farmhouse for as long as Franco would have them. But later that evening, events took a sudden turn for the worse when Cristo began complaining about his arm again.

'Is it still hurting?' asked Lizzie after the meal. Normally Cristo would be outside as soon as he'd finished eating. Vincenzo had taught him what to look for in nature; snail shells, birds' nests, caterpillars. He loved to explore, but this evening he had lost the colour from his cheeks and Lizzie couldn't coax a smile out of him. 'Let me look,' she said.

He was wearing a long-sleeved shirt, and when she touched his arm gently, he winced. Carefully she rolled up the sleeve to find his arm was badly bruised at the elbow and very swollen.

'I think it's broken,' she told Hugh later that night after she'd seen Cristo to bed in a cot upstairs.

'Broken?' repeated Hugh. 'Nonsense. It was just a bump. He'll be right as rain tomorrow.'

But Cristo was not. That night the throbbing ache kept him awake. Around midnight his whimpering turned to tears as the pain became more intense. He needed a doctor. First thing the next morning Lizzie told Franco.

'We have to go into town. Cristo's arm.' Lizzie pointed at the child, whose eyes were now red from crying.

The farmer raised his brows and said in English, 'Dangerous. The Germans . . .'

Hugh looked at her incredulously. 'You can't honestly think that's a good idea. If the place is crawling with Nazis, it would be madness.' He stroked his moustache briskly.

151

'What choice do we have? Cristo is suffering.' Lizzie turned to Franco. 'He must see a doctor, signor,' she pleaded. 'We have to get into town.'

Franco's smile disappeared as he puffed out his lips. Then he said, 'It is market day. You can come with me, if you want. Everywhere will be busy.'

'That's a good thing, yes?' asked Lizzie.

'Si.' Franco nodded. 'But if you get caught . . .' His eyes slid away.

'I know, we're on our own.'

'Wait,' protested Hugh, realising what was being arranged over his head. 'You're not going to town.' His face was very serious. 'I won't let you.'

Lizzie was afraid he might behave like this. He'd done it before when they were engaged. He seemed to think that because she'd worn his ring, he had some sort of ownership of her.

'I'm afraid this isn't your decision to make, Hugh,' she told him politely but firmly.

'But I'm responsible for you,' he blurted.

'No, you're not. As far as I'm concerned, we're no longer officially engaged. I told you, I'd rather we didn't rush into anything like last time.' She waved her ringless left hand and saw the frustration in his face.

'But you didn't mean it. You were tired, darling.'

Now, as well as trying to take charge of her actions, he thought he understood her emotions as well. Although Lizzie rolled her eyes in exasperation, she held her tongue. It was not the right time to make a scene.

The awkward silence was filled with a suggestion from Franco. He looked at Lizzie and Cristo. 'If you go into Castell'Arquato together, you must be mother and son. I shall drive my cart into town to sell my wine and eggs as usual. The German bastards won't suspect.'

'Very well,' she replied, letting out a long breath. 'Let's get started.'

Chapter 24

The ancient cart rattled along the dusty track. The early morning sun already threatened to be merciless. Lizzie sat next to Franco who held the reins, while Cristo sat on the other side clutching his arm in evident pain.

In a simple bleached-out black dress once belonging to Franco's wife, Lizzie hoped to blend in with the other women on market day. Geppetto, the mule, was proving to be a temperamental beast and now and again Franco had to poke it on the backside with a stick to shift him. Their cargo was big stone jars of red wine and a crate of eggs. Each time the cart went over a bump or a rut in the road, which was practically every few seconds, the jars knocked together and clattered. Lizzie feared the same was happening to Cristo's bone, if it was broken.

Hugh was still unhappy about the expedition and remained sulking at the farm. He hid in the hayloft of the adjoining barn just in case any neighbours got suspicious or, worse still, if the Nazis called by.

The journey into Castell'Arquato took them through the beech woods and down the valley onto a pitted wide track. They met the main road about two kilometres outside the town. The medieval Rocca with its huge tower perched high upon a rock loomed above them. Surrounded by ancient buildings and a maze of tight streets, it brooded over the newer town on the flatter ground below.

The first they saw of the Germans was at the large bridge over the River Arda on the outskirts. Franco warned of a roadblock and because it was market day, there was a queue of carts, together with the odd motor vehicle, waiting to cross the bridge. When Franco pulled the reins, Geppetto slowed to a stop behind another cart carrying firewood.

'Papers,' snarled a bull-necked German soldier.

Lizzie, wearing a headscarf to hide her pale hair, tried to quash her nerves as Franco handed over the documents. He'd given Lizzie his late wife's papers. Meanwhile, another soldier inspected his cargo, removing a stopper and sniffing the wine. A moment later, the cart was waved through.

As they clattered over the bridge, Lizzie could see an imposing school with an ornate facade that seemed to be the hub of German activity. Several military vehicles, including two tanks, were parked outside. Franco urged the mule on until they came to a stop at a farm cooperative building on the Via Guglielmo Marconi. It was where he was to unload his wine and eggs.

'If we are not back by the end of the day you must leave without us,' Lizzie told him. He did not protest, but simply nodded and wished them good luck.

Franco had given Lizzie the name of a doctor in the old town. Lizzie took Cristo by his uninjured arm and together they walked underneath a stone arch. They were not alone. Franco was right. As it was market day, there were many other women and children about so Lizzie and Cristo did not stand out. As the road rose, they walked as briskly as Cristo could manage, threading their way past smoking braziers of roasting chestnuts and stalls selling shiny apples and pears.

Already the red-and-black Nazi swastikas were flying on all the municipal buildings. The Germans had wasted no time in stamping their authority on the town. The cobbled hill up to the old hospital was steep and grew steeper after they passed under a portcullis.

'How much farther?' Cristo pleaded as they rounded a sharp bend.

'Hold on. Not far,' she replied, even though she had no idea. All she could do was head straight for the address Franco had given them, but when they reached it, Lizzie was dismayed to be greeted by a handwritten note on the door. *Gone away*. The doctor had upped and left, probably fearing the Germans. She bit her lip as she looked down at Cristo's crumpled face as he clutched his arm.

'It hurts so much, Miss Lizzie,' he moaned.

'I know. I know. We'll find another doctor, soon,' she told him, even though, in reality she was completely at a loss.

She decided to return to Franco, hoping he could suggest an alternative. Back down the steps they went and into the market square, which was even busier than before. German soldiers were posted on the perimeter, and some were patrolling, stopping shoppers and looking in their baskets.

Panic rose, and then . . .

'Cristoforo.' Lizzie froze. A woman's voice. With her head spinning, she turned to see Violetta.

When the maid realised the peasant woman with the child was in fact Lizzie, her eyes bulged out of their sockets.

'Miss—' she blurted.

'Violetta,' Lizzie cut her off. Her look was enough to silence the maid, until they were all safely round the corner and in an alley away from prying ears. 'Cristo is hurt.' Her eyes dipped to his arm. 'He needs a doctor.'

It was a huge gamble. Violetta could betray her, just as she had before, but there was something in her eyes that told her that she could trust her now.

'This way,' said the maid. She took them into a quiet lane

155

leading from the market square. 'I know a doctor. He is just two streets away. Come.'

Lizzie, clutching Cristo's uninjured arm, followed the maid up some narrow steps to a large house with heavy wrought-iron gates, but just as she was about to open them, two German soldiers emerged from the front door.

'Keep walking,' said Violetta.

They stopped at the corner of the street until the soldiers were out of sight, then retraced their steps. The girl rang the doorbell and after a moment an elderly woman in a headscarf and apron appeared.

'Yes.' She looked her callers up and down then said, 'The doctor's surgery is at five o'clock. Come back later.'

Despite the door starting to close in their faces, Violetta persisted. 'Please. The child . . .'

'No,' said the woman, emphatically, starting to shut the door again, but just before she could, an equally elderly man with a shock of white hair shuffled towards her.

'There is a problem?' he asked.

The woman huffed. 'I told them to come back later, *dottore*.'

He smiled. 'I thought you were those Germans again. They told me to be on the lookout for any English prisoners. A lot of them have escaped from their camps, apparently.' He chuckled. 'But none of you look English, so how can I help?'

Cristo's arm was broken. The doctor gave the child a sedative and set the bone in a splint. But when it came to pay, Lizzie only had half the fee on her.

'Here,' said Violetta. 'That should be enough.' The maid counted out the notes. It was clear to Lizzie it was the house-keeping money Maria had given her for food and supplies from the market.

'Thank you,' said Lizzie. 'For all that you've done today.'

Violetta's eyes filled with tears. 'I want you to know,' she began, her throat scratchy with emotion. 'You have to know I didn't want to betray you and Signor Baldini. It was the count. He made me.'

Lizzie nodded. 'I know. Remember you told me he threatened you with dismissal?'

Violetta's lips quavered. 'He did more than that, miss.' Her eyes betrayed a terrible truth.

'What? You mean . . .?' asked Lizzie, suddenly realising Violetta was trying to tell her what happened but was struggling to find the words.

The girl took a deep breath. 'Il Duce's visit . . .' She broke off as Lizzie cast her mind back to that night and the following day, when Violetta had behaved oddly.

'After Il Duce left, I went to see if there was anything else and he . . . he grabbed me and forced . . .' She turned away, too ashamed to relate what happened next.

'Oh, Violetta,' said Lizzie, laying a hand on her arm.

'After that he thought he owned me. He made me swear to spy on you and Signor Baldini.'

Lizzie nodded and silently hooked her arm through the maid's in a show of sisterly understanding. She knew Violetta's ordeal at the hands of the count would take a lot longer to heal than Cristo's broken arm. Together they walked to the edge of the old town.

'Thank you,' said Lizzie, just before Violetta turned to go. 'Not just for helping Cristo, but for telling me the truth, too.'

Franco was waiting for Lizzie and Cristo when they returned to the farmer's cooperative later that afternoon.

'You had success?' he asked, looking at Cristo's bandaged arm in a sling. He was sitting on the tailboard, chewing on a ciabatta.

Lizzie nodded. 'Cristo was very brave,' she told him, helping the child up onto the cart. Violetta, meantime, set off back to Castello di Castiglione on foot. If it hadn't been for her, Lizzie knew things could have worked out very differently.

Chapter 25

As they began their journey back into the foothills, Lizzie noticed more German trucks were coming the other way, from the north, down the Via Emilia. In front of them was a large mountain range which Lizzie hadn't noted properly before. It contrasted sharply with the flat, fertile plains they'd crossed to get here. Beyond the hills covered in golden trees and occasional black firs lay purple peaks and dark, treeless crags. It struck Lizzie then that those forbidding mountains might be the only route to safety for her and Hugh.

Franco had sold all his wine and eggs and seemed in a good mood. As they began to ascend the track to leave the relentless sunshine for the cooler woods once more, he even broke out into song.

'*O sole mio*,' he began in a beautiful baritone. He'd just reached the second verse when from among the trees two men jumped out of the shade. Their rifles were aimed at them.

'*Fermati proprio lì!* Stop!' cried one. Two more armed men, with ammunition belts slung over their shoulders, appeared from the undergrowth. They were younger and looked alike.

Franco tugged at the reins. 'Whoa!' he told the mule, which for once did as he was told. The men were unshaven, and their clothes dusty. One wore a curious Alpine-style hat and one a green bandana. Lizzie tensed and glanced round to see Cristo looked equally scared. Robbers, she assumed. Franco, on the other hand, seemed relaxed. He transferred the reins to his left hand and held out his right.

'Carlo, my friend. It is good to see you again,' he cried to the man in the bandana.

In unison the rifle muzzles tilted down and Franco turned to Lizzie. 'A teacher at the elementary school in town.'

Carlo's face split into a smile to reveal a missing front tooth. 'Franco, you old crook,' he replied, shaking his hand firmly.

'So, you are back!'

'We were in Modena, but they let us go as soon as news of the Armistice came through.'

Franco let out a throaty laugh. 'You were the lucky ones. So now you fight the Germans, yes?'

'We fight all fascists,' came the reply from the man in the Alpine hat as he stepped closer.

Carlo chuckled. 'This is my good friend Ernesto from Piedmont. He's a great shot, but a lousy cook.' He patted his friend on the back then looked at Lizzie and Cristo.

'Perhaps you would introduce us?' Carlo said, with a disarming smile.

'The lady is English,' replied Franco, inclining his head to imply that Lizzie should be treated with respect. 'She speaks very good Italian,' he added, possibly as a warning she thought, just in case the men were tempted to say anything vulgar. 'And the boy is the son of Count de Falco.' Franco turned to pinch Cristo's cheek.

Carlo's expression changed instantly. His smile disappeared, like a fingerprint on a misted window pane. 'De Falco, eh?' he mumbled disdainfully. 'What are you doing with him?'

Lizzie had to step in. Not content to be talked about in the third person, she decided to show she was not to be trifled with. 'Like you, I am a teacher, sir, and I tutor Cristoforo,' she explained in flawless Italian. 'My name is Miss Thornton.'

Carlo's eyes opened wide before he dipped an exaggerated bow. 'Then we are honoured,' he teased in broken English. Lizzie had to hide a smile when he made a great effort to pronounce the aitch in *honoured*.

His companion in the curious hat wasn't so gracious. He'd sidled to the back of the cart. 'You have food?' he asked, poking the muzzle of his gun into the sacks on the trailer.

'Some polenta and salami. Take a sausage,' Franco told him, still smiling. He gestured to the two younger men, brothers Lizzie assumed, who'd stayed in the shade to join them. 'Pietro. Paulo. *Avanti!*'

So, these were the men Franco had spoken about before – the fighters who might be able to help her and Hugh escape. Was he really suggesting they entrust their lives to them if they were to stand any chance of leaving Italy? Right now, for all intents and purposes, these men seemed little better than bandits. The thought of placing her future in their hands filled her with alarm.

'Better still, why don't you come back with us?' suggested Franco. 'There is an English pilot with them. He escaped from Fontanellato.'

Carlo nodded. 'We heard about the prisoners round here. Hundreds of them. The Nazis are rounding them up.' He glanced at Lizzie for a moment and smiled. 'Yes. We'll come back to yours,' he agreed, nodding to the other three men.

All four of them hitched a ride aboard the cart with Cristo and started raiding the provisions in the sacks. They clearly hadn't eaten in a very long time.

'So no banquets in jail?' teased Franco.

Lizzie watched as the men ate ravenously. She assumed they'd been political prisoners; victims of the OVRA like the man in the street she'd seen beaten. Like Vincenzo.

The sun hovered like a red ball over the hills as Geppetto delivered his load safely up the steep valley track to the farmhouse.

They arrived back a little under an hour later. The clatter of the cart alerted Hugh. Lizzie glanced up at the hayloft to see his anxious face looking down on them. She knew he would be worried when she returned in the company of strangers.

'It's all right. They're on our side,' she called up. On the way back she'd discovered not only that Carlo was a teacher but that the brothers were both students. One was studying law, the other architecture. These were the sort of people Vincenzo had spoken about in his network. Their only crime was being good and decent and speaking out against fascism.

As the men and Cristo jumped down from the cart, Hugh emerged from the shadows.

'*Inglese!*' shouted one of the young men with a beard, pointing to the bewildered pilot.

Hugh moved forward slowly, frowning. 'What the hell's going on?' he asked Lizzie.

'They're our friends, Hugh,' she replied, going up to him. Without thinking she hooked a reassuring arm through his. 'They've been discharged from the Italian Army and from prison. They're the ones who might help us.'

Hugh remained unconvinced. Narrowing his eyes he said, 'I wouldn't trust that bunch of reprobates as far as I could throw them.' As he spoke, he scowled at the men, but they appeared oblivious to him and were in high spirits as they headed into the farmhouse with Franco.

Lizzie understood Hugh's concerns, but she also knew they really had very little choice. Trekking more than a hundred miles over mountains to the coast without a guide or any support network – let alone with the Nazis on your tail – was a tall order.

'We need their help,' she persisted. 'They're from this region. Franco says they know the mountains like the backs of their hands. We'd be stupid not to accept it, if it's offered.'

Hugh sighed heavily and thrust his hands into his pockets. 'I suppose you're right,' he conceded grudgingly.

'Come and meet them,' she urged, again finding herself tugging gently at his arm. 'And please, do try and be nice.'

It appeared the men had quickly made themselves at home. A flagon of beer was already being passed round among them and they'd raided the larder to find stale hunks of bread and smoked sausage. One of the brothers remained outside, perched on the top step of the granary to keep guard, his gun over his knee. The other three were sitting at the long table. Ernesto with the Alpine hat was lending Franco a hand finding cups in the dresser.

'You want wine?' he asked Lizzie, catching her eye by lifting a bottle.

'Thank you,' she replied.

Hugh raised a brow. 'But the sun's not over the yard arm yet, old girl,' he protested.

Her lips twitched. 'When in Rome,' she replied, taking a full cup from the fighter.

'And you?' asked Ernesto in Italian.

'*Si*,' said Hugh with a nod, following it up with a grudging, '*grazie*.'

'That wasn't so difficult, was it?' teased Lizzie, as Hugh made an effort to speak Italian for the first time. Raising her full cup, she chinked Hugh's. '*Chin chin*,' she said.

Carlo laughed when he saw her make the toast and decided to join in. The next moment they were all standing up, clinking each other's cups and smiling before they sat to eat. Over plates of cheese and slices of salami Lizzie managed to follow the talk as best she could. Ernesto's accent was harder to understand, and they spoke quickly. Now and again, Carlo made an effort to involve her and Hugh in the conversation. 'Before we can help you, we wait for Il Gufo,' he said.

'Il Gufo?' repeated Lizzie. The word meant *owl* and confused her.

'Our commanding officer,' explained Ernesto. 'We were all in jail together for a time.' He smiled broadly to show her that, like

162

Carlo, he also had missing teeth. 'Fingernails, too,' he said, proudly flashing a hand. 'They tore them out as well, but we didn't crack.'

Lizzie flinched at the thought. These men had endured unspeakable torture at the hands of fascist OVRA. And now they wanted their revenge.

'Why do you call your leader the Owl?' she asked.

Ernesto formed his fingers into two circles and put them up to his eyes.

Carlo intervened. 'Our commanders all have battle names to protect themselves and their families.' He slapped his chest. 'We fighters only use our first names, too.' He pointed to the brothers. 'That's Paulo with the scar and Pietro has the beard.'

'What would your battle name be, miss?' asked Cristo in English, sitting at her side. 'If you were a commander.'

The unexpected question caused her to raise both brows in surprise. 'I don't know.' She shrugged. 'I really haven't thought . . .' she began then paused and said with a smile, 'Wait. I would be Rosa.'

'Rosa?' repeated Hugh. 'Why not just Rose – the good old-fashioned English version?'

'Because,' said Lizzie, rather too playfully for Hugh's liking, 'I may look like an English rose, but I love Italy. I like to think of myself as a daughter of Tuscany.'

He flashed his disapproval, but she ignored him. 'So, this Owl,' she carried on, 'are you expecting him to join you soon?'

Ernesto nodded. 'We had word yesterday. He is on his way, but the plains are crawling with Germans.' He turned to look at Hugh. 'Many English prisoners have been recaptured.'

'What did he say?' Hugh asked Lizzie.

She bit her lip. 'I'm afraid he said that some of the men who escaped have already been recaptured by the Germans.'

Hugh made a fist with his hand and hit the table hard, sending the crockery clattering. 'Damn the Jerry bastards,' he muttered through clenched teeth. Lizzie put a comforting arm on his.

163

There was an awkward silence before Franco glanced up at the wall clock. It was half past eight.

'It is time,' he said, knocking back the rest of his wine before rising and lumbering over to the alcove. Drawing back the curtain, he opened the cupboard door and pulled out the shelf where the wireless set sat.

The men drew up their chairs and stools and gathered round. Excitedly they watched as Franco switched knobs and dials and a high-pitched hum turned into noises that sounded like bubbles underwater. A moment later they became clearer. A burst of military music played before a dramatic voice made an announcement.

This is the voice of EIAR. It is with great pride that we report His Excellency Benito Mussolini has been freed from imprisonment in the Abruzzo mountains and is being flown to safety. The mission to rescue Il Duce was carried out by . . .

'What?!' Ernesto began shaking his head. 'This can't be true,' he mumbled, taking off his hat and scratching his head.

'It's a lie!' declared Paulo. Pietro bared his teeth and growled. Carlo took a slug of wine. 'God damn him!'

'For God's sake, Lizzie, will you tell me what's happened?' snapped Hugh, a look of panic spreading across his face. 'What did they say? Something about Mussolini.'

Lizzie took a deep breath. She could barely believe the news herself. 'Oh, Hugh. The Germans have rescued him,' she told him earnestly.

'What!' he blurted. 'How the devil?'

'Gliders. It seems they used gliders to storm the hotel where he was being held, then they flew him out in a plane.'

Hugh looked at her open-mouthed. 'I don't believe it. They can't have. It's impossible.' He was shaking his head as he spoke. 'This changes everything.'

Cristo moved closer to Lizzie as the other men bickered among themselves about how such a mission could have succeeded. 'Does that mean my father will come home soon, Miss Lizzie?' he asked.

She looked down at him and put an arm around his bony shoulder. 'Perhaps, Cristo. It's hard to tell. But I'm sure he'll be all right.' It was so difficult for the child. He still seemed to care for his father, even though he must've known most people feared and hated him.

The boy nodded, but still seemed troubled. Lizzie wasn't sure if he would be happier knowing his father was in jail or free to return to the estate to find him missing. He pulled back again to stack some of the dirty plates.

'Now what do we do?' asked Hugh, watching Cristo walk to the sink. It was more of a rhetorical question, aimed at anyone who understood him, which, of course, meant primarily Lizzie.

'I suppose we wait,' she suggested. She was half listening to the men's conversation. They were angry and confused about the situation.

'What are they saying?' Hugh nodded at Franco and the others.

'Carlo is telling them there is nothing they can do until the Owl arrives.'

'Which is when, remind me?'

'They hope tomorrow.'

'Tomorrow,' grunted Hugh, looking deep into his mug of wine. 'And until then we're sitting ducks, sat here when Jerry's rounding up chaps left, right and centre.'

Hearing him talk like that made something inside Lizzie stir then. An old feeling. A comfortable feeling. And she felt the urge to console him. She found herself putting her arm around him. 'All we can do is trust in these men,' she told him. 'Our fate is in their hands.'

Hugh lifted his hand and brushed her cheek. For a moment she thought he might try and kiss her again. Instead, his hand went to his moustache, and he stroked it slowly as he studied the gathering in front of him. The men, appearing sobered by what they'd learned, were sharing the two cigarettes Franco had handed out. They seemed at a loss, shaking their heads in despair as they digested the news of Mussolini's escape. After a moment Hugh turned to Lizzie and put his hand on hers. 'That's precisely what worries me,' he replied.

Chapter 26

Hugh bedded down with the other men in the hayloft that night, while Lizzie and Cristo remained in a bedroom inside the farm-house. The Italians had drawn lots to decide who should keep watch. Ernesto and Pietro got the short straws and took it in turns to stand guard, stationed by a shrine on the track above. Lizzie slept – or tried to – in the rickety double bed, while Cristo lay on his back with his broken arm resting on his stomach on the wooden cot in the corner.

The horsehair mattress was lumpy and the men's snores from the adjoining hayloft were so loud they kept Lizzie awake – those and the constant buzzing of mosquitoes that dive-bombed her with the precision of RAF planes. But much more pressing than these niggling distractions was the fear. Beyond the irritating snores and flying insects, she listened for engines, for footsteps, for birds disturbed in the woods – the tell-tale signs that would alert her to German intruders. She thought about Hugh, too. In the convent she'd hoped against hope that when they were finally reunited, Hugh's feelings towards her might have cooled. Not a bit of it. His desire still burned as brightly as it had at the Café de Paris. But he'd looked death in the eye and cheated it. And he'd been incarcerated for much longer than her. No one could emerge the same after what he'd endured. Her time in Italy and witnessing first-hand the brutality of the fascists had changed her, too. Their different experiences must surely have altered them both in ways which weren't yet obvious. Neither of them could be the same as they were in the summer of '39 before the war blew everything apart. All that she knew for certain, right now, was keeping one step ahead of the Germans had to be their priority.

As dawn broke, she dressed quickly before Cristo woke. Pulling on the slacks and short-sleeved shirt she'd washed and dried the previous day, she scurried unseen downstairs. After lighting the fire in the range, she walked outside and stretched out her arms to feel the cool morning air on her skin. The red sun could be glimpsed in the V of the valley floor to the east and in front of it lay a carpet of fields the colour of polished copper. Her gaze lingered on the sight, relishing her freedom once more. Then as if to remind her she shouldn't be idling, a cockerel crowed, telling her she needed eggs for breakfast. When she returned to the kitchen, her hen-house mission accomplished, she was surprised to find Hugh poking the fire.

'Good morning, my darling,' he said. He put down the poker and, without warning, put his arms around her and kissed her on the lips.

She braced herself against his chest before pulling gently away. 'Good morning to you, too,' she said.

'I wanted to apologise for yesterday,' he told her.

'Apologise?' She sounded surprised. 'What for?'

'I was rather beastly to you. It's just that we're caught in a sort of limbo. I'm the one used to giving orders and now I need to take them from those . . . those . . ?' He waved a hand towards the hayloft where the men still slept.

Hugh's tone reminded her that he really could be terribly pompous. It was the way so many English officers behaved towards anyone who wasn't – well – English, believing themselves to be far superior to any other nationality. It was just their way.

Unthinkingly Lizzie lifted both her hands to straighten his shirt collar. It's what she used to do when they were engaged. When she realised what she was doing she stopped immediately. She mustn't slip into her old ways. 'I know the men may seem a little lively, but let's just wait until this Owl arrives, shall we?' She shrugged. 'You never know, you might be quite impressed with him if he comes up with some *wise* plan.'

The sound of the water pump being yanked into life outside reminded Lizzie they were not alone. A glance through the door revealed two of the men had stripped off to their waists. Paulo and Carlo were taking it in turns to shave with a cut-throat razor in front of a broken mirror propped up on the branch of a tree.

Franco shambled downstairs then, looking distinctly the worse for wear.

'You sleep well?' he asked Lizzie. His eyes, she noted, were pink, and his greying hair stuck out at all angles.

'Yes, thank you, signor,' she said, trying not to wince at the smell of alcohol lingering on his breath. She lifted up the basket of eggs. 'I thought I would make us all some breakfast.'

'Yes. Yes,' he replied, clapping his big hands together. 'And the boy?'

Just then footsteps could be heard hurrying along the corridor upstairs and Cristo appeared, trying, but failing to button his shirt with his one good hand.

'Good morning, Cristo,' said Lizzie with a smile, rushing to him. 'How is your arm?'

'A little better,' he replied with a shrug.

'Good, then you can fetch bread from the larder, while I fix breakfast for everyone.'

Thirty minutes later Lizzie was dishing out omelettes to the men as they sat at the long table.

'*Buono!*' said Carlo with a smile when he saw Lizzie looking at him. He'd dispatched his green bandana to reveal tufted silver hair.

The men spent the morning cleaning their rifles as they waited for news of Il Gufo. Cristo watched them with interest. It saddened Lizzie that he was so keen to learn everything he could about a weapon. She hoped he wouldn't ever have to use one in war.

Later that afternoon, when she was at the stove stirring a sauce, a cry went up outside. Paulo, who'd only recently replaced his brother as lookout, was running towards the house.

'Il Gufo!' he called. 'Il Gufo sta arrivando.'

Hugh, who'd been resting in the corner, turned to Lizzie, as the other men scrambled up outside. 'I take it the Owl has landed,' he commented drily, looking out of the window.

Lizzie nodded and wiped her hands on her apron. 'I suppose we ought to greet him, too.'

They joined the others outside. A few metres from the farmhouse, where the road rose at the edge of the woodland, a man on a mule was cresting the hill. Another man rode behind him wearing a flat cap. Paulo trotted excitedly at his side, patting the animal's flanks.

As they drew nearer, Lizzie saw one of the men had a beaked nose and high cheekbones. She stared at him quizzically, then realised, he'd been her contact for the newspaper in Lucca after Vincenzo was taken.

'Il Gufo!' called Carlo, raising an arm. The others joined him, punching the air and cheering.

The other rider, wearing a dusty, wide-brimmed hat, acknowledged his compatriots with a wave, then pulled at the reins and dismounted. He was immediately surrounded by the small welcoming party in the shade of the farmhouse. For the next minute or more there was mayhem. The air was thick with greetings and slaps. Embraces were thrown like confetti. Hugh held back, a wallflower at a dance. Lizzie understood he took a dim view of the men's rowdiness, so she held back too, just watching the reunion with a bemused detachment. Cristo, taking his cue from Lizzie, also remained by the farmhouse door while Paulo tugged at the mule's reins to lead it to the water trough. The man with the large nose Lizzie recognised was also welcomed with handshakes and embraces as he dismounted.

'Miss Thornton,' he said, immediately walking over to Lizzie. 'We meet properly at last, Miss Elizabeth Thornton.' He held out his hand and she took it. He was the link in the resistance chain; the contact she'd met in the café in Lucca who had connected her to the *Freedom & Justice* network.

'I am Stefano. Part-time lawyer, but full-time freedom fighter,' he told her.

'It is good to see you,' she replied. 'Is there . . .' She was just about to ask if he's heard any news about Vincenzo when he was called away by the other men.

It wasn't until the welcoming party turned to face the farmhouse and surged towards them with Il Gufo in their midst that Lizzie thought there was something familiar about the visitor as well. The confident gait and the long arms reminded her of someone. Sweat had darkened his shirt in places, and from the haze of stubble on his face it was plain he hadn't shaved for several days. But it wasn't until he took off his hat and put on a pair of round-framed spectacles that she realised just who Il Gufo really was.

'Vincenzo.' The name escaped from her mouth on a short, sharp breath. Standing before her was a vision. A ghost. A memory made of flesh. But as much as she wanted to feel his breath on her skin, his hands on her body; as much as she wanted to embrace him and never let him go, so she had proof he was real and not a hallucination, she held herself in check. Flexing her toes to stop herself rushing forward, she remained rooted to the spot. It wasn't the right time.

'What?' snapped Hugh, shooting her a puzzled look.

Lizzie didn't answer. The colour was leaching from her face, and her eyes were burning into the man who drew closer with each step. Cristo, too, recognised his old teacher. He broke ranks first. 'Signor Baldini!' he cried, running towards him.

Vincenzo's head lifted and when he saw the boy a look of delight burst across his face. 'Cristo! Cristo! What are you doing here?' he exclaimed, bending his knees. He was about to sweep up the boy to whirl him round until he saw his arm in a sling.

'I fell off my bike, sir,' Cristo said. 'But now you're back it doesn't hurt so much.'

They all laughed at the remark. But it was only when Vincenzo left Cristo to glance around that he caught sight of another person close to him. His smile disappeared to be replaced by an expression so intense the other men feared he might be in pain. Seeing the look was aimed at Lizzie, they fell silent, and their eyes switched to her.

'Signor Baldini,' she said formally.

'Miss Thornton,' he replied, sounding confused and quickening his pace as he approached.

Hugh's gaze bounced from one to the other like a tennis ball and his stiff voice stopped Vincenzo in his tracks. 'You two have met before, I take it.'

Vincenzo frowned.

'Yes. Yes, we have, Hugh,' replied Lizzie, her eyes still clamped on Vincenzo's. 'The signor was Cristo's tutor in Lucca.'

'Was he now?' said Hugh, scratching the back of his head and sounding distinctly unimpressed. 'What a coincidence.'

'Yes. Yes, it is,' said Lizzie, forcing a smile, when all she wanted to do was weep with joy and relief. 'It's so good to see you again, signor,' she told Vincenzo, finally moving forward. 'I thought . . . I feared . . .' She dipped away to hide her glassy eyes.

'And you. It's been a while. I've lost count of the time,' he replied. He seized both her hands in his and kissed them one after the other, sending electric shocks through her body. 'I just know it's been too long.'

Briefly she closed her eyes, but she had to maintain control in front of Hugh and Cristo. 'Yes. Yes, it has,' she replied, still not quite believing what was happening.

Vincenzo's gaze played on Lizzie's face for a moment longer, understanding that something wasn't right before he switched to Hugh. 'And this is . . .?' he asked, looking directly at him.

'Forgive me,' blurted Lizzie, trying to come to her senses. 'This is Flight Lieutenant Hugh Codrington.'

Vincenzo threw Lizzie a questioning look. 'Ah,' he said. 'But I thought you . . .'

Lizzie jumped in. 'Yes. Hugh had a miraculous escape.'

'That's right. Got shot down, but bounced back like a rubber ball,' said Hugh. He stuck out his chin as he offered his hand.

Vincenzo took it in his left, while his right hand remained at his side. Looking at him more closely, Lizzie noticed three of his fingernails were missing, leaving scabby stumps in their wake. He'd been tortured and the thought made her want to rush to his side. Forcing her body to go rigid, she fought off the urge. All she could do, for now, was remain restrained.

'I am pleased to meet you,' Vincenzo greeted Hugh in English, before switching to Lizzie and adding in Italian, 'So your pilot is alive.'

Lizzie managed to laugh lightly. 'Yes, as you see, he survived. He was taken prisoner,' she replied in Italian. 'It's a long story and . . .'

Franco patted Vincenzo on the back. 'And perhaps one to be told inside over a drink,' he urged. His eyes scanned the woods. 'The Germans . . .'

Once in the farmhouse, Franco reached for a bottle of grappa on top of the dresser, kept for special guests. He poured the clear liquid into squat glasses and the men drank a toast to their leader.

'Il Gufo,' said Franco and the Italians slugged back the liquor in unison.

'So what news do you bring us, my friend?' asked Carlo, sitting astride the kitchen bench. 'We know the Germans have freed Mussolini.'

Vincenzo, accompanied by Stefano, coughed as the last of

the grappa seemed to scorch his throat. He set down his empty glass and addressed them in Italian. 'The Gran Sasso raid. Very daring,' he said. 'And now they have restored Il Duce as head of the Italian Social Republic at Salò on Lake Garda.'

Carlo and Ernesto groaned in unison. Pietro slapped his forehead. His brother cursed. Franco's head dropped into his hands.

'*Santa Maria*,' he mumbled.

Lizzie translated for Hugh as his features tightened with every word. They'd gone back to the beginning. It was as if nothing had changed. The pain and grief and deprivation endured by the people of Italy weren't over, as they'd hoped just a few days before. The hatred and the fighting might soon be replayed all over again. Mussolini's release could mean civil war.

Hugh reached out and put a comforting arm around Lizzie. She flinched at his touch, until she realised he wasn't comforting her at all. Following his gaze, she saw he was looking at Vincenzo. He'd already marked him out as a rival. With his gesture he was telling the man they called Il Gufo that she belonged to him.

Cristo, perhaps not fully grasping the possible fallout from the news about Mussolini, waited for a moment, eyeing up the adults' reactions. When no one asked the obvious question, he decided to step up. 'So what must we do, sir?' he said to Vincenzo.

The boy's words seemed to jolt everyone back into reality.

'A good question, Cristo,' Vincenzo replied. 'And the answer is we carry on the fight. Only we must fight with our heads, as well as our hearts.' He touched his temple. 'The Germans have many more weapons and men than us, but they do not possess knowledge of this area, or its people. That is where we have the upper hand.'

Hugh's frown deepened as Lizzie translated for him. 'Are you talking about a guerrilla war?'

Vincenzo looked at him squarely and replied in English, 'That is exactly what I am talking about, flight lieutenant.'

Lizzie saw Hugh's lips twitch in a sneer as he waved a

haughty hand. 'Good luck with that, old chap. I think we'll leave you to it.'

Vincenzo's lips also twitched, but in a smile. 'It's you who'll need the luck if these men choose not to escort you and Miss Thornton to safety,' he countered.

Lizzie caught a flash of disbelief in Hugh's eyes. He wasn't used to being challenged. She patted his hand to calm him. 'We will be very grateful to you and your men if you can help get us to the coast,' she told Vincenzo quickly. 'Hugh needs to rejoin his squadron.'

'The coast?' The Italian raised a quizzical brow.

'There was talk in camp of landings at La Spezia,' Hugh chimed in. 'If your men can get us there . . .'

Lizzie rolled her eyes. Hugh was like a dog with a bone. Franco had already discredited the information. Now Vincenzo did, too. He shook his head.

'I have heard no such intelligence.'

Even though he was sitting, Hugh drew himself up at the table, as if to pull rank. 'Well, I have, and I'd be most obliged if your men could get us there.'

Vincenzo tilted his head and glanced at Lizzie, shifting awkwardly in her seat. Hugh could sound so arrogant at times.

'As you wish,' he said graciously. 'The brothers will escort you to Bardi, about eight hours on foot. There they can hand you over to some of our associates.'

'Associates?' Hugh baulked at the term.

'We are not properly organised yet, flight lieutenant,' explained Vincenzo. 'It's less than a week since the gates of the inferno were opened, but we know who we can count on in the locality.'

As if on cue, a shout was heard from outside. It was Paulo. Carlo and Ernesto scrambled to the window, expecting the worst. But instead of a German truck or Nazi jackboots marching up the drive, a young girl with long dark braids, white ankle socks and a ragged skirt stood outside.

'Lena!' shouted Franco.

The girl – Lizzie guessed she was much younger than Cristo – smiled at the sound of his voice. 'Uncle!' she replied, running up to the farmhouse door.

'What is it, child?' Franco asked her at the doorstep. 'Is your mama all right?'

The girl nodded. 'I have a message for you,' she said breathlessly. 'I am to tell you that the Germans have issued a decree.'

'A decree?' repeated Carlo, joining Franco at the threshold. 'What kind of decree?' By now everyone was gathering around the door, and some spilled out onto the path at the front.

The girl looked straight ahead and recited parrot-fashion. 'Anyone who gives food or shelter or clothes to British or American prisoners will face the severest punishments,' she said, taking a deep breath at the end of the long sentence.

For a moment no one spoke, as everyone digested what they'd just been told. Vincenzo broke the silence. 'Thank you, Lena,' he told the child. 'You have done a good thing. We are all grateful to you.'

The girl smiled, then rushed to her uncle, who hugged her and handed her an apple from a nearby basket. 'Now, go back to your mama,' he told her. 'Uncle Franco can take care of himself.'

The men and Lizzie all watched the child skip back down the track, munching her apple as if she hadn't a care in the world. They, on the other hand, had plenty.

Vincenzo chewed his lip. 'We're putting you in danger, Franco. We shall leave at first light.'

'But you are welcome here as long as you need,' insisted the farmer.

'I know and we are most grateful, but we have much work to do in the valley,' he replied, glancing in the direction of Castell'Arquato. 'We shall be joined by more men tomorrow, so we won't trouble you anymore.'

'Whatever is best for you,' Franco replied.

176

Vincenzo was going. Only a few hours after he'd blown back into Lizzie's life like a storm, he was intending to leave again. She couldn't bear it. She needed to open her heart to him. To explain everything. To be with him. Alone.

Chapter 27

The thick tomato sauce reminded Lizzie of blood as she stirred it in the pot over the fire that evening. She looked over at Vincenzo. He was drinking with his men. The red wine seemed to relax them all. It also loosened their tongues and the more they drank the darker their recollections became. Questions crowded in on Lizzie as she listened to their conversation. She needed to fill the gaps during the time she and Vincenzo were apart. His suffering had changed him, not just physically, but mentally, too. She sensed it. She'd heard rumours the prisoners were made to drink castor oil. Many died slowly from dehydration. Had Professor Lodato survived such cruelty? In her cell at the convent at night, the thought of Vincenzo's suffering had kept her awake so often. She'd pictured him writhing in agony, calling out. *Did he ever call out for her?* she wondered.

They all ate heartily and afterwards Ernesto led them in some old military songs often sung before battle. Pietro accompanied on a tin whistle. Now and again, Vincenzo would join in with a chorus, but there were times when she felt his gaze burning into her. She longed to sit next to him, to ask him about those missing months; to hear what happened, no matter how hard she knew it would be. She longed to touch him, too; to feel his heartbeat, his arms around her. Hugh was also watching her, she knew it, guarding her jealously from beneath his heavy brows. But there would be a chance. There had to be. Come hell or high water, she had to be alone with Vincenzo.

Later that evening, as the men continued to drink, Lizzie saw an opportunity and seized it. Vincenzo accepted one of Franco's precious cigarettes. Carlo lit it for him, and he went outside to smoke it.

Franco stirred. 'I better go, too, or the fox will get my chickens.'

Lizzie jumped in. 'I can put them in the coop for you,' she volunteered, rising to her feet. By this time, Hugh had drunk far too much red wine and seemed happy to let her go. In the darkness, she followed the trail of smoke from the cigarette for a few metres until she saw Vincenzo sit down on a flat rock. Below, the valley was silvered by a full moon. The night was clear, but the distant roar of tanks and flashes of gunfire were reminders the war was close by.

Lizzie stopped short to study Vincenzo in the darkness. He was bathed in a shaft of moonlight that threw his profile into silhouette. It wasn't the one she knew. His face had been turned into a map of pain, a permanent reminder of what he'd suffered at the hands of the OVRA. A million words floated in front of her like stars in the night sky. If only she could find the right ones.

When he heard footsteps, Vincenzo spun round then turned back again, exhaling smoke as he went. She wondered if he realised it was her, standing there in the darkness, wanting him so badly.

'Vincenzo.'

Yet instead of acknowledging her, he remained staring out at the valley, a plume of smoke feathering the night air.

Lizzie's heart froze in her chest. She took a few more steps towards him. 'I can explain. I didn't say anything. I couldn't because . . .'

Vincenzo's shoulders jolted in a laugh. 'Because you are glad your fiancé is back in your life?'

Shocked by the callous remark, Lizzie recoiled. She couldn't deny Hugh had supported her. Without his help her escape would certainly have been harder. The trouble was he still loved her. He'd made that very plain. Falling back into Hugh's open arms would have been the easy option. But she'd resisted it because in her heart of hearts she knew she could never love anyone like she loved Vincenzo. But he wouldn't even look her in the eye right now. He was hurting, she could see that, and people said cruel things when they'd been wounded.

'Hugh did propose to me again, as soon as we escaped,' she admitted. 'But it's over between us. I hoped, I prayed you were still alive.'

She saw his shoulders heave in a shrug. 'And here I am. So now you have a choice to make, but it's not that simple, is it?' He switched back to look her in the eye for the first time. 'Be with me, and, if we're arrested, we die together, or stay with your pilot and try to escape. You may die that way, too, but at least you'd die free.'

Her breath juddered as it left her mouth. 'Why are you being like this?'

He stood then and threw away his half-smoked cigarette, grinding it in the dirt with his boot. Turning to face her he said, 'Because I love you. Because every time they beat me in jail, every time they pulled a fingernail out, I thought of you and Cristo, and you both kept me going.'

'I love you, too, Vincenzo.' She rushed towards him then, but when she wrapped her arms around him, he kept his own by his sides and looked beyond her when he spoke.

'But as much as I love you, I can't offer you a future because I'm not sure I have one.'

Frowning, she took a step back to look into his eyes. 'What? Vincenzo, what are you saying?'

He answered with a cold stare. 'I may be a good teacher, but I could never be a good enough husband.'

180

Lizzie wanted to cry. 'Don't say things like that.' She leaned in again and nuzzled her head against his chest. 'Please, Vincenzo. Don't be like this.' Her sudden tears were wetting his shirt.

'I cannot offer you security. A big house. Nice clothes. I cannot offer you the life you deserve.'

'But that's not what I want, my love. I want you,' she protested, running her hands over his shirt, feeling his chest muscles under her fingertips.

He grabbed her wrists to stay her hands. 'You are English, Lizzie. And you always will be. You belong with your own kind.'

Horrified, she looked up at him as he let her hands drop. His quiet, cold words echoed in mid-air then hit her heart like a hail of bullets. She retreated, unable to believe what he'd just said, what he'd just done.

'You'd better go,' he told her on a long breath. 'Your pilot is waiting.'

She shook her head incredulously. She would try one last time. 'It's you I love. I need you, Vincenzo,' she pleaded. She tried to reach out to him, but yet again he pushed her away. Once more she came back. 'I'm not the same person Hugh proposed to in England. Italy has changed me. The war has changed me. You have changed me.'

Another half-mocking laugh. 'I have changed you?'

'Yes. You taught me to be myself. Not what other people want me to be.' She moved closer again. 'I love you, Vincenzo. I've never loved anyone more.'

He shook his head and turned away from her again. 'No, you don't love me, Lizzie. You love yourself.'

She was so shocked that when she opened her mouth to tell him that was a lie, the words wouldn't come.

Vincenzo filled the stunned silence.

'You and me,' he said softly, and her heart leapt. He didn't really mean what he'd just said. He was going to tell her he loved her, too.

'Yes.'

He shook his head. 'It was a mistake.'

The spell was finally broken.

A mistake?

The air left her lungs, and dazed, she felt her legs weaken beneath her.

'You have found your pilot again and we must go our separate ways.'

His heartless, brutal words knocked her to the ground. It was the final blow. This time his callous remarks sent her reeling. With her heart breaking into a thousand pieces, she realised that perhaps Vincenzo was right. Maybe a part of old Elizabeth remained. She didn't want to quarrel; didn't want to fight with him. She may have felt Italian, but that fire; that uncontrollable Latin passion wasn't in her blood. If Vincenzo had been testing her to see if she was the woman he thought she was, then she'd failed. Lizzie had lost the fight.

Tears crowded in her throat and once again threatened to spill down her cheeks, but she choked them back as she marched out her despair returning to the farmhouse. Hugh was now sprawled in a chair and clapping along to songs he'd never heard before, while Cristo sat on the other side of the hearth. He was watching the men, too, but didn't join in. Instead, he seemed miserable, and not just because of his painful arm. Lizzie understood why. His own future was uncertain, too. She was going to have to break the news to him herself and he wasn't going to like it.

As the men helped themselves to more wine and continued to swap stories from prison by the fire's glow, Lizzie went over to the boy. He smiled when he saw her, and she sat beside him on a stool.

'What time shall we leave tomorrow?' he asked, wide-eyed. The question cut Lizzie like a knife. He was in denial.

'Oh Cristo,' she replied, her hand reaching out to touch him lightly on the shoulder. 'My dear Cristo.'

His mouth turned down at the edges.

182

'I am coming with you, aren't I?' he asked, piercing her with his innocent look. But his words only twisted the knife.

'I'm sorry, Cristo, but where we are going is very dangerous. We have to go alone,' she replied, her voice quavering as she spoke.

The child's lips pouted. 'But what about me? Where shall I go?'

'Back to Maria and Giuseppe, of course. Your papa will probably be coming home soon. He will want to see you.' Lizzie tried to sound positive, but she knew Cristo had no wish to return.

'No. No. I want to be with you!' His voice rose above the men's drone. When he leapt to his feet, they turned to see what was going on just as Vincenzo returned. Realising all was not well with Cristo, he strode over. When she heard footsteps, Lizzie looked up to see him standing above her.

He gazed at her blankly before addressing the boy. 'Something wrong, young man?'

Cristo wiped away a tear that was coursing down his cheek. 'Miss Lizzie says I can't go with her tomorrow.'

Vincenzo also sat down on the floor and lifted his glasses to the top of his head. 'She's right,' he agreed. 'It is too dangerous for you. And with your broken arm . . .'

'But . . .' the boy protested.

'But' – Vincenzo raised a hand to calm him – 'there is something else you can do.'

Cristo's head jerked up. 'What's that?'

'You are needed here. I need you.'

Lizzie now regarded Vincenzo with questioning eyes.

'What do you mean?' asked the boy.

Glancing furtively over his shoulder, he leaned in towards Cristo to make him feel he was taking him into his confidence. Speaking softly, he said: 'I need you to be my messenger and my spy.'

Cristo's eyes widened. 'A spy,' he repeated. 'You want me to be a spy?'

Lizzie's face fell. 'What do you mean?'

Ignoring Lizzie, Vincenzo squared up to the boy. 'You remember the nature trails you used to follow around the lake? You'd always pick up clues. Notice things. Feathers, seeds. And you remember I always said facts have to be discovered by observation.'

'Yes. Yes, I remember,' he replied, suddenly excited.

'Well, now I need someone I can trust to deliver messages for me and make observations about what is going on.'

'What?' gasped Lizzie, but Vincenzo dismissed her with an impatient hand.

'Do you think you can handle the responsibility?'

'Yes. Yes, of course, sir.'

'Then it is settled. You stay here. With me.' Vincenzo leaned back, the deal done.

Lizzie flashed an angry look at him. Not only had he just banished her from his life, it seemed he was even prepared to put Cristo in danger. It was not the action of the man she'd fallen so in love with back in Tuscany. Now it seemed his suffering had made him a stranger.

Chapter 28

Lizzie cried herself to sleep that night and when she woke at dawn and remembered what had passed the night before, she cried some more. But she knew what she had to do and, drying her tears, she rose from the bed.

The sun was cresting the far hills as she slipped into the same plain black dress that once belonged to Franco's wife. In front of a cracked mirror, she caught sight of a weary, life-worn woman. Her eyes were red rimmed and the surrounding skin was puffy. After splashing cold water on her face, she scraped back her fair hair and hid it under a black scarf. She needed to look Italian. No one must suspect she was English. It was vital to blend in with the other women in the region in case they encountered any German patrols. Vincenzo's comment about being more English than Italian echoed in her head. She had always known that with her privileged upbringing in England came responsibility. Her late mother had taught her that. She'd never intended to take her own comfortable circumstances at the villa for granted and, seeing the suffering and resilience all around her had made her feel far more Italian than English.

Over in the corner she could hear Cristo's gentle breaths as he slept. She'd managed not to glance over at him right up until the moment it was time to leave. She knew that if he woke, her parting would only hurt them both even more. Instead, she slipped off the silver St Christopher medal she always wore around her neck and laid it gently on his pillow.

'May God protect you, my Cristo,' she whispered and kissing her fingers, she blew towards the child. For a second, he stirred, as if he felt the kiss land on his cheek. But then he rolled over and Lizzie picked up her bag and hurried towards the door, before tears blurred her vision.

'Come on, Elizabeth.' Hugh beckoned impatiently. She hurried down the corridor where he was waiting at the end, but instead of letting her pass, he took her in his arms. 'This is it,' he whispered into her ear. 'We'll soon be free.' He found her cheek and planted an unwelcome kiss.

Choking back her emotion, she noted he was wearing a slouch hat and patched clothes. His once-neat moustache was still unruly, and Lizzie thought he could just about pass for an Italian. On his back was a rucksack full of provisions and a blanket, and in his hand, he held a long wooden staff.

'Will I do?' he asked her, looking down the length of his own body.

'You'll do,' she agreed, brushing off the moment with a laugh, even though inside she was in turmoil. The one-hundred-mile journey to La Spezia on the coast would be hard. They were on the run from the Nazis. That would be terrifying enough, but Lizzie knew she was also on the run from her old self. It would be so easy to slip back into her past ways with Hugh, especially after the hardship of the convent. Vincenzo had rejected her. Cristo couldn't come with her, and Hugh was all she had in the world. Yes, it would be so easy and so tempting.

Bidding farewell to Franco, they set off up the track that wound above the farm. The brothers Pietro and Paulo were already by the shrine, eager to make a start. The path rose sharply through the woods, zig-zagging between steep limestone walls on one side

186

and a sheer drop on the other. Below lay a thickly wooded gorge. After about thirty minutes they emerged from dense beeches into the sun and a view on the Val d'Arda.

Lizzie stopped to get her breath back and take in the sweeping panorama of mountains and the fertile river valley. But rising above the river on a plug of volcanic rock lay the great tower of the Rocca, surrounded by three smaller ones at Castell'Arquato. At its foot, medieval buildings clustered around it. As the nearby church chimes rang out across the valley, she feared she might never see Cristo or Vincenzo ever again.

Hugh brought her back into the moment. 'Come on, darling,' he urged up ahead. 'We can't afford to dawdle.'

'Coming,' she called, wiping away tears. Hugh mustn't see her cry. Chin up and all that, he'd say. So that is what she did.

For the next few hours, they plodded on, taking an old drover's track that was bordered by tumble-down stone walls. Each footstep carried her further away from those she cared for so deeply and chafed the skin on her feet into painful blisters. But every time Hugh turned and asked her how she was 'bearing up' she would smile and tell him she was 'fine'. Her life was with him now – at least until they'd both escaped. He was the one giving her courage to face the future and she was going to have to accept him and work with him. But still the doubt remained.

That first night they made camp in a ruined summer-grazing house. It smelt of damp and mould. Pietro found some old hessian sacking for bedding and they ate the bread and cheese Franco had given them. Afterwards the two brothers went outside, taking it in turns to keep watch, leaving Lizzie and Hugh to lie on the sacking, side by side.

'I love you, my darling,' said Hugh, as they stared up at the broken rafters above them. Beyond lay a starry sky, but below, in between them, sat embarrassment. They'd never shared a bed; never strayed into the realm of married couples. In England it was a given they'd remain virgins until their wedding night but lying so close to Hugh made Lizzie uncomfortable. In the gathering silence he waited for a reply to his declaration, but she couldn't give him what he wanted.

If she said she loved him back, would he take it as a sign she was agreeing to give herself to him? She tensed at the thought and simply said, 'Sleep well,' before turning on her side with her back to him.

They lay in silence, apart from the mosquitoes that flew regular sorties over them. Now and again the stutter of gunfire sounded across the valley, reminding them why they were hiding in a stone hut. They snatched a couple of hours' sleep, but they were both restless.

'We made good progress today,' said Hugh, during one of the times when they were both wide awake. 'Only another three or four nights after Bardi and we should make it to the coast.'

He sounded so certain that Lizzie believed him. Almost. Without access to a radio or any means of communication, she wondered how he could be so sure they'd be rescued at La Spezia. Hugh was asking her to put her blind faith in him. Once upon a time she would have. But not anymore. War had shaken her belief in everything. Nothing could ever be certain again.

'We'll see.'

The following day there was more cloud cover. The air was cooler, and the sun only made the occasional appearance. For that Lizzie was grateful as they marched on. She padded her shoes with large leaves to stop the blisters rubbing, but she still found the track hard going. Now and again, when the path dipped down into a valley, they would pass some *contadini* working in the small, cultivated patches of ground that dotted the hills. As well as sheaves of corn drying in the sun, there were baskets piled high with zucchini and apples to take to market. Usually, the peasants in their bandanas and wide-brimmed hats would either ignore them or simply wave, but once one of the women handed Paulo a bag with a knowing look. Inside were tomatoes, cheese and a loaf. It was gratefully received.

On the third day the track began to descend and towards evening they reached a large farmhouse nestling in a wooded valley. Paulo and Pietro made Lizzie and Hugh wait a few metres away in the trees as they knocked. They were greeted by a squat man with a large belly and an even larger laugh. The men talked animatedly for a few moments then Paulo turned and signalled Lizzie and Hugh to join them.

'*La mia case è casa tua*,' greeted the jolly farmer, motioning around him with his hands. Everyone smiled at that and even Hugh didn't need a translation.

The signor, it turned out, had connections in London where one of his sons worked in a restaurant in Soho. He even had English words and phrases which were delivered with a very strong Cockney accent, much to Lizzie's delight. But amid the laughter, there was fear too, as he warned them they could be betrayed by a *spia* at any moment.

'Be careful,' he told them, his finger aloft. 'All around.' His eyes slid to the left and right. 'But I know people. They help you.'

After a good night's sleep in proper beds, and a hearty breakfast, the four of them moved off the next day with the address of a safe house about twenty kilometres north of Bardi. Pietro said they should reach it before nightfall.

'You're doing well, old girl,' Hugh told Lizzie after they'd been walking for a little over three hours. He made her sound like a work horse, she thought. 'How are those blisters of yours?'

Lizzie smiled. 'Not too bad,' she lied. She was still in agony.

They'd been following the river since they left the farmhouse that morning and the water looked so cool and inviting that Lizzie longed to take a dip. Towards midday Paulo veered off the track and crouched by the riverbank to fill his canteen with water.

'Can we stop here for a while?' Lizzie asked Pietro, as he drank long and hard.

189

He shrugged and delivered a reluctant *si*. Lizzie sat down on a smooth rock to take off her boots. Peeling off her socks, she revealed two huge, raw blisters, one on either foot just below her ankles. The sensation of the cold running water on her skin took her breath away at first as she stood in the shallows. It reminded her of a time she had once dabbled her feet in the lake at the villa with Vincenzo after lessons. The smooth pebbles felt cool and slippery under her soles as she began to walk along the riverbed, and the vivid green reeds tickled her ankles. Fat blue dragonflies darted all around her and small birds skimmed across the water's surface. The cold made her feel alive and she walked on further around the bend where the bed dropped, and the river became deeper. The hem of her dusty dress grew darker and heavier as the water reached her knees. It was such a thrilling sensation that she found herself reaching for her skirt on a whim and pulling her dress up over her head, leaving her with nothing on but a flimsy shift. Throwing the dress onto the bank, she decided to take the plunge and dipped down into the flowing water to immerse herself up to her neck. As she leaned back the current swirled around her scalp and her hair floated out behind her. For a few moments she felt cleansed; as if the water was baptising her, washing away all the black thoughts that had stained her over the past few months. Lifting her face to the cloudless sky she began to float, her body becoming completely weightless and free. But then . . .

'Elizabeth! Elizabeth, what are you doing?'

Clamping down her feet on the riverbed, she pushed herself up to see Hugh on the bank.

'Why don't you come in, too?' she suggested with a wave. 'It's so . . . so invigorating.'

The next moment Hugh was stripping to his underpants. She was shocked by how thin he was. Only once before had she seen him in trunks. It was at a country club pool, and she'd been impressed by his muscular torso. Now however, his ribs showed, and his chest was blindingly white and almost concave. His back, too, was badly scarred by burns from the air crash. It was a reminder that he, too, had suffered. He slipped in further up the bank and winced as the cold mountain water lapped his body. As soon as it was deep enough, he launched himself off to swim towards her.

'Isn't it wonderful?' she called out, treading water.

Hugh reached her and suddenly put his arms around her. Quickly she smoothed her wet hair away from her face to see his lips close to hers. At first, she tensed, shocked by the long-forgotten sensation of his embrace and her thoughts flew to Vincenzo. But he'd made it plain he wanted nothing more to do with her so she told herself she needed to banish him from her mind.

'It certainly is,' Hugh replied, moving closer to reach her lips. But she couldn't let him. It was too soon. Instead, she broke away from him playfully, to float on her back and look up at the sky. When she righted herself and found her feet a moment later, she caught his expression; a mixture of desire and fascination. Did he think she was flirting with him? Leading him on? It was only then that she realised the water had turned her flimsy white shift transparent. It was clinging to her breasts and thighs.

'Oh dear!' she cried, crossing her arms over her chest. But Hugh laughed and waded back through the water towards her. She was almost within reach when a cry went up.

'Germans!'

It was Pietro. He'd been keeping watch from a perch overlooking the road that ran parallel with the river.

'Bloody hell!' shouted Hugh, grabbing Lizzie's hand and lunging for the bank. Scrambling out of the river, they dashed towards the nearby reeds as the roar of an engine approached. Shivering with cold, Lizzie looked up to see, through the trees that lined the road, first one truck, then another. She counted a total of ten German military vehicles. They were rumbling

191

south, heading in the same direction as them – towards the town of Bardi.

As soon as they were sure the convoy had passed, Lizzie found her dress and struggled into it, while Hugh tugged on his trousers. The four of them regrouped by the riverbank.

'What do we do now?' asked Hugh.

In Italian Pietro told Lizzie it would be best to carry on to the safe house as planned. There they would be able to find out more intelligence via a wireless.

'But we must be very careful,' Paulo warned. 'The Germans may have left men in the villages on their way. *Spia*. We'd better keep to the higher mountain tracks.'

Their plan to reach Bardi by nightfall was in tatters. Seeing the German convoy was a wake-up call. From then on, they ascended steeply up through the deciduous woods and into the pines on the higher ground. The track was uneven and disappeared completely now and again under bracken and rocks. Lizzie's lungs burned as they went higher. Ropes of pain ran up her thighs. It was hard keeping up with the men and her feet were rubbed raw.

'Easy does it, darling,' said Hugh, holding out a hand as she tried to negotiate a large rock blocking the path. 'How much further?' he called to Pietro up ahead.

Below them the valley was hazed with smoke and from the height they were at it was impossible to say if it came from the customary corn stubble burning by the *contadini* or if the Nazis were laying waste to another farm. Lizzie translated Pietro's reply. 'We can't risk going to Bardi tonight, but we'll make camp there.' The partisan was pointing towards the forest and not long after they reached a clearing just below the tree line. In it sat a log cabin with a steep-sided roof.

'Come. We stay here,' Paulo told them.

There was a small stove, but they all knew lighting a fire was out of the question. Any smoke could draw the Germans to them. Instead, Hugh brought out the provisions the farmer had given them. Just as Lizzie was dividing the food carefully, a crack splintered through the forest and ricocheted around the steep valley walls.

'What the hell . . .?' said Hugh.

The birds roosting in the trees overhead took flight and, seconds later, Pietro slid down from the vantage point, a scowl on his face.

'What was that noise?' asked Hugh.

Paulo cursed and spat on the ground. 'Firing squad.'

'No!' Lizzie closed her eyes at the thought. 'You mean the Germans . . .?'

Pietro nodded.

'Can you tell where they came from?' she asked.

The Italian shot her a piercing look.

'Not the signor at the farmhouse.'

'*Forse.* Perhaps.'

Lizzie hadn't even known the jolly farmer's name and when Pietro said the shots might have been aimed at him, she saw hatred fill his eyes.

'No. Oh no,' she rasped. A selfless stranger had sacrificed himself so they could escape. She would be eternally grateful.

As the evening drew on, the wind got up and whistled around the hut's chimney. The surrounding pines started to creak and when Lizzie closed her eyes, the noise was so loud she could have been on a galleon in a storm. She huddled in a corner to keep warm, and Hugh came to sit by her, putting his arm around her. She was glad of the warmth and instead of tensing at his touch, she found herself relaxing into it. Outside Pietro and Paulo took it in turns to keep watch.

'What happens if they were wrong at the camp, Hugh, and there aren't any landings at the coast?' she asked.

He paused for a moment then said, 'If I'm wrong, we'll work something else out. But it'll all be fine, you'll see.'

The old, eternally optimistic Hugh was back. Once she'd

believed everything he said. If he'd told her the moon was made of ripe Gouda, she'd have swallowed it. When everything around was bleak and threatening, a word from Hugh could make the sun shine once more. It was one of the reasons she'd loved him in England and for a second, just a split second, a chink of light crept through a crack in her feelings. Now that Vincenzo had rejected her, perhaps she should follow where her broken heart took her.

'Yes, we'll see,' she agreed, looking up in the twilight just as Hugh leaned down to kiss her. But, as his lips brushed hers, she returned only a peck. Despite Vincenzo's rejection, it seemed she still wasn't ready to take the leap back to Hugh.

Chapter 29

In the early hours of the next morning Lizzie was wrenched awake by Paulo when he burst into the cabin. She sat up blurry-eyed as Hugh sprang to his feet.

'More trucks! Tanks,' cried the fighter in broken English.

Pietro joined in, this time in Italian and Lizzie translated. 'The Germans are in control of Bardi. They're everywhere. They crawl like ants.'

'But we can't stay here,' protested Hugh. 'There's no water.' He glowered at Paulo. 'No *aqua*.'

Paulo narrowed his eyes, resenting the English officer stating the obvious.

'We go next village,' he replied, his scar now darkened by dirt.

'There is a house,' Lizzie translated. 'Just outside the town. We will wait there until the others come.'

'The others?' questioned Hugh. 'Does he mean Allied soldiers?'

'There are groups of us,' Pietro told Lizzie. 'We are organising ourselves. The jurisdiction of the Emilia-Romagna group ends here and another one begins.'

Hugh bristled when he heard Lizzie's translation. 'So, you're going to hand us over to strangers?'

'Strangers, *non*,' Pietro corrected him with a frown. 'They are our brothers.'

Lizzie could tell Hugh was about to protest and, once again, she took him by the arm to calm him.

'Thank you, Pietro,' she said with a smile. 'We appreciate everything you and Paulo are doing for us.'

Hugh flexed his fists and growled at Lizzie. 'But is there any news from La Spezia? Have the Allies landed yet?'

At the mention of the town, Paulo shook his head. 'Nobody knows anything about any Allied landings, apart from the ones around Salerno. But there's talk about Naples being next,' he told Lizzie in Italian.

Lizzie saw Hugh's neck redden and his anger rise as he picked up on the place names. 'Salerno? Naples? But that's preposterous. We heard about La Spezia on Radio Londra, from the BBC.'

Paulo's features set hard. 'No landings there,' he said in English.

'Maybe the BBC was mistaken,' suggested Lizzie. 'But it won't help arguing.'

'I don't like this one bit,' snarled Hugh.

'What choice do we have?' she asked, trying to calm him. 'These people are putting themselves in danger to help us. They don't want to take any more risks than they have to.'

For the first time that day she saw his face dissolve into a gentle smile. 'You're right, my love,' he told her. 'I'm used to being in charge and it's hard for me—'

'I know,' Lizzie broke in. 'It's hard for everyone, Hugh. But we must trust these people.'

'Yes,' he replied, picking up a rucksack. 'But if our chaps aren't landing at La Spezia, should we go to the coast anyway? I just need to get back to my squadron. Quite frankly, I don't care how.'

It was a question that had troubled Lizzie, too. Their whole journey was now in doubt. Was there any point in carrying on if they couldn't be certain someone was there to rescue them?

'*Avanti!*' called Paulo.

* * *

They kept just under the tree line for most of the morning. Every now and again, Pietro would check out the lie of the land with his binoculars. No one spoke. They were all listening to the rustling of the wind in the trees and to the occasional squeak of a squirrel or the call of an eagle high overhead. After a while they began to drop down. A waterfall gave them a chance to fill their flasks before they moved on through denser undergrowth. They waited in a small cave until night fell and then soon picked up a trail that led directly to a farmhouse on the outskirts of Bardi. Pietro went ahead and a moment later beckoned to them.

Inside two men were waiting. Like the brothers, they were dressed in Italian Army trousers and wore ammunition belts slung over their shoulders.

'This is Bruno,' said Pietro, gesturing to a tall man with a lantern jaw. 'And this is Alberto.' He was younger with dark stubble covering a swarthy face. 'They will take you somewhere safer.'

'Does this mean you're leaving us?' Hugh asked Pietro.

The brother nodded.

'Thank you. Thank you for everything,' said Lizzie, shaking his hand.

It was clear their new escorts wanted to get going. They said nothing, but both nodded towards the door. It was almost dark, and the men led them behind the house and onto a riverbank. Bruno pointed towards a steep embankment on the other side, but there was no bridge. After a long, hot summer, the river levels were low and they could wade across, the water only coming to Lizzie's knees. Once on the other side they began their ascent through cinnamon-coloured trees before following a track that wound around the hill. The moon was almost full. It meant their progress was much easier. But it also made them more visible to Nazi troopers. They trudged on through the night for what Lizzie guessed were five or six kilometres before they finally stopped at a ruined building.

'You stay here,' said Alberto in English, pushing open a flimsy door that creaked at his touch.

Lizzie wasn't expecting to join anyone else, but before her eyes adjusted to the darkness, she could hear something shuffling in the far corner.

'What the . . .?' Hugh scowled and turned back to Alberto. 'Who . . .?' They were not alone.

'Your fellow Englishmen,' he replied with a grin, his teeth visible in the darkness.

'Gentlemen,' said an English voice. 'We have company.'

A match was struck, and a lamp lit, and Lizzie suddenly saw what she'd thought were farm animals taking shelter were in fact British soldiers. There were three of them and they scrambled to their feet when they realised they were being joined.

'Good Lord! Tuffers!' cried Hugh, forgetting the need for quiet.

'Hugh! You old devil!' The two men slapped each other on the back, then Tufnell gestured to his companions. 'And Flash and Pelham.'

Hugh extended his hand in the darkness to the two others, also at Fontanellato. One, Lizzie noted, was smoking a cigarette in a holder, while the other looked impossibly young.

'So, the little lady didn't hold you back too much,' sniped Tuffers, as soon as he noticed Lizzie standing at Hugh's side.

'No. She's actually done rather well,' replied Hugh, wheeling Lizzie round and nudging her forward to introduce her to the other men. 'Miss Elizabeth Thornton – my future wife when all this ghastly business is over.' He winked at her and added in a whisper, 'If she'll have me.'

Lizzie bit her lips. Hugh seemed to be taking it for granted she'd agree again to marry him eventually, and everything would be as it was before. This time she let it pass, but her smile was self-conscious. Aware she'd become an object of curiosity, she felt irritated and uncomfortable. There was resentment on the other men's faces.

'How the devil did she get here?' asked the one with the cigarette holder, called Flash. His question was directed at Hugh, as if Lizzie was incapable of answering. She soon put that impression to bed.

'I can speak for myself, you know,' she replied sharply. 'I was working as a tutor in Tuscany before the war, then interned in a convent in Fontanellato.'

'The one next door to us?' asked Pelham.

'Yes. That's the one. I discovered Hugh was there, and a priest agreed to become our messenger.'

'Had to keep it all very hush, hush,' interjected Hugh, tapping the side of his nose confidentially.

'You sly old fox.' Flash chuckled, then gestured everyone to sit down. Lizzie saw there was a log pile in the corner and perched on the timber.

'So, what are you doing here? What are your plans?' asked Hugh.

'As soon as we got away, we heard Jerry was coming for us. That's when we scarpered,' explained Tuffers. 'Word has it they're rounding up our chaps in football stadia to send them to camps in the east. We want to go north.'

'What about you? Where have you been?' asked Flash, looking directly at Lizzie.

'We've relied on the kindness of strangers,' she replied.

'We're trying to get to La Spezia,' Hugh butted in. 'We heard the Allies are landing there.'

Flash barked out a laugh. 'They fooled you, too,' he said.

Hugh frowned. 'What do you mean?'

'I know we heard it on the BBC, old boy,' said Tuffers sheepishly. 'But it turns out it was a decoy, to fool the Hun.'

'Oh no,' murmured Lizzie. It was as she feared, as if someone had turned out the light. Hugh's expression dropped.

'Sorry to burst your bubble, but there is no Allied landing north of Rome – yet. We're thinking of heading to Switzerland.'

'Switzerland,' Lizzie echoed.

'Neutral and all that,' Flash explained. 'And I do quite fancy a spot of skiing if they intern us.'

Hugh was shaking his head. Lizzie was glad to see he shared her scepticism. 'But the weather's on the turn. Winter's only three or four weeks away. Do you think you'll make it before then?'

'Who knows? But we've got to give it a go, eh Pelham?' Flash eyed the young man in the corner, who'd barely said a word. When he looked up, Lizzie could see fear on his face.

'Yes, sir,' he replied, half-heartedly.

They talked late into the night, arguing about which escape routes were the safest or quickest and how the Special Operations Executive was expected to get involved soon to provide help to the growing resistance groups. Lizzie decided to keep out of the conversation. She'd already made up her mind to talk to Hugh alone, away from his friends. They would be safer staying in the region, she would tell him. Ordinary, decent Italian villagers had no interest in supporting fascism. They were the best allies anyone could hope for. They'd be safer in the company of the fighters, too. These men knew the territory like their own back gardens. Staying put was the best option, and while they were waiting for news of the Allies' progress, they could make themselves useful. Why not give back a little of the generosity they'd received? As she laid down her head on a folded sack for a pillow, she formulated a plan. After that, all she had to do was make Hugh think the idea was his.

The weather turned shortly afterwards. It was too late to head north, so Tuffers, Pelham and Flash decided to stay put for the next few weeks. The whole operation was carefully planned over the biting winter. Much of December and January were spent holed up in another farmhouse, a few kilometres to the west. It was higher up the mountain and owned by a man with a terrible limp and a small dog that followed him everywhere. There were no roads, no villages, few houses and even less food. Snow blanketed the peaks in an eerie silence. The occasional clatter of machine guns in one of the nearby valleys was the only sound to break it. That and the incessant coughing of those suffering from bronchitis.

Despite the inactivity and their inability to leave the farm because they could so easily be tracked in the snow, the men managed to fill their days. Lizzie called on her long-idle skills with a needle to darn shirts and socks. Hugh whittled draught pieces from spare wood and marked out black and white squares on a board, while Flash set a daily crossword, which occupied them all for a couple of hours each day. Pelham always finished first. Yet no matter how busy Lizzie kept herself, Vincenzo's ghost still haunted her, appearing at times she least expected him. When she made pasta dough, she was back in Maria's kitchen with him or when grinding spices in a pestle and mortar, she would recall him preparing compounds for Cristo's chemistry lessons. He may be gone from her life, but she feared he could never be forgotten.

On New Year's Eve, while the other men went down into the farmhouse cellar to fetch wine for the evening's celebrations, Hugh hung back to talk to Lizzie on her own. She was sitting by a sickly fire, sewing on a button when he said, 'Elizabeth.'

She'd grown used to the name again. Lizzie was from her other life. Lifting her head, she noticed a glint in his eye. 'You look so contented there,' he told her. 'Just how you should.' He reached out and took her hand. 'You remember when I asked you to marry me just after we escaped from Fontanellato?'

Lizzie's stomach flipped. Of course she did. She'd thought about it every day. Slowly, she nodded.

'You said you needed more time. That we needed to get to know each other again.'

'I remember,' she replied, dread creeping through her veins. He wanted a decision. He deserved a decision.

'I've been very patient.'

'Yes. Yes, you have,' she conceded.

'Well?' He was kneeling at her side now, a gentle smile on his lips. 'I still love you, you know.' He held her hand tighter.

When she replied her voice was thick with emotion. But there was still confusion, too. 'I know you love me,' she replied softly. 'But give me until spring. Please. I'll tell you my answer then.'

His head dropped. She knew he'd take it badly, but seconds later when he looked at her again, he chuckled.

'Well, I shan't be going anywhere without you.'

She smiled at him and, to her own surprise, pecked him on the lips. Encouraged by her affection, Hugh held her and kissed her long and hard and instead of resisting him, Lizzie allowed his warmth to seep through her body. Perhaps she could love him again, after all. Perhaps. But she wanted to be absolutely honest with Hugh, and that would take courage. A different kind of courage. Not the sort that made you pick up a rifle or print propaganda leaflets on pain of death. She *needed* to tell him how she felt; how this war had touched her in ways she could never have imagined. How she'd realised that not everything was black and white – sometimes things were grey – and that evil could bring out the best in people as well as the worst; that honesty was to be cherished above all because without it, friendships, relationships and even governments were built on sand and could come crashing down at any time; that life was far too fragile and precious to waste a moment of it. She needed to tell him all this; to open her heart entirely to him so that he understood what effect Italy and its people had made on her. Hugh needed to know she was no longer that starry-eyed young woman who'd be content to live in a large house in leafy suburbia, manage the household, entertain his business associates and raise his children. Once she had dreamed of such things. Now they were her nightmares. She just had to tell him all this if she were ever to agree to marry him.

That had been a few weeks back. In early January they'd heard about the formation of a liberation committee from the partisan known as Bruno. Lizzie had managed to persuade Hugh they should do what they could to help the resistance. It hadn't been difficult. She'd argued they were safer staying in the Morfasso area, under the guardianship of the men they knew and trusted, rather than going it alone, heading north in the winter snows.

Tuffers, Flash and Pelham disagreed. As soon as the thaw set in, they decided to take their chances and set a course for Switzerland. They'd left the week before. No one had heard of them since.

Chapter 30

The night was cold and crisp. A thousand stars lit the cloudless dome of sky above them as the partisans waited for the signal. It was to be the newly formed unit's first raid. The fascists were transporting an important resistance member from the notorious Le Nuove in Turin to a prison near Bardi. The plan was to ambush the truck and its Carabinieri escort, rescue the prisoner and bring him back to safety.

There were seven of them on this mission. Lizzie and Hugh were guided down the mountain to join up with the partisans in the woods just outside a town that straddled the main road from Bardi to Parma. Hunkered down in a nearby ditch, Lizzie squinted at her watch as the moon kept disappearing behind squally clouds. Almost midnight. Adrenaline coursed through her body and her heart beat faster. She was angry. Not just with the Nazis and the fascists. But with Hugh, too.

Any minute now, she told herself.

Bruno had taken Lizzie and Hugh to a small house on the outskirts of the village, surrounded by pigs and chickens, where more partisans had gathered to go over the plan one more time.

There'd been a tip-off from the Castell'Arquato unit – Vincenzo's unit, Lizzie noted. A map was unfurled on the kitchen table and Bruno pointed to various points where he believed German snipers could be stationed. The truck was scheduled to pass near the town just after midnight.

A pot of face cream mixed with powdered charcoal appeared beside the map on the table. Much to Lizzie's delight, two women were joining the raid. She knew them only by their code names – Tigrona and Carma. There'd been no time to talk to them, but just having a sisterly presence made her feel more confident. They were more practised at applying the charcoal, and helped the men camouflage their faces and hands before they also followed suit. Lizzie applied Hugh's, too. But when it came to her turn, and she dipped her fingers in the pot and began to smear the cream on her own face, Hugh spluttered.

'What do you think you're doing?'

Lizzie baulked. 'Camouflaging, of course. Like everyone else,' she replied. The other women had finished smearing their faces and were already tucking their hair under dark caps.

Hugh laughed. 'Don't be so ridiculous, darling. You don't think you are coming with us?'

Lizzie bristled. 'Of course I am. I've already been assigned. I'm to be stationed here.' She leaned over the table to point at the map and to a sharp bend by the junction where there was a roadside shrine, just outside the town. 'And these are . . .' She reached for a heavy canvas bag containing the metal stars she was to throw across the road to puncture the enemy's tyres.

'I know. I know,' Hugh said, shaking his head and grabbing the bag. 'I played along to please you, but perhaps you should give me that.'

She snatched it back. 'I can't believe you, Hugh. There are other women in this team.' She threw a glance at them, and saw they were watching the spat with interest. 'Would you like them to remain here, too?'

Hugh floundered. 'No, but they're not you.'

'So, I'm less capable than they are? Is that it?'

'No, but . . . You're not cut out for this sort of thing. It's dangerous.'

'So only men can do work that is risky. Is that it?'

'I want to protect you, Elizabeth, and besides . . .' His eyes dropped.

'Besides what, Hugh?' Lizzie wasn't going to let him get away with this.

'Besides, you'll ruin your skin,' Hugh replied, looking at her straight. His delivery was light-hearted but he added sternly, 'And I forbid it.'

It was Lizzie's turn to laugh. 'You forbid it?'

Meanwhile, on the other side of the room, Bruno and the others were arming themselves. There were only three rifles between them, so the best shots took those. The partisans were to position themselves on strategic rooftops. There were two hand grenades and three knives.

Bruno noticed Hugh and Lizzie were arguing. 'Something wrong?' he asked in Italian.

'Flight Lieutenant Codrington says I am not allowed to join you,' replied Lizzie, staring angrily at Hugh.

Bruno smiled. 'I am in charge here. You are needed. You will come,' he replied with a nod.

'What did he say?' asked Hugh, half understanding that Lizzie had been given the green light to take part in the operation.

Lizzie dipped her hand in the charcoal. 'This is what he said,' she replied, sticking out her jaw defiantly and proceeding to plaster her face until only the whites of her eyes were visible.

'*Andiamo*,' said Bruno, standing armed by the door. 'Let's go.'

Even underneath a layer of black, Lizzie was willing to bet Hugh's face would be bright red right now.

* * *

Keeping to the shadows they fanned out from the edge of the town, ducking low along the hedgerows until they reached a junction about two kilometres east of Morfasso. Alberto had a motorcycle. The plan was to ambush the escort from a side road, then the others would move in. They all took up their positions. Hugh, Lizzie could tell, was still sulking. 'I'll stay with you here,' he told her as she stopped close to the little roadside shrine. It housed a statue of the Madonna and child.

'Don't let everyone down, Hugh,' she warned him. 'You know where you should be, and I don't need you.'

His pride was wounded, but he flattened his palms in an exaggerated surrender and backed off throwing her his hang-dog look as he went. She watched as he lay down in a ditch on the opposite side of the bend in the road where visibility was poor for oncoming traffic.

On schedule, five minutes later the roar of engines could be heard speeding along the main road. Pinpricks of slatted head-lights from an escort vehicle advanced, followed by a larger truck behind. Tigrona flashed a torch beam, and Alberto twisted the throttle of his motorcycle to surge across the junction. The car in front, a Mercedes, screeched on its brakes, and swerved off the road, shuddering into the ditch. Realising there was an ambush, the truck behind started to accelerate. It was gaining ground when Lizzie leapt up from her position and hurled several iron stars onto the road just a few metres ahead of it. It was too late to brake. As soon as the truck's tyres hit the razor-sharp stars they burst, each puncture splitting the air like a bullet. The vehicle spun out of control, zig-zagging across the road until it clipped a tree and careered into a ditch, toppling onto its side.

As smoke roiled from the smashed truck, the two guards in the Mercedes crouched down behind it and drew their pistols to fire into the dark. Bullets hailed across the road but were answered with fire from partisans in the ditches. Bruno hit one of the guards as he tried to flee, while the other was brought down by Tigrona.

Crawling on her belly to the truck Lizzie peered through the windscreen. The driver and a guard were sprawled unconscious on the front seat, blood pouring from under the guard's helmet. At the back she could hear someone kicking at the crumpled doors. She prayed the passenger was still alive.

'Easy! Easy!' she heard Bruno call as she dashed round to the back. Hugh and one of the men were tending to the elderly prisoner. He seemed very frail, but she couldn't be sure if he was injured.

Both guards came out with their hands above their heads, but then one tried to make a break for it and a partisan coshed him hard and he fell. The other also tried to escape but was grabbed by the legs and brought down.

Meanwhile, Carma, a trained nurse, was examining the prisoner on the verge. He seemed very confused and moaned a lot but didn't appear to have any broken bones.

From out of the blackness a call went up from the junction.

'Someone's coming,' cried one of the lookouts.

'Here,' yelled Tigrona, heading up a track.

A tall, muscular partisan known as Orsini hefted the prisoner onto his shoulders like a flitch of bacon and hurried up the path behind the woman. Hugh followed but stopped to look around. When he spotted Lizzie behind him, he shot out his hand to help her up the steep bank. She could have managed but accepted his help as a peace offering. As she tucked her hand in his, she noticed relief in his eyes.

'I'm sorry I doubted you,' he mumbled as they scrambled up through the trees.

By now a German patrol vehicle had discovered the ambush and the Nazi machine was set in motion. The barks of half-starved dogs echoed round the valley. Flashlights criss-crossed the road and fields nearby. Anyone they encountered would be shot on sight. No questions asked.

It wasn't safe to return to the farmhouse above the town where

208

they'd sheltered in the cellar before. Instead, they headed for a mill house, about three kilometres upstream. Every time Lizzie took a breath, the air burned her lungs. Her legs felt like lead, but she knew she had no choice. She had to keep going. When she and Hugh finally made it to the rendezvous, two partisans were already there, but there was no sign of Carma and the two men who stayed with Orsini as he shouldered the rescued prisoner.

A woman with an eye patch was ready for them. She ushered them through a trapdoor leading down to a cellar. There they waited in silence, listening for any sound until a few minutes later, the door creaked open, and voices could be heard. Italian voices.

Lizzie let out a great sigh. 'They've made it,' she said, as the trap door opened, and Bruno's face appeared.

'We need help,' he called down.

Hugh jumped up, alongside the other two partisans as the prisoner was lowered gently down the ladder. He was barely conscious, but Lizzie quickly made up a bed for him using old sacks and sheep's wool and they laid him down on his back.

'We need more light,' said Lizzie.

Hugh brought over a lamp and held it aloft so Carma could tend to the man. He groaned again but at least it meant he was conscious.

'It's going to be all right,' Lizzie told him in Italian as the nurse loosened his shirt to help him breathe. Bruno offered a blanket and Lizzie laid it gently across him, but it wasn't until she looked at his face to offer him water that she realised.

'My God!' She rocked back on her heels, reeling from the shock.

'What is it?' asked Hugh.

'I know him,' muttered Lizzie, then louder. 'I know this man.' She'd glimpsed him in the botanical gardens in Lucca and seen his photograph in Vincenzo's newspaper. He was the leader of the Action Party in the city. Leaning forward, she stroked his head and whispered in his ear. 'You're safe now, Professor Lodato.'

*　*　*

209

The Nazis and their slavering dogs paid the mill house a visit, two days after the ambush. They smashed chairs and broke crockery. They even slapped the woman with the eye patch across the face. But she did not waver, and the Germans went away empty-handed. Professor Lodato remained recuperating in the cellar. Some of the other partisans returned to their homes nearby but Lizzie and Hugh stayed. Before long, their patient was sitting up and drinking chicken broth. Despite suffering with his jaw which had been broken and left untreated a few months back, Professor Lodato was managing to talk. Almost immediately he asked about Vincenzo.

'Baldini. Does anyone have news of him?'

Lizzie's heart jumped in her chest but mention of Vincenzo's name was bitter-sweet. 'Baldini?' she repeated. 'Yes. Yes. I saw him.'

'You saw him? So, he escaped?' The professor's bruised face lifted for a moment before pain replaced his smile with a grimace.

'He did,' replied Lizzie. She'd tried not to think of him over the cruel winter months. The memory of what he'd said to her was still too painful. 'He's . . . he is leading a partisan unit near Castell'Arquato,' she told him. 'He tipped us off about a transfer from Le Nuove.'

'I certainly owe my life to you and your friends, dear signorina . . .' He paused, looking at Lizzie. 'I don't even know your name. You're English, aren't you?'

She nodded. 'You may not know me, but I feel I know you, Professor Lodato. Vincenzo spoke very highly of you. And yes, I am English, and my name is Lizzie Thornton.'

'Miss Thornton. *Si*, Baldini spoke highly of you also,' he replied, lifting his shoulders to manage a lop-sided smile. 'You may be English, but you have the heart of an Italian!' he told her.

Lizzie smiled, too, at this ironic remark. Vincenzo believed she remained English at heart, and always would. And Hugh wanted it to be true. She turned to see Hugh's eyebrows lift, even though he could only vaguely follow their conversation. She switched back to the professor. 'I do what I can,' she replied, 'but it's your fellow Italians who planned your rescue and when you are better, they will get you back to Lucca.'

'What was all that about being an Italian?' asked Hugh when, a few minutes later, Professor Lodato was asleep and they'd both settled themselves in a corner lined with sacks. Lizzie looked at him in the lamplight, assuming he was intending to remind her she was an Englishwoman. But no. She was wrong.

'I underestimated you,' he told her, an apology in his voice.

Lizzie thought for a moment then nodded. 'Yes, you did rather,' she agreed. 'You should never underestimate a woman, Hugh,' she told him, reminded of what Vincenzo had told her once. '*We need strong women like you to help our cause.*'

'And that's why I love you,' he replied, producing a small coil of wire from his pocket. '*Now* will you marry me?'

Chapter 31

The fire could be seen for miles around; orange flames leaping up from the mountain ridge to lick the sky. Coils of black smoke rising. The Nazis planned it that way. It was a signal. A warning. Two Carabinieri were dead and two Germans badly injured. An important prisoner had escaped, and the Nazis wanted revenge. Late at night they torched a home where they suspected one of the partisans lived. A woman and a child had died in the blaze. They were Alberto's wife and daughter.

'They're after us, but they can't beat us,' Bruno told the small group as they assembled nervously. They crowded into a shepherd's hut two kilometres north of Morfasso the following week. 'More and more fighters are joining us, leaving the fascist army as they return from abroad and despite what happened with Margherita and the baby' – he glanced at Alberto who was wiping away silent tears – 'or maybe because of it, we have the support of the local community and many others wanting to join.' Bruno rose to open the door. 'Please welcome our newest recruit,' he said, as a petite young woman with short dark hair and elfin features entered.

It took a moment to recognise the girl without her short veil and habit but when she caught the familiar bewildered expression,

Lizzie shot to her feet. 'Cecilia?' she cried, leaping up. 'Is it really you?'

The girl, now dressed in trousers and a battledress jacket, blinked and Lizzie recognised her instantly. Hurrying forward, she hugged her slight frame.

'What happened?' asked Lizzie, leaning back to inspect her dress.

Before she could answer, Bruno interrupted. 'Everyone, this is Cecilia Olivetti. She is joining us in the fight.' He turned to her. 'Do you want to tell us all your story?'

Lizzie was curious. Something had happened to her friend; something to make her question her life behind the convent walls and her wholehearted commitment to the authority of the church.

Cecilia's large eyes swept nervously around the room.

'I want to join you,' she began, but her throat was croaky, and her words grated. 'I want to join you because my brothers . . .' She faltered again. Lizzie remembered how only two remained after the other two were killed. 'I had four brothers. Two died fighting in Tunisia and the other two . . .' She paused to compose herself. 'My two remaining brothers were both murdered by the Nazis in Cephalonia.' Finally, the words were spat out so forcefully that they surprised Lizzie. Loss seemed to have turned a mild-mannered novice who'd put all her faith in God into a fierce warrior. Lizzie had heard there'd been a massacre of Italian troops on the island last September. The Nazis, regarding the Italians as traitors after the Armistice, had executed almost all the soldiers by firing squad. More than five thousand men were murdered.

'When they told me at the convent, I knew I would be failing my brothers if I stayed inside those walls and hid myself away.' She turned to Lizzie. 'I needed to be part of the fight and I remembered what I said to you.'

The words suddenly echoed in Lizzie's head. *Listen to your heart.* What Cecilia advised her was true, but it was proving so hard for her to follow its instructions. When she sensed the girl's eyes on the wire coil on her left hand, she felt embarrassed. She'd surrendered and accepted Hugh's proposal, finally allowing him to slip a makeshift engagement ring on her finger. It was as if by returning to Hugh, Lizzie had let down not just herself, but Cecilia, too.

'That's when I knew I had to act,' the girl continued.

Stepping forward, Lizzie took Cecilia by the hand. She admired her bravery more than she could say. 'It can't have been easy to leave,' she told her. Courage, she knew, wasn't necessarily about picking up a gun to fight. So often the struggle was inside and the means to overcome it had to be found within. 'But you have done the right thing.'

Cecilia nodded. 'I think so,' she replied. 'I believe God will understand.'

There was a spontaneous round of applause for the young woman. Even Hugh clapped. 'Welcome,' he said in English.

Cecilia's face lit up. 'This is Hugh?' she asked.

'Yes,' replied Lizzie. 'The one and only.' She smiled as she turned to him to explain in English. 'Cecilia was the novice I told you about. She kept me sane while I was in the convent. I told her all about you, too.'

'And are you to be m—?' began the girl in stilted English.

Lizzie didn't dare to look at Hugh. 'Yes,' she cut in. 'Yes, we are to be married.' She could barely believe it herself, but somehow it was true. Over the past few weeks, she'd seen a change in his attitude towards her. He was far more caring and attentive and once again, she'd come to realise why she'd wanted to marry him in the first place. He was what her late mother would have called 'a good catch'. Handsome, debonair and witty. He could also give her the kind of life that would be the envy of most women. What was it Vincenzo had said? '*You are English, Lizzie. And you always will be. You belong with your own kind.*' Perhaps he was right.

Of course, now and again, the old Hugh had resurfaced – *the stiff-upper-lip* Hugh who looked at her as a delicate flower one moment, then as a cook and a laundress the next. But at least her future with Hugh gave her security and stability. She'd made a logical decision, hadn't she? Even so, she still couldn't look at Cecilia, fearing it might seem she was just using her ex-fiancé to help her escape. Thoughts whooped and whirled like starlings in her head. Throughout the winter sensible Elizabeth had nagged in her ear, then nudged her forward. Hugh would never be a match for Vincenzo, but she'd been rejected by her one true love. In her head she'd replayed Vincenzo's cruel dismissal so many times that she'd given up any hope of a reunion with him. Hugh was the wiser choice. Her only choice.

She just wished she could be as brave as Cecilia.

'What did Mother Superior say?' whispered Lizzie as she lay on her back, looking up at a thin stripe of stars between the broken roof rafters. The weather had turned warmer and that night Lizzie, Cecilia and the other two women slept on a bed of straw in the adjoining hayloft, while the men bedded down in the nearby woods.

Cecilia was silent for a moment then replied, 'She was cold towards me, but I did not expect her to understand. The church demands obedience, not love.'

'It must've been a hard decision.'

In the darkness the young woman sighed heavily. 'I thought long and hard about leaving, but in the end, I couldn't stand by and ignore what was going on in the outside world.'

'So you just walked out?'

'Yes. A week after I heard about my brothers, I went to my parents' house in Castell di Castiglione. They told me about the partisans and how people were forming groups to fight the Nazis. I knew then that was what I had to do. I had to leave the Order.'

Lizzie rolled over onto her side and propped her head up on her hand. 'Then where did you go?' The mention of Castello di Castiglione had rung alarm bells in Lizzie's head, making her think of Cristo.

'A friend of my parents introduced me to someone who knew about a group of fighters in the area. They were looking for *staffette*, messengers. Boys and women, mainly.'

'*Staffette*,' repeated Lizzie. 'Did you come across a boy called Cristo de Falco?'

'Cristo?' Cecilia repeated. 'Why, yes. He was very good, one of Il Gufo's favourites.'

A gasp escaped Lizzie's lips in the gloom. 'You know Il Gufo, the Owl?' Her heart began to race.

'Yes. He commands the Castell'Arquato unit.'

No matter how hard she tried to forget him, Vincenzo's memory refused to leave her. Her pulse still raced at the mere thought of Il Gufo. It was so good to know he and Cristo were still alive, and for that she was grateful, but the very mention of his name still stirred something inside her that she was trying so hard to banish.

'So why did you leave his unit?' she asked.

'I knew they needed fighters over here and I wanted to be more than a *staffetta*. My brothers taught me to shoot when I was twelve. So, here I am.'

Cecilia's disembodied voice sounded so young in the dark. It was hard for Lizzie to imagine her toting a gun. 'And you will be a great asset, I know,' she replied. She turned onto her other side then, as if to signify she wanted to sleep, even though she knew she wouldn't be able to. Her mind was crammed full of thoughts, but of one man in particular.

Heavy clouds were dimming the stars on a warm April night by the railway track between Morfasso and Rocchetta. This time the target was a German supply train. The goal was to derail it and salvage as much food and ammunition as the partisans could.

'Nervous?' Lizzie asked Cecilia as she blacked her face with charcoal that evening.

The young woman shook her head. 'I still put my trust in God,' she said with a shrug. 'If I die, it is His will that I join my brothers.'

Such courage tugged at Lizzie's heart. 'Good luck,' she said, lifting her lips into a smile to mask her deepest fears. Like the last mission, there was no guarantee they'd all make it back alive.

They walked in pairs to the track and split up. Lizzie and Hugh were to station themselves on a rocky ledge overlooking the line and signal when the train was about to approach. Bruno and Alberto would loosen the fittings on the track to derail it. Once the locomotive was off the rails, the rest of the fighters would loot whatever weapons and supplies they could and disappear into the hills as fast as possible. It was Cecilia's job to provide covering fire, alongside Orsini.

There had been a heavy rain shower. The ground was slippery underfoot. Hugh, armed with nothing more than a pair of binoculars, kept watch for the train from the vantage point, while Lizzie constantly scanned everywhere else. She was to signal with her flashlight as soon as she saw the train. It was due to pass at 03.28 hours. At 03.20 the men moved onto the line with wrenches and spanners and set to work loosening the nuts and bolts. It wasn't easy but eventually the fixings yielded, and the rails slackened. They had two minutes to spare. Diving behind bushes on the embankment the men waited for the signal.

'Here she comes,' growled Hugh, as the train rounded the bend. The roar of the engine grew louder, and Lizzie turned and flashed her torch three times down the track. The next few seconds were a blur, but the brakes shrieked like banshees. The train was screeching to a halt. This wasn't supposed to happen. Something was wrong. Concentrating the torch beam on the rails, she glimpsed, to her horror, two helmeted Nazis waving frantically.

'They're onto us!' she cried as one of the soldiers fired his rifle into the air.

'Quick. Let's get the hell out of here!' Hugh exclaimed, scrambling down from the rock. He landed on the rough ground below with a thud. 'Hurry, Elizabeth,' he cried, reaching up and tugging her down, so that she almost fell into his arms at the bottom of the outcrop. 'Come on!'

Hand in hand they hurtled down a steep bank away from the railway line. Lizzie stumbled over a slippery rock, but Hugh snatched at her arm before she hit the damp ground. 'This way,' he yelled, yanking her towards a track that led away from the valley floor. But Lizzie hesitated. The darkness had closed in, but she knew the others must be in trouble. A dozen or more rapid flashes of machine-gun fire exploded in the blackness. The sound echoed round the valley.

Lizzie looked at Hugh in dismay, the noise beating against her skull. 'We need to go back,' she cried above the gunfire, but he just tugged at her wrist. Her reply was to dig in with her heels. 'We can't just leave them,' she pleaded.

Hugh yanked at her arm again. 'Are you mad?' he cried. 'Come on. We need to save our own skins.'

'No, Hugh. They need us. Cecilia could be in trouble.' She jerked her hand away and started running down the railway track towards the shooting. Hugh's cries were soon drowned out by the sound of automatic fire. Pitching down behind some reeds a few metres from the last train carriage, she tried to make out what was happening. It seemed at least two partisans were cowering under one of the railway cars as endless rounds of German bullets were fired at them. The rusty rifles were no match for the enemy sub-machine guns. Lizzie thought quickly. If she could create a diversion to draw away the Nazi fire, it would give whoever was trapped a few seconds to escape and run for cover. A pile of scree lay at the foot of the exposed cliff nearby. Crawling over to them on her hands and knees, she picked up the biggest rock she could find and hurled it as far as she could into a bush near the carriage. The reaction from the Germans was immediate. Their fire was redirected at the bush. Lizzie threw another stone in the opposite direction, then another to confuse the soldiers. To her side she caught movement; two, maybe three figures dashing from under the rail car and slumping down in the undergrowth. But she wasn't the only one to notice. One of the soldiers twisted round, too, firing randomly into the scrub. A piercing cry tore through the air before something hit the ground. The two men were powering towards her now. Lizzie had to run, too. Clambering up the bank of scree was like climbing up a wall of treacle. She kept losing her footing until finally she reached the rocky path and managed to hoist herself up onto a solid ledge. The two partisans followed close at her heels, but she daren't stop running. Her lungs were burning but still she climbed, hefting herself up over the rocks with her hands. She kept going for as long as she could. The guns had long fallen silent, but she could still hear the German commands. Then, from out of the blackness, a figure blocked the path.

'Hugh!' she blurted, her hand palming her chest.

'What the hell's going on? Let's get out of here!' he hissed at her, thrusting out a hand. Even in the dark she could see the fury tightening his features, but she was furious, too. A surge of adrenaline pulsed through her and instead of taking his hand, she whipped round just as the two partisans caught up with her. Squinting into the gloom, she could make out Bruno and Orsini. Slung over the big man's left shoulder was what Lizzie first thought was a sack.

'Where's Cecilia?' she asked.

Bruno stepped closer; the whites of his eyes glinting. Orsini shook his head, laying a respectful hand on the precious bundle. Lizzie's heart stopped when she saw a jacket drenched in blood.

'She didn't stand a chance,' he muttered.

'No! No!' cried Lizzie, lunged forward to embrace Cecilia. Hugh tried to pull her back, but she shrugged him off. 'Don't touch me!' she yelled.

As Bruno lay the body gently on the ground, Lizzie dropped to her knees. 'My dear, dear Cecilia,' she kept saying, over and over, first feeling her wrist for a pulse, then her neck. When no signs of life were found, Lizzie held her hand over her mouth to stifle another cry. Biting back tears, she studied her child-like face, then traced her nose and mouth with her finger. Despite the blood on her chest, Cecilia's expression was peaceful. She could almost have been sleeping.

'You are with your brothers now, sweet Cecilia,' she whispered.

Bruno laid a hand on her shoulder. 'We must get out of here,' he told her.

'Yes. Yes, we must,' she said, returning to the moment.

They would be next in the Nazis' sights if they didn't hurry.

Hugh held out a hand to help her to her feet, but she shunned it and scrambled up unaided. Orsini lifted Cecilia as if she were a bundle of rags and together all four of them began their ascent up the steep path to the shelter of the forest, while below them tracker dogs snarled and growled.

It seemed like an age before they stopped to rest once more. The higher they climbed, the colder the air, but inside Lizzie was burning; running away from the flames of hurt that were lapping at her heels. Cecilia was dead and Hugh had deserted her when she'd needed him most.

'Elizabeth. Elizabeth, please,' he implored, frantically gulping for breath when he finally caught up with her. 'I know you're angry with me, but . . .'

She heard him panting behind her and wheeled round to face him. Her fury and exhaustion spilled over.

'You're a coward, Hugh,' she cried, tugging at the flimsy wire on her finger and throwing it to the ground. 'It's over between us.'

Her words hit him like a slap. He shrunk back.

'You don't really mean that.'

Lizzie looked heavenward. 'Yes, I do, Hugh. I don't want to be your wife. Not now, not ever.'

Still, he persisted. 'I was thinking about you,' he pleaded. 'We could both have been killed.'

She shook her head. 'We weren't the ones in immediate danger.

We had a duty to take care of the others. Didn't you learn that in the RAF?'

Hugh's face was a mixture of shock and indignation. 'My first duty was to protect you, Elizabeth. Please, don't be like this. We've been through too much together.' He held out a hand as tears gathered in her eyes once more. She wiped them away with the back of her hand and growled.

'You barely think about anyone but yourself, Hugh. All you want to do is get us out of here so you can rejoin your squadron, but we can't just walk away from what's happening around us. We owe a debt to the people who've kept us alive so far.'

By now Bruno and Orsini, still carrying Cecilia's body, had caught up with them. Alberto had joined them, too, and he put out a hand to lean on a tree trunk and catch his breath.

'What do you say to resting here for the night?' he asked Lizzie in Italian. 'I'm sure we've shaken off the dogs.'

Lizzie nodded. '*Si*,' she told him and scanned the ground for a suitable spot to take some rest. Hugh moved forward and, gathering they were planning to make camp, pointed to a hollow in the ground that was lined with dead leaves.

Inside, Lizzie was still screaming at him, but the hollow would shelter them both. Silently she settled herself down on the ground and Hugh took off his coat and laid it over her. It was still warm from his own body and once again, she picked up his scent on the heavy wool.

'Please forgive me,' he whispered in her ear as she lay with her back to him. 'I just had to protect you.'

'Well you don't have to any more,' she replied flatly. 'I'm no longer your . . .' She paused. 'Responsibility.' Right then she was far too angry to forgive him. Yet while she'd accused him of being a coward, in reality, she had to acknowledge she had been, too, when she agreed to his proposal a second time. Even though it offered her little comfort, it seemed Cecilia's death had given her the courage to finally come to her senses.

221

Chapter 32

Lizzie scooped up a handful of earth and tossed it onto the wooden coffin in the ground below. 'Rest in peace with your brothers,' she whispered. A cold shiver coursed down her spine as an unexpected breeze whipped up the fallen leaves on the path. Cecilia was saying farewell.

A priest intoned the final prayer as dawn broke. They were gathered in the tiny cemetery in a hamlet midway between Castell'Arquato and Morfasso. The distant moan of bombers overhead reminded them all why they were there. At the end of the short ceremony the mourners adjourned to a room at the back of the church.

Lizzie dried her tears and took a seat at the long table. Cecilia would want to keep fighting and that was exactly what she intended to do. Hugh sat next to her, stroking his moustache pensively. She'd tried to keep her distance from him, although it was hard, given they were both on the run and relying on the partisans for their survival. But she could tell he still expected her to relent and fall back into his arms once more.

Bruno, Alberto and five other unit members filed into the room with them to await the arrival of the other partisans. They were coming from the neighbouring unit. It would be the first time the two divisions had met up since they'd both been created six months before. There was talk of forming a new brigade to cover the whole of the Arda Valley. Bruno was in favour of the idea. He'd lost six members in as many weeks, including Carma, who'd been executed in nearby Piacenza. Combining forces seemed like an obvious course of action. He'd also heard there'd been contact from the British. Regular air drops of welcome supplies and weapons to the groups were life-savers.

'The Allies have approached us,' Bruno announced. 'They want to establish escape routes for former prisoners of war. A Special Operations Executive officer had been assigned to the region.' He looked directly at Hugh and Lizzie. They both leaned forward. 'I have met with the Englishman. He is coordinating activities,' he told them. 'He wants to meet with you and . . .' Bruno turned to Hugh.

'What's he saying?' asked the pilot, his dark brows knotted in a frown.

'It's all right,' Lizzie replied. 'There are plans to get us out of here. There's a British officer on the ground. Once we liaise with him, he'll help to get us home.'

For the first time in months, there was hope that she and Hugh might be able to escape occupied Italy. Bruno continued to talk about what he called the Rome Escape Route, but he was only five minutes into his address when he was interrupted by the sound of motor engines. Alberto was at the window in a second. He turned back with a nod and shortly after some familiar faces appeared at the doorway. Stefano, Carlo, Ernesto, Paulo and Pietro walked in, accompanied by three men and another woman, who were strangers to Lizzie. She held her breath, waiting for Vincenzo to come through the door. She wasn't sure how she'd react to seeing him again. When he finally appeared, he was dressed in a khaki uniform. Stubble hazed his face, and his hair was longer and tousled, but he was instantly recognisable. He took his seat at the table and cast around, nodding and greeting the other men by name. When he saw Lizzie, his gaze rested on her for a moment. Their eyes locked and her whole body went rigid, but then another partisan entered the room, looking grave. He strode straight up to Vincenzo to whisper something in his ear. Whatever it was, the news made Il Gufo frown. He rose immediately from his seat. 'Forgive me,' he said, pushing himself away from the table. 'I need to talk with Miss Thornton.' He fixed her with a worried look.

Lizzie frowned, too, as he strode over to the door and opened it, motioning her to join him outside. Everyone's eyes lanced into her. Bewildered she rose, but Hugh tugged at her arm.

'What do you think you're . . .?' he began, clearly forgetting he no longer held any power over her. She simply glared at him and pulled herself free to follow Vincenzo out of the room.

'What is it?' Her mouth was dry with worry.

'I've just had bad news. It's Cristo.' His face was tense and drawn and he spoke softly as he raked his fingers through his hair.

'What's happened? He's not . . .?'

A quick shake of the head reassured Lizzie the boy was still alive, but Vincenzo's expression did not change. 'He's been arrested by the Nazis.'

'No!' Lizzie gasped. 'How? Why?'

'Lizzie, is everything all right?' Hugh had left the hall and was striding towards her.

'Please, Hugh. Leave us,' she snapped, turning her back on him.

'I would ask for privacy, if you please,' said Vincenzo.

'Now look here . . .' huffed Hugh.

'It's all right, Hugh,' Lizzie insisted.

'If you're sure . . .' he replied uneasily.

'I am,' she told him.

Vincenzo carried on. 'Cristo was supposed to deliver a message about a mission, but he was stopped and . . .'

Horror spread throughout Lizzie's body. 'I knew this would happen if he became a *staffetta*.' She shook her head. 'How could you let him?'

Vincenzo lifted his palms in a gesture of resignation. 'I couldn't stop him. He loved what he did.'

Lizzie hit her forehead with the heel of her hand. 'Where is he now?'

'In custody.'

Lizzie's eyes widened in horror. 'You mean he's in prison.'

Vincenzo nodded. 'In the Rocca.'

Lizzie recalled the medieval tower that dominated the town of Castell'Arquato. It was a notorious fascist prison and no place for any human, let alone an eleven-year-old boy. 'We must get him out of there. Does de Falco know?'

'No,' he told her, a dark shadow passing across his face. 'I don't believe so. But you're right we do have to get him out of there . . .' He hesitated. 'Before they shoot him.'

A terrible wail escaped Lizzie's lips. 'No! No, they can't!' she cried, knowing full well the Nazis could and did execute children. Cristo had to be rescued before he was hauled in front of a firing squad. 'We must go now!'

'And do what?' Vincenzo's palms were upturned. 'We can't just turn up at the prison and demand they release him.'

Lizzie acknowledged he was right, but her mind was so clouded with worry she couldn't think straight, imagining what hell Cristo must be going through right now.

Vincenzo began to pace, his fingers pressing his temples, then stopped dead and snapped his fingers. 'We could go . . .'

'Just a minute.' It was Hugh. Without warning he'd reappeared at Lizzie's side and had picked up on Vincenzo's intention to leave. 'You're not going anywhere without me.'

Vincenzo took a deep breath, his face wreathed in dislike for the Englishman.

'However we decide to spring Cristo from jail, we have to do it quickly, so we need to get going,' Lizzie intervened. 'We can talk through ideas on the way.'

'Very well,' the Italian conceded, clearly thinking on his feet.

225

'We'll need a driver, but first we have to get back to Castello di Castiglione.'

'Wait. To the count's estate? Why there?' asked Lizzie.

'There is a way we might be able to free Cristo,' said Vincenzo. 'I'll explain my idea as we go.'

Chapter 33

Vincenzo drove them through the back roads as the rising spring sun broke through rain clouds. Lizzie had seen him brief his men about the situation before setting off, but she was anxious to know more herself.

'Why are we going to Castello di Castiglione?' she pressed, sitting in the front passenger seat, while Hugh was relegated to the back. 'Where is de Falco now?'

'We think he's joined Il Duce in the north. Obviously, he's no idea Cristo's been working as a *staffetta*. We need to keep it that way for the time being. At least until I have posed as the furious father demanding the release of my son.'

Lizzie's mouth dropped open. 'Wait! Are you serious? You're going to pose as de Falco to get Cristo out of jail?'

Vincenzo took his eyes off the road for a second and shrugged. 'If you can think of anything better . . .'

Hugh, annoyed he wasn't in the front passenger seat, leaned forward. 'Lizzie, will you explain what's going on?' he fumed. He couldn't hide feeling threatened by Vincenzo's sudden re-appearance on the scene.

'Yes,' replied Lizzie. 'I will, although you're not going to like it.'

* * *

They left the car on the edge of the count's estate and set off on foot, about a two-kilometre walk through vineyards. Soon the ground started to rise towards the count's castle. Minutes later it emerged from trees some way ahead of them.

'This is madness,' muttered Hugh at Lizzie's side.

'What else can we do?'

Cristo's life was at stake. Every option had to be considered. The Nazis had no qualms about killing children and young people. They would make no exception for an eleven-year-old partisan messenger.

'Once this is over, we're out of here,' Hugh told her. 'I've just got to get back to my squadron.'

She did not reply.

Vincenzo led the way, a few paces ahead, unaware of what had happened between Lizzie and Hugh. Watching him, Lizzie was seized by a tremendous ache in her chest. Half her heart belonged here, with Cristo and Maria and Giuseppe. Leaving them would be like leaving her family behind. And as for Vincenzo – she would still give herself to him, body and soul, if he only asked her. Escaping from Italy, she knew, would tear her in two.

Up ahead Vincenzo stopped dead. Two fascist guards were posted at the main gates. He signalled to take cover.

'The wall round the back has collapsed,' Lizzie told him, remembering that she and Cristo used to climb over it to reach a path into the woods.

Keeping to the shadows, she led the way round the perimeter. Sure enough, a small section of the wall had fallen down, leaving just enough room for them to squeeze through the stones and enter the castle gardens.

'You go for the Lancia,' Vincenzo told Hugh in English, pointing to the garages where the vehicles were kept. Lizzie saw her ex-fiancé's expression. He wasn't used to taking orders, but she looked at him so sternly, he acquiesced without obvious complaint. 'You, come with me,' Vincenzo instructed Lizzie.

Skirting the pale walls that were glowing gold in the early morning sun, Lizzie reached the castle courtyard unnoticed. She peered in through the kitchen panes. She was relieved to see Maria in the kitchen, making pasta as she'd hoped. A moment later the cook turned and saw her, almost dropping her rolling pin in surprise. Lizzie put her finger to her lips then hurried to the kitchen door.

'Signorina Lizzie, it is so good to see you,' Maria whispered, hugging her tightly. 'But what are you doing here?'

It was hard to be the messenger. 'Have you not heard? Cristo has been arrested.'

The cook's hands flew up to her face. '*Santa Maria!*' she crossed herself. 'No! No, this cannot be. He told me he was staying with a friend.'

'They're holding him in the Rocca, and we're going to get him out,' said Lizzie, looking squarely at the cook. 'But we need your help.'

Maria nodded with terrified, wide eyes.

'I need some of the contessa's clothes,' Lizzie told her, looking down at her own dirty battledress top and torn trousers. 'A coat and shoes, if nothing else. Do you think you can do that?'

The cook nodded eagerly. 'All her clothes are still in her room. But . . .'

'But?' repeated Lizzie, sensing Maria's reluctance.

'The count.' She pointed up to the ceiling.

'He's here?' asked Lizzie incredulously. 'But he can't be.'

Maria nodded again. 'He came last night and later today he is being escorted to Salò in the north. It's where Il Duce has set up his new republic.'

Lizzie's chest tightened and she clenched her fists in thought. She'd been about to ask Maria to fetch one of the count's uniforms for Vincenzo, too. But that was now out of the question.

Just then Bianca, the tall housemaid from the Villa Martini, entered the kitchen, rubbing the sleep from her eyes. She'd evidently only just dragged herself out of bed.

Maria put her forefinger to her lips. 'Say nothing,' she instructed the girl when her eyes snapped open at the sight of Lizzie. 'She can be trusted,' the cook assured. 'Her brother is a partisan.' Then switching back to Bianca, she said, 'Go to the contessa's room and bring down some of her clothes and shoes for Miss Thornton.'

As the maid scurried off upstairs, Lizzie headed out of the kitchen. Her next stop was the count's study. She crossed the hallway and, certain she wasn't being watched, entered to make a beeline for de Falco's desk. The room smelt of cigar smoke. Half of last night's Havana lay in an ashtray. She needed papers; any official document that could be presented as proof of identity when they were challenged, as they surely would be, at the prison. She rummaged in one drawer. The search proved fruitless. Then another. Until on the fourth attempt she came across his fascist party membership card. On it was the count's personal details and his signature, but crucially no photograph. Slipping it into the top pocket of her jacket, she was just about to close the drawer and make her exit when a shadow fell across the desk. Her head jerked up. Count Antonio de Falco stood before her, a pistol pointing straight at her.

'Have you lost something, Miss Thornton?' His voice was cold.

Lizzie froze under his icy stare. 'Count de Falco. I was looking for something for Cristo,' she blurted, caught completely off guard.

'So, you know where my son is? I returned last night to find he'd gone missing.'

Her stomach flipped. The count must never uncover the secret – that in his absence his son had been working for the partisans.

'Well, Miss Thornton, what have you to say for yourself?' Impatience tinged his voice.

'I, well . . .' Lizzie's eyes dropped to the pistol. It took all her composure to remain calm when she knew de Falco could pull the trigger at any moment. But it took even more willpower not to cry out when she saw Vincenzo appear behind him in the study doorway. She tried to keep talking as she saw Vincenzo grab a bronze paperweight from a nearby bookshelf. A second later, it struck the back of de Falco's skull hard, and he fell unconscious to the floor. Lizzie rushed to his side to check for a pulse.

'Still alive,' she pronounced, leaving him sprawled on the ground.

Vincenzo nodded. 'You got the papers?'

'Yes,' was all she could manage through her shock as she watched Vincenzo start undressing the count. 'Help me,' he whispered, and, willing herself into action, she set to work unbuttoning the count's tunic as Vincenzo slid off the polished knee-boots.

They were close to each other; closer than they'd been in more than two years. Lizzie could feel the electricity fizzing around Vincenzo as he unbuckled the stricken count's belt. But then, as if sensing her gaze, he stopped and returned it. 'I've missed you,' he told her, his eyes piercing into her.

She didn't have to think about her reply. 'I've missed you, too.' Only a few inches separated their lips, and she felt Vincenzo's warm hand cup her face. She closed her eyes to await his kiss, but a shout from outside broke them apart. It was Hugh at the window.

'Someone's coming!'

'Let's get out of here!' said Vincenzo, gathering up the trousers, boots and jacket.

As they hurried from the study with the scavenged uniform, Bianca negotiated the stairs, her long legs bending under the bulk of a large bundle of clothes. Lizzie met her halfway to grab a heavy fur coat, and a few other items. Plumping a hat on her head, she ran out of the back door with Vincenzo to the Lancia. With its fascist pendant fluttering from the hood, it was waiting on the driveway, its engine revving. Hugh, wearing a chauffeur's cap, was at the wheel.

As soon as they were both inside, they ducked down, and the car accelerated up to the huge gates. It stopped for the guards to open them. Hugh kept his foot hovering over the accelerator,

231

ready to hit the floor just as soon as he could. Lizzie dreaded being stopped but the guards, assuming the chauffeur was leaving on official business, waved the car through without hesitation.

'Where to now?' asked Hugh, shifting the gears and flattening the pedal to the floor.

'To the Rocca. Castell'Arquato,' replied Vincenzo, righting himself in the back seat.

'To Cristo,' whispered Lizzie, now wearing the contessa's mink. The weather was too warm for a fur coat, but at least it meant that underneath it, no one could see she was shaking with fear.

Chapter 34

Speeding across the plain, rows of infant vines about to burst into bud on either side, Hugh grudgingly followed Vincenzo's instructions. He turned off the main road about two kilometres out of the town. In a quiet lane the Italian finished changing into the count's uniform. Lizzie, wreathed in the scent of the late contessa's perfume that lingered on the coat, examined her features in the car's rear-view mirror. She began to apply her lipstick.

'That perfume,' said Vincenzo, adjusting the buttons on de Falco's uniform jacket.

'What of it?' asked Lizzie, studying him closely as he sat beside her on the back seat.

'Nothing,' he replied, even though she could tell it seemed to stir something in him that he did not wish to share. Now that he was in uniform and with his dark hair slicked back with oil, she found Vincenzo's resemblance to the count quite unnerving.

Hugh craned his neck to catch Lizzie's reflection in the rear-view mirror. 'I hardly recognise you,' he said.

The fur coat and toque hat made her feel like someone else, too. For the past few months, she'd been a prisoner and a fugitive, but posing as Count de Falco's wife terrified her more than any of the partisan missions she'd undertaken. This was even more audacious. Or was it just plain insanity? One false move, one slip and their cover would be blown. There was only one way, she knew, that scenario would end.

The three-span bridge across the Arda was blocked by a checkpoint. The car was flagged down. The guards were Italian, not Nazis. Lizzie and Vincenzo, sitting side by side in the back seat, exchanged relieved looks. The town was under shared control. The red-and-black swastikas had once more been joined by the image of a bundle of sticks with an axe over it. Lizzie prayed the *fascista* were still in charge of the prison, too. Anyone was better than the Nazis.

'Straight on,' directed Vincenzo as the cobbled road rose through the town. The Lancia had to work hard as the gradient grew steeper, belching out leaden exhaust fumes as it squeezed through lanes that grew ever tighter approaching the old town. Then, without warning, Hugh swerved.

'Christ!' he cursed, as a small boy ran out in front of them. The tyres clipped the kerb as the child's mother yanked him out of harm's way just in time. The Lancia's sudden braking launched Lizzie sideways. A panicked breath escaped from her mouth, as she found herself pressed hard against Vincenzo. He held her for a moment until she righted herself once more, but it was enough to tell her what she needed to know.

A minute later the criss-cross gate of the portcullis came into view. It marked the start of the old town. Once they'd sped under it, the lanes narrowed even more, and the stone buildings crowded in on each other. Escape would be harder. The fear must've shown on Lizzie's face because the next thing she felt was a warm palm. Her eyes dipped to see Vincenzo's hand on hers, while his gaze remained straight ahead. Something stirred at his touch, and she trembled inside, but she left her hand where it was.

A few metres further up the cobbles the road forked left to open out in front of the main gates and the castle fortress loomed up ahead. Lizzie shivered. The thought of Cristo being held captive in the medieval tower filled her with outrage; the thought of him facing execution by firing squad, with terror.

Four soldiers in the dun-coloured uniform of the *fascisti* stood smoking in a huddle outside the makeshift guardhouse, their rifles slung over their shoulders. One of them threw his cigarette to the ground, stamped it out on the cobbles and marched out in front of the approaching limousine. The Lancia pulled up, but it was Vincenzo who wound down the rear window, flashing the stolen party card.

'Count Antonio de Falco wishes to see the prison governor,' he ordered. He sounded in full control.

The guard's eyes bulged. Instantly he stood to attention, his arm outstretched in a stiff salute.

'Excellency!' he cried.

He goose-stepped to the guardhouse to make a telephone call. A moment later a small, balding man emerged from an ornate building just outside the castle gates, shrugging on his uniform jacket, as if he had been caught napping. Vincenzo's intelligence was that the man was new to the job of prison governor. His predecessor been shot after a break-out. By all accounts his successor wasn't much better. Crucially, he had never met de Falco in person, although, of course his reputation as a powerful Mussolini loyalist preceded him.

As the governor strode towards the Lancia, he buttoned his tunic. 'Count de Falco. What an honour,' he greeted. He gave his jacket a final tug before lowering his head to look through the back window. The elaborate epaulettes on the count's uniform worked their magic. 'I am honoured, Your Excellency. How may I assist you?'

Vincenzo kept his cool. He turned to the man with a cold, hard look. 'I must inform you, you have made a terrible mistake.'

The official's Adam's apple bobbed in fear. 'A m-mistake, sir. Please, tell me what I have done, Excellency, so I can put it right.'

Vincenzo snorted through his nose like an angry bull. 'You are holding an eleven-year-old boy in your prison.'

The governor straightened and smirked as if he had personally bagged a trophy. 'Yes, sir. He is a *staffetta*. He was caught red-handed with a message for a partisan group.'

Vincenzo shook his head. 'You are mistaken. He is not and never will be a *staffetta*.'

The governor seemed deflated. His shoulders slumped. 'You can prove this, sir?'

'He is my son.'

The man's eyes widened once more, only this time he turned a distinct shade of grey as well.

'You will release him straight away,' commanded Vincenzo.

'Of course. Of course. I don't . . . I cannot . . .' the governor spluttered, his head dipping woodenly up and down like a puppet. 'Please, come this way, sir.' He barked orders to a waiting guard who sprinted to the main prison gates.

News that the child prisoner was Count de Falco's son ran ahead as rapidly as a telegram down a wire. It sent the *fascisti* into a frenzy. Footsteps quickened as gates were unlocked and bolts slid back. Then came the thunk of ancient keys protesting in rusty holes.

Danger cloaked the courtyard as Vincenzo and Lizzie left the Lancia. The governor, jabbering nervously, escorted them through the massive entrance, over weed-hemmed cobbles and into an ante room at the foot of the tower.

'You will wait here, please, Your Excellency,' said the little man. Two guards stood to attention before they were ordered up the stairs to fetch Cristo.

Left alone with the governor, Vincenzo took his chance. Hands behind his back and jaw jutting, he channelled Mussolini as he circled his anxious prey. 'Il Duce would be outraged if he were ever to hear of this,' he told him. 'He is close to the boy.'

Lizzie saw the governor swallow hard at this revelation. Vincenzo was putting on an award-winning performance. But she knew they were still not out of danger. She drew the edges of her mink coat round her, even though under her hat, she felt sweat prickle her scalp. She, on the other hand, did not need to put on an act. Her anguish was genuine; that of a mother fearing for the life of her young son.

The governor's eyes slid to Lizzie and saw her evident distress. 'Of course, sir. I appreciate your understanding. I will see to it that whoever is responsible is punished severely.'

Footsteps could soon be heard echoing down the mossy stairwell where walls dripped with water. A moment later, in walked a bewildered Cristo, his hands in shackles. He was flanked by the two guards. The moment he recognised Lizzie and Vincenzo he bounded towards them. Lizzie, too, rushed forward to hug the child. One of the guards unlocked the shackles and Cristo flung his arms around her.

'It's all right. You're safe now,' Lizzie whispered through her tears as he buried his head in the fur coat. 'Say nothing,' she whispered, bending low. 'Keep calm.'

'My sincere apologies, once again, Your Excellency,' said the governor, this time wringing his hands.

Vincenzo, instead of acknowledging the apology, looked past him. 'Arrest this man,' he ordered the guards.

The governor's jaw hit the floor. 'What? No. Please, sir . . . I . . .'

Vincenzo remained steely. 'You said yourself whoever was responsible for my son's detention should be severely punished.'

'No. I . . .'

And with those words and the governor's protests ringing in their ears, the three of them walked back calmly to the waiting limousine as soldiers moved in to arrest the hapless fascist.

The Lancia was facing downhill, its engine running as instructed. Under the watchful gaze of the guards, Lizzie shepherded Cristo into the car. 'You're safe now, my darling,' she repeated in his ear.

It was only when they'd settled themselves on the back seat, Cristo's curly head nestled against her like a frightened puppy,

237

that Lizzie heard a telephone ring in the guardhouse. A guard took the call and as soon as she saw his startled glance target the Lancia, she knew. The game was up.

'Hurry, Hugh. They know!' she cried.

'Let's get out of here,' yelled Vincenzo as Hugh put his foot down on the throttle and the Lancia shot off, gathering speed in a billow of black smoke and hurtling over the pitted cobbles. A sharp left turn took them down a narrow backstreet where a flower seller jumped for her life. The car bounced along, and Lizzie feared it might take off at any minute. Landing, it shaved the kerb and began fishtailing as Hugh wrestled with the steering wheel.

Vincenzo twisted round, eyes to the rear window, picturing guards rushing to their trucks by the prison. Orders would be bellowed, but right now it was looking as though they might just . . .

'Bloody hell!' yelled Hugh.

The first shot whistled past the Lancia, smashing a shop window, sending shards of glass shattering across the street. Then a second and a third.

'Get down,' screamed Vincenzo, throwing himself sideways on top of Lizzie, forcing her and Cristo to lower their heads and cower below window height.

The portcullis came into view, but on the other side of it two Germans leapt out onto the road. Hugh's pilot training kicked in and he instinctively drove towards them. Before they had time to aim, he'd forced them to dive out of the way. But it didn't stop them from firing their semiautomatics as he passed. Bullets were falling like rain. Harsh cracks sounded as two or three ricocheted off the bonnet. Hugh put his foot down, then came another hail. This time the right wing was clipped.

On the back seat Lizzie clung to Cristo. With each wrench of the wheel, they were tossed left and right. Throttle. Brake. Throttle. Brake. With every swerve, the child screamed, like a passenger on a fairground swing boat.

Vincenzo, daring to raise his gaze and look behind, saw guards huddle together then disperse, their rifles primed. 'Faster,' he yelled. 'Faster.'

The car continued to lurch and pitch through the back streets, only just avoiding a bent old woman. Up ahead lay the archway that marked the border between the old and new towns, the impossibly narrow lanes and the wider, smoother roads. Hugh's foot hit the throttle harder, but just as he did, a shower of bullets rained down from a balcony above. A shot shattered the rear window. Vincenzo flinched. Lizzie screamed as a thousand spears of glass burst through the air and a heavy weight fell against her. Only when she saw the spatters of blood on her fur coat did she realise Vincenzo was hit. Cristo screamed at the sight and struggled to sit up, but Lizzie gripped his shoulders down like a vice.

'Get down,' she snapped, at the same time trying to stem Vincenzo's blood with her scarf. Then to Hugh, 'He's been hit. Hurry, Hugh. Keep going.'

Another bullet shattered the Lancia's wing mirror as it continued to career down the street, heading for the bridge. Lizzie prayed the message from the prison hadn't been radioed down yet. At the checkpoint, the fascist guards were still milling around, shouldering their rifles. The car was gaining speed ahead of the bridge, but it clipped a dustbin, sending it flying and alerting the soldiers. Two of them took aim and began to fire as the Lancia powered past them.

'Keep going, Hugh. Faster!' she screamed, suddenly realising they were now being followed by a truck.

A bullet glanced off the windscreen, cracking it, but not penetrating the glass.

As Cristo cried hysterically, Lizzie cradled Vincenzo's head in her lap. Blood drenched her fur coat. It was streaming from below his peaked cap, as the car sped along the main road.

'Where now?' cried Hugh.

Lizzie had to think quickly. 'Franco's. We'll have to go back there.'

'What? The road's just a track,' he yelled, glancing up into his rear-view mirror. 'Besides, they're following us!'

'We'll have to ditch the car and go on foot.'

Both his hands left the wheel in anger, before he slammed them down again. 'You expect me to carry . . .'

A flash burst just as she spoke. It came from the verge. She ducked as something exploded a few metres behind their car. Hugh flinched but kept on driving. Whipping round, Lizzie realised someone had thrown a hand grenade onto the road in front of the truck in pursuit. Partisans. Amid the smoke and debris, the vehicle swerved and hit a tree. At the same time, up ahead, two armed men appeared on the road. Hugh slammed on the brakes and the car shuddered to a screeching halt.

'What the . . .?' Lizzie looked up to see the men approaching the car. It wasn't until one of them looked in through the window and she saw his green bandana. *Carlo.*

'Follow us, quick,' he shouted. He pointed to a waiting van up ahead that had just appeared from a side road.

'Il Gufo's hurt,' cried Lizzie, winding down the window.

Carlo looked inside again and to his horror saw Vincenzo lying prone across her. 'Quick!' He started running to the van and climbed in as it began moving off.

Hugh followed as the vehicle picked up speed and almost immediately turned off the main road into a farm drive, lined by trees on both sides. All the while Lizzie was watching out for Germans, but the road behind them was now impassable after the grenade attack.

The van came to a standstill outside a small house in a clearing. Carlo's wife and Ernesto were waiting, alongside Paulo and Pietro. The shattered windscreen of the limousine signalled there'd been trouble.

Carlo and the other partisan jumped out of the van. 'Quick,' he told his wife. 'Il Gufo is injured!'

Wasting no time, they flung open the car's back door to find Vincenzo slumped and bloodied leaning against Lizzie.

'Be careful,' she pleaded, as gently Carlo righted Il Gufo's body, and she tried to protect his head. Ernesto hooked his arms under Vincenzo's and lifted him out, while Pietro took his legs. Cristo, still in tears, was comforted by Paulo.

They laid Vincenzo on a bed inside and Lizzie knelt beside him. Carefully she eased off his cap.

'Send for the doctor,' Carlo ordered Pietro.

'It looks like he needs a priest, too,' muttered Paulo.

Lizzie heard the remark and knew what Paulo said could be right. Blood was still pouring from the wound. Ernesto handed her a towel and she pressed it to Vincenzo's head to stem the flow.

'Don't go, my love. Please don't die,' she whispered, realising that she'd been lying to herself for the past few months. Only now did she realise accepting Hugh's second proposal was a way of trying to banish Vincenzo from her life when he was the one she really loved with all her heart and soul.

Hugh arrived then. He'd driven the Lancia into the woods. Another partisan had been waiting to hide it under bracken and leaves, away from Nazi eyes.

'How is he?' he asked, approaching the bed.

Lizzie looked up at him, eyes brimming with tears. She shook her head.

'And you, darling?' Hugh rested his hand on her shoulder, and she winced at the same time swallowing down the cry that had been hovering in her throat.

'Don't worry about me,' she told him, trying to sound in control when all she really wanted to do was scream at the top of her voice. 'Perhaps you can get Cristo something to eat.' She bobbed her head to where the boy sat sobbing, cross-legged by Ernesto.

'Very well,' he mumbled, skulking off to the kitchen in search of food. Carlo clapped a comforting hand on Hugh's shoulder and left the room with him.

Vincenzo lay on his back, his face a bloodless white, his breath lengthening by the second. It was only because Lizzie watched his chest rise and fall that she knew he was still alive. The doctor could not come soon enough.

'Hold on, Vincenzo,' she whispered, taking his cold hand in hers. Looking around she saw Cristo, now wiping his eyes on his sleeve. He was so thin and drawn, but at least he was alive. Leaning close to Vincenzo's ear she said: 'Cristo is safe. You saved him and he wants to see you.'

It was then the miracle happened. At the mention of Cristo's name Vincenzo's eyelids fluttered. Lizzie gasped and leaned over him. 'You can hear me? Oh, thank God!' She craned her neck. 'Cristo,' she called softly. 'Cristo, come here.'

Bewildered and upset, the child hesitated for a moment, then scurried over to kneel by the bed.

'Say something,' pleaded Lizzie.

Cristo took Vincenzo's other hand. 'Signor,' he said softly. 'Signor Baldini. It's Cristo.'

Lizzie watched, wide-eyed, as Vincenzo seemed to lift his lips at the sound of Cristo's voice. 'Keep talking,' she urged the child.

'You saved me, Signor Baldini. They wanted to shoot me and . . .'

When Lizzie felt Vincenzo's hand twitch in hers, she instinctively squeezed it. 'He's safe,' she whispered, her heart aching as she spoke. His lips twitched again, then, not in a smile, but trying to form a word. A sound came out, but it was muffled, so Lizzie lowered an ear to his mouth to listen. When Vincenzo repeated what he'd just tried to say, the words sent a shock through her entire body. She jolted upright, unable to believe what she'd heard. But there was no mistaking the words Vincenzo had uttered. No room for doubt. He hadn't been faking his heart-felt fury when

242

he'd posed as the outraged de Falco demanding Cristo's release from the Rocca. Born on a laboured breath and mumbled in a tremulous voice, he had delivered a secret kept hidden for eleven years when he let loose two words to Lizzie.

'My son.'

Chapter 35

For a moment Lizzie was speechless. Could Vincenzo really be Cristo's father? Slowly the mist began to clear. The more she thought about it, the more it made sense; why he took the position of tutor at the Villa Martini, how he reacted to the lingering scent of the contessa's perfume, why he looked at Cristo the way he did sometimes, why there was such a bond between them. They were father and son. Vincenzo must have had an affair with de Falco's wife and Cristo was the result. But the clearer things became, the more questions were thrown into the air. Did de Falco know that Cristo wasn't his? Who else knew of the infidelity? Lizzie was still reeling from the revelation when in stomped a breathless Hugh. He was followed by Carlo and another man – a stranger with short, sandy hair, wearing a cravat at the neck of his battledress jacket. There was a neatness about him that made her think he might be English.

'Lizzie.' Hugh was excited, hurrying round to where she was kneeling by the bed.

'You are a doctor?' Lizzie asked in Italian, addressing the stranger.

Hugh picked up on the word *medico* and let out a laugh. 'No, no,' he said, shaking his head.

Lizzie frowned. 'Then who . . .?' Her eyes cast over the stranger.

'This is Lieutenant Kennard,' Hugh announced. 'He's come to help us.'

The officer, who Lizzie guessed was in his early twenties, leaned forward to shake her hand, but when he saw hers had blood on it, he withdrew awkwardly. 'Pleased to meet you, Miss Thornton,' he told her in a cut-glass English accent.

Hugh spoke quickly. 'Kennard's from the Rome Escape Line,' he told her, a broad grin splitting his face. His mood only irked Lizzie. It was inappropriate. She frowned.

'I don't understand,' she said. 'Why? How?' The lieutenant's arrival had taken her by surprise. There was so much going on in her head she was finding his sudden appearance confusing.

Hugh was still beaming and stroking his moustache vigorously. 'He's come to get us out of here. He's going to help us get home, Elizabeth.'

The words crashed into her skull and buffeted her brain. 'What? No!' she cried, leaping to her feet. 'I can't leave here. Not now. At least not until we know Signor Baldini will survive.' She pointed to Vincenzo, the blood-soaked towel on his head.

Hugh grimaced. He seemed stunned by her reaction. 'The doctor will be here soon, and he'll be fine,' he replied, dismissing the injury like it was a slight graze. 'This is our only chance, Elizabeth.'

'But we can't leave yet.' She threw a look at Cristo, now standing on the other side of the bed. 'And what about him?'

Hugh rolled his eyes. 'The boy's really not your concern anymore. There are people here who'll take care of him,' he shot back.

His remark stoked Lizzie's anger, making it flare to fury.

'How dare you say that about Cristo? He is my concern. Would you have let an eleven-year-old boy be shot by a firing squad?' She pointed at the bewildered child as his eyes darted from Lizzie to Hugh.

245

'Of course not,' he blustered, appearing to retreat under Lizzie's salvo. 'But if we stay here, we could end up in front of a firing squad ourselves. Don't you see?'

Lizzie's head jerked back as she looked heavenward in a silent prayer. With clenched fists, she replied through gritted teeth, 'My duty lies here, Hugh. Vincenzo needs me. Cristo needs me.' She fixed him with a glare.

'You're being preposterous, Elizabeth,' Hugh growled.

Following the ill-tempered spat, the English officer intervened. 'Sorry to interrupt, but I must point out that Flight Lieutenant Codrington is a serving member of His Majesty's Armed Forces, and his duty lies in returning to his squadron in the Royal Air Force.' He held up his hand. 'I have forged papers, bus tickets and cash here. For you both.'

A bolt of shock made Lizzie gasp as she switched back to Hugh. 'You planned this?' It was an accusation, not a question.

Hugh nodded. 'I told you about Kennard before. We'd already made contact over the winter. I didn't mention it again because I was afraid to get your hopes up. Tuffers and the others are already on their way back home.' Hugh's stern look drilled into her. 'You know you can't stay here. If the Nazis find you, you're as good as dead. Now, come with me. Please.' He held out his hand.

Before Lizzie could deliver another refusal, an elderly man in a Homburg hat, carrying a small case, appeared. 'Where is the patient?' he asked urgently.

'*Dottore* Gambetti,' Carlo greeted the elderly man, who'd just taken off his hat to reveal a shock of white hair.

Lizzie instantly recognised him as the man who'd treated Cristo's broken arm. She shifted to one side to allow him access to the bed.

'Thank God you're here, doctor,' she said.

'You have accident-prone friends,' he told her, drily, before rolling up his sleeves. He was soon at work, checking Vincenzo's pulse and heart, then examining the wound.

'What happened?'

'He was shot.'

The medic sucked through his teeth, then began to clean the wound. As he did so, Vincenzo started to move. His back arched and his breathing became laboured. Lizzie tried to calm him, taking his hand in hers.

'I'm here,' she soothed. 'And so is Dr Gambetti. You'll be more comfortable soon.' She switched back to see the doctor delving into his case. He brought out a hypodermic syringe and filled it from a vial. A few seconds after he'd delivered a sedative into his patient's vein, Vincenzo seemed to relax.

While Hugh and the other men were out of the room, Carlo's wife remained, working at her rosary beads. Cristo stayed at the foot of the bed, but the doctor was too preoccupied to notice him. Lizzie's whole body trembled as she awaited the verdict. She'd been chewing her lip and realised the coppery taste in her mouth was blood. 'Will he? Is he . . .?'

The doctor straightened his back and frowned. 'It's hard to tell until the swelling goes down a little.'

'But the bullet,' said Lizzie.

'Bullet?' repeated Gambetti, frowning. 'Ah, yes. You said he was shot, but I couldn't see a bullet in there. It looks like a flesh wound to me.'

Lizzie let out her pent-up breath and Carlo's wife crossed herself.

'A flesh wound. You mean he's going to be all right?'

The doctor shook his head as he finished bandaging the wound. 'He's lost a good deal of blood, but his chances of survival are greatly increased if there isn't a bullet lodged in his brain, obviously.'

A little later Carlo's wife accompanied Gambetti out of the room. Drawing Cristo to her, Lizzie kissed the top of his head and looked at Vincenzo. 'He's going to be all right,' she whispered, raising her eyes to the crucifix above the bed. 'I know he is.'

As if he'd heard her words, Vincenzo's eyelids began to flicker again. Lizzie leaned in and took his hand. To her delight, she felt him squeeze it and when she looked at his face, she saw his lips twitch in a smile.

'The doctor says it's a flesh wound,' she told him. 'You were lucky, this time.'

He licked his lips. 'Yes,' he whispered. 'Yes, I was, my love.'

'My love,' she repeated under her breath. He still loved her. She realised now he had all along. And she had never stopped loving him either, not deep down. She'd just tried to hide the way she felt because it hurt too much.

Vincenzo's voice trailed off and she thought he was about to sleep but then he seemed to rally. His eyes opened again. 'I want you . . . to do something for me.'

She squeezed his hand tighter. 'Anything. Anything, Vincenzo.' She curled her fingers round his hand.

'Go with the pilot.'

His request was met with silence at first, then outrage.

'What? No!' She retracted her hand and shook her head.

Vincenzo tried to focus on her through blurry eyes. 'You must escape, Lizzie.'

'Never. I will never leave you and Cristo,' she cried.

'It's your only chance. I beg you.'

More tears broke loose, only this time she was angry. Why would he tell her to go?

'But you need me, Vincenzo. Cristo, too.'

'We will be looked after,' he told her, his voice fading again. 'We are . . . there are trusted people who love us.'

She shook her head, trying to process what he'd just said. Was it true that he didn't need her? That Cristo didn't need her, too? When she stood upright again, her full heart felt so battered and bruised she thought it might burst. More tears spilled as she gazed on Vincenzo's peaceful face. He was drifting off to sleep.

Hugh returned at that moment to catch her staring at the bed. Without looking away she said, 'You must go without me, Hugh.'

He stopped abruptly just inside the threshold. 'What?'

She switched to him. 'You heard me.'

'Are you mad? No. No, I will not go without you, Elizabeth.' Cristo put his hand in hers then. 'I want you to stay, Miss Lizzie.'

She kissed the top of his head. 'Of course I will,' she replied.

But then she noticed the boy was shaking his head. 'I want you to stay but you have to go. What Signor Baldini said was right. We will be cared for here.' His large eyes settled on Carlo's wife. She held out her hand to him. 'You will be trapped if you stay here,' he told her. 'And if the Germans catch you, they will kill you.'

Lizzie didn't realise that Cristo had heard Vincenzo's words. Now he was echoing them. They were both telling her to leave, and she knew it was because they both loved her. But it was the toughest love of all. It was for her own safety.

The English lieutenant entered the room then.

'The bus leaves in less than twenty minutes,' Kennard interrupted. 'As I said, I have your papers here.' He waved a sheaf of documents in front of her.

'Elizabeth, please,' urged Hugh, putting his arm on her shoulder.

She shrugged his hand away to take Cristo in her arms. 'When this is all over,' she told him, 'I'll come back. I promise.' Looking into his huge brown eyes, she said, 'I know you'll look after Signor Baldini, because you are so strong and brave.' She straightened his shirt collar, as she bit back more tears. 'Take care, my dearest boy,' she whispered. Kissing him softly on the cheek, she prayed this would not be the last time she saw him; that she could be true to her word and return some day. Then turning, she leaned over the bed to take Vincenzo's hand one last time. It was warm against her skin. Her prayers had been answered. He seemed to be out of danger. At least this wound would not kill him. But then . . .

Outside the sound of someone running broke into her thoughts. A second later Carlo was at the door. 'Nazis! They're searching everywhere. Leave now!'

Cristo stood. 'Upstairs. The loft,' Carlo told him, pointing above.

And then, Hugh's pleas sounded in Lizzie's ears again. 'Elizabeth, for God's sake!'

'We need to go now,' urged Kennard, halfway out of the door.

In a fog of bitter sadness Lizzie kissed Vincenzo one last time. Even if they could never be together again, at least she could leave her love on his lips.

'*Arriverderci, caro mio,*' she whispered as Hugh yanked at her arm.

Chapter 36

The bus took them westward, through the mountains and along the Ligurian coast. It was packed with travellers; even luggage racks were fair game for the more agile passengers. For the first part of the journey Lizzie kept her eyes firmly on the window, afraid if she looked at Hugh, sitting at her side, her tears would flow again. She'd been forced to abandon the people she cared for most; torn away from them so quickly there hadn't been time for proper goodbyes.

Seeing her distress, Hugh reached across and held her hand and regarded her with such tenderness that she could no longer contain her tears. She was grieving the loss of loved ones who weren't dead. Or at least she prayed not, although for all she knew Vincenzo could well have fallen into Nazi hands already. The thought weighed heavy like a stone in her chest as her shoulders heaved in silent sobs.

Much to Lizzie's relief, many of the passengers disembarked at Parma. She and Hugh could speak more freely, even though it was hard above the noise of the bus's ancient engine.

As soon as they moved off again, out of the blue he said, 'Baldini.'

Lizzie's head jerked up.

He was stroking his moustache in thought and regarding her with a strange look. 'Is there . . .' He hesitated and Lizzie's pulse began to race. 'Is there anything I should know about you and him? It's obvious you two have history. And after he was shot, well, it seemed . . .' He cleared his throat. 'It would appear I would only ever have been second best.'

Lizzie appreciated how hurt Hugh must be feeling. He'd thought the sole reason she'd broke off their engagement was his behaviour during the disastrous mission that led to Cecilia's death. Now the truth was out. Vincenzo was the light in her life and had been for a long time. Despite his rejection of her when they were reunited at the farmhouse, and despite her agreeing to Hugh's proposal again, she had never stopped loving her Italian soulmate. Fearing he would die only confirmed to her that part of her heart would die with him. The plain fact of the matter was it was true. She did love Vincenzo and always would. If that meant Hugh abandoning her, then so be it. Somehow, she would survive, with or without him. She was no longer the woman who needed a man to make her complete. But if it meant they were to continue to the coast together, it would be on her terms. Whichever way she looked at it, she was dangling from a precipice by her fingernails. She had to cling on or face falling into a dark void.

'I'm sorry, Hugh. I don't think we would ever have made each other happy.'

She held out her other hand and touched his by way of an apology. To her surprise, he didn't withdraw. Instead, he concentrated on it in silence for what seemed an age, then said: 'I think you just need more time to come to terms with what's happened,' he told her with a tight smile.

It wasn't the reaction she'd expected. Did that mean he still didn't take her seriously? Had he not understood what she had just told him? She couldn't be sure, but she decided not to question him further. She was too emotionally exhausted. She rested her head on the back of the seat again and took a deep breath, not wanting to meet Hugh's gaze.

'Sometimes I think it would have been easier if I'd died when my plane was shot down,' he mumbled.

If his remark was intended to wound her, it did. But she wasn't going to rise to such cruel and unnecessary bait. She lifted her head again. 'Oh Hugh, you know that's not true, but if you want us to go our separate ways, then so be it. I don't want you to think you need to be my protector any longer.' It felt satisfying to get her feelings out into the open.

She saw his eyebrow arch. 'What sort of a man do you take me for?' There was an angry edge to his reply. 'An Englishman would never abandon a woman, let alone one he once thought would be his wife.'

He was needling her again, so she made her position plain. 'I don't want you to feel obliged to stay with me.'

Hugh huffed. 'Well, I do,' he told her. 'You wouldn't last five minutes on your own.'

She bit her lip, feeling her own anger surface once more and turned her head to stare – unseeing – out of the bus window.

Summer had finally arrived, and the weather was much warmer as the road left the mountains behind to skirt the shoreline. A carpet of deep blue unfurled before them as the Ligurian sea shimmered in the sunlight. This time, Lizzie did look at Hugh. They both smiled. It meant they were nearer to the Allies and to freedom, even though they were under no illusion that the rest of their journey would be easy.

The bus pulled up in a cloud of leaden smoke at the terminus in Genoa. Lizzie's stomach tightened. It was here they were to meet one of Lieutenant Kennard's contacts and give him a pre-arranged password. People swarmed forward like bees to greet loved ones and friends. There was much hand-waving and shouting under the watchful eyes of armed Nazi guards stationed by the entrance,

253

but when the reunions and the meeting and greeting had died down, there was still no sign of a contact. A few minutes later, when Lizzie had almost given up hope, a young man in a long white apron and cap, worn at a jaunty angle, approached them. He was dressed as a baker but when he delivered the coded message and Hugh replied with the password, they followed him to his van outside.

They were driven in silence to the outskirts of the town, then along the gentle curve of coast until they turned off up a smaller road. The hills here were terraced with vineyards and the vines were a vibrant green.

'What I wouldn't give for a glass of red right now,' remarked Hugh.

As they ascended into the foothills, the pot-holed lanes twisted into corkscrews and narrowed. Through tiny hamlets and past derelict farms, they went, gaining height the whole time. But although the little van coughed and spluttered, it proved a worthy match for the steep incline until they reached the end of the track. It just stopped. In the middle of nowhere.

'Someone will meet you here soon,' the driver told Lizzie.

'Here?' she repeated. 'But there's nobody . . .'

The driver leaned across her then to open the passenger door. '*Buona fortuna*,' he said.

'Now look here,' objected Hugh, reluctant to budge.

'Are you really that surprised?' Lizzie asked him, sliding out of the van. She opened the back doors to allow Hugh to exit before the van sped off the way it had come.

It seemed they were being abandoned; marooned on a high track, seemingly miles from anywhere. But barely had the cloud of dust from the retreating van settled, when they turned to see they were no longer alone. A leathery man with a cigarette wedged in the corner of his mouth was eyeing them suspiciously. To her alarm Lizzie noticed a pistol in his hand. It was trained on them.

'*Inglesi?*' he asked.

'*Si*,' said Lizzie.

'Password?' he asked in a thick accent.

Hugh gave it and the pistol was replaced into a holster. The contact seemed satisfied and beckoned them to follow him. By now it was getting dark, and the track wound into a wooded area. They walked on for another hour until finally they arrived at a dilapidated old farm building, its walls and roof smothered in ivy. The man nodded to the door which was falling off its hinges and Hugh managed to prise it open. Lizzie followed and blinking into the darkness was shocked to find they were not alone.

Half a dozen partisans sat round the embers of a log fire. As her eyes adjusted to the gloom, Lizzie noticed three of them were in uniform and three of them were in shabby labourers' clothes, but they all wore a distinctive red scarf knotted around their necks.

'Welcome. Welcome.' An older man with a paunch and a lazy right eye greeted them. A large revolver was stuck in his belt, and he walked with a swagger towards his visitors. But his smile was broad and, to Hugh's delight, he spoke a little English. 'You hungry? Yes?'

Over thin stew and hard biscuits Lizzie heard the men were members of the Garibaldi Brigade – communists – but they were working with the British. When it was her turn to put them in the picture, she recounted the raids carried out by Vincenzo's unit in Emilia-Romagna, and of course, their rescue of Cristo.

Immediately the leader's expression changed. 'We hear about that on radio,' he told her, his eyes alight. 'Il Gufo is a hero, yes?'

Lizzie's lips lifted into a smile. 'Yes. Yes, Il Gufo is a hero,' she agreed.

Chapter 37

Word came of the next rendezvous a week later. The partisans had moved from the old farmhouse because of reports of Germans combing the hills. While they trekked deeper into the mountains, they headed west. The weather was on their side. During the day the skies were an unbroken blue and at night the temperature was warm enough to sleep under the stars. With the fall of Rome to the Allies in early June, the mood had changed, too.

'We'll drive the Nazi bastards out before Christmas,' growled one of the older men as he cleaned his rifle.

The partisan unit was under instruction from the Rome Escape Line to deliver Lizzie and Hugh to a village about forty kilometres north up the coast. There they would meet with some other escapees and rendezvous with a Royal Navy submarine. A British agent was expected to arrive shortly to brief them.

That evening when they all gathered to eat, the leader approached Lizzie. She noticed the expression on his jowly face and didn't like it. He propped himself up against a stone ledge near where she sat. 'We hear news,' he told her in a low voice.

'What news?' said Lizzie, instinctively knowing whatever it was, it was bad.

'Il Gufo.'

Recognising the name, Hugh's head jerked up. Lizzie swallowed hard.

'Yes? What did you hear?' Her head was suddenly pounding.

The leader's mouth turned down at the edges.

'Please tell me.'

Since leaving Castell'Arquato, her every waking hour had been spent thinking about Vincenzo and Cristo. She'd been assured Vincenzo would recover. It was only a flesh wound, the doctor had said. *There was no bullet*, she reminded herself.

Still, the partisan looked grave. 'Il Gufo,' he said. Then in English, 'He dead.'

An invisible hand gripped Lizzie's neck, choking her. Barely able to breathe, she shook her head. 'No. No,' she spluttered. 'He can't be. You must be mistaken.'

'They say on radio,' the leader butted in, lifting both hands and showing his palms to the sky. 'The Germans came and . . .'

'I can't . . . No.' The blow winded Lizzie. She couldn't speak. Couldn't think. It was only a flesh wound, the doctor had said. *There was no bullet*, she reminded herself once more. The unexpected news plunged her into darkness. There must be a mistake.

Hugh, sitting beside her, twisted round. 'Elizabeth, I'm sorry.' Reaching out, he put a comforting arm around her. She was too numb to react to him. Too shocked. Nor did she hear him mumble, 'Too bad,' as he turned his head away.

Three days later the British Special Operations Executive officer arrived at the camp like a bullet. Short with dark hair, he could easily have been mistaken for an Italian. The partisans gave him a good welcome and he seemed popular with them. He spoke extremely quickly, as if each sentence could be his last. It was said he was constantly on the move, never remaining in the same place two days running in case of detection by the Germans.

In his very rapid delivery, he outlined a proposal to his eager audience, then Lizzie translated for Hugh. The plan was simple.

Rubber dinghies from a Royal Navy submarine were to land equipment at a suitable point on the coast at night. The exact date and location were still to be arranged. On their return journey the boats would take passengers – Lizzie, Hugh and any other Allies in the group.

'That sounds straightforward enough,' remarked Hugh when she told him.

Lizzie remained silent. She feared it would be anything but.

In the intense heat, the track rippled in front of Lizzie as she walked in heavy silence. The orders had come through the previous night, and they were on the move south. Her heart still ached with such a sense of loss that it alarmed her. The guilt had surfaced, too. If she'd stayed with Vincenzo, perhaps he wouldn't have died. Now she'd never hear his voice again or see his lips twitch into his enigmatic smile. She thought of Cristo, too, having to face the wrath of the count. She also recalled what Vincenzo muttered in one of his last breaths. 'My son.' Did he get a chance to tell Cristo he was his real father before he died?

'Look, Elizabeth.' Hugh's voice broke into her thoughts. 'The coast again.'

Five days into the journey, they stood on an outcrop, high up, just above the town of Bordighera, where the air was cooler. The piercing cry of an eagle ripped through the sky as it swooped overhead. The day was clear and below them lay the sea. A patrol boat, presumably German, cruised across the bay.

'Soon we'll be out there,' Hugh told her. When she didn't react, he turned and scolded her. 'Oh, do cheer up, will you?' She lifted her gaze and felt Hugh's rough fingers pinch her cheek. 'Let's see a smile on that pretty face of yours, eh?' he told her with a grin.

While Lizzie nodded, she couldn't manage a smile. Inside she was still numb. This was not how freedom was supposed to feel. If she'd opened wide her arms, she should have felt like the eagle overhead, lifted by the joy of the wind under her wings. But right

258

now, she knew she would drop like a stone if she'd tried to fly. All she could see was not the breathtakingly beautiful view of the coast, but Vincenzo's bloody head. Her thoughts took her to other dark places, too. She pictured Cecilia's corpse, Alberto's wife and child burned in their home, and Cristo's torment in shackles facing death by firing squad. All these tragedies now piled one on top of the other, like logs on a funeral pyre. If she'd loved Hugh, setting foot on French soil with him would be like lighting a match and setting fire to them all; making the horrors of the last few months go up in flames.

'Frightening, isn't it?' he remarked suddenly.

Lizzie frowned, unsure what he was referring to. Did he mean the sea crossing, the prospect of trying to get back to England through hostile territory, or just life in general? It was all so terrifying that if she gave it too much thought, she'd simply hurl herself off the cliff. But she didn't have to wait long before everything became clear.

'The future,' he said. 'Now that Baldini's gone and you have to leave the boy, what will you have in England?'

The sheer starkness of his remark shocked her, even though she had to admit what he said was true. She wasn't staring at a beautiful vista, but into a black void.

'I don't know,' she replied. Inside she felt she was shrivelling up, like a dying flower wilting in the heat.

'I mean what is there for you at home? What will you do? Where will you go?'

Vincenzo's loss had bandaged her from reality. She'd been so caught up in it she hadn't been able to see much beyond her immediate present. Hugh was only rubbing salt into a raw wound. 'Please don't ask me all these questions. I can't think about the future right now,' she replied with a shake of her head.

Hugh was silent for a moment, then inhaled loudly, as if an idea had just landed in his lap. 'My offer is still there you know. Once we get over there'– he nodded towards the French coast – 'it'll be our chance to begin again; to start anew as man and wife. All those plans. All those dreams.' His lips lifted in a smile. 'You know we could still make them happen.' He turned back to her then to catch a tear rolling down her cheek. 'Darling, you're crying,' he said, wiping it away with his forefinger. He put a comforting arm around her then and kissed her temple. She didn't shy from his touch, and when he stroked her hair, she let him. After the news of Vincenzo's death, she simply couldn't find the will to fight anymore.

Chapter 38

The closer they came to the coast, the heavier and more frequent the exchanges of heavy artillery fire. More Allied planes could be seen overhead as they arrived just north of the appointed rendezvous with the submarine. A group of about ten partisans would accompany them to the beach. Their job was to unload all the supplies sent by the sub, then see that Lizzie, Hugh and the other escapees who were yet to join them were sent back.

'So, nearly there,' said Hugh in a low voice as he and Lizzie sat huddled around a fire in yet another abandoned farmhouse. For the past ten days they'd been guided by a new company of partisans. Through the mountains the going had been tough. They'd rested during the day and trekked at night. Food hadn't been a problem thanks to Allied airdrops, but water was in short supply because high up in the hills, there were few streams.

'What I wouldn't give for a pint of bitter,' said Hugh wistfully. 'And a gin fizz for you, eh, darling?' He nudged her gently with his elbow.

Darling. He was calling her *darling* again, but she didn't protest. Three weeks had passed since they'd been told of Vincenzo's death and ever since, Hugh had been more attentive to her. She'd felt so wretched and alone that she hadn't fended him off. Her defences were down. No, more than that, they'd completely collapsed and been trampled underfoot.

The fire's glow threw long shadows against the stone wall of the farmhouse kitchen. Lizzie stared into the embers, still thinking of Vincenzo. The partisans were fetching supplies, so she found herself alone with Hugh.

'You really are very beautiful,' he whispered, drawing her towards him.

This time she felt herself stiffen. He sensed her reluctance to his touch and gave an odd little laugh. 'You know we were meant to be together,' he told her. 'It's only a matter of time before you say yes to me again.'

Only a few weeks back she would have taken his words and thrown them into the fire right there and then. She would have let them go up in smoke, along with any notion Hugh still harboured of marrying her. But she did not. Tragedy and despair had worn her down to the ground so that instead of berating him for his arrogance, she remained silent. She simply shrugged as if she was accepting the inevitable: that after Vincenzo her own happiness would be as far off as the White Cliffs of Dover were at that moment. But just as Hugh was about to kiss her, they both heard footsteps at the doorway. Hugh pulled back as the commander of the new unit approached. Il Ciclone was a lawyer in civilian life, with a bald head as brown as a hazelnut and an easy smile.

'Please,' he said in English. 'I am about to make an announcement.'

The landings, he told the gathered unit, were on schedule. Intelligence suggested some German units would be in the area, although the beach was still clear. A few minutes later, under cover of darkness, everyone prepared themselves to move off. Lizzie packed in a daze, still too upset to make small talk with Hugh. Now he believed he was in with a chance of wooing her back, he'd resumed his campaign. He even volunteered to carry her canvas bag for her. She declined.

They'd only been going about an hour when, at a point where two tracks converged the unit was joined by another, smaller one, consisting of five men and two women. Under cover of some nearby trees, the commander gave them all a briefing in Italian.

Lizzie looked up at the moon as they filed out of the wood and began the steep descent towards the coast. It was half-hidden by clouds that kept scudding across it, blown by a stiff breeze. Darkness, she knew, might be their only protection as they made their way to the beach. The route had been carefully chosen and sentries were posted in advance to give early warnings, if necessary. But they made it to the coastal town without incident.

'Now for the hard part,' said one of the women to Lizzie with a smile. 'I'm Ada,' she said. She was in her mid-twenties, Lizzie guessed, with cropped blonde hair and a dark mole on her cheek.

'I'm Lizzie, battle name Rosa, and he is Hugh,' said Lizzie.

'You two are together?' the other girl asked. She was younger than Ada and her dark, curly hair was tamed by a bandana. She had an air of recklessness about her that came with her youth. 'I'm Rita, by the way.'

'Hello, Rita,' said Lizzie. 'Together? It's complicated,' she replied with a shake of her head. Hugh was walking a little way ahead.

'He is very handsome,' said Rita, flashing her dark eyes at Hugh. 'He is a pilot, yes?'

Lizzie nodded. 'He wants to rejoin his squadron and carry on fighting.'

'Of course,' agreed Ada. She was tall and slender, and her rifle was slung over her shoulder like a fashion accessory. 'We all want to carry on fighting. It's our futures that are at stake.'

'You're right,' agreed Lizzie. 'But what you do still takes courage. I think you're very brave.'

Ada shrugged. 'Brave or foolish?'

The question was left hanging in the air.

They reached a little ridge and could just about make out the houses and shops below. Lizzie counted the number of vehicles, wheezing trucks, throbbing motorcycles and the occasional staff car. Not impossible to cross without being seen, but not easy either. They organised themselves into small groups and waited for lulls in the traffic before they ran across the highway when a sentry signalled the all-clear.

'Now just the railway line,' said Hugh, taking Lizzie by the hand.

They skipped over the iron rails then together scrambled down a slope to the beach. The wind seemed to have dropped and all they could hear apart from the low rumble of trucks on the main road behind them was the lapping of the waves on the shore. Lizzie squinted at her watch. It was nearly midnight, the time of the rendezvous.

'Not long now,' she whispered to Ada, crouching in bushes a few metres from the water's edge.

Ada was the signal operator. She lit her lamp, and, at exactly midnight, she pointed it out to sea to begin signalling to the submarine everyone prayed was just off the shore. But as the minutes passed, and no further noises were detected, a current of unease moved through the partisans. A dozen pairs of eyes scanned the bay for any incoming boats, but ahead lay only an inky void. No one said anything but Lizzie watched the smudged outline of men in the shadows, shifting their weight and shaking their heads, when, from out of the black, came the sound of a ship's engine.

Lizzie looked at Ada as she redoubled her signalling, but then . . . the gates of hell opened. Flares rocketed into the sky lighting up the beach as if it was day.

'Get down!' shouted the commander and Lizzie and Hugh flattened themselves on the shingle as the firing started. Gun shots tore through the air, mercifully not directed onto the beach but out at sea.

For the next ten minutes the whole unit remained frozen to the spot, not daring to move as the barrage continued firing on some unseen target out in the bay. But then it stopped as soon

264

as it had begun, and an eerie silence fell upon the beach. The waves could be heard once again, gently lapping the shore as if nothing had happened.

'They knew about the sub,' Hugh said, pausing for breath as they retraced their steps back up the hillside. For the past two hours hardly anyone had spoken, as if they'd all been stunned into silence, aware they were lucky to escape with their lives. The Germans must have known something was happening, if not exactly what. The hillside would be crawling with soldiers. They could even be lying in wait to ambush their group at any moment. Not daring to return to their farmhouse base, they trekked to another derelict summer lodge higher up the mountainside and reached it just as dawn broke over the high peaks.

Il Ciclone was in a dark mood. He stood looking out over the valley, his hands behind his back, deep in thought. Lizzie watched as his second in command approached and the two men leaned in towards each other. She could guess what they were saying. The shocking truth was, there was a traitor in their midst. There had to be. How else would the Germans have known about the rendezvous? As reality dawned along with the day, a cloud of suspicion began to settle on the unit like fog. No one dared say a word and they were all told to stay close to camp. No one was allowed to leave under pain of being shot until Il Ciclone had decided their next move.

'Who could it be?' asked Hugh, twiddling his thumbs as he propped his head on his rucksack. He was trying to rest in the shade as they waited for news. Lizzie sat beside him, watching him silently and realising she'd allowed herself to fall into a trap. What could she have been thinking? She wasn't. That was the trouble. She'd been so concentrated on Vincenzo and on Cristo that she'd allowed herself to be swept away once again on Hugh's relentless tide. She hadn't possessed the strength to battle his unremitting current, but now she could take courage from the other women; from Ada and Rita.

'The traitor?' she replied, adding sarcastically, 'I've no idea. I'm only a woman.'

Hugh grunted and ignored her. 'All I know is, I wouldn't like to be them when the chief finds out,' he said.

Lizzie understood the commander was making enquiries as they spoke. All day long he'd been summoning partisans individually to interrogate them about the events leading up to the beach attack. Someone had to know the truth. Someone had to be a traitor.

As the sun began to drop slowly behind the jagged mountains Lizzie joined Ada and Rita to cook dinner over the makeshift range. The packages from an air drop contained rice and salt, and five rabbits were gutted for a stew. That evening, as they put the finishing touches to the meal, Lizzie noticed the other women were in a sombre mood, too.

'They think it was me,' confided Ada. She sat and watched Rita stir the stew. Lizzie noticed her skin was a pearly grey.

Lizzie was shocked. 'What makes you say that?'

The signal operator shrugged. 'The way the chief looks at me. I only joined three weeks ago. He's doesn't trust me.'

'How can he not trust you?' protested Lizzie.

Ada shook her head. 'Men do not trust women, Rosa. We are easy targets,' she replied wearily, glancing out of the paneless window. Beads of sweat had gathered on her forehead, and she mopped them away with a handkerchief.

'Are you all right?' asked Lizzie.

At that moment Ada leapt up and made a dash for the door. A second later a retching sound was heard. Lizzie looked at Rita, but the younger girl returned to the stew without a word.

The men had all gathered around in a circle a few metres away. Seated on the ground, they listened to their commander. It seemed the women had been excluded from what he had to tell them. Lizzie could see them through the window and bristled at the sight.

When Ada returned, wiping her mouth, Rita didn't even look up. It was as if her friend's vomiting was completely normal. Lizzie didn't remark either. Instead, she continued her original line of questioning, as Rita added more herbs to the stew.

'But you must have an alibi, Ada?' she said tetchily.

'We have been at each other's side all the time, but an alibi is not proof,' she came back. 'They probably suspect both of us,' she said, looking at Rita.

'Surely not!' Lizzie was growing angrier by the second.

'I'm a signal operator,' Ada pointed out. 'I could easily have sent a message to the Germans.'

'Why would they suspect you of doing that?' asked Lizzie, horrified.

'That's easy,' interrupted Rita. 'Women are to blame for tempting Adam in the Garden of Eden. Everything bad that happens, happens because of us.'

Lizzie shook her head. 'I can't believe they'd accuse either of you.' She comforted herself with the thought that Il Ciclone was a lawyer and would judge fairly. 'As soon as the investigation is finished, hopefully we'll know the truth.'

Supper was eaten in an ominous silence. Normally the men would talk and joke among themselves and sometimes sing partisan songs, but tonight Lizzie sensed the air was thick with tension. She sat with Ada and Rita, away from Hugh, making a show of sisterly solidarity. Oddly Hugh hadn't encouraged her to sit with him as she usually did. She wondered what he meant by distancing himself from her.

After the food, the men went their separate ways; some bedded down for the night; in the open or inside the lodge, while others chatted. No mention was made of a second attempt to reach the coast. Lizzie supposed it would be at least a few more days before everything could be rearranged.

'I'm going to turn in, Hugh,' she called as she headed for the lodge. They were sleeping in the same hut, but no longer side by side. The female partisans had retired to an adjacent, smaller shepherd's shelter. But Hugh seemed reticent.

'We've got a game of cards on,' he told her, even though she'd never known him join in with the partisans before.

'Very well,' she replied with a nod, trying to sound accepting. She looked over at the shelter as she walked back to the lodge. The women would have bedded down in the hay for the night. She hoped they slept well. She knew she wouldn't.

Chapter 39

The August morning dawned clear and bright, but Lizzie's sleep had been fitful. Not only was the heat still almost unbearable, the sound of distant gunfire had also kept her awake. They were tantalisingly near France, but the border also formed the German line, and the Nazis were well dug in, with outposts and guards at all strategic points. Rumour had it the Allies were making great progress. Ports, docks and bridges were being bombed ahead of a possible landing on the French Riviera. The sounds of war were all around, but then there'd been a couple of gunshots closer to home. They'd come cracking through the night air so close that Lizzie had bolted upright, fearing snipers nearby.

'Hugh. Gunfire!' she'd called out. She could tell from his reaction he hadn't been asleep.

'Only the partisans bagging rabbits,' he'd assured her. 'Not to worry. Go back to sleep.'

Lizzie found it hard. From now on, she knew, they would be playing the waiting game. Yesterday's aborted operation not only meant that she and Hugh were still stranded, but it also left the partisans without vital supplies of equipment and food.

Later that morning, when she was brewing morning coffee

from ground chestnuts on a primus stove in the lodge, Lizzie made a suggestion.

'Maybe we ought to try something different.'

'Such as?' asked Hugh.

'A boat, perhaps.'

'That's just plain silly,' came his swift reply, followed by a hasty, 'I'm sorry. I didn't mean . . .' when he caught her wounded expression. 'The problem is Jerry has ordered all small boats to be confiscated or ordered inland. They're dashed hard to come by.' He huffed. 'Besides, where could we go? Corsica's the nearest friendly place, but even then, it's over a hundred miles away.'

Lizzie thought for a moment as she poured pale liquid into an enamel mug. 'How about an outboard motor?' She handed coffee to Hugh.

'And how would we get one of those?'

She hated to admit it, but their situation was looking increasingly bleak. There was nothing for it but to sit tight for the moment and pray the Allied forces would make a breakthrough very soon.

As more partisans appeared from various bushes and shelters around them that morning, Lizzie wondered why Ada and Rita hadn't surfaced yet. She decided to visit the barn where they'd spent the night.

'Where are you going?' asked Hugh when she made a move.

'I'm going to tell the girls I've made what passes for coffee,' she told him lightly.

Hugh frowned and his hand flew up to his moustache. 'Arrgh,' he grunted. 'I wouldn't do that if I were you.'

Lizzie laughed. 'Whyever not?'

'Let them have a lie-in,' he told her with a wink.

Lizzie frowned. Was Hugh really implying that they were sleeping with other partisans – other men?

'Oh,' was all she said, agreeing that perhaps they might appreciate their privacy.

It was much later on that day when all the partisans came together to eat that Lizzie noticed Rita for the first time. She was sitting a little apart from the rest of them, having refused food. When Lizzie approached her and she looked up, it was obvious she'd been crying.

'What's wrong? Where's Ada?' she asked, sitting down beside her.

Rita said nothing but shook her head, then rose and stormed off in tears.

Lizzie turned horrified towards the men who'd been watching the encounter. 'What did I say?' she mumbled to herself.

The other partisans looked at each other conspiratorially. The Americans looked away. But no one spoke until, Hugh, eyes sliding awkwardly left to right, said ominously, 'I need a word with you, Elizabeth.'

He took her aside, thrust one hand in his pocket and began to stroke his moustache vigorously. 'There's something,' he began, turning and cupping his hand round the back of his neck. 'There's something you need to know.'

'It's about Ada, isn't it?' she guessed. 'Where is she?'

Her question was met with a sickening silence. Hugh could barely bring himself to look at her, but when he did, she saw tears in his eyes. Then she remembered the shots she'd heard in the night. They'd been troubling her all day; worming away. Something, she'd suspected, wasn't right. The mission had been disrupted by the Germans. Someone had tipped them off. There had to a spy in their midst, but Il Ciclone's investigation was dragging on. Lizzie frowned, and as she frowned another thought prompted a shiver. Could he have reached a conclusion and meted out a punishment already? Had he pronounced a verdict without telling the women?

'Oh, no. No, they didn't. They couldn't! No!' Lurching forward she pummelled Hugh's chest with her fists in fury. 'They had no proof. They had no proof.'

271

Hugh grabbed her by the wrists. 'It's war, Elizabeth. You don't need proof. Suspicion is enough.'

She looked up and made an odd sort of growling sound that came from somewhere deep inside, then punched him once more on the chest before thundering off.

'Where are you going?' he called after her.

'To see Rita,' she shouted back.

Lizzie found the partisan sitting on a rock, looking out to sea, tears streaming down her face. Without saying anything she put her arms round her and both women remained for a long time, simply holding each other.

Rita broke the silence. 'It wasn't her. I know it wasn't.'

'Of course it wasn't, but can you prove it?' asked Lizzie, searching the girl's tear-stained face and sensing she was holding something back.

Wiping away tears, Rita looked at Lizzie and said, 'She was pregnant.'

The news stunned Lizzie at first, then she recalled how Ada had looked unwell and vomited the evening before. In her own mind, she'd dismissed it as a stomach bug, a regular hazard of partisan life. She hadn't wanted to pry. Maybe she should have.

'Do you know . . .?'

Rita sighed. 'She had a boyfriend who lived in her village. When she told him she was joining the partisans he got angry. He tried to stop her, but when she said she'd made up her mind, he . . .'

'Oh God,' mumbled Lizzie.

'About two weeks ago, she started throwing up. She had to dash off sometimes. The men saw she was acting strangely.'

'And they started to suspect her.'

Rita nodded.

'And when the mission went wrong, they needed someone to blame, so they blamed her.'

Lizzie knew when a woman was tried by a court of prejudiced men, there could only be one outcome. If Vincenzo had been in charge, fairness would have been his priority. He would never have sanctioned an execution on such flimsy grounds. If he couldn't be there, maybe it was time she fulfilled his legacy. What she was about to do, she would do in his name. Reaching out to Rita again she said, 'I am so, so sorry.' She laid her hand on her arm. 'Will you tell Il Ciclone?'

The girl shrugged. 'He wouldn't believe me. No one would. They'd say I was just making up an excuse for her.'

Slowly Lizzie started to shake her head, unable to believe what she was hearing. Rita wasn't even going to protest about her friend's shooting. She'd already decided there was no point. She'd surrendered before she'd even aimed her rifle. But Lizzie wasn't ready to wave a white flag. From deep inside her a rage welled up. It had been simmering before; a sense that women were second class, never to be taken seriously. Hugh, Count de Falco and now these partisans had all regarded her as beneath them merely because of her sex. Outwardly she had tolerated such attitudes, not wishing to be a nuisance, or regarded as difficult. Since news of Vincenzo's death she'd capped her feelings; even submitting to Hugh's advances. But now Ada's execution caused her emotions to boil up inside her. Ada's death was murder. Cold-blooded murder. She could not stand by and let it pass.

'Where are you going?' cried Rita as Lizzie stalked towards the main camp.

Lizzie turned. 'Someone has got to get justice for Ada,' she protested. 'They've executed an innocent woman without any evidence. They cannot get away with this.' And with that she broke out into a run towards the farmhouse, powered by her own rising fury.

Il Ciclone was stooping over a map on an old table when Lizzie tore inside. One of the armed partisans barred her way and thrust his rifle in her chest when she called the commander's name, but Il Ciclone waved her through.

'What have you done?' she cried. She glared at the other four men in the room. 'What have you done?'

'Leave us,' the commander told his men with a nod.

'But Il Ciclone,' protested Roberto, one of the bulkier partisans with a goatee who'd been eager to exclude Lizzie. 'This English . . .'

'Go,' snapped the lawyer. His eyes met Lizzie's across the room. Her chest was still heaving from running and her arms were rigid by her sides as she tried to rein in her anger enough to collect her thoughts.

'If this is about Ada . . .' he began.

But that was as far as he got.

'Of course this is about Ada,' cried Lizzie. 'An innocent woman is dead – shot by your men – and you treat it like was a complaint over food rations. Do you not understand that Ada was murdered? She wasn't even put on trial. How could you, a lawyer, have let that happen?'

He puffed out his chest to meet her challenge. 'I asked my men.'

She narrowed her eyes in contempt. 'You asked your men? Since when has rumour and prejudice been the basis for a fair judicial system?'

Il Ciclone floundered for a defence. 'They said she was always going off into the bushes. Disappearing for minutes on end. She could have been sending radio messages.'

Lizzie coughed out a mocking laugh. 'She was pregnant, Il Ciclone. She was being sick.'

But instead of making him relent, the news seemed to embolden the commander. 'So, she was a whore!'

Lizzie instinctively tugged at her hair at the accusation, as if being pregnant out of wedlock was a justification for Ada's death. 'She was raped, Il Ciclone. Raped when she told her boyfriend she wanted to leave her village and join the partisans.'

At last the revelation seemed to deflate him. 'I . . . I didn't know. No one . . .'

'No one knew, apart from Rita. So you based your judgement

274

on flimsy evidence and allowed your men to dispense Mafia justice. Rita says two of them came in the middle of the night and claimed you wanted to speak to her. Ada went to her death because she thought she was being summoned by her commanding officer. Does that make you proud, Il Ciclone?'

The lawyer was grimacing, and unable to meet Lizzie's damning gaze.

'Does it?' she repeated, the hot fire of righteousness burning inside her.

He shook his head, and wrung his hands, until he admitted grudgingly, 'Perhaps I was too hasty. My decision—'

'Your decision was wrong,' Lizzie cut in. 'You sanctioned cold-blooded murder.'

His head jerked up and he lifted his palms heavenwards in a shrug. 'We are at war,' he protested.

'We are at war,' Lizzie chanted mockingly. 'How many times have I heard that excuse? Perhaps we *are* at war, but afterwards, when this is all over and the Allies have won, there will be a reckoning, Il Ciclone, and the daughters of Italy will want justice, believe me.'

Lizzie returned to Rita a few minutes later, kicking the stump of a dead tree as she approached. The flames of her anger may have died down, but they were still smouldering and now tears came to dampen the embers. She sat with her head in her hands on a nearby rock until Rita moved closer to her and reached out to hold her hand.

'Thank you.' The girl's eyes were still glassy. 'I heard. You spoke the truth. Il Ciclone needed to hear it.'

Lizzie looked up and forced a smile. 'But was he listening?'

'If we speak loud enough, the men will have to listen to us,' Rita replied.

Sighing deeply, Lizzie nodded slowly, hoping what her friend said was right. 'So, what will you do now?' she asked.

Rita sniffed and crossed her legs in front of her. 'I go on, just like Ada would want me to.'

Lizzie squeezed her arm. 'Yes, we must all go on,' she replied, knowing that somehow, she needed to find the strength to do just that. With Vincenzo gone there seemed little point in carrying on. But now Cristo would be her inspiration. She would return and be with him again. One day.

From then on, the mood in the camp turned. News of the Allied landings in Cannes and Saint-Tropez had brought momentary joy the other day. But now, after Ada's execution, suspicion and recrimination lingered as doubts about her guilt set in. It was as if someone had laid steel traps, and everyone was waiting to see who'd be the one to set them off. Ada may be dead, but she'd been sentenced by the court of men's prejudice. Now, after Lizzie's intervention, it seemed the men themselves had realised their grievous mistake, only it was too late. There were no guarantees the traitor, if there was one, wasn't still in their midst as they waited for more orders.

Lizzie spent more time with Rita, apart from the men during the day. Hugh came calling, but he knew better than to try to persuade her to join him. The battle lines had been drawn.

'I'm so sorry,' he told her the following day when he stopped by the lodge.

'Did you know, Hugh?' Lizzie challenged him. 'Did you know they intended to kill her? Is that why you stayed playing cards that night? Is that why you made some excuse when I was woken by gunshot?'

His head dropped. He couldn't bear to look at her, let alone answer her questions.

'Then you are as guilty as the rest of them,' she growled between clenched teeth.

'Now hang on, Elizabeth . . .' he protested.

But Lizzie was in no mood for his excuses. 'Go back to your friends, Hugh. I can't bear to look at you,' she shouted through the door she'd just slammed in his face. She could no longer carry on with this charade. How could she when the man who'd tried to exploit her grief to make her agree to marry him was complicit in the murder of another woman she regarded as a friend?

'Wait? What do you mean? What about us?' He sounded shocked.

Lizzie flung the door open wide. 'There is no *us*, Hugh.'

Hugh's grimace suddenly transformed into a smile. 'You're joking, yes? You don't really mean that. You're just upset about that girl.'

'Don't tell me what I mean, or what I feel, Hugh. It won't work anymore,' she fumed, about to slam the door in his face once more.

'Wait, please. Elizabeth, listen to me!'

'No, Hugh. I've done enough listening.' The storm that had been gathering inside her now erupted. When he'd talked of the future and she'd allowed him to put his arms around her once more, he'd caught her at her lowest ebb. She'd been vulnerable, given up the fight, and he'd tried to take advantage of her weakness by dangling the prospect of marriage in front of her during her bleakest hour. Now she saw clearly she would be the one to suffer if she had agreed to stay with him. 'It's your turn to listen to me for a change. I will come to France with you, but not to marry you. Once we are on Allied territory, we must go our separate ways.' And with those words, she hurled the door shut. This time there'd be no going back.

For the next few days, Lizzie hardly saw Hugh. In fact, she hardly saw any of the men at all. She and Rita kept themselves apart until one evening, the following week, Il Ciclone asked them to join the others. He was offering an olive branch. Lizzie had already realised she and Rita couldn't go on putting up barriers between them, so Lizzie took it. As the two women approached the meeting, the men, who were seated in a circle around Il Ciclone, rose, one by one. Puzzled, Lizzie looked at Rita, but she seemed equally confused, then Hugh started to clap. Slowly at first, before he was joined by the others. It was their way of welcoming the women's return. They were showing their respect for them. It couldn't bring Ada back, but Lizzie and Rita acknowledged the gesture with good grace. It was the first step on the road to reconciliation.

As soon as everyone was sitting, Il Ciclone made his announcement. News had just come over the radio.

'Allied forces have landed on the south coast of France,' he declared.

A spontaneous roar went up, followed immediately by a silence as everyone feared they might have alerted any nearby Germans. Thankfully they hadn't.

'What do we do now?' asked Roberto, the strapping young man with the goatee.

'We wait for our orders,' replied Il Ciclone. 'The coast is a dangerous place right now, so we hold back until it's secured.'

While the news was positive, it put Hugh in a disgruntled mood. 'More delay,' he mumbled later that evening. They were sitting on a rocky outcrop where a breeze from the coast cooled the air. The sun was a huge orange orb dropping slowly towards the horizon.

'We have to be patient,' said Lizzie. 'Conditions have to be right.'

'Yes, I suppose now the Allies have landed, we are in with a much better chance.' He smiled at her, almost as if everything had gone back to how it was before Ada's execution. To her astonishment, he even patted her hand.

It was then he turned to her with a proposition. 'I like your idea of the boat.'

Lizzie raised a brow. Usually, Hugh claimed her ideas as his own if he thought they were any good. 'Really?'

'Yes, really, Elizabeth. You're full of good ideas.' *Was he still trying to appease her, after everything she'd said?*

When Hugh put the proposal of the rowboat to Il Ciclone the

next day, the scheme was dismissed as far too risky. No immediate action was taken. Besides, they had no time to plan such an operation. They needed to move again.

Chapter 40

The cave they found for the night was cramped but at least Lizzie felt safer than if they'd slept outdoors. Their small unit had now been joined by another which included two American soldiers who, like her and Hugh had been on the run from the Nazis for months. The wiry, livelier one who seemed to have a constant smile on his face was called Ronnie, while the other, more studious one, was a Jew named Hertz.

A fire was lit away from the mouth of the cave where they could heat up some soup the partisans had brought with them. The Americans, both from Texas, had had a hard time of it and lost two of their fellow infantrymen on the way, gunned down during one of the brutal Nazi mountain raids. They'd escaped by diving into a pig pen and the smell of manure still lingered on their uniforms. Ordinarily they would have been cheerful company, but Lizzie kept her distance. The day when she would have to leave her beloved Italy – and, with it, memories of Vincenzo and Cristo – was drawing ever nearer. She wanted to be alone with her thoughts and still didn't feel she could talk about how she was feeling. It was as if she were drowning, but she didn't want to shout for help. Right now, she didn't want to be saved. She sat apart from the men, on her own towards the back of the cave. She wouldn't eat, although she still listened in on their conversation.

Over the meagre dinner Hugh asked, 'Where have you come from?'

'Both got captured in Tunis and sent to a camp up in Verona,' explained Ronnie. 'Come the Armistice we got out and walked to a small town where they fed us and dyed our uniforms. Then they put us in touch with these crazy guys and we've been on the road, dodging the Nazis for the past twelve months.'

'Partisans,' corrected Lizzie, breaking her silence. 'The crazy guys. You mean partisans.'

Ronnie turned to look at her. 'Sure do, missie. Better bunch of men you'd be hard to find.'

Hugh looked annoyed. 'Not certain about that,' he muttered.

Hertz joined in. 'Well, sir, we wouldn't have made it this far without them. They helped us over a good few hundred miles and seen that we've been fed and watered. If they were cowboys, I'd say they'd done a fine job on their horses, taking mighty good care o' them.'

'Sure would,' echoed Ronnie.

Lizzie edged forward then, finding herself much more interested in what the Americans had to say. 'If you came from Verona to get here, did you pass through Emilia-Romagna?'

Ronnie again. 'Sure did, ma'am.'

Lizzie leaned closer.

'Best food we've had. Salami and cheeses and those porcini. Tastiest mushrooms ever.' Ronnie kissed his cupped fingers, Italian style.

'Did you go anywhere near Castell'Arquato, or Morfasso, or Bardi?' she asked. She was aware she sounded like an interrogator, but she had to know.

'Bardi? We were there earlier. Same lot as these boys,' he pointed to the other partisans. 'The Garibaldi Brigade occupied it in June. They took big parts of the Ceno Valley, too.'

281

'Oh, good show,' said Hugh.

"Fraid not, sir,' Hertz retorted. 'The fascists got their own back soon after and went on a killing spree. Shot three priests and torched whole villages, then they retook Bardi in July.'

Lizzie frowned at the news. 'And Castell'Arquato? The Val d'Arda?'

'It was liberated for a short while, too. But then . . .' Hertz lowered his head and looked away.

Just then one of the partisan lookouts stationed on the ridge above signalled to them to take cover. A German patrol was passing on the track above the ravine. They rushed to the back of the cave and hid until they were given the all-clear.

When they hunkered down later that night, Hugh didn't even try to put his arm around her. She guessed why, of course. He must've caught her eagerness when she inquired about the partisans in the Val d'Arda and known she was thinking about Vincenzo and Cristo. Even though she knew it must have hurt him, she'd found it impossible not to rake through the ashes for the tiniest scrap of information about them before she remembered the embers were cold. There was no hope, and that night she sank back into the black.

The mood among the partisans was one of frustration as they awaited orders from the Allies. The British agent had visited twice, but there'd been no specific plans. So, when Il Ciclone came to Hugh one morning to tell him a contact of Roberto's had found a rowboat, spirits were instantly lifted. They were to make a second attempt to escape. This time they would row themselves.

'I heard about your plan with the boat,' Rita said, as they prepared to leave for the coast again. She was standing with her hands in her trouser pockets watching Lizzie buckle a small canvas bag of supplies.

'We're taking a look at it first. Do you want to come?'

Rita shook her black head. 'Better not. I could be spying on you. Sabotaging your plans,' she replied sarcastically.

Lizzie shook her head and patted her on the arm. 'I understand,' she said, agreeing it was probably wiser if she stayed in camp. She was just about to leave when Rita called her back.

'Is it true?' she asked.

Lizzie frowned, knowing exactly what she meant. 'About Hugh, you mean?'

'The men said they heard you arguing and saw you walk away.'

Lizzie nodded. 'I wish I could just walk away. It sounds so easy,' she replied wistfully. 'But yes, Hugh and I are no longer together.'

'But you are still leaving for France with him?'

'That is the plan,' she agreed. As she spoke, she suddenly realised she may have freed herself from one trap, but relying on Hugh to help her escape meant she was still caught in another. 'We leave together.'

It was only a two-hour hike to where the boat was kept in a small coastal village. Lizzie reluctantly accompanied Hugh in the advance party to check it out. But when they reached it, even to her untrained eye, it didn't look seaworthy. The wooden planking was cracked and a rollock was clearly loose. They'd made their way towards a quiet stretch of beach and rendez-voused with another group of partisans at a spot at the foot of the railway embankment. A French pilot and an Australian officer were to join them.

'Now we are six,' remarked Hugh.

'Six in that boat?' Lizzie queried.

'What choice do we have?' he asked, although she could tell he shared her concerns.

The operation was planned for two days later. Lizzie bid a tearful farewell to Rita.

'I don't like to leave you like this,' she said.

Fighting back tears, Rita replied, 'I hope you make it this time. I really do.' Although beneath her kind words, Lizzie sensed there was doubt and suspicion. Suspicion she shared. In truth, they both knew that if there was an enemy spy among them, this second attempt could also be thwarted. Not only did the boat not look seaworthy, the escapers could all be betrayed to the Nazis.

Chapter 41

The deserted villa had been found by the partisans on the earlier scouting mission. It lay a little way inland but less than two kilometres from the sea. From the cobwebs and the layer of dust, Lizzie guessed it had been abandoned a few months back. A discarded copy of *Il Popolo d'Italia* on the kitchen table confirmed the inhabitants had fled before Christmas. She looked in the cupboards. They'd been emptied of food, but a forage through the bedrooms rewarded her with a few finds. There was no running water, so a bath was out of the question, but Lizzie managed to help herself to a pair of slacks and a fresh blouse from a wardrobe. The long-forgotten touch of silk on her skin sent a thrill through her body. Searching around for more practical items, she pulled out a thick jumper. She suspected it would be needed once they were out on the water at night.

As darkness fell, Lizzie knew what she had to do. She caught Hugh standing on the veranda in the shadows, looking out to sea, silhouetted in profile. He wasn't a bad man. He was just doing what most men did – thinking about himself first. Hearing footsteps, he turned.

'Ah, there you are, Elizabeth. I'm glad you're here. I wanted . . .' He thrust his hands in his pockets. 'I hope we can still be friends.'

'Friends? Yes,' she said, finding herself relieved by the idea.

Now that she could see her way through the fog of grief, she understood he had been controlling her; exploiting her emotions to a point where she would almost have agreed to anything if it meant she could just be left alone to mourn. He simply didn't seem to be capable of taking no for an answer. But she was glad he appeared ready to be civil.

'After all, we're not out of the woods yet,' he reminded her.

Lizzie really didn't need reminding. They were just as likely to die attempting this crossing as they had been over the past twelve months, evading the Nazis. 'No. No, we're not,' she agreed.

Hugh moved closer to her then and for a split second she thought he might make a move on her again. But then . . .

'Flight Lieutenant!' Roberto was calling from inside the villa. 'You come now.'

Hugh was one of four men chosen to shoulder the upturned craft.

'That's me,' said Hugh. He winked and dipped a bow before disappearing.

Under a hazy moon they left the villa just before midnight and carefully they made their way towards a quiet stretch of beach. It was only another kilometre to the wooden rowing boat, which, despite its poor condition, was surprisingly heavy. As soon as they'd managed to lift it up and balance it on their shoulders, Ronnie joked he felt like a pall bearer. Normally the remark would at least have raised a smile, but this time, knowing they could all be dead within the next hour, nobody laughed. One of the partisans carried the oars, while the other scouted a few metres ahead. Lizzie, with a rucksack slung on her back, brought up the rear.

They knew there would be military vehicles on the coast road, but the area remained in total blackness, so they all wore dark clothes. One flash of white in the moonlight could be their undoing. To deaden their footsteps, they'd taken off their boots and tied strips of blanket round their feet. Although she'd originally proposed it, in reality, escaping by boat was a madcap scheme, but Lizzie had gone along with it because there'd been no other course. Even if the Germans didn't catch them before they made it to the sea, the boat could spring a leak and sink. Either way if they didn't reach Monte Carlo, Hugh said at least they'd have died trying. She'd agreed at the time. And yet something didn't feel right. In fact, it felt terribly wrong and was growing worse by the minute.

Manoeuvring the boat over fences and through gates was hard going, but once they'd reached the edge of the village, they began to make better progress. Once they'd crossed the railway track, they found themselves walking over waste ground; a mixture of scrub and shingle underfoot. They'd arrived at their destination.

Somewhere out in the bay, a dozen or more booms echoed consecutively. They wouldn't be safe – or safer – until they'd reached dry land on the Allied French side. On shore the night was calm, but as soon as the boat was launched, a stiff offshore breeze ruffled Lizzie's hair. Hugh saw her shiver.

'Take this, won't you?' He was wearing a military great coat that a villager had dyed black. It had been too hot to wear on land, but now he was glad of it.

'I'll be fine,' replied Lizzie. The coat was too big even for Hugh.

'Very well,' he said, shrugging inside its shoulders and fastening its buttons.

They were to take it in turns to row the fifteen miles to Monte Carlo and estimated they should reach their destination just before dawn. The earlier artillery fire was replaced by the more peaceful sound of water gently lapping against the shore. The Frenchman and the Australian volunteered to row first, but even before they pushed off, the wind began to strengthen. Sea conditions had been hard to gauge on land, but now, even in the shallows, they were undoubtedly choppy.

Immediately a swell rose. The boat was cramped, and Lizzie was elbowed to one side. She curled up in a ball at the bow, out of the way of the two rowers, but felt the boat roll and pitch beneath her. Then to her dismay, not five minutes from the shore, there was water around her feet. Glancing down she saw one of the planks had split. The vessel was leaking, and seawater was trickling in. Without a word, she snatched an enamel mug from her rucksack and began bailing as the trickle rapidly became a flood.

'Oh Christ,' said Hugh as soon as he saw her spring into action. He, too, began frantically scooping at the rising water.

The rowers pulled harder, but in their panic the oars caught the sea's surface at a difficult angle and instead of speeding up, the boat slowed down. By then the Americans had joined in, bailing with anything to hand, but it was no use. Seawater was flooding in so fast it was impossible to keep pace with it.

'We're going down,' shouted the joker, only this time, he wasn't joking.

The rowboat began to list to starboard and even though everyone leaned over to port, it was useless. One wave was all it took. One big wave. There was nothing they could do to save themselves from the black depths.

All around there was darkness. Darkness and cold. Seconds under water seemed like minutes until Lizzie finally rose to the surface and gulped for air. Through her coughs she scanned the sea. The boat was gone. An oar floated in front of her. But, more importantly, where was everyone else? From the corner of her eye, she spotted a hand, waving. Another went up in reply, followed by another a few metres towards the beach.

'*Ici*,' came a call from farther out. The Frenchman.

Lizzie forced her shocked brain to think. Someone was missing. 'Here,' she cried, battling against the saltwater stinging her throat like a hornet. But no one shouted her name. 'Hugh,' she called, frantically treading water as she turned round to scan the sea. No reply. Again, she called. Nothing.

The two men who'd waved turned out to be the Americans. They were swimming erratically towards her. The Australian, obviously a very strong swimmer, was powering out to the Frenchman. But of Hugh there was no sign, until ... A cry. Over to her left she saw something flailing in the water; rising then disappearing below the waves.

'Hugh!' she screamed. Adrenaline drove her arms and legs as she cut through the water towards the thrashing. When she was within a few metres she could see Hugh fighting with something under the water. One moment he would thrust his head and arm above the swell and cry out, the next he had plunged down again. As she approached, she realised why. His huge coat was weighing him down. Battling to get free of it, he was trapped inside. Lunging forward she grabbed hold of his lapels as he came up for air, then felt for the brass buttons, twisting them from their holes. There was more writhing as Hugh grasped hold of her arm, pulling her down with him. As she pushed him away, she pulled open the coat and he managed to struggle free, fighting his way to the surface just in time. With her last breath Lizzie somehow summoned all her strength to thrust herself upwards to break water close by. Although Hugh's head was above the surface, he sputtered and snorted, his thrashing limbs rapidly losing all strength. Seeing his exhaustion, she knew he could easily sink again. She also knew he might try and take her down with him, so swimming behind him, she gave him a gentle push. The next moment he caught a shoreward wave. It seemed what he needed to start swimming back to the beach. Lizzie followed behind, her breathing now under control. Soon after she felt the crunch of pebbles beneath her feet.

Up ahead of her, on the shore, the other men had all landed safely. Two were lying on their backs, the other two were sitting, hugging their legs up under their chins. There were other men on the beach, too, and she instantly feared they could be fascists, but soon realised they were partisans come to help.

The water was still chest high when she staggered towards the shore, her arms around Hugh's torso, careful to keep his face above the water. One of the partisans waded out to help her and lifted Hugh's arm around his neck to get him clear of the water before laying him, face down, on the shingle.

'Oh God!' he spluttered. Bending his arms, he tried to push himself up, but immediately collapsed.

'It's all right, Hugh. You're safe now,' she told him, slumping down exhausted beside him. Her own teeth were chattering with the cold, and she felt someone – a partisan, she supposed – lay a jacket around her shoulders.

As she peered at him through a curtain of wet hair, she saw Hugh turn his head and open his eyes.

'You saved my life, Elizabeth,' he gasped between coughs. His hand spidered across the pebbles and reached out for hers. It felt like ice. 'How can I ever repay you?'

Chapter 42

The partisans, it turned out, had been about to leave the beach when one of them spotted something was wrong in the water. They'd stayed on shore and watched with horror as the rowboat disappeared under the waves. Now they'd managed to shepherd all six of the escapers back inland, to the deserted villa. There they were able to dry their clothes and get some rest.

'I thought I was a gonna,' said Hugh as he slumped on a sofa at the villa. Lizzie sat next to him. He turned to face her. 'You really are a remarkable woman, Elizabeth,' he told her.

There was no doubt her quick-thinking had saved his life.

Hugh chuckled unexpectedly. 'That'll be something to tell the children, won't it?'

Lizzie suddenly pictured herself surrounded by squabbling children at the breakfast table while Hugh ploughed through his copy of *The Times*, oblivious. But the look on her face signalled to Hugh what he'd just said alarmed her.

'Sorry. I forgot,' he muttered. 'There won't be any children.'

Lizzie looked at him sceptically. Was it a genuine mistake or should she still be worried? It seemed her ex-fiancé still wasn't prepared to give up on her entirely.

* * *

They started early the next morning to meet up with the rest of the group in the mountains. But Hugh was finding it tough going. After almost drowning, his breathing had become laboured. He'd also twisted his ankle when he'd landed heavily on the beach and was limping badly. One of the partisans dropped behind and angled his shoulder under Hugh's arm to take some of the weight off his feet.

Much to her surprise, Lizzie found herself feeling sorry for him, after all he'd nearly drowned and was still suffering from the aftermath. Making sure he was cared for by of one of the partisans, she snatched the opportunity to walk with the two Americans. There were questions she needed answering. Ever since they'd made mention of the partisans of the Val d'Arda, her shattered thoughts had slowly mended themselves to form more questions.

'Flight Lieutenant Codrington and I were in Emilia-Romagna, too,' Lizzie started, beginning where she'd left off the other day. 'We were with the unit headed by Lieutenant Vincenzo Baldini.'

She waited for a reaction, but there wasn't one. 'Uh huh.' Hertz nodded. That was all.

A weight pressed so hard on Lizzie's chest she had to bite back the tears. It was true, then. Vincenzo had to be dead otherwise his name would surely have meant something to them if they'd been in the area. But she couldn't give up all hope. She mustn't. 'His partisan name was Il Gufo.'

Ronnie stopped in his tracks. 'Hell yeah!' He grinned broadly. 'Il Gufo,' he repeated, nudging Hertz. 'You remember him. Now he was a good guy.'

Lizzie's heart was beating so fast she thought it might explode. 'You met him?'

'Yeah,' agreed Ronnie. 'Sure we did,' he replied, looking down at his sleeve. To her embarrassment Lizzie realised she was tugging at it unthinkingly.

'Forgive me,' she said. 'It's just . . .'

'We saw him a few weeks back.'

'Really?' Hope kindled inside her. There'd been a mistake. A terrible mistake. Vincenzo was alive after all.

'Yeah. Too bad he got shot.'

The glimmer was extinguished.

'Yes,' was all she could muster at first. For a moment she thought she was about to soar through the air. Now she'd plummeted to the ground once more with a heavy thud.

'You knew the guy?' asked Hertz.

She nodded and a vice closed round her heart. 'Yes. He and I were both tutors in Lucca.' She looked Ronnie in the eye. 'Did you come across a boy, about eleven, called Cristo? Tall, with curly dark hair.'

'Cristo?' repeated Hertz.

'Cristo,' echoed Ronnie. 'Yeah, sure, we did.' He slapped Hertz on the arm. 'You remember. A *staffetta.*'

'Yes. That's him,' cried Lizzie.

'Poor kid,' mumbled Hertz.

Lizzie frowned. 'What do you mean?'

Ronnie stepped in. 'He was real low. He'd just lost his teacher. Pretty cut up about it, an' all.' He looked at Lizzie. 'Hey, lady, you OK?'

Lizzie's legs suddenly weakened beneath her. Vincenzo must have died before he could tell Cristo he was his son. But he'd always been more of a father to him than de Falco ever was. Of course, his death would have been devastating for the boy.

No longer able to contain her grief, Lizzie broke down in tears. 'Yes. Yes, it's just . . .' She couldn't find the strength to tell the men that she loved Cristo like a son and that she'd only left him because she was certain Vincenzo would recover. His place was with his father, but now he was dead. She dabbed her cheeks with the back of her hand.

'Everything all right, Elizabeth?' called Hugh, somehow finding the energy to put on a spurt and catch up.

Lizzie looked round to find him standing behind her. He couldn't know the despair she was feeling. Wiping away her sorrow alongside her tears she replied, 'Yes. Yes, it's fine. It turns out our American friends met Lieutenant Baldini and Cristo on their travels.'

Hertz leaned in. 'He helped us get as far as Morfasso. Things were getting pretty crazy round there.'

'They saw Cristo, Hugh. He's taken Vincenzo's death very badly.'

Hugh arched one of his thick brows. 'At least it'll toughen him up, I suppose,' he replied tartly.

Lizzie drilled him with a horrified glare. 'Is that all you can say?' she asked incredulously. Understandably, he'd resented her relationship with Vincenzo from the start, but he'd obviously felt cold towards Cristo, too. Perhaps he was jealous of them both. Hugh had been fiercely protective of her when he'd first met Vincenzo and Cristo. And his protection had felt increasingly like control. It seemed to suit him now they were both out of the picture.

'I'm sorry for the boy, of course, but he's not the only child to lose someone close in this bloody war and sadly he won't be the last.'

Deep down she had to acknowledge the harsh truth of what Hugh had just said. But it didn't mean she accepted it.

The group found the other partisans about three miles south of where they'd left them. Later that evening, they sat side by side on a rock watching the sun set over the Ligurian sea. But the silence between them was uneasy.

Now the Americans had confirmed, once and for all, Vincenzo was dead. Had he lived she would have stayed in Italy. They would have married and lived happily ever after in their very own fairy tale. But now Vincenzo was gone, and her happy ending had turned into a nightmare. Grief had blunted any dreams she had for her own future. Cristo was now all that mattered.

Glancing to her left, Lizzie saw Hugh stroking his moustache, a smug grin on his face. It was almost as if he felt satisfied Vincenzo no longer posed a threat; almost as if he still wouldn't accept her rejection.

After all that had happened, she knew she could never learn to love him again, but there was something she thought he needed to know; something to help him make sense of her decision.

'Hugh,' she began. Her stomach felt like the rowing boat just before it had sunk a few hours back. It was pitching and tossing, and she wanted to be sick. 'Hugh, there's something I need to tell you.' He turned and looked at her then, but before she could continue, he clamped a finger over her mouth.

'You don't have to say anything,' he told her, looking into her eyes. 'I already know.'

'You do?' she replied. Perhaps he was more perceptive than she'd given him credit for.

'Yes, I do, and there's no need to worry. I completely understand.' He was nodding his sleek head before looking straight ahead.

Lizzie was confused. 'I don't . . .'

'I know you've spent the legacy your mother left you, so I'm perfectly happy to give you a small allowance to tide you over when we get back to England.'

Lizzie could no longer stand for it. Once again, he'd drowned out her words with his arrogant bluster, but she thought it right that he should know what she'd decided. She should have told him after Ada's death, but she hadn't been able to look at him, let alone speak to him. Then she should have done it after the failed boat attempt, although Hugh had been too vulnerable to take the news and she'd felt drained of energy. Now that she knew from the Americans Vincenzo was definitely dead, she'd realised it was even more important she shared with him her decision.

'No, Hugh,' she began again.

'No, Elizabeth? Having second thoughts?' Suddenly he reached for her hand.

She regarded him wide-eyed. It was staggering to see he still believed he had a chance with her. But then . . .

'Codrington!'

Both Lizzie and Hugh twisted round to see Hertz striding towards them. 'Codrington, we're starting a game of poker. Come join us?'

Hugh threw her an odd look. 'I'll join you in a moment, old chap,' he replied, his eyes still trained on Lizzie. 'It's all right to change your mind, you know. Women do all the time.' He winked at her then and stood up to follow the American like an eager Labrador, leaving Lizzie to load up the burden of the secret she felt she ought to share.

Chapter 43

Quite by chance, two days later news came that a second boat had been located, just a few kilometres to the west. The partisans assured the six in the group that it was clearly well maintained and completely watertight. This time there could be no mistake.

They took to the quiet back tracks at dusk and were soon making progress towards the coast. The partisans planned to launch the boat at a place called Ventimiglia, just a three-hour journey on foot, avoiding the main roads. If all went to plan, they could be in Allied territory by dawn.

'You all right, old girl?' Hugh asked as they scrambled along a narrow gorge. They were following a stream that led down to the coast. 'You're very quiet.'

Of course she wasn't 'all right'. She still harboured the secret she'd been wanting to share with him for the past few days. It would help explain everything afterwards; allow him to process the situation. That night she would come out with it.

Another villa had been found as a base for the afternoon – not as comfortable as the first one, but a sound roof was a luxury for Lizzie these days. They all ate together in the kitchen – a cold meal of bread and cheese. Lizzie found it hard to swallow. Knowing what could go wrong had left her even more nervous about their escape. Every time she closed her eyes, she could see the black water swirling in front of her and feel her lungs burn. Her head would be filled with a sucking sensation and her ears would once again hurt. She looked across the table at Hugh. He'd barely touched his food, too. The brushes they'd had with the Nazis in the mountains over the past few weeks and his near drowning had unnerved him, but it had also left him with a steeliness. That night he was more determined than ever to succeed. She could tell it by the way he was going over everything with the British officer in charge of the operation. In front of him was a sheet of paper and he was sketching a map of the coast on it and going over the finer points of the plan once more. This time he was going to leave nothing to chance. He'd even insisted they camouflaged their faces and that they carry firearms. Normally only the partisans were armed, but that evening he was adamant. Hugh needed his own gun.

Il Ciclone wasn't happy. Guns were in short supply and ammunition was even harder to come by, but he ordered his men to fetch what they could find from a stash somewhere in town. An hour later they returned with a motley selection of ancient rifles and three handguns. The escapees were invited to take their pick. But when Lizzie's hand hovered over a pistol, she suddenly felt a grip around her wrist. Shocked she looked round to see Hugh's glare. His brows were knitted, but as soon as he saw the fury on her face, he laughed and let go.

'Come on, Elizabeth,' he said, chuckling. 'You don't need a gun. We chaps will protect you. Won't we?' He looked to the Americans to garner support and found it in their hearty laughs.

'Sure we will, little lady,' said Ronnie with a wink.

Lizzie, however, was past seeing the funny side of the situation. Whatever happened now, Hugh didn't deserve to know. He could remain in the dark.

*   *   *

A road ran parallel with the beach and there was only one way to reach it – via a pedestrian tunnel under it at a place called Vallecrosia. It was always guarded by Italian militiamen under German command, but the partisans had enlisted infiltrators at the nearby checkpoint. That night they'd been assured of a safe passage, so Hugh and the others were told by Roberto, whose friend would be on guard.

Lizzie was on high alert. Every rustle of reeds, every twig that snapped, every flap of a wing could mean danger. She kept the boat, carried on the men's shoulders, in her sights but held back far enough in case she needed to raise the alarm. After ten minutes they reached the main railway line running along the south coast. There were flashlights up ahead, but they faded into the distance, and the seven of them crossed the tracks without a problem.

Next came the embankment. It was steep, forcing the carriers to bend their knees to brake all the way down, against the weight of the boat. Once they'd made it safely to the bottom, the mouth of the tunnel opened up a few metres ahead. If all went according to plan, the partisan infiltrator would let them pass. Another few seconds and they'd all disappeared inside, leaving Lizzie to check they'd not been followed. Satisfied they'd been allowed through, she was just about to enter the tunnel when from out of the darkness a figure stepped in front of her. A helmeted solider in the field grey of a German uniform blocked her path. Her heart leapt into her mouth, but she forced down a threatened scream and simply froze until, that is, she saw the expression on his face.

'Buonasera, signorina,' he said with a grin before he ushered her on through the tunnel.

Now they were all on the beach; no longer sheltered by the gorse and the reeds. The wind was stiffer, too, and it laced the edges of the sea as it lapped the shore. Their destination lay just twenty miles to the west, but it would take at least eight hours to row there. The men had already righted the boat and were loading their backpacks into it. Hugh was sitting on the shingle, tugging on his boots while another partisan kept watch with his assault rifle prone.

'All good?' whispered Hertz. He seemed the only one who'd noticed her arrival.

She nodded and, letting the rucksack slide off her back, proceeded to unhook her boots that were tied by their laces and slung round her neck. She was reminded of Cristo again; the time she'd shown him how to tie his own shoes. The memory turned the dull ache in her chest that had troubled her for so long into a stabbing pain.

'There you are,' said Hugh, now standing behind her. 'Best look lively.' He pulled roughly at her arm, and she thought of the last time she'd held Vincenzo's hand to say farewell as he lay injured in the house near Castell'Arquato.

By now the boat was on the water. The waves came up to the other men's knees. Roberto was beckoning them, making sweeping gestures with his arms, pointing to something to their left. A pinprick of light out in the pitch-black bay grew brighter by the second.

'Come on, Lizzie.' Hugh's whisper had turned into a growl. 'For God's sake, do you want to get us all killed?'

But Lizzie couldn't move. She remained statue-still, her feet rooted in the pebbles on the beach. She had to tell him before he flung himself into the boat and they rowed out to sea. She had to let him know before he left everything behind. The volcano that had been simmering inside her all this time threatened to erupt. As tears brimmed from her eyes, she gulped down a lungful of air and braced herself. It was now or never.

'I can't, Hugh.'

Shock registered on his face. He opened his mouth to say something, closed it quickly then opened it again. 'What?' He narrowed his eyes. 'What the hell are you talking about. Get in, will you?' He pointed to the boat behind, the waves now slapping hard against the wood.

'No. No. I'm not coming with you.' Was that her voice? Was she really turning down the chance to escape?

'Just get in the bloody boat!'

A surge, now, as if she'd just caught a wave and it was rolling her back towards the shore and away from him. 'No, Hugh. I won't.'

'What? Are you mad?'

'Maybe I am.' But all that mattered, she told herself, was that this time she was listening to her heart, not her head. What she was doing wasn't sensible at all, insane even, but it felt right. She was staying for Vincenzo's son; the son Hugh didn't know his rival had. She was staying for the child who had meant so much to her before, but who meant everything now Vincenzo was dead. She was staying for Cristo.

Taking a deep breath she shouted, 'After I saved your life, you asked me how you could ever repay me, Hugh.'

'What nonsense are you talking?' he shot back.

But before she could answer, from out of nowhere, a blinding light lit up the sky, burning the backs of her eyes. A search light strafed the beach, making it bright as day and from out of nowhere a missile screamed through the air and landed in the sea, sending a column of water high above their heads. Lizzie and the two partisans behind her were blown off their feet and hit the shore instantly. Pebbles and sand rained down on them where they lay.

They'd been betrayed. Again.

As soon as the debris cleared, Lizzie looked out to sea. The explosion triggered huge waves that were breaking on shore. The rowboat? Where was it? Fearing it had sunk, she scanned the sea and made out two or three men up to their waists in water. They were steadying the boat as the sea crashed against its boughs. Meanwhile the Frenchman, the Australian and the Americans, who'd boarded before the explosion were waving and shouting at Hugh to hurry. They didn't understand what was happening with Lizzie.

'Hurry it up, will ya, Biggles?' shouted Ronnie, cupping his hand round his mouth.

'Elizabeth,' Hugh boomed again, turning back to shore; the high waves slapping his chest.

An arc of bright light swept across the beach again and Lizzie ducked once more but held her nerve. Better to die quickly at the hands of the Nazis than die slowly in suburbia, she told herself.

This time she was only given a second to respond and when she did not, Hugh swore loudly and waded out to join the others and clamber aboard. The partisans shoved hard, and the heavily laden craft was sent ploughing through the water in a westerly direction towards France. Five people were on board. There should have been six.

Search lights were now criss-crossing the beach, just a few metres from where the boat had entered the sea and the throb of an engine was heard above the waves. Lizzie squinted into the darkness, her eyes tracing the little boat as it bobbed westwards. Soon it would be out of sight and, she prayed, out of the Germans'.

'What do you think you're playing at?' shouted Il Ciclone. He'd crawled over to where Lizzie lay, obviously thinking she was one of his men. 'Good God. I'm sorry,' he said as she turned towards him.

'I couldn't go,' she told him. 'This is where I belong.'

He narrowed his eyes as he looked at her but remained silent. She was grateful he asked no more of her. She didn't have the energy to explain that she couldn't leave her heart behind.

'Then we better get you out of here,' was all he said, summoning the partisans as they rushed up the beach from the water. 'Back inland it is,' he muttered, shielding his eyes against another searchlight as it strafed the beach. 'Either that or a Nazi prison camp.'

Once again, they'd been betrayed. It proved Ada wasn't the spy in the camp. The men had summarily executed an innocent woman. Lizzie walked back up the shore, away from Hugh and from any chance of escape.

Chapter 44

'I need to go back.' Lizzie was lying on a bed looking up at the flaking plaster ceiling of another safe house belonging to a partisan's mother. The unit had been told they were moving out shortly, into the mountains once more. They were making the most of their last night under a proper roof by the coast.

Rita lay beside her, smoking a cigarette made of chestnut leaves. Her bandana was now relegated to her neck, exposing her wild black curls. Ada's execution still cast a long shadow over her – over some of the men, too, especially now the traitor had been uncovered. It was Roberto. His accomplice at the checkpoint at Vallecrosia had tipped off the Germans. They'd found him with signalling equipment, and he'd pleaded for mercy. But raw justice had been done and now the other partisans were drowning their sorrows in wine they'd found in the cellar. Rita had told Lizzie she couldn't bear to be near them anymore. Despite Ada's proven innocence, she still felt she was being judged by them all the time.

'Back where?' asked Rita, taking another drag of her cigarette. She turned away from Lizzie, so the smoke didn't blow in her face.

'To Emilia-Romagna. To Castell'Arquato.'

'What about your pilot?'

'I told you. We're over.' Lizzie sighed. 'We were over a long time ago. I just didn't have the nerve to end it.'

Rita frowned. 'So what made you stay, just as you were about to escape?'

'Ada,' Lizzie replied bluntly. 'Ada's murder tapped into something deep inside me. I knew I just had to stay.'

Rita nodded in silence, as if she, too, had just signed up to an unspoken oath after the execution of her friend. She took another drag. 'There is another man?'

There had to be a strong reason her English friend didn't seize the chance to get to freedom.

'Another man?' Lizzie repeated. 'Yes.' She was thinking of Cristo. 'And no. A boy, actually. He lives in Emilia-Romagna. A boy I regard as my son.'

'Aaah,' said Rita, flicking a cone of ash into a nearby saucer. 'But who is the father?'

'A man I loved. But he died.'

'I'm sorry,' said Rita. She lifted her hand and thrust the rest of her cigarette in front of Lizzie. Even though she'd hardly ever smoked, she took it, closed her lips around the end and inhaled. It tasted vile and triggered a cough. She handed it straight back.

'So, you want to return for the child?' asked Rita.

'Yes. I need him as much as he needs me. Perhaps more.'

Rita turned to lie on her back. 'So how will you go? It's not like you can get a train anymore. We've blown up so many lines.'

Lizzie had to admit her friend was right. The partisans were setting off charges on rail tracks almost daily to disrupt the German supply line. She could always walk across the mountains, but without a guide, she was putting herself at untold risk. The idea had come to her when she was remembering happier times with Cristo.

'I shall cycle.'

Rita spluttered on her cigarette. 'Cycle? Ha!'

'Why is that so funny?' Now it was Lizzie's turn to prop her head up on her hand.

Rita lifted her shoulders. 'It's just slow, I guess.'

Lizzie snorted through her nose. 'Not as slow as walking.'

'That's true,' Rita conceded.

'I reckon I could do it in two days. Maybe three.'

'But on your own? It's not safe.'

Another snort from Lizzie. 'Crossing the mountains on foot with a partisan unit isn't exactly safe, is it? What choice do I have?'

Rita sat up to stub out her cigarette on the saucer on the bedside table. She paused for a moment and said, 'I heard you once tell Ada you admired her courage.' She spun round to look at her. 'Well, I admire yours.' She drew her legs back up onto the bed and sat cross-legged for a moment, then asked, 'Is there room for one more on this new adventure?'

Lizzie traded the silk blouse she'd taken from the deserted villa for two bicycles the old woman had no use for. They'd belonged to her sons when they were much younger and were now too small for them. According to Rita, they were distantly related to her. Even though it seemed an unfair exchange, the woman also gave them two skirts. It was strange to get out of trousers after three months of wearing them. After a good wash and an application of mascara, courtesy of Rita who never travelled without it, Lizzie felt like a woman again.

Il Ciclone gave Lizzie the names of the towns to pass through on her way back to Genoa. *If you are stopped by the Germans, they will suspect you if you carry a map*, he'd advised. The route, he said, was straight forward to the city, at least. He neglected to mention the German lorries and trucks that took the hairpin bends at speed and often threatened to run cycles off the road and down sheer cliffs to the sea.

Their cover story was simple. They were refugees from Florence, keen to flee the Allied onslaught, and were staying with relatives in whatever area they happened to be pedalling through.

'I do have a cousin in Savona,' Rita chimed in.

'You seem to have relatives everywhere,' remarked Lizzie lightly.

The journey began well enough. The road, although busy with military vehicles, was reasonably flat and the cycling quite easy – if you avoided the shell holes. A few mules had been pressed into service along the highway, as well as old bicycles. They passed a fellow cyclist teetering along with a mattress delicately poised on his handlebars and waved. Unsurprisingly, he didn't wave back. But then, just outside Arenzano, a few miles west of Genoa, disaster struck. Rita's chain broke and there was no way it could be mended without arousing suspicion.

As they gazed forlornly at the chain, wondering what to do, some of the civilian lorry drivers started tooting their horns. Rita waved at one of them.

'What do you think you're doing?' scolded Lizzie.

'Why don't we hitch a ride?' Rita shot back. 'There are plenty of fruit and veg trucks on the road. I'm sure some of the drivers would welcome our company.' She winked at Lizzie as she spoke. 'We just stick to our story, don't talk about politics and before you know it, we'll be in Genoa.'

Rita stuck out her thumb. The third lorry – which was indeed carrying fruit and vegetables – slowed down as it passed them then braked and pulled up in a cloud of fumes nearby. Lizzie and Rita ran to it and the driver opened his door. The smell of sweat assaulted them.

'You want a ride, ladies?' asked the driver with a droopy moustache.

'To Genoa?' asked Rita, flashing a smile.

When he smiled back, they could see he had very few teeth in his gums. 'Sure. Hop in.'

The driver told them he was heading to market. A wooden set of rosary beads hung from his rear-view mirror and a half-eaten salami sat on his dashboard. To the right lay the coast, a shimmering carpet of blue in the sunlight. But as soon as he began chatting about his wife and his elderly mother, Lizzie

306

was uneasy. She let Rita do most of the talking, afraid he might detect her English accent. Then he mentioned his two sons, both in the Carabinieri.

'You have boyfriends?' he asked.

Rita and Lizzie both shook their heads. 'My sons are looking for good wives. Pretty ones, like you.' He stretched out his hand and squeezed Lizzie's thigh. 'I can take you to meet them.'

They were now just on the outskirts of the city. The Allies had bombed Genoa, but Lizzie hadn't understood the scale of the destruction before. Even though the docks bore the brunt of the attack, many buildings had also been reduced to rubble. People were wandering round in a daze, trying to salvage their possessions. A pang of guilt jabbed at her when she saw a young mother begging on the roadside with her baby. Allied bombs had reduced her life to rubble, too.

A German checkpoint lay ahead. Lizzie felt herself on edge as the truck was flagged to a halt. The driver pulled up, wound down his window and presented his papers.

'And these women?' asked the soldier, waving his finger at Lizzie and Rita.

'Hitchhikers,' the driver said.

Lizzie wished he'd said friends, or family, but calling them hitchhikers raised suspicions straight away.

'Papers,' snapped the guard.

He looked first at Rita's, then at Lizzie's. Then he looked up. 'You are married, signora?'

The colour rose in Lizzie's face. She'd presented him with the papers she and Hugh had travelled on from Castell'Arquato. According to those they were husband and wife. 'Widowed,' she replied.

The driver narrowed his eyes at her. 'You're a widow? You don't look like a widow. Or sound like one.'

Lizzie stared at the guard, her heart in her mouth.

'Your ring,' he snapped.

'My what?'

'Your ring.' The guard grabbed her left hand and when he saw no wedding ring, he said, 'Wait here.' He marched towards the guardhouse, clutching Lizzie's documents.

A surge of adrenaline flooded her body and one look at Rita told her they were both thinking the same thing.

'Run!' she shouted, jumping down from the cab. They split up, as they said they always would in such a situation. Rita headed west, along the harbour, while Lizzie dashed into the *caruggi*, the labyrinthine maze of shops in the old town, just as shots started to ring out. A bullet screeched past her ear and nicked a column ahead of her. She ducked and dived behind a rubbish cart, sliding down the wall as two German guards hurtled past. With the stench of rotting food clinging to her nostrils, she moved on, intent on reaching the cathedral. The women had already decided it was where they would rendezvous, should they be forced apart.

Sneaking along the nearest alley, Lizzie snatched a scarf from an overhead washing line to cover her hair and tied it under her chin. She carried on walking as calmly as she could until she came to a junction. A plump woman was leaning against her shop door, just as more Germans arrived. From beneath her wooden crucifixes and plaster saints hanging by their halos from rafters overhead, the shopkeeper eyed Lizzie. Knowing she was in trouble she stood aside and lifted the beaded curtain hanging across the doorway. Lizzie made it inside just as jackboots stomped past. There were more shouts, but the woman remained propped up against the door lintel in silence until the soldiers had dispersed. On the way out, Lizzie squeezed her arm to say thank you. She continued towards the cathedral.

By the time Lizzie reached San Lorenzo, a half hour had passed. There were guards on either side of the main cathedral doors. It would be hard to enter without raising suspicions. There were a few steps up to the front entrance and an old man, leaning on a cane, had just begun to climb them, but was finding it hard.

Lizzie rushed to his aid, talking to him gently as if she knew him well. The guards paid little attention. She was inside.

It took a few seconds for her eyes to adjust to the darkness, but the sense of serenity was such a relief. Sliding into a pew she sat and took deep breaths to regain her composure as she looked around for Rita. There was no sign of her, although it was a large cathedral, with many side chapels. She started to walk up the main aisle, but soon after spotted her friend kneeling by a shrine to Our Lady, a black mantilla covering her dark hair.

When Lizzie tapped her gently on the shoulder, she jumped but smiled as Lizzie knelt beside her.

'What now?' Rita whispered.

'Out of the city on foot, I guess.'

'Or find more bicycles?'

'Steal them, you mean.'

Rita shrugged. It was a tall order, she knew. 'But we carry on north, yes? We could maybe get a bus if the road is passable.'

'A bus. Yes,' said Lizzie. The commander had given them a few hundred lire. 'That is what we shall do.'

They waited until late afternoon to make their move and started out of the city around six, hoping to reach the outskirts before curfew. That night they found a deserted barn by the side of the road, where they ate the stale bread they'd managed to find and a bunch of grapes. As they settled down, Lizzie's thoughts turned to Ada again.

'Who did it?' she asked. 'Who pulled the trigger?'

In the darkness she heard Rita sigh. 'They drew lots,' she replied. 'It was Roberto.' Just hearing the traitor's name sickened Lizzie, but to think he, of all the partisans, the real traitor in their midst, was the one who shot Ada was despicable.

'I suppose she got justice in the end,' muttered Rita.

Lizzie said nothing. The death of Ada's murderer offered little consolation.

Chapter 45

The bus, they were told, ran once a day, but no one knew what time it passed through the village. So, the two women just sat and waited as the hot sky darkened and threatening clouds gathered over the mountains. Thunder rumbled in the distance and within twenty minutes the heavens opened, soaking both of them. A nearby tree provided little shelter, but then from the downpour appeared a dilapidated old vehicle, belching black smoke. With windscreen wipers barely up to the task, the vehicle trundled along the road, sending up spray. Rita held out her arm and it slowed to a stop just by them.

'Where are you going?' asked the driver, winding down his window.

'Bobbio,' said Rita.

'Get in.'

He opened the door and the two women poured themselves inside, dripping all over the floor of the bus.

'I will have to drop you before,' the driver told them as Lizzie offered the fare.

'Why?' asked Lizzie.

'You don't know?' he asked. The young man, who wore his peaked cap at a rakish angle, frowned.

'Know what?' said Lizzie.

'The partisans have just taken it. It is a republic now. I cannot cross the border in this. It's a state bus.' He smiled as he spoke, so Lizzie sensed it was safe to smile, too.

They sat side by side, excited by what they'd just heard. The partisans had captured the town and declared a republic. Were other communes doing the same? The Americans, Ronnie and Hertz, had spoken about the Ceno Valley and of Bardi. It seemed there were regions that were fighting off the Germans and taking back control, even if their freedom had been short-lived. Did that mean it would be easier to find Cristo again?

For the three-hour journey Lizzie and Rita were allowed to escape the ravages of war. The rainstorm cleared and the farther away from Genoa they travelled, the more beautiful the landscape became. The rain-washed road, although rutted, followed a river valley and took them along gorges, by waterfalls and through pines. The bus wheezed its way across bridges and barely passable roads. It stopped off at a few villages on the way; poor, forgotten places where the children were in rags and not a man under forty could be seen. Finally, as more rain threatened to fall, the bus arrived at its destination. Lizzie and Rita, together with a woman and her infirm mother, found themselves the only passengers left.

'Bobbio,' announced the driver as an ancient bridge came into view.

'The Devil's Bridge,' squealed Rita in delight. 'I've heard so much about it, but never seen it.' With its eleven arches dating back to Roman times, Lizzie found it impressive, but like so many bridges in Italy she could also see a checkpoint. Only this time it was controlled not by fascists, but by a group of partisans. It felt as though she was going home.

They left the bus and walked towards the bridge just as more mountain rain splatted on the road. The two women ahead of them were greeted with smiles and allowed to pass over the bridge, but the welcome the partisans gave Lizzie and Rita certainly wasn't as warm. Instead of the cordial greeting given to the others, guns were pointed at them as soon as they drew near.

'Papers!' one of three men on duty cried. His teeth were black, and he regarded them suspiciously, although the others looked on smiling. Rita smiled back, then pouted like a child.

'No need for papers, brother,' she replied. 'We are partisans, too. Blue brigade. Il Ciclone sends his regards. We've come all the way from Ventimiglia.'

'Il Ciclone, you say.' Another, older partisan, an ammunition belt slung across his torso, suddenly took an interest. He nodded at the others.

'We still need your papers.'

'They were taken by Germans, who wanted to arrest us,' Lizzie explained.

The men swapped glances and one of them said, 'Come with me.'

By now the rain was falling heavily once more. It was cold against Lizzie's bare arms. The partisans made them walk before him across the bridge then guided them to a municipal building on the other side. They were made to wait in a soulless room where damp seeped through flaking walls.

'Are we under arrest?' asked Lizzie.

'That depends,' replied the partisan.

'On whom?' she insisted.

'On me,' said a voice as another door opened and a familiar figure with a beaked nose appeared on the threshold.

'Stefano?' said Lizzie, not quite able to believe she was seeing Vincenzo's friend and fellow partisan again.

He smiled broadly. 'Here I am known as Justice,' he said, pulling a stern face. 'It is so good to see you, Miss Thornton, or should I say Rosa?' He offered his hand.

Lizzie took it and smiled. 'I don't care what you call me, or my friend Rita here. All we need is some food, a wash and clean clothes.'

312

'Of course. Then you can tell me your news. And I will tell you ours.'

Lizzie's expression darkened and a blade stabbed her heart once more. 'I heard about Vincenzo,' she told him. 'I blame myself. If I'd . . .'

'Blame yourself? For what?' Stefano seemed confused.

'For Vincenzo's death, of course.'

'His death?'

'Yes. After he was shot, I . . .'

'I don't understand.' Stefano was shaking his head.

'What do you mean?' The tone in Lizzie's voice betrayed her frustration.

'But, Miss Thornton, you are mistaken. I'm happy to tell you Vincenzo Baldini is very much alive.'

Chapter 46

September 1944

Lizzie woke with a jolt to the crunch of feet on stones. She blinked away the sleep. Twilight. She must have dozed off. Exhaustion had won the fight. Travelling freely by car for at least twenty miles from the edge of the new republic's border, she'd finally made it back to Castell'Arquato. Rita had gone with her as far as Rivergaro to stay with yet another cousin, then Lizzie had trekked a farther full day until she finally saw the familiar bridge and the formidable Rocca looming over the town.

Now she remembered she was back in Franco's farmhouse. Stefano had managed to reach Vincenzo's unit via radio, and she'd been told to go there. But she'd been shocked and saddened to find the place deserted. Bullet holes in the closed shutters evidenced a gunfight, while inside chairs were overturned. The broken mirror, once on the wall, lay shattered on the floor. Cold ashes scattered the hearth while mould grew on the wooden platters. Not even the hens pecked the dirt anymore. But now she heard a noise.

Shuffling upright in the closet where the wireless used to sit, she clutched a discarded shawl to her chest and held her breath. A curtain still separated the tiny room from the kitchen.

She'd found the front door unlocked and now cursed herself for not bolting it from the inside. A slow creak and a set of footsteps. Just one. The visitor was alone. A partisan or rogue Nazi? A deserter, maybe?

The footsteps retreated up the stairs, then sounded overhead, the floorboards creaking under unfamiliar weight. Back downstairs, but this time they drew closer. They were heavy, but slow. She closed her eyes, praying that whoever it was would make themselves known. But no. They were pacing at leisure, not opening cupboards or drawers. She imagined them sweeping their eyes thoughtfully over the dust and neglect of the kitchen. A moment later she saw the feet stop a metre away, pointing towards her. Whoever was looking at the pantry was thankfully not in jackboots. She still braced herself for the curtain to be drawn back. And when it was . . .

'Vincenzo!'

She hadn't dared to think he'd come alone in person, but now he stood before her she could barely believe it. Stars danced in front of her eyes and the next thing she knew was feeling strong arms bundle her up from the floor. The same thrill returned at his touch, but she thought she had to be dreaming.

'Lizzie, my love,' he whispered.

'I thought you were dead, Vincenzo, then when Stefano . . .'

'I know. I know,' he told her softly as he held her tight.

After a moment she eased herself back. 'Let me look at you,' she said, touching his arms and shoulders and tracing his cheeks and lips with her fingers. She only stopped when, on the edge of his hairline, she came to a livid scar and recalled the sorrow of their last parting.

He held her close again. 'Oh, Lizzie, I'm very much alive, as you see.'

'When I heard you were dead, I thought of Cristo. I couldn't bear . . .'

'Cristo is fine. He'll be here soon.'

'But I heard he was struggling after . . .' Her voice tailed off when she realised she must have misunderstood. 'A partisan told me you'd been killed a while back, but I didn't want to believe him. Then some Americans said Cristo's teacher was killed and I assumed . . .'

Vincenzo nodded. 'Carlo was executed for breaking curfew back in summer. Franco has moved into town to care for him.'

The scales of confusion suddenly fell from Lizzie's eyes. Carlo was a teacher in civilian life. The Americans must have meant him. He was the one who was shot. Everything now made sense.

'And have you told him that you are his father?' Vincenzo looked at her quizzically. 'I was with you after you were shot, remember? You called out for him. I heard you whisper, "*My son*."'

Vincenzo flung back his head to look upwards and laughed gently. 'You're right. And yes, I have told him.' He nodded. 'As I recovered, I realised that if I'd died, Cristo would never know the truth. So, yes, I let him know.'

'And what did you tell him, Vincenzo?' In spite of the time they'd spent together in the Villa Martini and everything they'd been through, Lizzie realised she still knew very little about the man she loved. She wanted to know more. Needed to.

He looked at her with his huge eyes and stroked her cheek. 'You're right,' he said with a nod. 'I owe you an explanation.' He invited her to sit, and he perched on the side of the table just by her.

Taking a deep breath, he told her, 'I'm not who you think I am, Lizzie. I'm not a teacher. I never was.'

She frowned. 'Who are you then?'

'I was originally an editor,' he began. 'But the fascists closed down my daily newspaper and I had to disappear for a while to avoid arrest. That's when Professor Lodato approached me. He knew of my political leanings and, as well as editing *Freedom & Justice*, he asked me to help the resistance by spying on de Falco.'

'So is that how you knew the countess?'

316

He shook his head. 'We'd met much earlier at some charity concert I was reviewing, and we fell in love. She'd been married to the count for five years by then. Five years of misery, and when she became pregnant, he knew the child wasn't his. He was furious, of course. There were rows. He was violent, but he wouldn't let her leave. He didn't want to be seen as a cuckold, so he passed the child off as his own. It got too dangerous for her and me to see each other, so she would write to me, pouring her heart out. De Falco was cruel. He threatened to take Cristo away from her so that she could never see him again. That's when we started making plans to run away with the boy; to make a new life. But then . . .'

'But then she died?' Lizzie had heard the story from Maria about how her mistress had taken ill one evening after dinner and three days later was gone.

'No,' Vincenzo countered. 'Everyone was told she died of some mystery illness. She didn't.' He bit his lip. 'She was murdered, Lizzie.'

'What?'

'De Falco poisoned her.'

Lizzie shook her head in disbelief.

'By this time there was a real possibility of Germany invading Poland and the Count found out she had links to the British via me and Professor Lodato. She wrote me a letter, using my pen name, Il Gufo, and gave it to Bianca before she died, but de Falco found it.'

Lizzie recalled the morning she discovered Vincenzo in the count's study. 'Was that what you were looking for when you said you wanted books?'

'Yes. She'd feared he was going to kill her and cover it up. And that is precisely what he did. So, when it looked like Italy was going to join the Nazis, Lodato asked me to take the job of tutor at the Villa Martini. I jumped at the chance. The count had never seen me. He didn't know me, and I wanted to be with my son.

As well as passing on vital information, I needed to produce proof that de Falco murdered the contessa. It was my way of finding closure after her death.'

Lizzie reached for his hand. 'I'm so sorry, Vincenzo. And now you have it? The letter?'

He laughed cynically. 'For all the good it does. I doubt de Falco will ever face justice for her murder. His war crimes will take priority when the Allies bring him to court.'

'But did he find out about you? Did he discover who you really are?'

Vincenzo nodded. 'When the OVRA raided the newspaper. Normally I would have been shot when they arrested me, but he wanted me tortured. He even came to watch once.'

'Oh God!' Lizzie cried, shaking her head as sudden tears sprang from her eyes. 'No!' She laid her head on his shoulder and her whole body shuddered in a sob.

He took a deep breath and held her in his arms. 'Don't, Lizzie, please. I will not let him win. He will never have Cristo.' Gently he pushed her back and she lifted her gaze to meet his. 'But what about your pilot?' he asked. 'Where is he?'

Now it was her turn to sigh deeply. 'We made it to the coast and Hugh escaped by boat to France.'

His face registered shock. 'What? Without you?'

'I couldn't go,' she told him, another sob gathering in her throat. 'Even though I thought you were dead.' She bit her lip and looked into his eyes. 'Standing by the shore watching Hugh get into the boat to row to France, I had this feeling that the tide was going out, taking it with me, pulling me away from everything I truly loved. There was an accident before. The boat we were in sank and Hugh nearly drowned. I got him back to shore and afterwards he said to me, *'You saved my life. How can I ever repay you?'* And I thought, *You must give me my freedom.* He acted like he owned me. All I wanted to do was rush back to Cristo.' She hesitated, looking at his hand in hers.

Vincenzo opened his mouth to reply but shut it again when they both heard a noise outside. 'Did you hear that?' he asked. To Lizzie it sounded like the crunch of a bicycle braking on pebbles. Heading over to the window Vincenzo peered out of the shutters, then almost instantaneously flung them wide to let in the light.

'Cristo!' he called. The boy smiled. 'We're in here!'

Lizzie leapt up and hurried to the door to see the child standing before her – now even taller than when she last saw him when she headed off with Hugh. As soon as he realised it was her, he ran into her outstretched arms.

'Cristo! Cristo! It's so good to see you!' She clutched him tight. 'I've been so worried about you.'

When she looked at his face once more, she saw that her own tears had triggered his.

'I never thought I'd see you again, Miss Lizzie,' he cried.

'I know. I know, but it's all right now,' she replied. 'I'm back and I'm here for good.'

Cristo hesitated, as if just struck by a thought. He reached up to the back of his neck and fumbling with something at his hairline, handed over the silver St Christopher medal. She recalled giving it to him when she'd left the farmhouse that autumn morning with Hugh. 'Just in case you do go anywhere.' He beamed. 'It protected me until your return. Now you must have it back.'

Lizzie held it in the palm of her hand and smiled. 'I certainly don't plan on leaving Italy ever again,' she told him, her fingers closing around the silver disc.

Vincenzo patted Cristo on the back. 'Now, why don't you go and tell Franco and the others Miss Lizzie is back? We must celebrate with a party!'

'Si! Si! Papa!' the boy replied excitedly. 'We can sing and dance.'

'Of course we can. Off you go,' urged Vincenzo, his face split into a broad smile.

They both watched Cristo remount his bicycle and pedal off.

'How did he take it? When you told him you were his real father?' Lizzie asked.

'We hugged. There were tears and he said he'd always felt I was more like a father to him than de Falco.'

'And where is the count now?'

Vincenzo let out a long sigh and raked his fingers through his hair. 'Right now, he's heading up a number of the Black Brigades.'

Lizzie knew of the brigades, some of the most brutal in the fascist army.

Vincenzo carried on. 'He's leading the offensive to recapture the liberated zones in this region.' He paused to look up at her, as a shadow travelled across his features. 'And he's out to get his revenge on me.'

Chapter 47

As the leaves on the beech trees in the Val d'Arda began to turn from green to gold, so, too, did the mood of the region's people. When, in August, Florence, just to the south, had been won back from the Germans, there'd been great rejoicing. The war would soon be over. Or so everyone had thought. But the Nazis had shown they weren't giving up that easily.

Lizzie and Cristo spent the next afternoon decorating the surroundings of Franco's farmhouse. They'd hung strings of coloured bunting and jars with lighted votive candles inside on branches of the orchard trees. Those who had any brought food, but a parachute drop from the Americans the day before also meant there was tinned meat and pilchards to enjoy. Plump peaches, plums and figs from the harvest were piled high in dishes and eaten with dollops of ricotta, while fat slices of Maria's polenta cake went down very well. As the wine flowed, Franco played a concertina accompanied by Pietro on his tin whistle. Vincenzo had rewritten the words of 'Giovinezza', the song loved by Mussolini and his followers. He'd parodied the lyrics, mocking the fascists mercilessly, and performed it with Cristo, much to everyone's delight.

When the applause died down, Vincenzo remained standing.

'Tonight is a very special night,' he announced. 'As you know, not only are we celebrating our freedom, again' – he paused for laughter because Lizzie had heard there'd been many celebrations over the last month – 'but we are also welcoming back one of our own, whom we thought lost.' He looked directly at Lizzie and beckoned her over. She'd been sitting on a tree trunk by Cristo and was reluctant to answer the call, feeling the colour rise in her cheeks. 'Dear friends, dear comrades,' he cried, taking Lizzie by the hand. 'Miss Lizzie Thornton may have been born English, but she has a fiery Italian heart.' There were cheers then and Ernesto put his fingers in his mouth to whistle loudly. 'Not only has she been a mother to my son Cristo, but she has fought for all of us, too, with courage and commitment and that is why tonight I am awarding her this.' From out of his pocket, he brandished a blue kerchief, like the ones worn by the partisans, the symbol of Vincenzo's brigade. 'Tonight, Miss Lizzie Thornton, we are proud to call you one of us: a true daughter of Italy.'

With a flick of his wrist, he folded the kerchief into a triangle and, drawing Lizzie close to him, he tied it around her neck to loud applause.

Lizzie's hands rose to her mouth. She'd never experienced such heart-felt warmth before and couldn't find the words to express her gratitude. These people, she knew, had little before the war and now they had even less, yet they were eager to share everything not just with her, but with all the other Allied escapees who'd sought refuge in the valley.

After the feasting came the dancing. A number of *staffete* had hiked up from town, together with some female fighters. Lizzie thought two of them looked familiar. They recognised her, too.

'Miss Thornton!' It was Nina, one of the housemaids from the Villa Martini. By her side was Bianca, last seen carrying the contessa's clothing at Castello di Castiglione.

Lizzie moved forward to hug them one after the other. 'It's so

322

good to see you again,' said Lizzie, marvelling at their transformation from giggling housemaids to armed partisans.

'We couldn't stand by and do nothing while we heard gunfire in the mountains each day,' said Nina.

'We had to join in, especially when we heard Signor Baldini was the leader of the unit,' said Bianca.

Lizzie smiled at that remark, knowing how popular Il Gufo was among the women. 'I'm so thankful you did,' she said.

The girls found eager partners in Pietro and Paulo, who'd now been joined by several more local men. Three couples danced La Bergamasca, a local rustic set-piece, while some of the men performed a sword dance using long sticks. Cristo threw himself enthusiastically into the fray and outlasted most of the other performers.

When the mood calmed and everyone was exhausted after all the clapping and foot-stamping, Vincenzo asked Lizzie to dance.

'May I have the pleasure?' he said, holding out his hand.

He led her to the makeshift 'floor' and as he put his arms around her, once again an electric charge pulsed through her.

'Are you sure you don't regret coming back here?' he asked her as they turned slowly to the music. Just holding him and swaying gently to the rhythm made her feel safe and loved. A longing rippled through her body as she nuzzled her head against his cheek. Echoing the words she'd once told him when she was about to join the resistance, she whispered in his ear, 'I've never been more certain of anything in my life.'

Chapter 48

Lizzie clutched the Carcano M38 rifle tight to her body. She willed her muscles to brace themselves as the blood pulsed through her temples. The metal was cold against her cheek as she readied herself. Her mouth was dry. She licked her lips.

'Aim!' cried Ernesto. 'Fire!'

Lizzie was one of the new recruits being trained to shoot a few kilometres away from the farmhouse. There were a dozen men, as well as Nina, Bianca and herself. Each of them had a battle name. Nina was Thunder and Bianca, Colt, because of her long legs, while Lizzie stuck with Rosa. The fascists would have forced the girls to marry shortly, and bear children, preferably sons, for *la patria*. But they wanted no part in Mussolini's plans for his 'little women'.

'We are a fire without smoke,' Nina told Lizzie as they set off on the long march to the next valley the following day. 'When the fascists get burned, they very often don't realise who did it.'

The last time Lizzie had handled a gun was as a child when she fired at a row of ducks at a fairground. After two days' training, with her blue kerchief around her neck, she was trekking south through the foothills on high alert for the enemy. In her arms she carried her rifle, and an ammunition belt was slung across her shoulders. Vincenzo was up ahead, at the front of the column of about fifty partisans. A neighbouring free-zone area needed help. They'd been called in to push back the baying German rottweilers who were refusing to give up their juicy bones. Several sabotage missions were planned, including blowing up electricity pylons and more railway lines.

It was hard saying goodbye to Cristo yet again. 'Your father and I plan to be away only a month or two, but while we are we want you to study hard,' she told the boy. 'You promise?'

'I promise,' replied Cristo. He was growing to look more like his father every day with his aquiline nose and determined chin. 'But you must promise me one thing, too,' he said as Lizzie turned to leave.

'What's that?' she asked.

'That you'll both come back.'

Lizzie, Nina and Bianca were in charge of logistics, collecting supplies of food, radios and weapons for the unit. Lizzie wondered how Hugh would react if he could see her now, in full battledress uniform, toting a loaded rifle and commanding a unit. At worst he would have tried to forbid her from playing an active role in the first place, and at best he'd have undermined her self-confidence, even though he did admit to underestimating her once. At long last she'd stepped out of his shadow to feel the sunshine of responsibility on her face. Although that autumn, sunshine, real sunshine, was in very short supply.

It rained. For several days on end. Water ran down the mountainsides, uprooting bushes. Mud collected in great slabs and slid at speed, taking with it boulders and sometimes trees. The Allies were bogged down near Bologna and the Germans were holding the Gothic Line that cut the country in two from north of La Spezia to Ravenna in the west. During those few miserable weeks Vincenzo was heading up another unit as well as their own. She barely saw him. Her small team was able to raid a factory to steal dozens of pairs of boots and smuggle meat from an abattoir, but in the face of the Nazi firepower, Lizzie understood their actions were as futile as spitting on a housefire. But she hadn't realised that much worse was yet to come.

One day in November, Vincenzo summoned all the partisan units in the area to a small church high up in the mountains. Lizzie saw him only briefly before he made his address. He was talking animatedly with another man. He looked battle-hardened. His features were gaunt and his skin sallow. She could tell he was angry, too.

'What is it, Vincenzo?' she asked, snatching a moment with him.

He glanced at a sheet of paper he held in his hand. A communiqué of some sort. 'The Allies have betrayed us,' he hissed.

'What?' cried Lizzie.

He did not reply but headed towards the pulpit to address the waiting partisans. It was then she realised the man who'd been talking with him looked familiar. When he turned and their eyes met, there was a flicker of recognition. It was Lieutenant Kennard, the British Special Operations Executive officer who'd helped her and Hugh escape towards the coast. Was there any news of him? she wondered. She wasn't surprised the officer hesitated. He surely wasn't expecting to see her in combat fatigues. Or with her skin darkened by both the sun and the wind. It was only when she said his name that his eyes almost popped out of their sockets.

'Miss Thornton? Good Lord! But I thought——?'

She broke in. 'Yes, Lieutenant, you thought I was with Flight Lieutenant Codrington, but I decided to stay.'

Kennard opened his mouth to ask the obvious question, but she stopped him.

'For reasons I'd rather not go into now,' she told him firmly. 'Has there been any word of the others?'

Kennard, clearly surprised by her news, nodded. 'Yes. As a matter of fact, I heard a few weeks back on the radio. All the men made the crossing safely and met up with an American division.'

Lizzie smiled. A weight had just been lifted from her shoulders. 'I'm so glad. Thank you,' she said.

For all his faults, Hugh was essentially a brave and decent man, who'd served his country well. She'd felt terrible ending their relationship how she did. But, at the time, she'd seen no other way.

'But if you don't mind me asking—' began Kennard.

Lizzie did. She cut him off. 'It's a long story, Lieutenant. I just realised Italy is my home now. It's where I belong, and I chose to stay.'

Turning to watch Vincenzo striding up the pulpit steps, the passion burning in his eyes, she knew she'd made the right choice. Raising his hand to call for silence, he looked out over the partisans as they waited anxiously. They guessed he was about to deliver bad news and braced themselves in anxious silence to hear Il Gufo's words.

'Comrades, friends, fellow fighters,' he began, 'the British commander, General Alexander, has sent a message to us declaring that the summer offensive is over.' There were nods – the summer was long gone – and confusion too. 'But he has also said we must go back to our homes for the winter.'

A collective gasp of horror echoed round the church. Were they really being asked to put down their weapons and go into hibernation like brown bears? Outraged shouts, accompanied by raised fists followed.

'No! Shame! We're not going anywhere!'

Lizzie watched Vincenzo scan the room as he fought back tears. Almost a hundred men and women had been dealt a body blow. They'd just been released from the battlefield, yes, but their courage was being treated like a light bulb – something that could be turned on and off at will. If they returned to their homes, they would be easy prey for the Nazis over the winter months. No one would be safe.

The announcement cut Vincenzo deep inside, she could see from his face, but she knew he wouldn't give in that easily.

He lifted his hands and called for calm. Silence settled once more. 'I can also tell you that Luigi Longo from the Communist Party of Italy, speaking for the Volunteer Corps for Freedom, has replied to this Allied command.' A few cheers rang out at the mention of the leader's name, even though most in the audience were not communists. '*Brothers and sisters, we will not be abandoning our struggle this winter. We will carry on the fight, no matter the cold, no matter the snows, no matter the cost, until Italy is free once again!*'

The roar of approval inside the church was enough to drown out the rumble of Allied bombers heading east overhead. The partisans of the Val d'Arda were not ready to give up for the winter, return home to their hearths and put on their slippers, Lizzie could tell. But she also knew that Vincenzo's call to remain at arms when the mercury dropped to minus ten, when the snow lay three metres thick and even milk froze solid in its pails, would be hard to bear. Especially when the Germans took advantage of their weakness.

Later that night, when the partisans had eaten and split up to take refuge in surrounding farms, barns and outbuildings, Vincenzo asked Lizzie to stay with him. They made their way up to a hayloft where a sympathetic farmer had provided a mattress and blankets.

Hanging a lantern from the rafters, Vincenzo sat down, stretching out his long limbs in front of him. Lizzie followed suit. Taking his glasses off, he rubbed his tired eyes, then putting his arm around her he sighed heavily. 'I didn't want to be alone tonight, Lizzie,' he told her.

'Nor I,' she replied, looking into his eyes as the lantern cast soft shadows on his face. Her heart was beating so fast she knew she never wanted to spend another night without him.

'Are we doing the right thing?' he asked. 'My people have been through such hardship, such suffering. Am I asking too much of everyone?'

Lizzie placed her hand on his. It was so cold to the touch. 'They love you, you know that,' she replied. 'You are Il Gufo. You are a wise leader, and you can be sure there are those who will follow you into the jaws of hell. But—'

Vincenzo cut her off. 'You are right,' he agreed, nodding. 'But there are those with families; ordinary men and women who need to rest and to restore themselves for the spring offensive. Is that what you were about to say?' He'd detected the tightness in her tone that looked beyond the present to the bleak and treacherous winter ahead.

She laced her fingers through his. 'Then you know what needs to be done. Some must return to the plains for the winter, while the rest of us continue.'

He kissed her fingers gently. 'You must go, Lizzie. It will be suicide to stay up here when the snows come. Go back to Cristo. Please.'

Her heart sank. 'Cristo will be fine with Franco,' she told him. 'My place is here.' She let out a nervous laugh. 'Besides, you will need me to keep you warm at night.'

Vincenzo smiled at that and leaned closer as if he were studying a painting or a sculpture for the first time. With his eyes he took in the curves of her lips, the sweep of her cheekbones, then reached up and felt the texture of her hair. And when she took a shallow breath to speak, he covered her mouth with his lips, softly, gently and lightly, so that she found her whole body craving his touch. Just like she had on his first kiss.

'You're right. I do need you to keep me warm at night and to be at my side during the day, too,' he whispered as they held each other. 'To give me strength and courage when my own fails me.'

'I want that, too, Vincenzo. I can't bear the thought of us being apart any longer.'

He pulled away a little and searched her eyes. 'But I want you with me on one condition.'

She returned his gaze, uncertain. 'What's that, my love?' she asked.

His arms were suddenly around her again, holding her even tighter. 'That it will be as my wife.'

Chapter 49

They were married a week later at the church where Vincenzo read out General Alexander's message and defied it with his own. The women from the neighbouring village rallied round, offering Lizzie a wedding dress made of parachute material and a bouquet of silk flowers. Stefano was Vincenzo's best man and Nina and Bianca, who'd decided to remain fighting over winter, acted as Lizzie's bridesmaids.

Lizzie feared this was the calm before the storm. Ahead loomed a huge dark cloud that threatened to deluge and destroy all the gains made over the summer. Almost as soon as they made it back to Val d'Arda, thousands of troops, including many Turkmen, Azerbaijanis and Mongols, joined the Germans to pour into the Apennine valleys. The ones from the Far East wore thick furs and rode on horses, which also pulled sledges, so they didn't rely on frozen gasoline. Those who saw them said the Mongols had long moustaches and wore inscrutable expressions. What's more, they were hunters.

The *rastrellamento*, as it was known, or the raking, usually began before the cold dawn. The new offensive most often started with German Stukas dive-bombing the mountain. When the aircraft had done their worst, there would follow a blitz of automatic fire and explosions as rapid and unrelenting as a mountain hailstorm.

That morning, the Stukas' sirens split Lizzie's deep slumber, waking her instantly to the panic of the other partisans scrambling to get clear of the barn. Then came Vincenzo's familiar tugging as he heaved her to her feet. She'd learned to shed sleep like a loose coat over the past few weeks. The freezing cold stung her exposed skin, her face and hands, but the routine had become easier, if not the exposure to terror.

'They're coming! Quick!' came the cry from below.

Casting round the straw, Lizzie gathered up her few possessions, a woollen blanket, a hat and a small bar of soap. Seconds later they were out of the barn and into the open. The snow lay thickly on the ground, reaching the ground-floor windows of the farmhouse. They split up; a group of about five choosing to head down the mountain, while three took a track leading east.

'This way,' shouted Vincenzo, grabbing her hand as she waded knee-deep through the snow. They scrambled up as a gunfight raged nearby. Lizzie clung to the mountain sides, crouching down every time a stray bullet came too close for comfort. She lost her footing when a large chunk of snow broke off beneath her. Landing awkwardly in a heap on a ledge below, she hurt her knee. Vincenzo held out a hand from above and hauled her up again. Ignoring the pain, she managed to make it to the cover of the woods where the snow was shallower. There they ran for ten minutes until they were sure no one had followed, and collapsed, their hearts leaping out of their chests. It had been like this ever since the Germans decided to treat the partisans not as enemy soldiers, but as vermin. They were rats and had to be eliminated, just as all those villagers who'd helped them had to be stamped out.

After a while, as the breath returned to them both, Vincenzo kissed Lizzie's forehead. 'That was close. Are you . . .?'

'Don't worry about me,' she replied. Her stomach was hollow

with hunger, the seams of her clothes were crawling with lice, the blisters on her feet were raw, and her leg hurt every time she moved it. She couldn't remember the last time she'd had a bath or enjoyed an unbroken night's sleep. But all these were minor discomforts. They paled in comparison with the feeling that overcame her when she thought she might never see Cristo again. That was verging on the unbearable.

'I'm with you,' she answered. That was what kept her going these days.

Hours passed before they dared venture back to the barn where they'd spent the night. They'd stopped there so often before that it almost felt like home to Lizzie, even though they never slept there more than two nights in a row – just in case the Germans were watching. Shortly before they cleared the woods, Lizzie stopped to sniff the icy air. Smoke. Vincenzo smelt it, too.

Quickening their pace, they trampled through the under-growth to reach the edge of the trees to arrive at the barn – or what was left of it. The flames had already died down. Now only one or two plumes of smoke curled in the air, leaving behind charred roof timbers that had completely caved in. The barn's walls were blackened, and the door and window frames were reduced to ash. It was too dangerous to go inside.

'Looks like we'll have to find a new place for tonight,' said Vincenzo, turning over a burned wooden beam with the heel of his boot.

Just then there came a cry. Lizzie's head jerked up. She and Vincenzo followed the sound to the far side of the barn where the wood continued to smoulder. Drawing closer they could see Paulo, Pietro and Nina standing a short distance down the track. They were bending over something, then Nina dropped to her knees.

Lizzie and Vincenzo approached and when she traced the long, thin legs up to the bloody face, Lizzie dropped down, too.

'Bianca!' she cried. 'Oh no.'

A bullet had pierced the young partisan's temple; her blood slicked red against the snow. As the tears streamed from her eyes, Lizzie made the sign of the cross. Forehead, breastbone, left then right. After everything she and the others had endured, she wasn't sure she even believed in God anymore, but she knew Bianca, the free spirit who'd inspired so many of other women and girls in the area, did. She was just twenty years old.

Lizzie, kissing the pads of her fingers, brushed her cheek lightly. 'Rest in peace, Bianca,' she whispered, before rising slowly.

'We better make sure she didn't die for nothing,' said Vincenzo, as he gazed at the girl's face.

Lizzie was too distraught to reply.

Chapter 50

They trudged down the mountain later that day to return to Franco's farmhouse. Pietro and Paulo and Nina strapped Bianca's body on Geppetto, the mule, and took her back to her parents' house down in Castell' Arquato. It was still too dangerous for Vincenzo to venture into town, so he remained at the farmhouse. Rumour had it the Germans and their Far Eastern henchmen had received orders to withdraw but wanted to go out with a bang. The 'raking' had been more like a bloody clawing.

Despite lying in the relative comfort of Franco's old bed and the luxury of three blankets, Lizzie could not sleep easily that night. Bianca's beautiful face swam before her every time she closed her eyes. She'd been everything that Lizzie hadn't been at that age; fearless, passionate, certain about her place in the world. Now she was gone.

Vincenzo turned over and wrapped an arm around her. He drew her close and entwined his legs with hers. The warmth radiated from both their bodies. 'You are so precious to me,' he told her, kissing her shoulder. But she failed to stifle a sob and gave in to tears. Propping himself up on one elbow, he lifted her hair gently from her face and she rolled onto her back so that he could see her tears in the moonlight.

'She was so strong. So passionate,' she said. 'When I think of myself at that age, well . . .' A weak, mocking laugh escaped. 'My life was mapped out for me. Five years as a teacher, then marriage to Hugh. A nice house. Children.'

Vincenzo laid his hand on her stomach. 'Doesn't that sound tempting now? All I've given you is a hayloft, constant danger and lice.' He scratched his head then, making her smile.

'You showed me that life is to be seized by the throat and lived, Vincenzo. I wouldn't swap it for the world.' Reaching up, she put both her arms around his neck and drew his face down to kiss him. They were so lost in each other that they didn't see the moonlight fade to a pale dawn, finally bringing with it sleep to them both.

It was Paulo who woke them. His shouts and the banging on the door would have roused the dead.

'Il Gufo. Are you there?' He was rattling the door handle as he yelled.

Vincenzo leapt out of bed and tugged on his trousers before flinging open the shutters.

'*Mama mia!*' he muttered.

'What is it?' asked Lizzie, scrambling out of bed and hurrying to the window.

'Come down quick, Il Gufo,' called Pietro. 'They want you.'

Lizzie's blurry eyes widened as she saw who 'they' were. Dozens of people, mainly women, had gathered outside the farmhouse and when they saw Vincenzo at the window they began to chant. '*Partigiani! Partigiani!*'

'What do they want?' asked Lizzie, standing behind Vincenzo. All these people had put themselves in danger to make the journey from town. Not only did they have to trudge through snow, but there were Nazi snipers in the woods, too.

'I'm not sure, but I'd better go and find out,' he told her. 'I'm coming down!' he shouted to the crowd.

A loud cheer rose on the cold air. Lizzie dressed quickly, too, and followed closely behind to find Vincenzo surrounded by a group of women. They were talking animatedly. Some were wiping away tears. Others were reaching out to touch Vincenzo, as if he were a film star. Lizzie saw him nodding his understanding.

Still unsure about the reason for the crowd, she beckoned Pietro over.

Cupping her hand round her mouth she leaned towards his ear and asked, 'Why are they here?'

'It's Colt,' he told her. 'They're here to honour Bianca's memory.'

Lizzie frowned. 'I don't understand.'

Pietro turned towards the crowd and opened wide his arms. 'They want to join the *partigiani*.'

A week later Bianca was buried. The Germans, still clinging to power in the area, ordered that only family members and close friends could attend her funeral, but the whole town turned out in defiance. Lizzie joined them, disguised as a peasant. Hundreds from the surrounding villages came, too, battling through the snow to pay their respects. Shops shut and people left their houses as the bell tolled for Bianca. Her coffin was carried through the streets from the church to the cemetery in silence, under the watchful eyes of steel-helmeted Nazis. It had been hard work digging a grave in frozen ground, but she was laid to rest in the presence of hundreds who deplored her brutal killing.

Lizzie returned to a safe house about a kilometre out of town that night. Vincenzo had said he would meet her there. What she wasn't expecting was a group of around twenty other men and two women all crammed into the basement, sitting on the floor.

As she negotiated the rickety steps, her eyes started to sting from the smoke of homemade cigarettes. Through the murk she spotted Vincenzo. He was standing pointing at a map somehow fixed to the wall. Heads turned as they heard the stairs creak to see Lizzie coming to join them.

'Rosa,' Vincenzo greeted her.

She raised a hand. 'Please, I don't want to interrupt. Carry on.'

Joining the others on the floor, she soon realised that the map on the wall was of Castell'Arquato. The unit had received word from a reliable informant that the Germans were planning to withdraw from the Val d'Arda any day now, but before they went, they would commit one final act of brutality. There was only one route into town passable to supply trucks. It was over the river bridge and the Nazis planned to destroy it. The people of the town faced being completely cut off if that happened.

'It's the only way in. We would all die,' shouted one of the women.

'You're right, signora. Everyone would starve. We cannot allow that. So what do we do?' He scanned his audience for answers.

'We play them at their own game,' called out Lizzie from the back.

Vincenzo pinpointed her against the far wall and smiled broadly. 'That is exactly what we do,' he said.

Chapter 51

Franco managed to scavenge some rotting vegetables from the dustbins outside the school where the Germans were stationed. He'd made soup from stinking cabbage and scabby potatoes. Lizzie, Vincenzo and Cristo all drank it as if it was the finest lobster bisque.

Chuckling and patting what was once a large belly, Franco pronounced, 'A feast fit for warriors!'

Lizzie smiled but prayed it wouldn't be their last. It was the evening before the raid. She and Vincenzo were on edge. Her husband had insisted they spend some time together before he headed back to the mountains where the partisan brigades were camped. He needed to be with his men – and women. It was his duty. Lizzie understood that.

Cristo, his once-plump face now gaunt and sallow, leaned over the table eagerly. War had turned him from a boy to a man in the squeeze of a trigger. He ought to have been in school, but alongside the periodic table he'd learned what it was like to face the death penalty.

'Will you let me come with you, Papa, please? I can . . .'

Vincenzo dipped his brows into a frown. 'How many times, Cristo? No. Your task is vital. Without you we will not launch the attack.'

Lizzie hated the idea. She'd spoken out against it, but Vincenzo knew that Cristo was desperate to be part of the operation.

'If he hadn't been included in the plan, then he would act on his own and put everything in jeopardy,' Vincenzo had told her.

She'd bowed to his argument, knowing Cristo could be as pigheaded as his father.

Vincenzo pushed away his soup bowl. 'There will be fighting tomorrow,' he told Cristo. 'A lot of gunfire and explosions and, after you've done what I've told you, the safest place for you is here, taking care of Franco.'

Lizzie could tell her husband was troubled. 'But we are prepared, and we have the numbers.' She tried to sound as positive as possible.

'We just need the Holy Virgin on our side.' Franco raised his eyes heavenward and crossed himself.

'And what about you two?' Cristo's large eyes were fixed on Lizzie and Vincenzo. 'Who will take care of you?'

Lizzie darted a look at Vincenzo and smiled. 'We can take care of ourselves,' she said, even though inside she was trembling at the thought of tomorrow's onslaught.

Franco showed Vincenzo out the back way. The side gate led to a lane with high hedges that provided cover until the track entered the woods. The snow on the trails had turned to slush, but it still loitered under hedgerows and on higher ground. Lizzie walked with him, her hand in his, until it was no longer safe to do so.

'You know what you have to do,' he told her, taking her into his arms.

'Yes. I know,' she replied, her head nuzzling against his neck. They'd been over the plan a dozen times. During the past few days all her unit had. 'I also know that I love you more than life itself, Vincenzo, and if anything happens . . .'

'Ssssh, *cara mia*,' he whispered, putting his finger to his lips.

'My life is worth nothing without you and Cristo. So, I will make sure I return tomorrow night and so must you.' He wiped away a loose tear from her cheek with his thumb. 'Be brave, my beloved wife. We are doing this for our son's future, remember.'

He kissed her urgently on the mouth and she clung on to him, wanting the moment to last. When he broke away, he didn't look at her again and for that she was thankful. If he had, she might have begged him to stay, but she had to be strong, for everyone.

Once Cristo was in bed, Lizzie slipped out of the house. Wearing a skirt and a threadbare coat once belonging to Franco's wife, she made her way to a house on the edge of town to rendezvous with her unit. There were about twenty of them. Lizzie recognised a few of the women who'd volunteered to join the partisans following Bianca's murder. They were still angry, and they needed to channel their fury in the only way they could. Ernesto was their commander, and he went over the plan one last time. Those who hadn't changed into their uniforms did so, then the firearms were distributed. The Carcano rifles were supplemented by pistols. There'd been an American air drop three days before and much-needed ammunition had been delivered alongside more rifles, although these remained with the brigade camped in the foothills. In just a few hours they would be converging on the town, if all went to plan.

The minutes between midnight and four o'clock dragged like an anchor. Some of the partisans grabbed a nap, others paced up and down. Some passed around precious cigarettes, while others wrote letters to loved ones. When the time came, they moved out in twos and threes to take up positions all around the town.

The Nazi patrols had been scaled back. The troops from far-flung lands – the Turkmen and the Mongols – had all gone so now only Germans remained, clinging on as news of Allied advances farther south made them start to retreat. But they wouldn't go quietly. Their final act of sabotage would be their most inhumane yet.

Lizzie and three others scurried over the fields to reach the riverbank where the snow had melted. The river was high with meltwater as it spewed from the mountains, taking boulders and small trees with it. The ground was soaked and perilous underfoot in the dark, but puffy clouds parted often to let the moon light much of the way.

At a fork in the track, about a half kilometre out of town, they started to climb, fanning out across the hillside. Lizzie reached her position just as a finger of light appeared in the cleft of two mountains. Dawn was breaking. All she could do was sit and wait for the signal. The partisans were to launch a full-scale attack before the Germans could detonate the explosives to destroy the bridge and cut off the town.

Sheltering under a rock she watched on high alert. Above her loomed the ancient towers of the Rocco. Below her a swollen torrent threatened its banks. The snows had gone from the lower slopes but in their wake, there was mud and slush, and the rocks were as slippery as fresh-caught fish.

From her vantage point, the town looked like a shell of itself. Through her binoculars she inspected the buildings. Castell'Arquato, she knew, was severely wounded. The once-magnificent town had lost its identity and its dignity, violated by the Nazi invaders. Doors were splintered and windows broken. Weeds choked the once-neat flower beds. Bullets had clipped cornices and pillars and ricocheted off statues and fountains. The ancient walls sagged as if the stones themselves were weeping.

A sudden flurry of sleet arrived from nowhere and stung her eyes. The sharp, cold rain pricked her gloveless hands, and she wafted flakes away like flies, praying they'd disappear as soon as they hit the ground. She shivered, but not with cold. Cradling her rifle, she knew she needed to stop shaking. *Had* to stop shaking. Her life – and everyone else's – depended on the success of this operation.

Reaching up to her neck, she felt for the St Christopher medal Cristo had returned to her and kissed it. At least she wasn't alone. Out there, unseen, dotted around on the ridge and further down towards the town, hidden behind trees and bushes, prone under parked trucks and lurking in alleys were scores of other partisans. Only the Germans didn't know it. While a column of Nazis listened out for the explosions on the far side of town before they moved off, two partisan brigades were gathering around them, waiting for a signal for the fightback to begin.

Until that signal came, Lizzie, Nina and several others were ordered to provide cover for those below. Looping her finger through the trigger once more, she focused. There were people down there she loved. The nausea rose in her stomach as she clutched the barrel tight to stop her hands from shaking. All she could hear was the sound of her blood as it pumped like an ack-ack gun through her body.

There was a sudden movement by the bridge. Through binoculars she saw a dozen or more Germans were providing cover for two soldiers who were wading, knee-deep, into the river. With cable reels clutched to their chests, they were aiming for the central span where they would fix their dynamite and lead their fuses to a detonator farther up the bank. If they were successful and the whole of the bridge was blown to smithereens, the entire Arda Valley would be cut off. No supplies could get through. Hundreds would die of starvation. That was the way the Nazis worked, Lizzie told herself. Their enemies were not human, but vermin to be starved out of existence.

An almost imperceptible gasp escaped her lips then as she tilted the binoculars down the slope. He was in her sights. A young boy with wild, dark curls on a bicycle. Cristo. One hand on the handlebars, the other cradling a paper bag of loaves. If he was stopped, he'd been told to say the bread was for German officers. That usually worked. *Harmless enough*, the guards would think.

'Steady, Cristo. Steady,' she whispered. Her heart raced and her head pounded watching Cristo pedal over the bridge, then turn right at the junction with the Via Guglielmo Marconi.

There, a hunched old woman was waiting. Dressed in black, she held a wicker basket. Cristo stopped. Looked round. Hesitated, then dropped a focaccia into the basket.

The signal.

Chapter 52

The first shots rang out almost immediately. Machine-gun fire, mortars, a chorus of artillery rounds as relentless as spring birdsong only a thousand times louder and a million times more deadly echoed through the hills. Partisans began to swarm from all directions towards the bridge, causing the outnumbered Germans to abandon their explosives.

Lizzie jumped up, just as someone was hit – with arms splayed wide they juddered before they hit the ground. It could have been her. *Don't think that way*, she told herself. But then a quick glance to her left to two other women told her she had to advance. They were up and running, scooting down the hillside in free fall. Their presence made her stronger. With her rifle slung over her shoulder, she joined the scramble down, down towards the bridge.

As soon as the brigades reached the bridge, the German column, waiting to retreat on the far side of town, started to splinter. Many withdrew, but some remained to stand their ground. Firing randomly, they spilled into the Via Guglielmo Marconi, lined with shops and houses. It was also where Cristo was last seen and Franco was hiding in his home; where she knew they were cowering, once again afraid for their lives.

Bullets whizzed past her ears as she flattened herself against a wall near the elementary school. Up again, she weaved between parked trucks towards the fighting. She rolled under an abandoned handcart in the square where she and Cristo once drank cream sodas. All the while the sound of war raged around her, pounding her skull, testing her courage. She pressed on with the others. The few Germans who hadn't already fled took up positions at the far end of town and were firing indiscriminately at anything that moved. Even the cats took refuge. Some of those who remained started overrunning the homes that lined the boulevard. Now and again a Nazi would appear from a doorway and let loose with a round of fire, but there were partisan snipers at all junctions, ready to pick them off. As the weak winter sun rose higher, the fighting continued.

Two German soldiers lay before her in the roads where they'd fallen. There was a partisan, too. He'd gone down in the doorway of the butcher's shop. His blood was running into the gutter. Clearly dead. She dared not look at him in case she recognised him. In case it was Vincenzo. She ploughed on, running from doorway to doorway, waiting until the partisans in front had signalled to proceed.

Lizzie fired off a round when she saw half a dozen fascists make a break for it from the farmers' cooperative store. A group of partisans pursued and managed to round them up. As more fascists and Nazis appeared in the main street with their hands raised in surrender it was clear the partisans were making headway. The constant gunfire had dwindled to intermittent bursts from lone wolves, hiding out in shops and homes overlooking the main street. Many of the Germans had already been taken prisoner.

Alongside Nina and a dozen other partisans, it was her task to sweep the civilian homes and shops, to ensure no enemy soldiers were lurking inside. Twenty minutes later she'd reached the house next to Franco's, home to an elderly cook. Peering through the window she caught her boiling oil on the stove, ready to throw over any fascist foolish enough to cross her threshold. The fearsome widow, Lizzie was certain, wouldn't hesitate.

Not far now, she told herself, the sound of her own heartbeat pulsing in her ears, amid the gunfire and the shouts. Franco's villa was only a few paces away. A single shot rang out from behind her. She pivoted to see a Nazi not ten metres away. Her heart stopped. He took aim again, but a second later he was splayed on the ground, bayonetted by another partisan. She moved on, rifle level, ready to fire. The mission was going well. Lizzie's group had made good progress, sweeping through the streets as the Germans beat their retreat. Franco's villa was next.

No one in the courtyard. Good. Cristo and Franco would be taking cover as she told them. If they'd followed instructions, Cristo would have rushed back after giving the signal and they'd have barricaded themselves in the basement until the fighting was over. Cautiously she kicked open the door and stood back for a moment to look and listen. When all seemed clear she went inside. To her left, the salon. It was empty and just how she remembered leaving it last night. Next, she picked her way through the dining room to the kitchen and the hatch into the basement. The rug was rolled back. *Good. But wait.* Her boot tested the bolt. It was drawn from the outside. She frowned. That could only mean . . .

'I was hoping you'd drop in to check on your pupil, Miss Thornton.'

Lizzie's head jerked round at the familiar voice to see an apparition in black appear from behind the pantry curtain. Count Antonio de Falco – the spectre of evil that had loomed over hers and Vincenzo's lives for so long – now stood in front of her. And he was not alone.

Lizzie's whole body went stiff. Her limbs froze, while fear grabbed at her throat, strangling a cry. De Falco's left arm was wedged vice-like under Cristo's head, pushing it upwards, half-choking him so the boy spluttered for breath. In his right hand the count held a Luger. It was pointed at the child's temple.

347

'Put it down, slowly,' de Falco told her, his head bowing to the Carcano now trembling in her grasp. The rifle had turned to stone in her hands; heavy and unwieldy, but she gripped it even tighter. Somehow, she kept it level, knowing if she fired it, it would hit Cristo.

Through her horror she hissed out her response. 'You harm him and I'll . . .'

'You'll what, Miss Thornton?' the count sneered. 'Believe me I wouldn't think twice about putting a bullet through the boy's head. As you now know, he is nothing to do with me. His mother was a whore.'

Cristo's face crumpled at these words and his eyes squeezed out tears. 'Please, Miss Lizzie . . .' he bleated.

The child's distress only spurred her on. She stabbed the count with a look of disgust and heard herself say: 'Your cruelty drove his mother to despair. Then you murdered her.'

De Falco's laugh was chilling. 'Baldini told you that, I presume. Where is he? Tell me where he is, and I won't harm the boy.' Again, he jabbed the Luger against Cristo's temple.

A choking sensation crept up Lizzie's throat; like rough hands around her neck, throttling her. Her legs, too, felt shackled. She couldn't move. Couldn't breathe. That same terrible fear she'd felt way back in Lucca when de Falco discovered she was a spy. A paralysing, engulfing sensation. 'No. No. You can't . . .'

The cold, calculating look he'd given her before contorted his features. The sneer became a grimace and his eyes burned with a kind of madness she'd never seen before. Suddenly she was certain he was capable of doing what no sane human could do – of putting a bullet in the head of an innocent boy he'd brought up as his own.

She swallowed down the bile convulsing in her throat. Cogs in her mind whirred again. A distraction. Franco. Where was Franco? In the basement. He'd been locked in the basement. Somehow she needed . . .

'De Falco.'

A voice boomed through the open door. In another instant Vincenzo stood in the room, sheathed in the smell of cordite, although, to Lizzie's horror, she soon realised he was unarmed.

At the same time the count switched round. When he saw Vincenzo, he threw back his head and laughed.

'So, you have come to see me kill your son, Baldini.' The click of the safety trigger above Cristo's left ear sounded as loud as a shot in the sudden stillness. 'Or are you prepared to hand yourself over to me?'

Lizzie couldn't believe Vincenzo had allowed himself to fall into the count's trap. He raised his arms in surrender.

'Leave the boy,' he said. 'Take me, instead.'

'Vincenzo,' Lizzie cried. 'No. No.'

'Please, Lizzie. You know this is the only way,' he told her, keeping his eyes trained on the Luger. Then to the count, 'Now let the boy go.'

'I have a better idea,' answered de Falco, his eyes glinting wildly. 'Why don't I kill you all? You, your son and . . .' He turned to Lizzie. But then . . .

It happened in an instant. A violent explosion erupted like a volcano in front of their eyes. Spurts of red and pink and pearl splattered across the tiles and splashed the walls. Cristo screamed as he lurched towards Lizzie and behind him the count staggered sideways and dropped to the floor. It only took her a moment to realise a shot had just shattered his skull. Her rifle clattered to the floor as Cristo hurled himself into her arms. Gulping down air as she held him, her horrified gaze tried to make sense of the scene.

'It's all right, my darling. You're safe now,' she told him, her voice trembling through the shock ripping through her body.

'Oh Cristo, Cristo!' Vincenzo ran to scoop them both into his embrace.

De Falco's body had been blown towards the walls. Blood

was pooling across the tiles and foamy pink tissue sprayed the plasterwork. Vincenzo steered Cristo's gaze away from the sight just as a partisan, dressed in a man's shirt and trousers, appeared at the doorway.

'Violetta?' gasped Lizzie.

'My God!' cried Vincenzo.

But the girl ignored them both. She simply walked up to de Falco's corpse and stared at his dead body.

'He'll never be able to hurt anyone again,' she muttered.

Just then a thumping sound boomed up from the basement.

'Franco!' cried Cristo.

Rushing to the trap door, Lizzie unbolted it to see the farmer emerge.

'*Santa Maria*. You are alive! Thank God,' he cried, flinging his arms first around Cristo, then Lizzie. The tears streamed down his face as he hugged the boy.

Vincenzo moved over to Violetta. Putting his hand on her shoulder as she stared at de Falco's corpse. He, too, stared at the body for a moment then said, 'Lizzie told me what he did. There are no words to express our thanks – and our sorrow for you.'

Violetta looked up at him; her eyes now overflowing with tears. She opened her mouth to reply, but the words caught in her throat. Instead, she just placed her hand on Vincenzo's as it lay on her shoulder.

'Now I need to get back to the fight,' he said. 'The fascists need to know their leader is dead.'

Walking over to Lizzie, he held her close and kissed the top of her head. 'Wait for me here,' he told her.

Lizzie nodded and watched him stride down the hallway with Violetta, his arm around her trembling shoulders, while she shepherded Cristo and Franco into the salon, away from de Falco's body.

'You're safe now, my darling. The count can't hurt you anymore,' she told Cristo. She stroked the child's head and as she did, a movement nearby caught her eye as a large scorpion scuttled from beneath the sofa. She stamped on it with her boot.

Chapter 53

Lizzie stood behind Cristo looking at his reflection in the mirror.

'Why are you crying, Mama Lizzie?' asked the boy.

Mama Lizzie was his name for her since she'd married Vincenzo. Every time she heard it, it brought her joy. Every time Cristo called her by it, she wanted to hug him. She brushed away the stray tear. 'I'm just so proud of you,' she told him.

It was true. She was proud of her stepson. He'd endured more than anyone should, no matter their age. But her tears were not for him, but for the empty space in her heart at a moment when everyone else was celebrating. Aided by the partisans, the Allies were advancing. Thousands of Germans were being forced to surrender as they were pushed north, but it was the absence of friends she'd made and lost along the way that was hurting her. She wished Cecilia, Ada and Bianca had lived to see this day.

Lizzie swallowed down her sorrow. 'Very smart,' she told Cristo, giving a satisfied nod. She patted both his shoulders simultaneously.

Since the count's death, back at Castello di Castiglione, Maria had busied herself with needle and thread to make Cristo a partisan uniform. Thankfully, his membership of the GIL was long behind him, but Maria said he deserved recognition for his service to the resistance as a *staffetta*. Of course, many of the partisans did not have a uniform at all, but she had sewn together a fine shirt with breast pockets. When she'd come to town to deliver it to Lizzie, she also brought Cristo's old GIL cap. Holding it at arms' length, as if it were a stinking rag, she said, 'I think we should burn this, don't you?'

The battle of Castell'Arquato had been the beginning of the end. The partisans saved the bridge and forced the Nazis out of town. The Allies resumed their offensive and just eight weeks later the American Fifth Army liberated the region's capital Bologna. Three days earlier the Germans had fled Fontanellato.

News came early that morning that Vincenzo's company had liaised with a United States division at the town of Alseno and thousands of German troops had been forced to surrender as they tried to flee across the river.

The citizens of Castell'Arquato came out into the street cheering and waving the green-white-and-red flags of the National Liberation Committee. The town still bore the wounds of the previous battle. While most of the broken glass and splintered wood had been cleared away, chunks of masonry and large beams of wood and steel still lay in some streets. Many of the younger townsfolk were readying themselves to walk to the Via Emilia. They wanted to welcome the columns of Allied troops that were streaming along the highway in trucks and tanks. Lizzie planned to carry on for another two hours to reach the town of Fiorenzuola, where a huge celebration was to be held.

They were readying themselves, packing water and what bread they could muster, when Lena, Franco's niece, burst in. New blue ribbons nestled in her dark hair.

'Are you ready?' she asked, holding a bunch of spring flowers. 'These are for the soldiers,' she explained. Then turning to Cristo, she said, 'What are you taking?'

Lizzie smiled. 'We have three bottles of your uncle's finest.'

Cristo was about to put the wine bottles in his bicycle basket. 'Shall we go?'

As soon as they crossed the bridge, they could see hundreds of people were already lining the main route. They could hear them, too, their cheers carrying over the steady hum of military vehicles as they trundled past. Flags were waving and girls were handing out flowers and bottles of wine to soldiers. In return some of them were given chocolate and candies by the Americans.

Somewhere nearby a voice said, 'You want a lift?' It was Franco in his cart, pulled by Geppetto. Maria was sitting alongside him, and old Giuseppe was in the back. 'Jump up,' he cried.

Lizzie and Lena climbed aboard while Cristo followed on his bicycle. They dropped in line at the end of the long column and reached Fiorenzuola in little over an hour. The Allies had sent word to the partisans that they should be the ones to liberate the major towns, and Vincenzo's unit had been the bearer of the great news.

By the time they arrived, the town was in chaos – ecstatic, jubilant chaos. Church bells were ringing, car horns were sounding and up above flocks of pigeons were circling because they were so alarmed by the noise they couldn't settle. Thousands of people were packed like anchovies into the town square, all their faces wreathed in smiles.

Cristo climbed up a lamppost to get a better view.

'What can you see?' Lizzie shouted up.

'I see partisans,' he replied. He looked up again, narrowing his eyes. 'Papa. I see Papa!'

A huge cheer rose into the air as, craning her neck, Lizzie could just about see movement on the steps outside the church. Hats were thrown in the air and there were cries of *'Viva i partigiani!'* as a group of men appeared and tried to calm the crowd.

Just then Lizzie felt a tap on her shoulder and turned her head to see Violetta, still in battle fatigues. For a moment the two of them just looked at each other. The pain was still etched on Violetta's face, but Lizzie saw something else, too. A smile was blooming behind the young woman's eyes. It would take time, but she was certain she would heal.

'We can never thank you enough for what you did,' said Lizzie, embracing her. 'You saved Cristo's life. And Vincenzo's and mine.'

Violetta nodded thoughtfully. 'I shall always take comfort from that,' she said, as the noise from the crowd died down.

An excited hush descended as, a moment later, a partisan walked out onto the middle of the platform to address them. It was Vincenzo.

'People of Emilia-Romagna,' he began. Another loud cheer rose into the air, startling the pigeons and doves once more. 'The fascist tyranny is over. You are free!'

Lizzie looked up to the sky as the world around her exploded with joy. The war was all but over and shattered lives could be pieced together again, but not as they were. She reached out to Violetta standing next to her. Somehow Nina had found her in the crowd, too, and was standing nearby. Italy would rebuild itself and she wanted to be part of that, but she also knew it had to build better. Women like Violetta and Cecilia, Nina and Bianca, Ada and Rita could no longer be ignored. After the courage they had shown, every bit as great as any of their male counterparts, they deserved to be treated as equals. That, she knew, would be the next battle – the fight for women's equality.

Chapter 54

Lucca, Tuscany

May 1946

The women came from all over Emilia-Romagna, from Tuscany and beyond. Some came from the mountains, some from the plains. Some from villages, some from towns and cities. Some were young. Some not so young. Some were smiling. Some had tears in their eyes. Even Rita made it to the event, travelling from Genoa, as did Violetta and Nina. But they were all united by one thing; each one of them had shown outstanding courage in the face of an incalculable evil.

Each had been a partisan.

Vincenzo took Lizzie's hand and kissed it. She was waiting to mount the stage erected at one end of the Piazza dell'Anfiteatro. Was it really six years ago that Mussolini's voice had called all Italian citizens to arms in this very square? To Lizzie it seemed like only yesterday that she'd pedalled back to the Villa Martini, terrified of what might lie ahead. Her fears had been more than justified. Countless lives had been lost and homes and businesses destroyed. But alongside the death and destruction, many friendships had been forged and now a new spirit of hope was rising from the ashes.

Once again, a nervous hum filled the large space, just as it did in June 1940. Only this time the atmosphere was one of joy, not hate. Of hope, not fear. The momentous task of rebuilding the beautiful country of saints and artists and poets, so shattered by division and war, had begun.

'Ready?' Vincenzo asked her, about to let go of her hand. She held on to it and squeezed it.

'Wish me luck,' she told him.

Her husband shook his head. 'You don't need luck. You have something much better. Strength.'

'You look beautiful,' said Cristo, standing beside her, dressed smartly in a shirt and tie and looking much older than his thirteen years.

'Thank you, my love,' she replied, before taking a deep breath to compose herself. 'Now go with Papa.'

Vincenzo led the way, and the applause was almost deafening as he strode onto the stage, followed by Lizzie. When the noise died down, he began.

'Women of Italy,' he addressed his audience. 'As Mayor of Lucca, may I welcome you to our beautiful city and say that we are honoured to have you within our ancient walls. Many of you have travelled a long way to reach us, by bus, by train, by car. But you are all united in your purpose; to celebrate the achievements of female partisans over the past three years.

'As many of you will know, I led a partisan division during the campaign, a body of courageous men and women who sacrificed so much so we could stand here today. And among them was a woman whom I am now proud and honoured to call my wife. She is not only that. She is my strength and my inspiration. And for her the war is not yet over. She will carry on fighting, and she is here to tell you why. Ladies, I give you your commander-in-chief and a true daughter of Tuscany, Signora Lizzie Baldini.'

Five hundred women rose to their feet to greet her with loud applause. Scanning their faces, Lizzie thought she would burst with pride to be among their number. Under the fascist regime their sole task was to produce and raise children to fight in Il Duce's army. *War is to a man what maternity is to a woman*, he'd once said. Well, now he could think again. By joining the partisans, Lizzie understood the women of Italy had not just been fighting to regain control of their country, but of their lost rights, too. Their bravery and courage hadn't been officially recognised. Most had even been excluded from official victory parades and the few who were allowed to march with the men at the back were labelled whores. This was her way of recognising their sacrifice.

When the clapping died down and the women were seated, Lizzie began the speech she'd prepared. But the script trembled in her hands and when she started to read from it, her voice sounded stilted and scratchy.

'This isn't right,' she said, and she tore up the paper into four pieces in front of everyone to a collective gasp. 'You haven't come here to listen to a stuffy speech, to sit stiffly as if you were in church, to clap politely when the speaker pauses for applause. I want to talk to you from my heart. I may have been born and brought up in England, but I now have the heart of an Italian. And an Italian woman at that. When Mussolini called us "*angels or demons, born to take care of the household, bear children, and to make cuckolds*", what did we do? We proved him wrong. When even an old Italian proverb tells us "*Words are for women, actions for men*", we proved that wrong, too.'

Shouts went up from the audience then, but Lizzie had only just started.

'They underestimated us at their peril. They underestimated us in Florence when we fought hand to hand to liberate the city and in Montefiorino where a republic was declared. In Turin we led strikes in supply factories. They underestimated us when we blew up bridges and railway lines, too, and when we carried secret messages across enemy lines. And when we were captured and raped, we didn't crack under torture. We defied them not with words, but with our actions. We showed them what we woman are made of and without us fascism would never have been defeated.'

Her voice rose as she spoke, and the hundreds of faces that looked up at her were lifted and inspired.

'So, I say to you, don't retreat to your homes like hens to your coops, content to lay eggs in solitude and silence. You have proved yourselves on the battlefield, now it is time to storm the ballot box.'

At her exhortation the women leapt to their feet, clapping and cheering. Vincenzo rose, too, followed by Cristo, and together they rushed over to her to kiss her. She nodded with tears in her eyes and motioned to her audience to return to their seats.

'And now,' she declared, 'the moment you've been waiting for. The awards to honour your courage, given out in memory of three brave women who should have been here today.'

Her eyes dropped to the front row. Seated next to Vincenzo on his right was Professor Lodato and to his left Giuseppe and Maria, cradling a sleeping baby girl in her arms. Violetta had been born to Lizzie and Vincenzo only three months before. But beyond them, three seats had been left vacant. One for Cecilia, one for Ada and one for Bianca.

'They all suffered under the fascist regimes both Italian and German, and like you, they were not prepared to accept the cruel injustices and brutality perpetrated by them. They gave their lives so that we might live in peace and redeem our freedom and dignity. They all died heroes.' She choked back tears. 'So now before I give out the awards, I would like you to take a moment to listen to my husband and son as they read out the names of those women who sacrificed themselves so that we may stand here to celebrate them today.'

She moved aside to allow Vincenzo and Cristo to take centre stage. They took it in turns to read out the grim litany of the female partisans who had paid the ultimate price. To the names of Cecilia, Ada and Bianca were added several more.

Luisa Calzetta.
Maria Macellari.
Lidia Gandolfi.
Teresa GullaceIrma Bandiera.
Gina Galeotti Bianchi.
Stefanina Moro.
Anna Maria Agnoletti.
Vera Arduino.
Libera Arduino.

No one stirred as they intoned the names of just some of the women who were gone but not forgotten. When the last was read a minute's silence followed before Lizzie addressed her audience once more.

'Let their names live on in history, alongside our brave men. All we are asking is for equality; that our sacrifices be recognised as just as important, just as courageous as men's.'

Lizzie paused for breath before she began again. 'Next month, you women receive the right to vote for the first time. This mile-stone goes some way to recognising the huge role you played in the defeat of fascism in this country. You can be justly proud of that achievement, but it is only a first step on the road to true equality. We still have a long way to go before our voices are truly heard, but together, we are stronger.'

Again, the women stood, clapping and cheering, and while Vincenzo readied the specially designed certificates to be awarded to those who'd shown outstanding courage during the war, Lizzie looked out over the audience once more. This time she didn't see the hundreds of faces staring up at her in admiration, applauding her, but three remarkable young women – Cecilia, Ada and Bianca – seated in the front row, all dressed in combat fatigues, and all having sacrificed their own lives so that others could live in freedom and in peace. While the future of women in Italy remained unknown – Lizzie was in no doubt there was still much work to be done – one thing was certain: Vincenzo, Cristo and now, little Violetta, would be by her side every step of the way. And she could finally make Italy – and Tuscany – her home.

A Letter from Tessa Harris

Thank you so much for choosing to read *The Tuscan Daughter*. I hope you enjoyed it! If you did and would like to be the first to know about my new releases, then follow me on X.

If you'd like to share your opinion of *The Tuscan Daughter*, I would be so grateful if you could leave a review. I always love to hear what readers think, and it helps new readers discover my books too.

Thanks,

Tessa

f: Tessa Harris Author
X: @harris_tessa

Beneath a Starless Sky

Munich: Smoke filled the air.

Lilli Sternberg's quickening heart sounded an alarm as she rounded the street corner. Lifting her gaze to the rooftops, a roaring blaze of thick flames engulfed the side of the building and joined the stars to fill the black sky. Her father's shop was no more.

Lilli Sternberg longs to be a ballet dancer. But outside the sanctuary of the theatre, Munich is no longer a place for dreams.

The Nazi party are gaining power and the threats to Jewish families increasing. Even Lilli's family shop was torched because of their faith.

When Lilli meets **Captain Marco Zeiller** during a chance encounter, her heart soars. He is the perfect gentleman and her love for him feels like a bright hope under a bleak sky.

But battle lines are being drawn, and Marco has been spotted by the Reich as an officer with potential. Lilli means more to him than anything and he knows he must find a way out.

With their lives on the line, will Marco and Lilli survive the growing Nazi threat, or do they risk losing everything in the fight to be free?

The Light We Left Behind

England: 1944

When psychologist **Maddie Gresham** is sent a mysterious message telling her to report to Trent Park mansion, she wonders how she will be helping the war effort from a stately home.

She soon finds captured Nazi generals are being detained at the house. Bugged with listening devices in every room, it's up to Maddie to gain the Nazis' trust and coax them into giving up information.

When **Max Weitzler**, a Jewish refugee, also arrives at Trent Park with the same mission, Maddie finds herself trapped in a dangerous game of chess.

The two met in Germany before the war, and Maddie's heart was his from the moment they locked eyes.

But Maddie has finally gained the trust of the Nazi officers at the house, and her love for Max must remain a secret.

When the walls have ears, who can you trust?

Based on the true events that took place at Trent Park during WWII, this is an emotionally gripping, and heart-breaking novel about love, sacrifice, and betrayal, perfect for fans of *The Rose Code* **and** *The Lost Girls of Paris.*

The Paris Notebook

A secret big enough to destroy the Führer's reputation . . .

January 1939:

When **Katja Heinz** secures a job as a typist at Doctor Viktor's clinic, she doesn't expect to be copying top secret medical records from a notebook.

At the end of the first world war, Doctor Viktor treated soldiers for psychological disorders. One of the patients was none other than Adolf Hitler . . .

The notes in his possession declare Hitler unfit for office – a secret that could destroy the Führer's reputation, and change the course of the war if exposed . . .

With the notebook hidden in her hat box, Katja and Doctor Viktor travel to Paris. Seeking refuge in the Shakespeare and Company bookshop, they hope to find a publisher brave enough to print the controversial script.

But Katja is being watched. Nazi spies in Paris have discovered her plan. They will stop at nothing to destroy the notebook and silence those who know of the secret hidden inside . . .

Acknowledgements

I love Italy and have visited it many times, but until I began researching this novel, I had no real understanding about the complexities of what went on during the Second World War and the deep divisions brought about by Mussolini's alliance with Hitler. Of course, the war also affected the many British citizens residing in the country, as well as British servicemen who were taken prisoner first by the Italians and later by the Germans before they could escape.

Of the 200,000 known partisans in Italy after the Armistice was signed in 1943, some estimates say up to a quarter were women. Most of them acted as *staffette*, or messengers. Children were also recruited, some as young as ten. Like the women, they were regarded as largely invisible by the fascists. '*You could be anybody. You were a fire without smoke or a flame,*' said one.

Several hundred women were also involved in armed combat. In Florence, for example, some 300 females took to the streets in the summer of 1944. They also fought in the town of Montefiorino, which was declared a republic in 1944. According to one American website, Italian Sons and Daughters of America, more than '4,600 of these heroines were arrested, 2,750 were deported to concentration camps, and 623 were killed by Fascists or Nazis'. However,

I have not been able to verify these figures. What I do know, is that female partisans in Italy have remained in the shadows for far too long. That is what inspired me to write this novel.

According to the Resistance Museum of Piacenza in Emilia-Romagna, around 200 women in the district have been recognised as partisans during the Second World War by the regional commission. Those killed amounted to twelve, although there were many more in other areas, as well. One of these real women who features in my novel was Luisa Calzetta. With the battle name Tigrona, she was a young primary school teacher from Parma, who commanded a detachment in Val Nure. She was shot in an ambush, while helping a fellow partisan. Maria Macellari, known as Carma, is also mentioned. A nurse, she was arrested during a mission and executed at just twenty-three years of age.

The list of female partisans in the final chapter names just a few of the women who were killed, many after being tortured, during the conflict. It is only relatively recently, however, that their stories have been uncovered and told. I am deeply indebted to Iara Meloni and Alessandro Pigazzini of the Museo della Resistenza, Piacentina, for their assistance in helping me shine a light on these extraordinary stories of female courage. For further reading on the role of the female partisan in Italy, I recommend Caroline Moorhead's *A House in the Mountains: The Women Who Liberated Italy from Fascism*. Also, Ada Gobetti's *Partisan Diary: A Woman's Life in the Italian Resistance* is her startling first-hand account of what life as a female partisan was really like.

Several Roman Catholic priests were executed by the occupying Nazis. Many memorials, together with photographs and information boards, remain outside the churches where they were shot.

At the end of the war in May 1945, Allied commanders were keen the Italian partisans were the ones to declare the defeat of fascism to local populations. However, for the many hundreds of women who had actively participated in the resistance, there was very little acknowledgement of their courage. Most were not even allowed to join in the victory parades. As one recalled in Moorhead's excellent book, female partisans were *'sent home like chickens to the coop to lay our eggs in solitude and silence'*.

There is much more written about the plight of the British prisoners of war who found themselves marooned in enemy territory after the declaration of the Armistice in September 1943. Malcolm Tudor's *British Prisoners of War in Italy: Paths to Freedom* is a fascinating read. Two first-hand accounts I recommend are *The British Partisan: Capture, Imprisonment and Escape in Wartime Italy* by Michael Ross and travel writer Eric Newby's memoirs, *Love and War in the Apennines*. The latter escaped from Fontanellato. Ross gives an account of a young woman being summarily shot when suspected of spying. My fictionalised accounts of attempts to escape from the coast were also inspired by Ross.

The former British prisoner-of-war camp in Fontanellato is still standing. It is now a mental health hospital. The adjacent convent where the nuns used to launder prisoners' clothes and did, indeed, place notes inside their returned washing, also remains. The fact that young women used to parade outside the prison on a regular basis and shots were routinely fired at excited prisoners by Italian guards, is also true.

Castell'Arquato is a beautiful medieval town that is well worth a visit. Here I was indebted to Manuel Preprost at the tourist information office for his guidance. The Rocca, or medieval tower at the castle, was where the fascists held prisoners throughout the war years. It remained a jail until the 1960s.

On my research trip to northern Italy, I first stayed at La Rondanina, at Castelnuovo Fogliani, a lovely hotel and working vineyard. In Liguria I opted for Agriturismo Risveglio Naturale, near Varese Ligure, which is owned and run by Emanuele and Francesa, whose hospitality I highly recommend. Francesa's grandfather was head of the Garibaldi Brigade in Genoa and Emanuele proudly showed me a partisan's metal star, once rolled onto roads in front of Nazi trucks to puncture tyres.

I would like to apologise to my tutor Marika Parisi and all my fellow students at South Gloucestershire and Stroud College where I undertook a course in basic Italian. I was a terrible student. But special thanks go to my dear friend and near neighbour, Franca Giampa, who more than compensated for my linguistic inadequacies. She also helped arrange my research trip, as well as corrected my written Italian on numerous occasions. Any errors are my own.

To my travelling companion, soul mate and husband Simon I must express my thanks for, among other things, driving me on perilous mountain tracks. And last, but never least, my gratitude goes to the team at HQ Digital and especially my new editor, Audrey Linton, for her invaluable input into the creation of this novel.

Dear Reader,

We hope you enjoyed reading this book. If you did, we'd be so appreciative if you left a review. It really helps us and the author to bring more books like this to you.

Here at HQ Digital we are dedicated to publishing fiction that will keep you turning the pages into the early hours. Don't want to miss a thing? To find out more about our books, promotions, discover exclusive content and enter competitions you can keep in touch in the following ways:

JOIN OUR COMMUNITY:
Sign up to our new email newsletter: http://smarturl.it/SignUpHQ
Read our new blog www.hqstories.co.uk

𝕏 https://twitter.com/HQStories
🇫 www.facebook.com/HQStories

BUDDING WRITER?
We're also looking for authors to join the HQ Digital family!
Find out more here:

https://www.hqstories.co.uk/want-to-write-for-us/

Thanks for reading, from the HQ Digital team